# Blood Rising

By

# Amber Anthony

**Paperback ISBN 978-0-578-46250-9**
**eBook ISBN 978-1-393-03961-7**

**Credits**
Cover Artist: Kelly Ann Martin, kam.design
Editor: Professional Editor Services
Published by Amber Anthony
Printed in the United States of America
August 2020

**Follow Amber Anthony on**
All Author
BookBub
BookSprout
GoodReads
The Romance Reviews
https://AmberAnthonyWrites.com

# Praise for Blood Rising

*"This book is a wonderful addition to the vampire folklore genre and sensual romance. I could not put it down once I started reading. I am a huge fan of the vampire genre, and Amber Anthony does not disappoint. The characters are very real, and the story of the shadowy underground of human/vampire sex and the longing for true love catches you from the moment you start. I can't wait to read the other books in the trilogy. This one is a must read for any vampire romance fan."* – J.R., Amazon

*"What a talented writer! Pacing, description, and emotions are thoroughly explored. The underworld of vampires and their lifestyle is exposed as in no vampire book I have seen before, and I've seen most. There is mystery entwined with the plot. Whodunit? And why? Are big questions. Will the semi-immortal Matt and his love survive manipulative vampires, and will the couple's love come out intact? I must keep reading to find out."* – P.S., Amazon

*"Blood Rising lured me in immediately with its lovable cast of characters and well-developed storyline. Cat Temple and Matt Brenner's chemistry is unstoppable."* – A.M.D., Amazon

# Brenner's Edicts for the Undead

1. Vampires are the ultimate Doms.
2. Stay out of mortal's relationships, *no good comes from intervening.*
3. Never get involved with mortal females, *they break too easily.*
4. Emotional relationships with mortals are difficult, *they can't detach.*
5. Immortality is an illusion, *vampires can be killed.*
6. The number one mannerism for appearing human: *inhale/exhale, repeat.*
7. To be irresistible to donors, *hang out with your fangs out.*
8. The first bite is the sweetest.
9. Pale is the new tan.

## The Vampire's Golden Rule

It's not the bite you get, *it's the bite you give.*

# Dedication

Natural pearls form when an irritant - usually a parasite and not the proverbial grain of sand - works its way into an oyster, mussel, or clam. As a defense mechanism, a fluid is used to coat the irritant. Layer upon layer of this coating, called 'nacre', is deposited until a lustrous pearl is formed.

This paperback edition of Blood Rising is dedicated to life's irritants that once inculcated, developed not only a shimmering pearl but the desire to create a necklace of four pearls.

Once Blood Rising was well received, Blood Emerald was the story's natural progression. When the characters kept peppering our inspiration with tales of a particular dragon shifter, Blood Dragon was written. By the summer of 2018, we had The Blood Trilogy.

Then there were questions, how did their friendships begin? We were inspired to tell their origin tale with the prequel, Appetite for Blood. A story that could only have begun in post-World War I and Prohibition-era Los Angeles.

We hope you enjoy the humor, adventure and magical realism of the romantic dramas of The Blood Trilogy. With paranormal Doms, the 'happy' *is* forever after.

# 1

"I'm so sorry," Cat rushed into the university art studio, banging the door into the wall in her haste.

"You're late," Brad's hands curled into fists at his side. "Tardiness will be punished." He suddenly looked as if he could follow through on that threat.

"Ornstein's class went long, and…" Cat was still in the middle of her breathless apology when his offensive words sank in, and she stopped abruptly. "Excuse me? Punished? Who the heck do you think you're talking to?"

Brad snarled down at her arrogantly from the classroom stage. "Watch your tone, Cat. When I want you to speak, I'll give you permission."

"Watch my…now hold on!" When did this guy, who'd seemed so charming and insightful on their first date, become such an ass?

He may have been every girl's definition of a fair-haired dream, but Cat guessed it was true—looks weren't everything.

"Strip." Brad jumped from the stage to stand intimidatingly in her personal space.

"What?" The shock left her gaping.

"I'm not in the habit of repeating myself. You're the class model tonight. Strip."

"You didn't say anything about modeling in the nude…"

"When and how I want you to model is none of your concern. Your job is to please me."

His audacity stunned her. She needed to set this guy straight right now. "Look, Brad," Cat's teeth clenched, "we're just getting acquainted, so I'm letting you know I'm the one who decides what I will or won't do with my own body."

Stress, fired by her resistance, intensified his demand. "That attitude will not be tolerated."

She didn't back down. "Oh, really, by whom? You?" Cat walked away. "I think you'd better find another model."

Brad's hand flashed out and grabbed her arm in an iron grip. "Don't you ever turn your back on me!"

Cat stared at him, amazed. He didn't strike her, but it looked as if he wanted to, which made the intruder at the door most welcome.

The man cleared his throat loudly enough to be a distraction. "She doesn't understand what you want. She doesn't understand submission, and it should be obvious by now, she'll never accept your domination." His voice was a low, resonant baritone with twice the authority of Brad's.

Cat flashed her gaze up to his with fascination as he leaned casually against the doorframe. He was probably mid-twenties, well over six feet, gorgeously built, with dark hair curling around an impossibly handsome face. He more than fit the image of a champion to a damsel in distress, and she sighed with relief at his intervention.

"What I do with my sub is none of your business…"

"Your sub?" The man snorted derisively. "Does she know she's supposed to be a sub?" He strolled forward to confront Brad.

Brad appeared flustered and wilted in the face of the stranger's cool confidence. "We haven't discussed labels…"

The man held out his hand to her, and Cat accepted it without a second thought. His fingers were cool, his eyes mesmerizing, large, deep azure, thickly lashed and slightly melancholy. "Stay behind me," he told her quietly and then turned his attention back to Brad. "I have no problem with a Dom/sub relationship. Whatever gets you off, that's your business, but this girl has no understanding of what you're after. If you were an experienced Dom and not a wanna-be poser, you'd have recognized that immediately."

Cat stared at them in confusion. "Dom/sub?"

They ignored her. Brad puffed out his chest in defiance. "I don't need instruction from you…"

"Clearly you do, or we wouldn't be having this conversation. Let me help you out." He turned to Cat. "Miss…uh…"

"Temple," she supplied quietly. "Catherine Temple. Cat to my friends."

"Miss Temple, do you have any intention of surrendering your body and safety to this man?" He glanced dismissively at Brad.

Cat's jaw dropped with alarm. "I…I…no! What are you talking about?"

He stared pointedly at Brad and shrugged. "She's not submissive, Brad. Wish her well and be done with it."

"Who do you think you are?" Brad challenged irritably.

"A new student in this class."

"Oh, yeah? Because I'm the Teacher's Assistant here, buddy, and you're getting off to a bad start."

"I see." The stranger considered that for a moment. "So, if the Dean were informed you were bullying a co-ed and then tried to intimidate a classmate who intervened, that wouldn't be a problem for you?"

"Fuck you!" Brad squared off against the newcomer.

Cat figured she'd better do something to distract them, or the two men were headed for an ugly fight. "Excuse me, you two do know I'm in the room, right? You can see me here? I mean, I haven't become invisible?"

"Yes, ma'am." The stranger gave her a nod, amusement in his eyes. "I see you very clearly."

He pointedly gazed from her face, over her breasts, waist, and hips, all the way down her legs to her toes. He drew in a long breath, bit down on his full lower lip and nodded appreciatively. "I'm Matt," he held his hand out in an introduction.

* * * *

Matt smiled as she took his hand again, trust and enchantment evident all over her face. Her touch was warm and electric, and he was smitten. She was stunning. A mass of long, blonde hair framed a heart-shaped face with deep-set, almond eyes and a flawless complexion. He couldn't remember ever having such an immediate attraction to a woman.

Cat flushed under his frank appraisal and ducked her head. She started to speak, and then lost the words and smiled shyly. Matt shifted uncomfortably. Was this what romantics described as love at first sight? He stared at her. Blue, he realized, drawn irresistibly into the depths of those dazzling eyes. They were a clear, cornflower-blue.

Brad scowled and clenched his jaw. "I need to get some supplies," he muttered, looking back and forth between the two of them.

"Good idea. While you're gone, maybe Miss Temple and I can discuss her modeling tonight."

"Oh, yeah, thanks a lot." Getting no rise with his jibe, Brad stalked away.

"What was all that about?" Cat demanded when he'd gone.

"Another discussion for another time," Matt deflected mildly before he seductively lowered his voice. "I'd love to paint you if you'd agree to pose?"

Her color rose higher at his compliment, and he wondered idly if her nipples were the same hue as her candy pink lips? Was their taste as sweet? His jeans grew uncomfortably tight at the thought.

"Not nude!" Her chin jutted out stubbornly from under a soft, full mouth.

Matt wanted to fall into her lips, could barely pull his gaze from them to answer. "No." He scanned the cluttered art room, and his gaze landed on a crumpled length of red satin. "Not nude, but maybe…a little bit of a tease?" He held up the fabric, unraveled several yards and offered it to her.

She accepted it with a quizzical look and disappeared behind a make-shift changing screen.

"You're sure you're not looking?"

"Wouldn't dream of it." Matt felt damned for a liar when his strongest desire was to tear down that barrier and dispatch what remained of her clothes. He'd lay her bare and sumptuous on the scarred desktop and sample every inch…

"I said, do you think it'll be long enough?" she asked, raising her voice.

Long enough? Matt jerked himself out of his erotic fantasy and refocused on the here and now.

"Sorry. Will what be long enough?"

"The fabric. You're sure it'll be long enough to, like, cover everything?"

Matt grinned. "I'm sure we'll manage." He waited for another few beats, sensing she was undressed but reluctant to leave the shelter of the screen. "Why don't you come out here and we'll see."

"I…"

"Come on. I won't let you be embarrassed. I swear."

His promise reassured her, and Cat emerged from behind the screen with a large swath of red satin wrapped around her like a sarong. The sensuous fabric hugged every curve of her luscious body. Matt swallowed and tried to keep his voice even.

"Good start," he praised. "Let's put you here."

He patted the high stool in the center of the stage. Cat darted an uncertain glance at him and worried her bottom lip. What would it be like to own those succulent lips? To have them fastened around his cock, her clear cornflower eyes gazing up at him? He gave his head a brief shake to clear it. *Impossible.*

"Now, you might want to cover your…" He gestured toward her breasts, grasping for diplomatic words to describe her lovely tatas.

Ordinarily, he had no problem being explicit with his sexual vocabulary. In his business, it was expected. Still, he sensed the young woman before him would be shocked and put off if he told her that. He slowly tugged the fabric away from her, giving her ample time for modesty. He'd love to make sure she had none left, and no need for it.

"What are you…" she began uncertainly, crossing her legs and using her hands to cover round, full breasts. "Oh, I get it." She breathed a sigh of relief as he worked. "You're going to drape it like an antique 'art' shot."

"Antique?" Matt gulped, remembering photos staged in just this way for Marilyn Monroe. "Uh…sure, antique. Anyway, I want mostly your back to the class with a hint of a profile over your right shoulder."

Cat posed as he instructed. "Like this?"

"Exactly. Now, I'm going to wind this fabric…"

Matt entwined the fluid, crimson fabric across her lap and between her legs. A flush crept up her torso to color her face. She wasn't as immune to his touch as she'd like him to believe, and he certainly wasn't to her soft curves over firm muscle. He sighed out a breath as he fought the impulse to caress her. Draping the fabric back across her lap, he wound it once around her body and then across her breasts, barely covering their tantalizing peaks.

"Hold on to the stool." He drew one long leg down in an artful line, and then draped the other over it to create a sensuous 'S' with her curves. "Balanced?" She nodded, and he pried her fingers from around the edge of the stool and then laid one arm at her side, the other held the fabric sweeping across her breasts and over her left shoulder. "You look incredible." She took his breath away! "Is this a pose you can hold for a while?"

"I suppose so." Her gaze searched his through her lashes.

Unspoken questions flew between them, but they would have to wait. The class was filling quickly with students.

"Maybe, I could thank you with a drink after class?" he suggested in a husky whisper. It was madness to even consider a relationship with this young woman, but one drink couldn't hurt.

"I don't know. With Brad and all…"

"Let me worry about Brad. You'll probably need a drink to unwind after posing in this position for an hour."

She slowly acquiesced. "Sure. A drink would be nice."

The sketch drew itself as Matt studied the angles and dimensions of her body. Her skin glowed peach with the simmering warmth of her blood flowing under it. It was soft as fine velvet and smelled of honeysuckle soap and lavender shampoo. He scented her even now, though he was several feet away. It was all he could do to keep his troublesome erection inside his jeans. As it was, he figured he was going to have a permanent zipper imprint on his cock.

Since actually bedding this girl was out of the question, he was going to have to take her out for a drink, have a nice fatherly talk about the dangers of men who thought they were Dominants. Then give her a polite kiss on the cheek at her door. He and his right hand were going to get real friendly tonight.

Matt studied her as she sat composed and graceful on the high stool, absorbing the admiration, not to mention the meticulous dissection of the entire class. What was she thinking about? What *was* her take on their odd meeting?

A crash at the back of the room startled the students and signaled Brad's return. He had made himself scarce during the actual class, and Matt thought it must rankle the guy not to be able to claim his prize as she sat posing prettily. Matt would bet the man was planning another confrontation of some kind. Was he aiming for Cat or him? Whatever, Matt was on his guard and standing sentry, waiting for her to change into her clothes.

"That is the longest I've sat still since, well…" Cat began nervously as she dressed behind the screen.

Matt listened to her charming chatter with half an ear, a knowing half-grin teasing his lips. His fuller attention was on Brad. Instinct told him the guy wasn't going to surrender her without a fight. Matt would rather not have to demonstrate his superior strength tonight.

"Of course, at school, the nuns were always making us stay put, but I guess I was about five, and I insisted on staying in the bubble bath… and I played and played and played until all the bubbles were gone and the water was cold."

Rancor seemed to be mounting in Brad. It indicated a level of confidence higher than average. Did he have a weapon? Maybe he knew martial arts? It wouldn't matter in a match between them but signaled to Matt a physical confrontation was inevitable. *What a jag-off,* he didn't want Cat to see that.

"And then, I realized my entire body was covered with gooseflesh. I was bumpy all over!"

Matt's mind flew to the image of her covered with gooseflesh, her firm breasts standing stiff and begging for attention. He shook himself back to reality. "How ya doin' back there?"

She exited from behind the screen, buckling her belt at her trim waist. "Ready!" She pulled her backpack over her shoulder. "Do you have a car? I walked."

"Oh, yeah. I'm in the lot right outside." He gestured her toward the door, noting Brad's sudden absence and certain they'd meet again in the dark parking lot.

Matt could scent her anxiety as he fell in step behind her. The thought had no sooner crossed his mind when she nervously fumbled her open backpack.

She bent down to retrieve her fallen books. "You know, I have an early class tomorrow. Maybe it'd be a good idea to just grab a cup of coffee at the student union."

Matt crouched beside her to rescue a rolling apple and scoop the books from her hands. She straightened warily, and he followed.

"Coffee keeps me awake at night, but whatever makes you more comfortable. I'd be happy to sit with you. I'm actually pretty harmless."

"Yeah?" She slanted a skeptical look his way. "What about that whole Dom/sub thing? For all I know you have a trunk full of ropes and gags."

Matt laughed easily. "Nice to know you have such a high opinion of me. Coffee it is then."

Cat stared an overlong moment into his eyes, uncertainty written all over her face "Oh, okay."

The light behind her lit her golden hair into a halo around her arresting face, and at that moment, she struck Matt as so compellingly real, not a contrived bone in her body. He caught her slight tremor as he placed a guiding hand at her back and walked them across the street to the student union.

Though it was not yet eight o'clock, most students and faculty had left the campus already, and the dimly lit streets were mostly empty. The usually chill January night was warmer because of a Santa Ana wind, which blew Brad's scent straight to him and warned Matt of his approach before he launched himself at them.

Matt had only a moment to push Cat to the safety of the curb before Brad was upon him. So far, Brad was textbook predictable. As pissed off as Matt was that they had fought in front of Cat, he was grateful the jerk took his aggression out on someone who could protect himself rather than her.

Now, Matt had to deal with the fact they were fighting in a fishbowl, right out in the middle of the goddamn street for anyone to see. He ground his teeth in frustration. Cat regained her footing after stumbling on her way to the curb and turned to watch them. Taller than his opponent by several inches, Matt feinted to the left and dodged a blow. Brad danced back and delivered a roundhouse kick to Matt's throat, drawing a horrified gasp from Cat. It was a blow meant to kill, but Matt absorbed it and shook it off to assume a defensive pose.

In a dark alley, this ridiculous 'fight' would have been over in seconds with the pretender Dom down—permanently. Here, Matt needed to be careful. He couldn't kill the prick, and he couldn't let his own ultimate victory look too easy.

Matt pegged his fighting style from the start. Brad was obviously versed in mixed martial arts. For the sake of authenticity, Matt let him land a blow to his left temple and open a cut which bled sluggishly. Body blows came next. Cat's attention locked on the furious volley of punches Brad threw at Matt's chest. Impossibly quick reflexes allowed him to evade them all. Matt landed one to Brad's gut and another to a kidney. He had to give it to the guy. Brad had some game. That last one should have put the little creep on the ground. They briefly danced around each other, Brad trying to catch his breath, Matt pretending he needed to.

What the…, man? Matt came to this class for fun, to work some long-dormant artistic muscles, not dip back into his Army training for hand-to-hand. Obviously, having gotten a second wind, Brad was on the offensive again, going after Matt's ribs with a vengeance. Matt let a couple blows land, getting more and more pissed at Brad's viciousness. This little pest was a potential killer. He needed to do something about it before someone, probably a woman, ran afoul of him.

What did Cat see in this arrogant prick? Hopefully, he wasn't what she wanted in a Dom, if she even knew the meaning of the word. Something was so off here. It was crazy-making, but one thing was sure—Brad needed to be taught a lesson harsh enough to prevent him from trying this bullshit on any other woman.

Matt moved in, determined to eliminate Brad's threats in a punishing way. They were engrossed in the ferocity of the struggle, and Matt didn't notice the speeding sedan bearing down on them until it was too late to avoid a collision. Brad dove for the curb while Matt jumped into the opposite lane. The driver veered into the oncoming lane, clipping him before he veered back and sped away. There was stunned silence and then a surreal moment as Cat's anguished cry elongated his name.

"Maattt!"

* * * *

Cat observed the carnage with horror. Brad lay still, his head bleeding against the curb. With a low groan, Matt rolled, making it slowly from his knees to his feet. He stretched what had to be battered muscles and bones. She sprinted to help him and stumbled mid-step at the sound of his guttural, threatening growl. She stood stock-still as he turned, and the light caught the glimmer from his eyes. They were as pale as opals. His face was an unnatural, deathly mask. Long, wicked fangs protruded between drawn lips.

In shock, and reverting to the solace of her childhood religion, Cat crossed herself while Matt's appearance gradually normalized.

He warningly reached out to her. "Don't come any closer," he said, his voice feral. "Give me a minute."

"What in God's name is going on?"

"I'm okay. You need to check Brad. He could be badly hurt."

"What?" She gawked at him as if she'd stepped into a waking nightmare.

He gestured toward Brad. "Does he have a pulse?"

Cat snapped out of her inertia and rushed to Brad, turning him over carefully and then checking his neck for a pulse.

She fearfully looked up at Matt. "I can't tell."

Matt knelt beside her and felt for the carotid. "Yeah, he's okay, just unconscious." He drew out his cell phone and then dialed 9-1-1. "Medical emergency in the street, the corner of Campus Avenue and Dowling. A man has hit his head on the curb." He worked his neck to the right and then the left, unkinking it. "No, I don't know him. I didn't see anything." He clicked off the call.

Cat stared at him accusingly. "What do you mean you don't know him? You didn't see anything?"

Matt hustled her up from Brad, and then propelled her toward the parking lot. "Really? You want to be involved in a police investigation?"

She immediately changed her demeanor from outrage to understanding. "Might not be a great idea. What if he tells them?"

Matt dismissed the thought with a shake of his head. "That he attacked me on the street? I don't think so."

"Tells them you turned into…God knows what?"

"Yeah, we probably need to talk." They reached the car, and he opened the passenger door. "Get in," he commanded. Cat hesitated and shifted uncomfortably from foot to foot. Matt rephrased. "Please. Get in, please."

# 2

Ambulance sirens spurred Matt to key the ignition. The incessant cry approached from an adjoining street and raced its way toward Brad. Matt wanted to get the hell out of here before the cops arrived.

Cat drew in a sharp breath as she looked him over. "You were worried about Brad, but…" She softly touched his ribs along his right side. "You're bleeding." She pulled her fingers back coated with dark sticky blood, then carefully peeled up his shirt, looking for the break in his skin. She felt gently, and then more firmly. "There's no broken skin!"

Matt winced and drew in a sharp breath. Her insistent prodding along his knitting ribs unexpectedly released the vampire, which would change his eyes from blue to opalescent. His fangs dropped. She arrested mid-stroke and gasped, withdrawing against the door of the car, flattening herself away from him. He hated the horrified look in her eyes. Not that he hadn't seen it before, but it got to him every time, revealing him to be the monster he always feared he was. She stared in shock -- which would wear off soon, and she would scream.

With effort, he normalized his appearance. "We'll talk. What's your address?" She didn't respond. "Cat? You're okay. What's your address?" He reached a tentative hand toward her, and she withdrew farther against the door.

Cat covered her face with her hands and curled into herself. Matt ignored her panic and reached for the backpack at her feet, withdrawing bottled water. "Here." He casually handed it to her. "The address on this thing, is that where you live?" She nodded and chanced a glance at him through the curtain of her fingers.

Just seeing the address in her tidy print unsettled him, ensuring the drive to her place was awkward and silent. As they pulled up to the crumbling façade of an art-deco apartment building, he sensed her salvaged composure. If only he could say the same for himself. The hairs on the back of his neck tingled at the memory of his last visit here. The building was a faded specter of its former grandeur. Now, it wasn't in the best area, and he wondered briefly if his car would be waiting for him on the street when he returned.

Cat cowered away from Matt's proffered hand when he bent to assist her out of the car, but she walked willingly enough by his side toward the building. Now, a key was required to enter, and he noticed her shaking hand as she inserted it.

They entered the hallway to an unexpected chill that seemed fitting, somehow. The cold stucco interior was cooler than the outside temperature by several degrees. Matt squinted at the glare of fluorescent lights off stark white walls. Where had the brass and crystal wall sconces gone? The mellow incandescent light on glowing mahogany paneling? Poorly plastered-over scars dotted the walls every ten feet of the formerly sumptuous grand foyer.

Matt strained to block out the cacophony of blaring televisions, crying babies and domestic quarrels, so different from the hip jazz trio which used to play in the lobby. The place smelled like mold, dust and last night's supper.

He glanced over at Cat. "Are you safe here?"

She led the way down the hall to her apartment, their footsteps muffled by cheap industrial carpeting which covered once gleaming marble mosaics.

A door opened immediately to their right, and a plump teenager dropped a soiled diaper bag outside her door and peered out at them.

"Hi, Amy! How are the twins?" The girl nodded, her inquiring gaze assessing Matt. "This is Matt Brenner," Cat continued, pronouncing his name clearly. "He's a student at the university."

A matronly woman from the apartment across the hall beamed at them from her living room couch. Obviously, she kept an eye on the comings and goings of everyone in the building through her open door.

"I didn't know you were taking night classes, mija?"

"Just tonight, Mrs. Gonzalez. I was modeling for the art department, in a class called Life Studies. This is Matt." Matt nodded genially at the woman. "He's just dropping me off at my door."

Matt trailed a look back at Mrs. Gonzalez as they passed, noting with concern her irregular, congested breathing.

They continued along the hall until they reached Cat's battered green door, and Matt wondered when they'd gutted the formerly expansive residences and replaced them with squalid studio and one-bedroom apartments.

"Well, you did a good job of that." He grinned.

She turned carefully innocent eyes up to him. "What?"

"Making sure everyone knew who I was and where to find me."

"It seemed polite."

He shook his head with another grin. "Right. So, ask me in. We still need to talk."

"Do I have to ask you in?" she whispered.

He gave her a flummoxed glance. "Uh…no, but I'm not the kind of guy to push my way into your place."

"Okay," she murmured, still cautious.

She opened the door to what might have been the smallest studio apartment he'd ever seen. It was neat, utilitarian and stark. Matt was struck by the large open space that dominated the middle of the small room until he realized the wood paneling centered on the wall was a Murphy bed. Cat gestured him onto the loveseat and leaned against the closed door.

She gave him a direct look. "Talk."

His stare back was just as direct. "Tell me what you think you saw."

"I know I saw you turn into something…in-human."

"In-human, huh?" he pondered. "Then…what would that make me?"

"Something I don't understand. Are you…an alien?"

Matt looked aside to squelch a smile, returning a serious face to her. "You mean, like from Mexico?"

"No, I mean, like…" She bit her lip and pointed upward.

"From upstairs?"

She laughed nervously. "No, I'm pretty sure everyone in this building has to prove citizenship."

"Ah…so, farther up? Like outer space?"

"Yeah, like outer space."

"No. I'm definitely from Los Angeles."

Cat paused and pondered what that could mean. "Then, what are you? Because what I saw…"

"I'm a vampire."

"That's impossible."

"You saw it for yourself. It's not the way I would choose to introduce my nature, but tonight's Murphy's Law in action."

She drew into herself again. "So, is this when you kill me?"

Matt buried a laugh. "Not tonight." And at her alarmed gasp, he added soothingly, "Not ever. I'm not ever going to kill you."

"Vampires are killers…"

"Maybe in bad B movies. Real vampires have a lot of different ways of eating, without killing. You'd be surprised."

"Oh. What's it like to be a vampire?" Her voice cracked as she pulled a pillow off the sofa and jumped back to the door. The upholstered would-be shield could do nothing to protect her. She feigned nonchalance. "Do you spend your life avoiding crosses and garlic? Is that why you're taking night classes?"

He looked at her from under his lashes. Her breath hitched. "Yeah, sunlight is a problem. It tires me out. I prefer nights."

Cat shifted fretfully and glanced toward the kitchenette wall. "May I get you a drink? I think I have some brandy left over from when I had the flu."

She nervously licked her lips, and in two steps, unearthed the barely touched bottle of Gallo brandy from a cabinet in the minuscule kitchen. Matt held up a halting hand.

"Well, I need a drink." She reached for a glass in the dish drainer and then poured a splash. She stood expectantly, her back against the metal cabinets, and waited.

"Look, I know you have a natural curiosity about me. The thing is, I overheard your conversation with Brad when I arrived for class tonight, and I didn't think it was right to leave you alone with him, so I got involved. Are you sorry I did?" She slowly shook her head. "I'm not sorry either. You know, if I'd been human…he meant to kill me."

"You must be invincible? I mean, first Brad and then the car."

"Yeah." He frowned, rejecting her line of questioning, and returned to the issue most on his mind. "Brad's a bad guy, Cat. I want you to stay away from him."

"Not that I'm arguing that point, but do vampires also order strangers around?"

He snorted and stared at her for a beat, his brows rising with concern. "How the hell did you get involved with a guy who has Domination fantasies? Do you really want to be a sub?"

"A what?" she asked with genuine innocence.

"A submissive." He paused. "You don't have a clue what I'm talking about, do you?"

She shook her head. "What are 'subs?'"

Matt pursed his lips. "It's a sexual fetish. I'm guessing you don't have much experience with them."

"I'm a writer," she declared before she drained the glass. "I should learn about everything."

He looked away, ruthlessly squelching a grin. "Stay away from Brad."

"Yeah. I already figured that out." She hesitated. "Do you mind if I ask, how did you become a vampire? Become, right? I mean, you're not born that way?"

Matt froze, an avalanche of memories stabbed his undead heart. His mortality ended in this building long before she was born.

"I don't want to be rude, but…" He rose. "There's nothing more you need to know. Stay away from Brad. Stay out of the art department. Have a good life." With vamp speed, he escaped the situation before Cat could react.

The convenience of vamp agility, which almost rivaled teleportation, allowed Matt to be nothing more than red tail lights in the distance by the time Cat reached the front door of her building. His supersensitive hearing caught her sudden indrawn breath immediately before he turned the corner and escaped her life forever.

As he drove, Matt considered his vow never to get involved with human females. They broke too damn easily. That was a truism he'd only needed to learn once, and much to his regret.

*What were the odds*, his mind raged. *What were the odds her apartment building would be that one? What were the odds the only human he'd taken an interest in for decades had led him to the site of his death? Against his will,* Matt's mind replayed her question. *How did you become a vampire?*

# 3

Los Angeles, July 1922

Los Angeles in the early 1920s had been exciting. The aftermath of World War I had brought damaged souls, too beautiful to work a trade, into the City of Angels to seek their fortune in moving pictures. Matt was born there and was immune to the temptations of the 'the business.' Good, solid work as a detective after his MP training in the Army was fine with him.

He didn't need the admiration of millions. The admiring glances of Ruth, the soda fountain girl at the Five and Dime on Broadway Street were plenty for him. She'd been flirting up a storm over the past week.

Assuming she agreed to a date, what would it take to get her horizontal? Matt's dick homed in on its favorite resting place, and that was not his hand. He'd always been popular with the ladies, but he recently hit a dry spell, and to tell the truth, he was parched.

"What have ya got to cool a guy down, Ruthie?" he asked, sliding onto the rotating counter stool.

"I thought you were the kind of guy who liked to burn?" She purred.

He grinned, infusing his look with a touch of wickedness. "That's for after hours. Why don't you join me tonight and find out?"

"Throw in a steak, and we'll burn the house down."

Matt swallowed around a lump of lust. "You got it, baby. Where and what time?"

* * * *

Matt was at the curb ready to pick her up on the dot of eight o'clock. His car looked great, he decided. Irritated by a tiny imperfection, he licked his thumb and then rubbed a smudge off the upholstery of the 1920 Model T. He'd spent an hour after work shining up this pussy-wagon. Never hurt to impress the girl. He leaned against the gleaming black fender, waiting for her, and wiped a drizzle of sweat off his forehead with a clean hanky.

"I could do that with my tongue," Ruth caught him off guard. She'd changed out of her drab soda fountain uniform and looked every inch the sexy siren in a clingy flapper skirt revealing way too much leg.

"I've gotta think about that all through dinner? Or were you thinking we'd go somewhere else first?" He greeted her with a kiss on the cheek, willing his cock into submission.

"Dinner first. You're gonna need all the energy you can get."

"Yes, ma'am." He swallowed hard. "Musso's has a prime rib with your name on it."

Musso and Frank's, famous for their Hollywood clientele, was also Matt's favorite steakhouse. He blew more than a little of his paycheck there every week, and that garnered him the special treatment he impressed Ruth with that night.

* * * *

Matt guided his date toward the back door. "Always a pleasure to see you, Detective Brenner," the maître d' called as they left.

The dinner conversation had been uninspiring, but the anticipation was razor-sharp. What did Matt care if she wasn't Einstein? She was gloriously willing, and intercourse of a different variety was what he had in mind now.

The stairs were just steep enough to make him catch the handrail for balance. Ruth stopped short ahead of him and ground her perfect backside against his hips. Matt ached to drill into that perfect ass. The air turned electric when they hit the sidewalk, and he hauled her against him for a plundering kiss.

"My place?" she whispered as they broke apart.

"Your place." He almost panted. She gave him the once-over, lingering long and interested at the bulge tenting his slacks. How the hell was he going to shift gears with a dick this hard?

"Yeah." She purred.

*Where does a girl who works at the Five and Dime get the coin for this frolic pad?* He pulled up at the curb, steps from her posh apartment building. The balcony lights of the lavishly landscaped art-deco structure beckoned invitingly. He looked at her askance.

"You some kind of heiress I don't know about?"

"I have terrific friends."

For reasons he couldn't quite name, Matt was suddenly uneasy. Instead of fishing for a key, Ruth stood beside the ornate wrought-iron door and removed a brass pad covering a speaking tube.

Confidently, with a sly look toward Matt, she addressed a disembodied recipient. "Not only the thirsty seek the blood."

"The blood, as well, seeks the thirsty," a voice intoned.

The heavy door drifted open, manned by a liveried servant. Music overcame Matt's senses as he eyed the tuxedoed jazz trio seated to his right. The elegant marble floors and massive chandelier glittered in the low light. He was becoming more impressed with his date by the minute. Apparently, she had terrific friends. He shuffled in anticipation, hoping her place was on the first floor.

She led him from the foyer and down a wide hallway. He lost count of the brass and crystal sconces dimly lighting their way. What was happening behind those heavy mahogany doors? She paused before a pair of massive ones at the corridor's end.

"You'll remember this forever," Ruth whispered over her shoulder as the doors swung open, seemingly of their own accord.

Matt struggled to see clearly through the dim light. A full orchestra played softly on the balcony, but these people were definitely not dancing. All around them translucently pale men and women grappled over richly upholstered ottomans and fainting couches. Were they doing the 'nasty' in public?

The man to his left had his face buried in a moaning woman's neck, her satin dress hiked around her waist while he delved his fingers deep inside her. Matt gawked. He considered himself a cocksman, but he'd never seen anything this blatant. To his right, a nude man kneeled submissively at the feet of a stunning naked woman, his arm lifted to her questing lips as he shuddered in sexual release.

Matt turned to Ruth in astonishment. "What the …?"

His words stuttered to a halt as a raven-haired beauty, hips and unbound locks swaying enticingly, glided toward them and locked gazes with him. She might have been the most exotic woman he'd ever seen. Delicately boned, café au lait skin and light celadon eyes, a perfect storm of dark and light.

The exquisite creature reached them and took Ruth's entranced face in her hands. She drew the girl's energy away with her touch. Her jade-eyed gaze assessed Matt from head to toe. His heart hammered. He wasn't sure he should touch a woman this beautiful, but he knew he wanted to. She spoke to Ruth, and he was captivated by the musical sound of a foreign language. He'd learned several languages during the war, but this was one he'd never heard before. It almost sounded French. Creole? Patois? Some other derivative of French?

An elegant hand reached out to touch his chest, red-tipped fingers playing over the knot of his tie. He glanced down at them, then back into her fathomless gaze.

At last, he found his voice and extended his hand. "Matt Brenner. And you are?"

She gave him a look somewhere between interest and disdain. "That's irrelevant," she said in perfect English. "Though, I suppose you should know my name before…" Her tongue played over her lips as she let the thought fade. Her words were replaced by a sinister chuckle. "It's Veronique."

A chill crept up his spine. Beautiful as she was, she gave him the creeps. This whole place gave him the creeps.

That delicate hand of hers slid up his chest and around his throat with more strength than he would ever have dreamed possible. Her steely fingered grip took him by surprise, and he moved with a pure instinct to fend her off. Hand-to-hand training rushed back to him as he grabbed her thumb, barely able to drag it back from his throat, peeling her hand away, and giving him mere seconds before she seemed to fly at him, her eyes opalescent slits. Her skin turned nearly transparent, emphasizing every blue vein, her nails elongated to wicked-looking claws and her even white teeth descended to sinister fangs.

Confronted with the monster before him, Matt swore. "Good god, what are you?" he demanded in a horrified gulp.

The punch he threw carried all his weight behind it. It barely slowed her down. Muttering broke out around them as a crowd of equally pale monsters watched the fight. She flattened him to the floor with one leap and then straddled him with both hands squeezing around his neck, choking the breath from him. His desperate punches fell impotently against her while his world dimmed from the edges inward. The last conscious impression he had as his world faded from gray to black was the slowing of his own heartbeat and the desperate need to draw breath into his faltering lungs.

* * * *

Matt's world returned in a rush of sensory overload. He lay against something soft and silky, and a ceiling fan spun lazily above him, churning heat-heavy air. His attention riveted to his throbbing dick. His vision cleared after a few blinks to see a head, hidden behind a curtain of dark wavy hair, bending over his groin.

Crimson lips ran the length of his rigid cock with a fierce suction threatening to pull the cum right out of his sac. He couldn't stifle a moan at the sweet pain her torment evoked. She smiled around his girth, sharp teeth grazing him as she lifted her head.

"Ah, I see you're awake." She drew her fingers daintily across blood-red lips.

Matt glanced down at his long, thick length, so aroused from the trail of gashes her fangs had excited.

"What fresh hell…?" he croaked.

"Oh, no, my darling. By the time I'm through with you, you'll be certain it's heaven."

Her lips descended to him again, and he was quickly convinced heaven was within his reach. She didn't stop when his cock hit the back of her throat. Matt shut his eyes and savored the sensation. She didn't gag or whimper as he thrust his hips up to meet her and his dick slid into the waiting column of her throat. The strangled cry was his as she repeatedly swallowed against him, her long tongue sensuously wrapping around him, driving him to the brink.

"Oh, fu…!" He gasped as she used her sharp nails to fondle his balls.

It was an act that should have taken him the last millimeter forward to a blinding release, and yet none came. Bewildered, he shuddered and plunged repeatedly into her icy mouth. He was right *there*. What was missing? The hot cum scorched out of his tight sac and edged up the length of his cool dick.

Veronique tore away from him for precious seconds. She exultantly leaned into his ear. "Bite me!" she begged. "Do it, now!"

21

*What in Satan's name is going on*, he wondered fleetingly until her lips surrounded him again and all thought ceased. In a desperate sexual frenzy, Matt sank his teeth into her wrist. The impact of her blood flowing against his tongue forced the scalding emission from his frigid body and into her waiting mouth. His orgasm suspended him in a vacuum, sensation thundered through every vein and sizzled along every nerve in his hypersensitive system. He shook, gasping, feeling disembodied.

Veronique lifted her head, smiling. Long, sharp canines splashed trails of blood down her neck to drip onto perfect breasts. That brought him back to earth, all right.

"Thunderation! What… are you? What have you done to me?"

Her smile was as tranquil as a stagnant pond. "Don't be trite. You know very well what I am. And now, what you are. Your innocent mind simply won't accept it."

Matt jumped from the bed in a panic. He was thirsty. So thirsty!

"Dry?" she simpered, seeming to read his mind. "Looking for something *red?*"

In horror, Matt realized she was right. He knew in an instant the name of the forbidden longing. It was blood. He wanted human blood.

"No!" he whispered in an agonized breath.

"Yes," Veronique countered, unperturbed. "Ruth." She'd raised her voice commandingly. "Come."

The bedroom door silently swung open, and Ruth, as if walking in a dream, drifted toward the bed. Veronique smiled at her unnecessarily.

"Come in, dear. I must express my gratitude. I asked for a man, and you brought me a god."

Ruth continued onto the bed and lay her head over the edge as if in mortal sacrifice. Veronique looked expectantly at Matt.

"What?"

"Now you may show your gratitude for the gift I've given you."

"Gift?" he began in confusion.

"Yes. Drain Ruth. Drink the gift of her blood, the life force you no longer possess but find in abundance within all the mortal creatures among us."

"Kill her?"

Veronique shrugged carelessly. "She's already brought me perfection. What chance is there she could do it again? Time for a new shill."

"You're mad! I'm not killing anyone."

Veronique gave him another sly smile. "It's not as if you can run down to the local market anymore, now, is it? If you don't kill, you're going to be very hungry, indeed. And cranky." She pouted suicide-red lips. "I don't like cranky men."

Dread and fury boiled up in him. He grabbed Ruth and thrust her away from the bed. "Get behind me and stay there," he growled, surprised by his own animalistic voice. To his dismay, she stood docilely rooted in place, making no effort to flee.

The husky timbre of Veronique's chuckle irritated him. "She's thralled, lover. She only hears my voice."

"I'm not going to let you hurt her! I'll fight you if I have to. Don't make me hurt you!"

"Oh!" Her giggle turned sultry, and Matt struggled to process her quixotic mood swings. "Are you courting me?"

His stomach turned, his thoughts churned. He didn't know much about vampire lore, but weren't crosses supposed to stop them? Where could he find one? Matt leaped from the bed, astonished at his strength and range. He found himself next to a dressing table, and as if it were nothing, he tore the legs from under it, forming a cross with the two sticks of furniture.

Veronique howled with derision. "What's that? A cross?"

"I-I thought vampires hated crosses?"

"Old wives' tale."

He grabbed Ruth and thrust her out the French doors and onto the balcony. "And yet you keep your distance from me."

"For now."

He snatched Ruth against him and jumped, not caring that they leaped from the top floor, not knowing whether either of them would survive the fall. To Matt's astonishment, he landed nimbly on his feet. Thinking she was still safely nestled against him, he pulled back to see Ruth's dead stare, her neck snapped.

Veronique was hot on his heels. "Come back, lover. You and I aren't finished."

"According to law, you have no right to hold him," a cultured voice from behind Matt intoned.

Matt spun around to find an elegant, athletic-looking man smirking at Veronique, delighting in her frustration. The man's whiskey-brown eyes watched them keenly as his lips curled up in an uncommon smile. He leaned against his gleaming Duesenberg with one booted foot crossed over the other.

"You must be Ronnie's au courant fledgling." The intruder straightened. "Why so glum?"

Matt defensively backed away, clutching Ruth's dead body, trying to guard his flanks against the two vampires, playing for time. Sick with regret, he laid her corpse down and turned toward the speaker.

"Who in blue blazes are you?" he snapped, trying to decide if the guy was an ally or enemy.

"Richard Hiatt," the man bowed his handsome head, "at your service."

"At my service? You're a little late. How do I get outta here, if you're at my service?" Matt glanced around, wondering what the hell weapon would keep these monsters at bay.

Richard's head jerked around to give Veronique an incredulous stare, and his voice dripped disdain. "Not again!"

"Oh, but he's so beautiful, Richard! Look at him," she whined, circling Matt as if admiring a stallion purchased at auction.

Richard's voice dropped dangerously low. "You must be certifiable to do this again, Ronnie. One Council re-education is all a vamp gets." Veronique dismissed Richard's words with a casual wave, but he was dogged. "Another rape-turn is going to earn you a sterling silver straight jacket and a stake."

"I'll leave the country." She eyed Matt sadly, hating to leave him behind. Over her shoulder, she added, "In a couple hundred years, he'll thank me. They always do."

Matt's flesh crawled, his mind struggled to adjust to his new incarnation. "I wouldn't thank you in a million years."

Richard's jaw clenched in anger. "You'll skip the country and leave your new turn with whom? Abandoned fledglings get put down."

"Fine. I'm ready," Matt spat.

"I'm not sure you really want that, dear boy," Richard intoned seriously. "In any case, you're in no condition to make that kind of decision at this point."

"I'll risk it. How much worse can it be?"

Richard inhaled a curious breath, his gaze roving over Matt's naked body. He shook his head. "Are you up for having her prosecuted?"

"I'm up for anything that puts the screws to her." Matt's furious gaze landed on Veronique, and his muscles twitched. His fangs dropped to score his unguarded lips and draw his own blood. It tasted raw and angry. "She deserves the gas chamber."

"Oh, dear boy." Richard shook his head. "You have no idea."

Matt watched the unfolding events with astonishment. Richard slid his hand into his breast pocket to retrieve what looked like a switchblade. With a flick of his thumb, a gleaming silver stake sprang out, and in a blur of movement, Veronique was caught and staked. Richard laid her prostrate on the lawn and turned to Matt.

"You've been ushered into a dark world, not of your own choosing. I'm sorry about that. Still, you'll see, there's justice here." He eyed Matt. "So, what's your name?

# 4



From that day to this, Richard, or "Rick" as he was now called, remained a fixture in Matt's life. Now, when he most felt the confines of his supposedly limitless existence oppressing him, he'd see Rick. Business partner, best friend, the annoying truth was, Rick persisted as his go-to guy for cockups.

Matt drummed his fingers on the steering wheel in agitation. His world had imploded. If there was ever a time, he needed the counsel of his best friend and more experienced vamp, this was it.

One luscious blonde not only stirred his libido and warmed his heart, but she'd also brought him face-to-face again with the unwanted brutality of his existence. He took a deep unnecessary breath as if the additional oxygen would calm him. He needed the rush of air, needed to feel the wind. With a flip of a switch, the Jag's rag top folded neatly away. Yeah, it would net him some curious looks from other drivers this time of year, but what the deuce? It was a singular car. They'd think he was a rich asshole showing off his swanky convertible.

Wasn't that a bitch? He was a member of the most powerful species on the planet, and still, he had to be careful not to stand out, not to cause suspicion, not to have anyone look at him too closely. And what had he done? He'd fought a mortal who'd been severely injured, without actually killing him, and without having the responders eliminate the evidence. Worse, he'd done it in the presence of a mortal woman. That was just goddamn stupid. Rick would know what to do.

What was today? He glanced at his watch. Yeah, of course, Wednesday, nine o'clock in the evening. Rick would be at The Gaoler, the flagship of the BDSM clubs they jointly owned. Wasn't there a demonstration tonight? Matt begged off because of his class, but Rick would be there. He needed to get in quietly, find Rick and get out again. There was a good reason for the BDSM clubs, Matt admitted. Still, he was in no mood for a demonstration tonight. Vampires needed donors who willingly offered their blood in exchange for the sexual high of the vampire's bite. Most mortals, male or female, weren't sexually adventurous enough to deal with the question, "Listen, would you mind if I drank about a pint of your blood? It'll really get you off."

On the other hand, mortals who frequented BDSM clubs, especially submissives, found this kind of thing right up their alley. A little pain, a big orgasm, great fun! The vamps got fed and laid all in one hot night.

For Matt, it was getting old. He was starting to believe the entire human race was kinky. And while that might be true to some extent, he didn't want another female who got off on pain and being ordered around. Fuck the power exchange. He wanted a woman who wanted him, the man he was, not just the ultimate sexual partner. He wanted a woman with heart and guts and brains. While he was sure those qualities were possessed by many in the submissive community, a BDSM club wasn't where he thought he'd find her, not that he'd been looking for a *mortal* woman, anyway.

Rick's warning echoed in his mind. *Avoid emotional involvement with mortals. They can't detach.* Matt found that only too true, and avoided relationships with mortal women until one soft, naive blonde with candy-pink nipples and more guts than sense wormed her way into his undead heart. *Now what?*

* * * *

Matt entered the Consort Group International building, home of the mega-conglomerate he owned with Rick, which housed its central financial office on L.A.'s Miracle Mile. The building was meant to showcase the company's wealth in the most impressive light possible. It was through the imposing glass and marble structure he strode purposefully past the chic cocktail bar which was the beard for their first S&M club, as they were called in the 1920s. The lounge was just as popular today as a watering hole for the building's execs and hopeful assistants.

The clubs—both legit and clandestine—began as speakeasies and flourished once the mob learned better than to interfere. They had morphed into S&M playgrounds and enjoyed their current incarnation as BDSM clubs. They'd made Matt's fortune and expanded Rick's substantially. He and Rick had a blend of talents which proved phenomenally successful. Matt managed security, personnel, and physical plants, and Rick managed guest relations, business, and finances.

One set of clubs grew to more than eighty in cities all over the world. If one vamp required several donors, a million vamps required legions, and they all needed a home. Little by little, Consort Group became Consort Group International, and they expanded their reach into other areas until now Matt and Rick owned a diverse number of businesses.

All this prosperity meant an extremely comfortable lifestyle for both of them, but Matt felt a creeping ennui, which was the reason for his foray into an art class tonight. One abbreviated meeting with Cat banished it, that was sure, but he wasn't so confident its uneasy replacement was a good trade.

Matt continued into the sleek chrome and slate elevator and caught his reflection in the wall's high polished shine. *You're the top of the food chain*, he reminded himself, ironically. He didn't feel like it just now.

A press of the button marked Consort started the car on its descent, and as the overhead numbers descended past Basement, Matt touched his hand to a security pad. Immediately, the lights dimmed to a deep red glow. The temperature dropped precipitously, and the canned elevator Muzak converted to the thrumming of a human heartbeat that reverberated against the walls and all through him.

The Gaoler featured another bar and lounge, one dealing in booze and blood and socializing, an exclusive dining room with both human and vamp cuisine and a demonstration room used for public submissions. Then, there were long hallways of privately owned and publicly rented dungeons.

The elevator doors opened with a discrete *swoosh*, admitting Matt to the hallway of dungeons. He automatically scented the area. The aroma of willing humans swirled with anticipation, fear, and excitement. He combed his gaze over the crimson leather wallpaper and thick, black carpet. Here again, the lights were muted, meant to mimic flickering carriage lanterns. Soundproofing kept the various moans, pleas, and screams from mortal ears, but he felt them viscerally, his vampire hearing catching every mortal response.

Being the owners of the clubs gave Rick and Matt the privilege of position and convenience. Their dungeons were almost directly across from the elevators, and a few steps from the bar.

"Why are you so upset?" Rick narrowed his eyes when Matt barged into his private dungeon. "The guy had a head injury. Even if he has the memory and balls to tell someone, who would believe him?" Rick sensuously ran a cat-o-nine tail across his palm several times as they talked.

His cute little sub, Bambi, waited impatiently for him, shackled in place over the spanking bench.

"Maasster?" she whimpered, longing evident in each drawn-out syllable.

Rick and Matt turned heavily censorious frowns her way.

"You wait for me without complaint until I'm ready, sub," Rick corrected. "I guess you're not ready for the big bite tonight, after all."

Her whine was pitiful. "Why? Because of him?" Her look spewed venom toward Matt.

Matt shrugged. "Oh, hell, Rick, give her what she wants. I did interrupt the party."

Rick's eyes flashed opalescent at him, letting Matt know he tread on dangerous territory. "You never were any good at dominance games, dear boy, but you should know better than to get between me and a sub in training." He walked Matt to the door of the dungeon. "You need to go to the lounge, get some blood and have that girl who's so hot for you. What's her name?"

"Anna," Matt muttered glumly.

"Right, Anna. Have Anna fondle your knob, feed a little and dial it all down. When I'm through here…should be about an hour…I'll join you. We'll talk about this thing and see if the girl needs to be eliminated or thralled or just left alone."

Matt nodded and left. Rick was right. He needed to calm the f' down. His mood was as dim as the light of the hallway as he left the dungeon. Mortals, who frequented the place, were grateful for the low lighting—not all that eager to be recognized—and vamps required no extra light. He headed toward the bar and lounge. Maybe a vampire woman would be there. Maybe, her sweet lips around his cock would calm him down. His footsteps slowed as he neared the door.

Two feet away he changed his mind. He didn't want a vamp's lips on his dick. That was a first. He'd never turned down oral pleasure in his existence. The truth was, the one pair of lips he wanted belonged to a sassy mortal co-ed with a knack for staking him on the horns of his own desires. Sometimes life sucked. He would grab a quick pint from the bar, and then wait for Rick in his playroom. Maybe, there was a game on television tonight.

The first sound Matt heard as he reached to open the padded leather door was female laughter, hot and raucous and a little drunk. He listened for a second. *All women. No men. No vamps,* either. Hmm. This could get interesting. It'd been some time since he'd had a party for six, and him the lone male.

"Don't get me wrong," the woman continued. "He's hot as Hades to look at, and from what I hear, he has great equipment, but you know what, he doesn't know how to use it."

"That's not true." It was Anna's voice. "He does have great equipment—unbelievable equipment—every time he bites me, I feel so…so spectacular. I come so hard. He's ruined me for any other man. Nobody gets me off the way Matt does." There was a derisive laugh from one of the other women. "Matt's just…he's too…too tenderhearted for all these domination games." Her words were met with more derisive laughter.

"A tenderhearted vampire? C'mon. None of them are."

Matt peeked around the edge of the opaque window with just enough clear glass to show him the speaker—Tina, a strident bleached platinum-blonde a few years past ripe. He'd pitied the woman more than once for spending the majority of her time at The Gaoler. Word was, her blood was laced with drugs and artificial hormones. Only the truly desperate even considered biting her. He guessed it was sour grapes talking.

Anna's gasp was genuine. "I think you really mean that! You can't honestly believe all vampires are cruel. And if you do, why are you here every night begging for a bite?"

"Oh, don't listen to her," admonished a dark-haired woman in a nearly invisible jumpsuit cinched by a thin gold chain. "She's drunk. She doesn't know what she's saying." The brunette checked her makeup in a compact mirror. "Matt's a good guy, vamp, whatever. He's just…" she flicked one acrylic nail against another, "boring, and way too cautious."

Matt's eyebrow shot up.

Anna angrily turned her way. "Matt is not boring. He's just not into

BDSM, and he would never want to hurt a mortal donor. Has he ever fed from you?" The other woman shrugged non-committedly. "He hasn't, has he? So you can't possibly know"

"Why are you here?" the dark-haired woman challenged. "You're the world's worst submissive, though you pretend to like it. Why do you come here?"

Anna waited a long beat before she answered truthfully. "The bite, and if the rest of you are honest, you're here for the bite too."

"Nope." The brunette closed the clasp of her purse with a finite click. "I was playing dominance games long before I learned about vamps. I'll be doing it with my husband long after vamps are gone from my life. Some of us are dedicated to the lifestyle. You're obviously not. Please excuse me."

She rose regally and strolled out, having the good grace to cast her eyes down as she slid past Matt. He guessed this was his cue to get Anna out of there.

* * * *

Cat finally succumbed to sleep after her over-stimulating day, but it was restless and stained by dreams of a handsome man with haunting eyes and long wicked fangs, standing over her, his dark curls wild in a phantom wind. She awoke with a start, a cry on her lips, and lay in the semi-darkness, listening to an infant's plaintive wail.

Matt Brenner was a vampire. She'd been in shock, she supposed, when it had all happened. Now, clarity replaced her fear with curiosity. More accurately, she corrected herself, he thought he was a vampire. She'd heard of instances where psychosis affected physical appearance. Opalescent eyes? Translucent skin? Fangs? That seemed unlikely.

Another possible explanation? Hypnosis? Hmm. She'd have to research that one. Drugs? Had he drugged her into seeing him change and then revert to normal? When? They'd never had that coffee. The only thing she ingested around him was her own brandy, and he'd been several feet away when she'd poured it. Even if he had managed to drug her somehow, why? He seemed to want to get away from her, not forge a relationship, which again begged the question, why? Why go to the trouble of hypnotizing and/or drugging her only to leave before the payoff?

What possible payoff could there be? Sex? He was awfully knowledgeable about that whole Dom/sub thing. Cat looked up sexual dominance and submission on the Internet after he left. She'd never imagined such things, and to find there were actual BDSM clubs and conventions…well, that was all too much for her.

She acknowledged her sexual experience was limited to some thoroughly hot kisses and a little light petting, but that was just because Mr. Right hadn't come along yet, and she didn't want Mr. Right-Now. Maybe, it was the Catholic boarding school in her, but she wanted a sexual relationship built on mutual trust and respect, and she was willing to wait for it until she found love.

She disciplined her thoughts back to the topic. Maybe a priest would know if vampires truly exist? No, someone higher up – a bishop? A cardinal? There were mystical secrets known only in certain circles of the church. Was it possible? Who did one ask? And if she did, would they lock her up, thinking her mad? She flopped over in frustration, pounding her pillow into submission.

It would be dawn soon, and she didn't think she could face the new day. If he really was a vampire, would Matt be going to bed now?

She wanted to fall back asleep and dream of a handsome man with a deep, warm voice and raw animal power he leashed with a gentle manner. She wanted him to have clear cobalt-blue eyes. She started to drift into dreams. She wanted his lips on hers, not snarling over dangerous-looking teeth. She wanted his hands on her…she descended into the dream and didn't awaken again until the sun was high in the sky.

* * * *

Matt's swift and silent appearance next to Anna caused her to gasp in surprise. "Come with me," he commanded warmly.

She looked at him, concern evident in her soft green eyes. "Those women, they don't…"

"Come with me," he repeated, taking her arm before leading her into a waiting elevator.

"Where are we going?" The doors closed, and they started ascending.

"What are you doing?" Matt cut directly to the heart of his concern.

"I…you said I should come…I…"

"What are you doing in this place? In this life? Anna…" He prowled forward, vamping out as he went, snatching her against him before she could brace herself. "Don't you understand how much danger you're in from me and every other vampire in this place?" His face as animalistic as his growl.

"You wouldn't hurt me, Matt." She glided her free hand down the side of his transformed face. "I know you wouldn't."

"If you really believe that, you're naïve. And wrong." He let his features return to normal. "Donors die feeding us, Anna." She shook her head. "Yes. It happens more frequently than anyone will admit. Everyone feels bad, but from a vamp's perspective it's only the loss of one more mortal." His stare bore into her. "Is the high of the bite really worth it?"

Anna shrugged, reluctant to reply. "No one makes me feel the way you do when you feed, Matt. No one else even comes close."

Matt sighed heavily and looked away, studying her unguarded reflection in the metallic finish of the elevator wall. The doors opened with a muted *swish*. Without regret, he came to a firm decision. "You're going home, right now." He hated to see the tears that immediately sprang to her eyes. "You're no longer welcome at the Gaoler."

She gasped at his pronouncement and stared at him in shock as if she'd just received a mortal blow from the last person on Earth, she thought would hurt her.

"Why?"

"Because you're addicted to the bite, and if you don't stop now, you're looking at the kind of future Tina has. Is that what you want? A barfly at some vampire lounge? C'mon, baby, you're too good for that. You're too good for us."

"It's not the bite I'm addicted to," Anna corrected. "It's the biter."

Oh God, he didn't want to have this conversation tonight. It was never pleasant, and he wasn't exactly at his best right now. Well, hell-fire, it looked as if he had no choice. He spoke the words to reinforce his resolve. "I will never get romantically involved with a mortal woman, Anna. Never."

"How do you know if—"

"Anna, please." She shivered slightly as he placed cool hands on her shoulders and turned her to face him. "Don't waste your life on me or any other vamp. Find your thrills doing worthwhile things in the mortal world." He shook his head and paused to press a consoling kiss against her temple. "Don't look for a life in the Vampire Nation. Life doesn't exist here."

With a distinct thud of her car door, Matt closed his final episode with Anna. He turned to find Rick at the high-rise's entrance, still dressed in his

Dom leathers. Something must be up.

"What was that all about?" Rick nodded toward Anna's retreating car.

"I banned her from the club."

Rick raised a brow. "You banned her from our club?"

"She's sweet and smart and could have a brilliant life in front of her. If we don't get her out..." Matt shook his head. "I don't want that on my conscience."

"Your conscience works overtime, dear boy," Rick replied flippantly and then relented at Matt's irritated look. "All right, I'll see what I can do. You really must stop rescuing the donors. It's becoming a bad habit." Rick glanced up at the impressive high-rise that his business acumen, learned over centuries, built. "Consort Group must have a position somewhere that would satisfy her."

"Somewhere without vamps," Matt decreed.

"It's a mystery to me why you hold our kind in so little esteem." Matt's gaze didn't shrink from the older vampire's withering look. Finally, Rick gave a curt nod. Matt clapped a hand on his best friend's leather-clad shoulder and turned to leave.

"Wait." Rick's hand on Matt's arm stopped him. "Aren't we going to discuss that little dust-up you had earlier this evening?"

Matt turned back, looking chagrined. "You know, you were right. I just needed to dial it all down. Mission accomplished. Nothing for you to worry about."

"Okay, either you took my advice and let Anna get you off before you put her in that car or you're a lying bastard."

Matt clenched his jaw. "Neither. I came to my senses, that's all. Sorry, I hit the panic button. This girl, Cat, unnerved me. It's nothing. Go back to your party."

"Come with me," Rick insisted. "Catalina's here. She's been asking for you. For both of us, actually. That's the kinda party I'm talking about."

"Not tonight. I'm beat. I'm going home."

"Indulge me. It's been a long time since I've been between Catalina's dark, smooth thighs. She says she's a vamp in search of a good vampire thrill and chill. Who are we to refuse?"

Matt shook his head. "You shouldn't refuse." He nodded toward the door. "I can only imagine the fun I'm missing out on. Catalina is seriously hot, but I'm not good company tonight, man. I'd damper the party, and you and Catalina would be pissed. So, tell her we'll do it another time, and we'll have a threesome until her toes curl. Just…not tonight. Okay?"

Rick studied him speculatively. "I have a feeling we're going be talking about that co-ed soon. Okay, if it's not tonight, Catalina and I will send a toast your way. Your loss."

They rode the elevator down together as far as the garage. "Please tell me you at least got some goodbye touch from Anna tonight."

"C'mon." Matt shifted uncomfortably under his scrutiny. "You don't expect me to kiss and tell?" Rick knew perfectly well Matt never bedded a donor.

The door to the garage level opened. "I do indeed expect you to kiss and tell, and I want to know everything, dear boy."

Matt sighed as the elevator doors closed and then walked to his car. He knew Rick had given up "vanilla" sex over a century ago. Now, it was non-stop kink for the five-hundred-year-old vamp, who pointed out more than once uninspired sex became boring after a few hundred years.

Matt supposed that was possible. Hard to conceive, but possible. He still couldn't imagine himself being attracted to all the things Rick was into. He loved women too much to want to control them, vampire or mortal. He loved the scent and sound of them, the soft, receptive feel of them. BDSM couldn't offer what he needed in the bedroom. As friends went, Rick was like a brother, and their friendship meant the world to him.

# 5

Cat awakened in the mid-morning with a new sense of purpose. Where the heck did Matt Brenner come from? If she intended to be a crime novelist, which involved detective-level research, surely, she could find one man? She started at their only common contact—the university.

"Student information is restricted," the disinterested registrar's clerk said.

"Well, what if it's an emergency?" Cat wheedled.

The older woman fastened her with a skeptical stare. "Is it an emergency?"

"No."

She'd been raised by nuns. Lying was nearly impossible for her. With a sigh, she turned away from the counter, slinking from the woman's derision.

A gawky young man in a mismatched shirt and tie followed Cat out of the office. "Hey, I, um, couldn't help overhearing your problem." Admiration and interest were evident in his earnest face. "There's a way to get that guy's information, you know."

Hope surged. "There is? How?"

"Go to the library. Behind the computer banks are the stacks. Look for big blue binders containing the class rosters. They have the names and contact info on every student in every class. You have to look closely. All the information is run together. I guess they think we're too stupid to notice they are addresses and phone numbers, but that's where you'll find his info. What'd he do to you, anyway?"

Cat looked up at him with a wry grin. "He gave me a flash of epic proportions. Thanks a million!" She punctuated her gratitude with a quick, hard kiss to his cheek, leaving him startled but delighted.

"Hey, any time!" he called after her. "If you need anything, ask for me. My name's Troy."

* * * *

In the library, Cat took the time to see what she could find online about Matthew Brenner. Birth certificate, military service—service in World War I? Can't be. Property ownership, tax records, newspaper articles, all contained his name. None of the confusing mish-mash of dates made sense. How could he have a military record from 1914 and own a condominium in this decade? Was he a suffix? Jr, III, IV? She needed answers, and the source would have to be Matt himself.

"This can't be right," Cat whispered as she pulled open the etched glass door to a 1920s condominium building that still held a majestic spot on the Miracle Mile.

She was immediately struck with a blast of nearly frigid air from the overworked air conditioner. Gold-veined black marble played in swirling patterns across the floor and marched up the walls. A dignified concierge stopped sorting mail behind the heavily carved walnut reception desk and looked up inquiringly at her approach.

"I need to see Mr. Brenner, please. I'm not sure what unit he's in."

The concierge looked down his considerable nose at her. "I'm sorry, miss. Access to Mr. Brenner's unit is restricted."

"Oh…uh…" She pulled a book from the backpack at her side. "Well, he accidentally left his textbook on his desk, and I…"

"If you would care to leave the item with me, I'll see that Mr. Brenner receives it."

"You will? Um…well…I owe him some money too, so…"

The man slid a pad of embossed stationery her way along with a pen. "Why don't you write a note with your name and number? I'm sure Mr. Brenner will be happy to call you about money."

Cat stifled a frustrated retort and bit her lip. "Yeah, I'm sure." She jotted her name and number on the pad and then turned briskly on her heel without another word.

"Oh, miss." He stopped her before she reached the door. "I could give you the name and location of Mr. Brenner's office if that would help." He nodded toward the street. "It's not far from here on Wilshire."

"You could? Oh, thank you!" She smiled and danced back to the desk.

* * * *

Cat entered the tasteful and expensively decorated private offices of Consort Group International where the glare of the winter sun was nothing but a dim memory. She was surprised to be shown to Matt's office with so little fanfare since his name was on the wall as a partner. A pretty receptionist looked up from her desk as Cat walked through the door to a suite of offices, specifying Human Resources, Security and Property Oversight. She was directed toward his private office.

Cat looked around in awe. Not since Disneyland had she stepped into a more themed environment. From the lettering on the door to the heavy mahogany and leather furnishings and the Jean Harlow look-alike at the desk reserved for Matt's assistant, the place screamed 1920s elegance.

"Wha'cha need, doll?" the platinum-blonde behind the desk asked brightly, startling Cat.

She would have expected someone with a little more sophistication in such a swank setting. "What?" Cat struggled with the time warp.

The woman looked her up and down. "You sellin' something?"

"No. I…uh…I need to see Matt Brenner."

"Oh, sorry, doll. He's never in this early. You lookin' for a job? I can leave a message for you. Here." She slid another pad and pen toward Cat. "Leave your—"

"Name and phone number, I know." She had a stare-down with the sultry platinum-blonde and finally relented. "Okay, fine! Here!" She jotted her name and number almost illegible in her frustration.

The secretary squinted at the pad and crooked a brow. "I'll give it to him. Don't know if he'll be able to read it."

"Just tell him to call, please."

* * * *

Cat ordered a fancy cup of coffee, all she could afford, as she stared determinedly at the metal-webbed door guarding the entrance from the adjacent garage to Matt's condo building. She glanced at the clock above the serving counter, ignoring the aggravated glances of the barista, who'd watched her monopolize a table for the past hour. Five fifteen. People should be coming home from work soon, and, if he really was a vampire, Matt should be getting up. How did he manage to run a multi-national corporation at night? Maybe he had 'people' for daylight hours. She laid fifty cents on the table for the persnickety server and then headed across the street to put her plan into action.

A string of Mercedes, Lexuses, and Porsches rolled through before Cat could secret herself behind a huge Cadillac SUV and sneak into the adjacent garage. She followed a smartly suited woman into the locked elevator, trying hard to look as though she belonged. She would have to trust unit 1001 would be on the tenth floor, probably the penthouse. When the door slid open, the plush green carpet led into a richly decorated hallway with three massive heavily carved walnut doors, but no unit numbers. Which one should she approach? She gnawed her lip in indecision, and finally resolved to knock until she got an answer.

* * * *

Matt leaned against the cool wood of the door, feeling her warmth penetrate it. He inhaled. Honeysuckle and lavender mixed with vibrant young woman. He knew, without consulting the security monitor, it was Cat. He'd never forget her scent. They were victims of happenstance. His smile faded. Along with the delicacy of her pheromones, he detected frustration, confusion and uncertainty, none of which he'd be able to relieve.

Sensational intensity welled inside him, his longing so acute he'd willingly walk through that door to get to her. Why? Why her? He'd been tempted by hundreds, maybe thousands, of beautiful human women in his long life. Most of them wanted him. Some were more beautiful, feature for feature than Cat, but no one had ever affected him the way she did. He was desperate. Afraid she'd find him. Afraid she wouldn't.

He knew what Rick would recommend. Bed her, bite her, turn her. That was what vampires did. Not Matt. He remembered only too well the devastation he felt over his own unwelcome turning. He'd never do that to another soul. He'd never been a sire. Had never wanted to, even with a willing participant.

He sensed Cat's pain and resignation as she looked up at the camera guarding his door one last time before she turned, shoulders slumped with defeat and headed back into the elevator. She couldn't know the fate he protected her from. Even though it was decades ago now, he vividly recalled the night Veronique changed his life forever, and in the process changed her own.

* * * *

Los Angeles, July 1922

Matt had stood in the sultry July night, naked and vulnerable, surrounded by murmuring vampires and confronted with Richard's tart sympathy. Richard had tossed him a trench coat from the front seat of the Duesenberg, and while Matt donned it, the older vamp had engaged in a quiet but intense conversation with some grim-faced vamps in blue uniforms.

Before his appalled gaze, two of them grabbed Veronique's paralyzed arms while another insured the silver stake through her heart was secure and effectively immobilized her. They lifted her supine onto a stretcher and then loaded her into what appeared to be an ambulance.

"W…Where are they taking her?" Matt stammered when he could find his voice.

"To trial…"

* * * *

Matt found the lengths to which vampires went in duplication of mortal courts impressive. If he hadn't known better, he would have been sure they sat in a California superior courtroom, save for the immediacy of the trial. This court played for keeps, and Veronique's sentence was more than a slap on the wrist, even by vampire standards.

The judge seated upon his bench intoned Veronique's fate. "In as much as rehabilitation has not reformed your behavior, it is the decision of this court that you be staked for a period of not less than one hundred and fifty years. If, after that time, there should be a reoccurrence of the crime of siring without consent, the penalty will be termination."

Veronique sat un-staked, but head bowed as the judgment was made. Matt almost felt sorry for her…almost. After all, she hadn't killed him, after a fashion. He did continue to exist, but in some ways, an existence as a monster was worse than death.

"Richard Hiatt…" the judge continued.

"My lord?" Richard stood and answered brightly.

"I have here a petition for protection, giving you legal authority to mentor one Matthew Brenner?"

41

Matt rose slowly to his feet and stared at the man beside him in slack-jawed surprise.

"Yes, my lord," Richard confirmed. "The incarceration of Miss Moreau has left Mr. Brenner an orphaned fledgling. In an effort to protect him from becoming feral, I beg the court to allow me to mentor him until he reaches vampiric majority."

"Your paperwork is in order." The judge pursed his lips and studied Matt. "It's a generous offer." He spoke to Matt as if speaking to a child. "Do you agree to Mr. Hiatt's mentorship, young man?"

Richard turned toward Matt with a smile. "Say yes or face certain death," he urged pleasantly.

"Uh…yes?"

"That's a yes?" the judge questioned dourly.

"Yes," Matt said more firmly, realizing he needed help in this strange parahuman world. "Yes, sir. I'm grateful for the help."

* * * *

Matt sat awed that first sunrise when Richard's chauffeur pulled the Duesenberg up to the mansion's shaded doorway. The curbside arrival allowed them to step from the indulgence of the car into the comfort of a truly spectacular house without encountering sunbeams. Matt stared agog at the luxury around him.

"Who are you? Rockefeller?"

Richard shrugged. "I've lived a few centuries, and I've accumulated a few toys."

"I guess so."

"I advise a glass of champagne before the purging begins," Richard said light-heartedly.

"Purging?"

"Yesss." Richard drew the word out slowly, glancing at his watch. "It's been approximately seven hours since you were turned. Within this next hour, your body should purge itself of everything human. That means bodily waste, I'm afraid. We'll get you settled in a loo straightaway."

"Great," Matt mumbled disheartened.

"There, there. Think of it as a brief bout with sprue. You'll be completely right again within a few hours when all the unnecessary material is out of your system."

Matt looked at him suspiciously. He had a dim memory of his mother referring to a violent stomach malady as sprue. "You mean I'll be vomiting and having—"

"Dear boy!" Richard raised a hand. "No need to go into graphic detail. We all know what I mean. Ramon," Richard beckoned his young majordomo. "Tell the donors to be ready to service Mr. Brenner any time he asks in the next day or two."

"Very good, sir," Ramon agreed with a bow. "Before you head upstairs, Mr. Brenner should call this number." He handed a paper to Matt. "The court bailiff has rung several times."

Richard gestured Matt to the phone while Ramon left to make arrangements.

On the phone, Matt had vamped uncontrollably, nearly crumpling the heavy receiver as he spoke. "What can they do to nab her?" He snarled. He'd chuffed out a breath and humanized. "Call me when you know."

Matt had looked from the phone into Richard's inquiring stare. "Veronique's on the lam."

* * * *

Los Angeles, Present Day

That was the last anyone in North America saw or heard from Veronique Moreau. Even after all this time, gnawing anxiety churned Matt's gut whenever he thought of her. So, no, vampirism wasn't something he'd inflict on any mortal, certainly not Cat. The only way to protect her, despite his inexplicable attraction to her, was to stay completely away from her, and that's exactly what he intended to do.

Moonrise found Matt on the phone with his assistant. "Sorry to get you on the I-5 late, Jonesy."

"That's okay, boss. I was waitin' for my nails to dry. What's the word?"

"I'm taking a breeze. I need to cancel some meetings, but you have the appointment book."

"It's that big?"

"Ice my appointments for tonight and tomorrow, will you?"

"Gotcha, but…"

"You can leave after that. Tomorrow, have Giles take over security. Marlon and Justin can handle personnel and maintenance. I'll be gone until…" he thought for a moment. "June."

43

"Hey, uh, does this mean I'm out of a job?"

"No, you've still got a job, kid. I need someone to take care of the office." He grinned at her delighted shriek.

"What do I tell folks about why you left?"

Matt frowned. "Do I have to give a reason?"

"Only if you wanna stay in business, see? I mean, boss, people get really annoyed without an explanation."

"Well, okay, I don't care what you tell 'em. Just don't tell anyone where I'm going or when I'll be back."

"You got it. Where are you going?"

"See you in June." He disconnected the call.

More calls followed to the cabin caretaker, his Red Cross contact and the building super. He'd see Rick in person in the morning. Leaving without a goodbye would really piss off his partner. Besides, they owned the cabin jointly, and he'd need the ski plane.

* * * *

Veronique Moreau pulled off her Armani shades and watched avidly, if uneasily, as her crew guided her yacht, *Escape*, toward her berth at the California Yacht Club. The boat was both ironically and accurately named. A yacht had been her escape from capture since 1922, and though she was on her sixth generation of *Escape*, the strategy still worked. She never lingered in any port longer than necessary, she banked on scores of lonely sailors available to parlay their lives for her beauty.

For companionship, Ronnie had family, or at least, her first cousin, Elise. She and Elise had dallied their way around the port cities of the world several times in the past decades, although they avoided the coast of the western States. Now, there was a bigger, more legitimate reason to risk capture in Los Angeles.

When she and Elise concocted the idea, which would take them beyond the dreams of avarice, it was a lark, and they had been simple partiers. Now, it was so much more. A venture begun for kicks became a deal pursued for a fortune's sake. Their designer drug attracted the crème de la crème of Euro-trash vamps, who couldn't get enough of the stuff and circulated the code word for their scores to their American cousins.

The chance to feel human, to expose their immortality-numbed senses to the blood rush of adrenaline was a hot commodity that would inevitably draw

Veronique before the judgment of the tight-assed Vampire High Council. That would mean scrutiny and the revelation of her arrest warrant in the United States. The Council was already iffy on whether her little moneymaker posed a danger to the Vampire Nation. She couldn't risk re-capture so Matt Brenner and his charge of siring without consent would have to be dealt with.

Then the nay-sayers would kiss off. Once she and Elise were done, there would be no more kowtowing to her family for money; no more acceding to the will of the Vampire High Council. The money from this endeavor would make her so powerful, no one would dare touch her again, especially if she won the forgiveness of that ingrate, Matt Brenner. Then, the world would be hers.

* * * *

Rick snarled only slightly when Matt barged into the meeting with the Taiwanese delegation. What difference did it make? He and Matt owned it all, anyway. It wasn't as if they wouldn't wait for him.

"Yes, your highness." Rick sneered when they were alone in his private office. "How may I serve you?"

Matt snorted and self-consciously rubbed the back of his neck. "Sorry to interrupt your meeting." He ducked his head. "I'm going to the cabin for a while. I told Jonesy to expect me back in June—"

"Wait!" Rick raised a hand. "My razor-sharp vampire instincts tell me this mysterious co-ed is somehow involved in your decision."

"No…well, maybe." He shook his head. "Damn, I don't know."

Rick folded his arms over his well-muscled chest and stared blandly.

"All right, all right. You got me. I confess. Somehow she got into my building last night."

"She got into your home?"

"Not exactly, no." Rick's silence prompted him. "She got to the door."

"Oh, horrors! I immediately see your need to flee—"

"Don't rag on me, Rick!" Matt's eyes flashed quickly opaline and then back to blue. "I don't know why she bothers me so much. I just have to get away from her. She…she makes me feel things…I don't want to feel."

Rick considered him seriously for a moment, realizing this was not all impulse on Matt's part. He narrowed his eyes at his friend. "Dear boy, I could take care of it, you know. One call, she disappears forever."

Matt was outraged. "No! God, no! That's the last thing I want! I swear to God, Rick, you harm one cell of her body and I'll—"

"Whoa, whoa!" Rick held up his hands in surrender. "Okay. She's safe as a fledgling, okay? Bollocks, you've got it bad, you poor bastard! Why don't you just turn her and be done with it?"

"Take her life as Veronique took mine?" Matt demanded with renewed horror.

"Actually, I was thinking more that you might ask her nicely, but your call."

"No. Don't ask me that again."

Rick shrugged. "So, what are you gonna do when you get back, and she's still here?"

"Yeah…" Matt rubbed his neck again, a surefire signal to Rick that he was about to ask for something outrageous. "I think it's time for Consort Publishing to sponsor a writing contest. Something with big prize money and a relocation to the office in New York where the winner gets a free semester or great internship or something…" He gestured vaguely. "She's a writer. I looked up some of her stuff on the university website. She's pretty good. This is a contest she's gonna win."

"And we're footing the bill for all this? What's in it for the company?"

"I think she'll make Consort Publishing money over time, but whatever; I'll put up the hundred thousand prize money if you want. You just make sure she enters and wins that contest. Take her stuff from online if you have to. I don't give a flip what. Just get her out of here and on a career track."

Rick considered him for a long beat. "Yeah. Okay. And meanwhile, you're going to hibernate in the wilds of Alaska? Live off expired Red Cross blood?"

"What does it matter?" Matt shrugged. "I haven't had a vacation in ten years. A little downtime will do me good."

"Right." Rick gave him a jaded glance. "I give you two weeks, tops before we're scraping you off the ceiling, but whatever, dear boy. You'll need to take the ski plane this time of year to get up there."

"Yeah. I already scheduled the flight for this afternoon. I figured you wouldn't mind."

Rick gave him an indifferent nod. "Don't get eaten by a polar bear. I'll see you in a couple weeks."

"A few months, Rick, I'll see you in June. Thanks, man."

# 6

Cat noticed Matt immediately in the most unexpected place possible. He was standing in line at the bank across from the medical center. This wasn't her usual branch. In fact, she and Maria only stopped in because Maria needed help covering the outrageous cost of her medication. Cat felt energized by finding Matt here. What a coincidence. After all the searching she'd done to find him yesterday, what were the odds she'd bump into him at a bank she never used, in a part of town she never frequented? *This must be a sign!*

*He's so easy to pick out of a crowd.* He was the tallest man in the room for one thing and by far the most handsome. Those wide shoulders and that powerful chest of his stretched full and strong under his leather jacket. She had reason to know his chest tapered from bulging sinew to a trim waist without an ounce of fat. It was a chest and arms she longed to step into and wrap hers around. She imagined his embrace would feel like home.

Shortly after they walked in, Matt scented the air, turned and look directly at her. His smile was wan and little sheepish. She whispered to Maria, who looked at Matt, smiled and whispered back. He nodded politely in their direction, and Cat thought he looked woefully as if he wanted to cut and run. *What is he doing here?* His gaze caressed her, lingering disconcertedly at her neck. *Wow, cut and run or caress, those are mixed signals for sure.*

After a beat that perfectly illustrated his conflict, he abandoned his place in line and joined Cat in hers, ignoring the irritated glares of the customers behind them.

"Miss Temple. I understand you've been trying to contact me."

"Mr. Brenner! You are a hard man to find."

He dug his hands deep into his jeans pockets. "I'm a busy guy. In fact, I'm headed out of town on business now, won't be back for quite a while."

She cleared her throat and skittered her gaze away from midnight-blue eyes that read her mind. "Oh? Ah… You remember Maria," she continued inanely.

"How could I forget?" He winked at Maria whose sudden blush gave color to her sickly pale face. "You don't look as if you feel well, Mrs. Gonzalez. I know you weren't wearing oxygen when we met."

"Yes, you're right. I became ill that night. The doctor thinks I have a little pneumonia."

Matt watched her with true concern. "I'm sorry to hear that. Maybe, you should sit while we wait in line?" he suggested kindly, starting to guide her to the chairs lining the perimeter of the space.

"That might be best." She took his arm. "I'm trying to get my strength back, and Catarina was so kind to bring me to the clinic today." She leaned into him, looking paler by the moment. "Mija must be glad to see you. She's talked about finding you since the night you met."

He glanced at Cat, who tried in vain to suppress the sudden blush she felt climb up her neck and emblazon her face. His grin as he guided her friend toward the chairs told her he hadn't missed it.

"Really? Well, she's a persistent young woman."

Unable to resist the conversation she could no longer hear, Cat joined them as he stooped to settle Maria's oxygen next to her on the chair. "What are you two so cozy about?" she inquired over-brightly as she leaned down to her friend with a warning look.

* * * *

Matt always found it necessary to filter out information supplied by his vampire senses. If not, the deluge would overwhelm him, but some sounds were too hard-wired to his nervous system to ignore. The sound of a shotgun bolt being drawn back was one of them. He heard it before anyone else in the bank even realized there was a problem.

His voice dropped to a low growl as he spoke intensely to Cat, pulling Maria out of her chair and pushing them both toward the door. "I want you to get out of this bank right now." Too late. Before he could propel them two more feet, the shouting began.

Matt zeroed in on the bank robbers at the teller's window, noting the pallor on the teller's face, the scent of adrenaline telegraphing her fear, her pounding heartbeat and the erratic ones of the two men in front of her. He heard the silent alarm, alerting the police, as the teller tried to pacify the men by putting money into the bag, they shoved at her. The thieves were riding drugged highs. The scents of meth and sweat diffused above them.

Matt realized with heartsick dread that the drug would escalate their desperation and recklessness. The tallest one, the one dancing from foot to foot, stroked the barrel of his shotgun, eyes wild as he glanced around. The teller pushed the bag toward his partner, hiccupping back tears, and without compunction, the animal leveled the barrel at her and shot. She crumpled.

"No more hiccups." He turned to the crowd. "Anybody else got the hiccups?"

There were gasps as people collapsed to the floor in a deathly hush. Matt pushed Cat and Maria down behind a desk.

"Stay where you are!" the tall gunman shouted. "I'm gonna come around with a bag. I want all your money and jewelry right the effing now!"

"No, man! C'mon, we gotta get outta here," the second man protested but was ignored.

The asshole was spoiling for a fight. If they weren't all incredibly careful, someone else was going to wind up dead.

"Stay down," Matt whispered to the women. "Keep your eyes down and give them whatever they ask for."

One by one the gunmen came around, demanding money and jewelry from the terrified patrons. A wail of sirens in the background drew closer. The tall gunman sneered and turned on the crowd. He grabbed a young and pregnant mother, who protected a stunned little boy, to use as human shields.

"You're coming with us!"

"Wait!" Matt's voice was calm and commanding. "Take me instead." He gestured at the mother and child. "They'll only slow you down. They can't run. Take me."

"He's right, she can't run! Look at her!"

The gunman shoved the pregnant woman hard, sending her careening into a counter, and then down to the floor. Matt wanted to rip the guy's head off, and without a crowd watching, it was exactly what he would have done.

"Get over here, then!" the gunman ordered Matt in a panic as the sirens drew nearer.

Matt walked toward the men, his arms raised in surrender. A loud burst of static from a bullhorn outside startled the robber, and he fired. Matt's body spun with the shot through his shoulder. He heard the ricochet, and the sound of a bullet hitting flesh, but he didn't dare take his gaze off the gunmen to see who'd been hit. He simply prayed it wasn't Cat.

"W…We gotta get outta here, man!" the second gunman stuttered. "The back door! You!" He grabbed the hapless bank manager by the collar. "Open it for us!"

Wild-eyed and out of control, he pushed the frightened man and Matt toward the back. They were past Cat and Maria, almost to the door. Matt willed them away from the terrified crowd of people, away from Cat. In the doorway, shielded from view, the panicky bank manager tried to delay them. The door was open. They had only a few feet to go when Cat let out a piercing scream. Matt closed his eyes with dread. Had she been hit? The hopped-up gunman beside Matt turned on her, millimeters from firing. Matt went feral with rage. Unable to stop it, he welcomed the vampire within with all its frightening physical manifestations. With his head down, he pushed the bank manager and lesser thug out the door and then slammed it hard, effectively locking them outside. He turned on the shooter with a snarl. In a frozen moment, he took the shotgun blast to his chest.

The currish gunman stood immobilized, a horrified stare in his eyes as Matt stalked toward him and grabbed the shotgun out of his now slack hands. Their gazes met over the weapon. Matt issued a low growl from the depths of his chest, and the thug silently pissed his pants.

Cat's face reflected her stunned horror when Matt transformed. She sat frozen with fear, watching him coldcock the shooter, who now lay unconscious with a broken jaw. Blood pooled from Matt's chest wound. He was still vamped out, head tilted to the sound of the approaching SWAT team.

He roared his contempt at the thug on the floor and then turned to Cat. "Are you hurt?" He bent down beside her. She wonderingly touched his face as his features became human again.

"I'm okay, but you're not. You've been shot. You're bleeding."

"It's nothing, a flesh wound."

"That can't be…"

Her eyes were huge as she stared at him. He could sense hysteria rising in her. He had no choice but to thrall her. *You're calm*, he thought urgently, mastering all his concentration in her direction. *You saw the gunman shoot at me but miss. You're concerned about Maria.*

Cat turned immediately to Maria and began to cry. "We have to help her! She's the one who was shot! We have to help her!"

Matt examined Maria, knowing before he reached her it was futile. He heard no pulse, no respirations. Half her brain lay on the floor. She was dead.

Cat knelt beside her friend, frantic. "We have to start CPR!"

"No, Cat." Matt drew her into his arms and stood, removing her from Maria's corpse. "She's gone, baby. I'm sorry. There's nothing you can do for her now."

The wounded look she gave him was pathetic. "But…but she was getting better…she was getting well…"

"I know. Shush." He rocked her in his arms. "I know."

The SWAT team entered the bank ready for anything, only to find they had nothing left to do, except call the coroner and an ambulance for the gunman.

Uniforms, detectives and the CSI team followed next. "Get that moron out of here," the lead detective ordered as SWAT cuffed the remaining robber. He'd given up without much of a fight. An ambulance took his unconscious cohort away for treatment. "Have the EMTs check the manager out, and then get his story."

Statements were given by the witnesses and evidence was bagged. Matt flanked Cat, helpless to soothe her pain, but protective, nonetheless. They sat on an EMT gurney, where Matt pulled a blanket around himself to conceal the quickly knitting hole in his chest.

The detective pressed Cat to repeat her statement, looking for inconsistencies. Matt set his jaw. "Release us and get that typed up." He nodded at the detective's notes. "She can come down to the station tomorrow and sign it." The detective blanched at being directed. Head lifted, he started to reiterate his question. Matt's patience snapped. "You have great tenacity, buddy, but a pathetic lack of compassion. Miss Temple witnessed two murders today. She's had enough. We don't need an inquisition." He drew Cat closer, and she buried her face in the crook of his neck. He sensed her exhaustion and tears developing. "We're done here."

Grinding his teeth, the frustrated detective released them.

A squad car drove them to Matt's condo, where the concierge studied them with concern as Matt carried a blood-splattered Cat inside.

"No visitors, except Mr. Hiatt, Barney."

"Of course, sir." The concierge bowed discretely.

Cat, coated with the blood of an innocent, lay in his arms shocked and unable to function. He released her into an overstuffed chair, and then shoved a glass with two fingers of whiskey into her hands.

"Drink this," he ordered kindly.

She accepted the glass and then stared down at the liquid as if she couldn't imagine what to do with it. He tipped it up to her lips, and she obediently swallowed the fiery stuff. Matt hovered while she drank it all, and then carried her upstairs to the shower.

"Arms up," Matt directed as he stripped off her clothes.

She mutely complied. Still fully dressed, Matt fought the urge to drag her to the floor and lick the clotted blood from her fingertips. He'd never be able to stop if he tried. Her luscious body caught the blood where it pooled in the shell of her ear, the crease of her eyelid. The sanguine invitation wasn't lost on him, merely sublimated. He wouldn't succumb to it today. The warm shower he drew her toward mercifully washed away the day's violence. Once clean, he toweled her dry before he wrapped her in a robe.

"Will you be all right while I shower?" he asked, dripping rivers of bloody water over the cream-colored carpet. Cat nodded, shivering violently, though not from cold. "I'll be right back." He returned to the shower, wincing slightly as the water hit his healing gunshot wounds.

Primal hunger prodded Matt. He urgently needed blood. Physical wounds increased his need one-hundred-fold. Still, he pushed his craving aside until he was certain Cat was recovering. He was back to her in minutes, a robe fastened tightly in front of him, hiding the superficially knitted holes in his chest. She stared vacantly, but her heart beat steadily.

"Cat?" She looked up at him. "Let's go downstairs. You need another drink, and so do I." She nodded and followed him.

The easy chair provided a haven for Cat while he prowled the kitchen. Pouring more whiskey for her, Matt glanced into the living room to make sure she couldn't see him and then pulled a pint of blood from his refrigerator. Three grateful gulps of the life-giving liquid gave him a rush of fortitude and pain relief. He'd drink the rest slower when he could disguise his condition. Wiping traces of blood from his lips, he thought with relief that he'd gotten away with his taboo act. Matt poured the remainder into an opaque cup and then paused when he heard her gasp behind him. He turned to find her standing in the kitchen.

"You were drinking blood, weren't you?"

His shoulders rose as he tucked his chin. He couldn't look at her. "Yes." His voice was deep and filled with the fear of rejection.

"You were shot back there at the bank." It wasn't a question. She knew.

"Yes." He winced at the admission.

"You took the bullet meant for me."

"Cat…" His voice was husky.

"You saved my life, and what I saw…it was real, wasn't it?"

"Yes."

"You *are* a vampire." The words were simple and implacable.

He turned to face her, his fangs descended. He felt shaky and weak. God, he really needed more blood. "Yes."

She walked into his arms and held him. "Thank you. Thank you for saving my life."

Matt stood rigidly within Cat's embrace, uneasily comprehending her gentle words. She caught him doing the second most intimate thing a vampire could do—feeding from a cup. Not nearly as visceral as tapping a vein, but damn, his bloodstained lips gave away what was on his menu. He admitted to her, hell, he showed her, he was a monster who lived off the blood and vital force of mortals, and she was…thanking him? He wasn't thralling her. She wasn't under the influence of his bite. She was just accepting him?

Cocooned in their moment of peace, it took him a few seconds to realize Cat was crying, dousing his chest with her tears. He consolingly wrapped his arms around her and held her in a secure embrace, rocking her. *She is too innocent to be exposed to all this.*

At last, she pulled away, looking up at him through tear-drenched lashes. He seemed drawn into those fathomless blue pools, and before he thought about it, he was kissing her. Strongly, eagerly, his arms wrapped around her as if it would allow him to better absorb her absolution. Her scent was exquisite—a mixture of virtue, gratitude, and comfort. Her mouth was warm and welcoming, and when the kiss ended, he gazed at her with such longing, she stroked a soothing palm down his cheek.

She shut her eyes and turned her face up to him for another kiss. Matt glowed, cradled it between his hands and lowered his lips to hers again. He licked gently along the inner ridge of her upper lip, and she gasped, mesmerized by the feeling as he slipped his tongue inside and explored her mouth. Cat welcomed the dance. She broke away from the kiss, panting.

They were both overwhelmed by the emotions arcing between them. Matt gathered his wits. He needed to explain to her why this was completely impossible.

"We should sit, and I should tell you some things about myself…about vampires." He meant to seat himself safely away from her in the easy chair while he placed her onto the facing sofa, but Cat would have none of that.

"If you're gonna sit there, you'd better make room for me on your lap." He grinned at her a little painfully. "Or, we could both sit on the couch."

He relented and sat beside her while she settled herself close against him. She leaned her head on his shoulder as he spoke in a low rumble.

"In 1922, I was just another Los Angeles cop, the youngest guy to ever to make detective…"

Within an hour, she heard his tale of Ruth, Veronique, Rick, and of becoming a monster.

"This has been awful for you, hasn't it?" she asked.

He frowned. "Some of it, yeah. Just like anyone in any unusual circumstance, you learn to adapt."

She nodded, her cheek rubbing the soft terry cloth of his robe. "I understand." Minutes ticked by in silence, and she simply let him hold her.

Matt was reassured she was out of shock when she sat up with a start. "What time is it?"

"About four thirty. Why?"

"I have to get over to Maria's. I have to call her son, Jorge. He should be home from work sometime after five. She has a dog. I'll have to look after him now or find someone to take him."

Matt nodded. "I'll call a friend to pick us up. We can get my car, and he can follow us in yours."

Rick arrived at Matt's penthouse in the limo. Matt changed into street clothes, but Cat still stood awkwardly in his oversized robe.

"Cat, this is Richard Hiatt."

Rick unleashed his charm and kissed Cat's hand rather than shaking it. She giggled slightly at the old-world gesture. "Co-eds are so much more beautiful than I remembered."

"You're Matt's partner at Consort Group International?"

"The same."

"We can stop at your apartment first, so you can change." Matt scowled at Rick flirting with his girl.

"Sure." She preceded them out the doorway.

"Now, I see what the fuss is about," Rick whispered as he passed Matt. "She's exquisite."

"Yeah," Matt returned grimly. "I don't know what the nucking futs to do about it. I need her to win that contest. Now!"

Rick nodded. "I'll see what I can do."

"What am I going to say to Maria's son? Do you think the police have already contacted him?" Cat asked nervously as they drove to her building.

There was a long delay in rush hour traffic, and Matt was glad. It would give her time to compose herself.

"You'll just listen, mostly. You'll comfort each other as best you can. It's the only thing you can do, Cat. Where does Jorge live?"

"Santa Barbara. He and his wife have a little girl. They were coming down to visit Maria next week…" She started sadly, and then suddenly looked up at him. "How old are you?"

He gave her a sideways glance. "That's a zinger of a segue."

She blew a breath out in a laugh. "I guess it is. I was just thinking you look a little younger than Jorge. You look as if you're twenty-five or so, but that can't be right. If you were made a vampire in 1922, how old are you really?"

Matt paused. "I'll be over one hundred and twenty years, soon." He wished he could have evaded that question.

"But…but you're so modern!"

He chuckled low. "Well, I try to keep up with the young folk."

"Is Rick a vampire, too?" Cat sighed.

"I have a friend, my best friend at boarding school, but she moved to Brooklyn a few years ago. I know I'd be welcome to stay with her, but I can't afford a ticket…"

"That sounds perfect to me. After you talk to Jorge, you call your friend and pack. You can stay at my building tonight. We'll both need to finish our police statements tomorrow, and then I'm putting you on the corporate jet to New York. It will do you good to get away for a couple weeks."

"But…the expense, the time away from school…I can't afford…"

"I'll take care of all that. Don't worry. You just concentrate on recovering."

She stared at him uncertainly for a long beat. "Why are you doing this? Why are you going so far out of your way to help me?"

"Do I need a reason?"

"You've always been so kind to me. You don't even know me. I don't understand."

Matt shook his head, baffled by the complexity of his need and emotions. "Maybe, I'm just a nice guy."

"Yeah." She nodded. "I think you probably are a nice guy, but this is way beyond nice…this is kind of…extravagant."

He smiled. "From your perspective, but Rick and I have some far-reaching resources and more money than we'll ever be able to spend, so just relax and enjoy someone helping you, okay?"

"Okay." she agreed, the bewildered, careful look still clouding the clear blue of her eyes.

# 7

Matt used the keycard and swung open the door to the opulent suite across the hall from his penthouse. By financial agreement with the management, it was used exclusively for Consort Group International guests. Though the maids cleaned it regularly, it hadn't been used for almost a month.

"Oh, wow!" Cat said. "This is gorgeous!"

Matt pursed his lips and nodded, glancing around, and then his gaze fell on her, by far the loveliest thing in the room. "Why don't you take your bag into the bedroom? I'll fix you something to eat."

"I'm really not hungry…"

Matt eyed her skeptically. "Have you eaten anything at all today?"

"No," she admitted reluctantly. "I don't think I can stomach food, yet."

Matt negated her fears with a shake of his head. "You have to eat. Put your bags away. I'll cook."

"You cook?" Her head swung around in amazement.

He shrugged. "I think I can remember how to scramble eggs. You like eggs? I can call out for something heavier if you want. I just thought with everything that's happened…"

Cat nodded. "Eggs sound okay."

* * * *

Cat heard Matt cooking as she pulled her toiletries from her bag and lined them up along the bathroom vanity. She was unexpectedly enticed by the aroma of sizzling bacon. Her stomach rumbled, and she rolled her shoulders, trying to relieve the tension centered there. She sighed, hung her clothes in the closet, and ran a brush through her tangled hair. Maybe she'd sleep tonight, after all.

She wished Matt would lie next to her in the elegantly upholstered bed. She almost laughed aloud at the thought. Sister Mary Immaculate would have her on her knees, rosary in hand for days if she heard that impure thought. Well, no need to worry. After those two sweet, hot kisses, he withdrew and did not attempt to kiss her again or give any indication their relationship would be anything other than platonic. Cat had no idea what to do about it.

* * * *

Matt set the table and turned on the sound system, so Debussy played low as he piled eggs and bacon from the frying pan onto a plate. Cat emerged from the bedroom, nervously rubbing her palms down her thighs.

"Smells good." She'd accepted the wisdom of taking some sustenance.

"Glad you think so." He flashed her a crooked smile and pulled out a chair for her. "I've scheduled a masseuse for you after dinner. A massage should relax you—"

"You could give me a back rub."

His face went almost grim before he caught himself and gave her a truly ingenuous smile. "Naw…I have a poor massage technique."

"Uh-huh." She glanced up from her food as he sat across the small table from her. "Aren't you going to eat…er…I mean…"

He smiled again and toasted her with the thick ceramic beer mug holding his blood.

Cat's lips formed a silent "Oh," and she grinned.

Matt squirmed awkwardly as Cat grasped his hand, crossed herself and bowed her head for a brief grace. She restarted the conversation as if it'd never been interrupted. "So…a massage, huh? That sounds…interesting…I've never had a massage before."

"This would probably be the right day to try it out."

He watched her test her eggs with the smug secret knowledge that he laced them with just a touch of Melatonin. He intended for her to be relaxed, asleep and beyond his immediate reach for the rest of the night until she got on that plane tomorrow.

Matt rinsed and piled the dishes in the sink for the maid. The female masseuse, dressed in scrubs, knocked on the door, carrying her massage table strapped over one shoulder and her bag of oils over the other. The woman introduced herself before she set up the table in the living room, placing scented candles around the perimeter.

Before Matt could clearly imagine Cat's glistening peach skin, soft and rosy from the oils and a therapeutic rub-down, he beat a hasty retreat. With a quick hug, which he kept as impersonal as possible, he was out the door and walking quickly toward his own unit, cursing the blood flooding to his eager dick.

Matt stopped in the middle of the hallway and inhaled. Someone was here. He glanced around warily, registering the scents of several vamps immediately before a hood was thrown over his head, and the world went black.

Matt woke to a swaying motion and the smell of the ocean around him. This scent was promptly replaced by a stronger one. Another vamp, not one he recognized. Or… wait…he inhaled again. A scent he recognized from long ago. *No, it couldn't be. Abso-fucking-lutely, especially not tonight*. His usually sluggish vampire's heart sped up as the hood was pulled from his head, and he felt a shove forward. He braced for a fight. Veronique sat on an elegant S-shaped couch in the lounge of a yacht. She looked up at him with compelling jade eyes and a radiant smile. With a flick of her hand, she motioned away the thugs guarding her.

"Matt!" she purred, as he tried to steady himself and get his bearings. "Look how you've grown!"

"Veronique," he began evenly. "Long time," his jaw clenched, "no see."

A surreptitious glance around the room provided no weapon, but no imminent threat, either. A vampire like Veronique was deadly if provoked. Matt had learned to more than hold his own in a fight, but she had two things on her side—she was older and perhaps stronger, and she was his sire. Killing one's sire was innately abhorrent to any vamp. He didn't want to fight her. Was she in the mood for a fight?

"You're looking so well! Vamp life obviously agrees with you."

She curled long legs under her, and Matt distractedly wondered if she would gouge the finish out of her leather sofa with those five-inch stiletto heels. She wasn't dressed for a fight, that was sure. Only a black, silk jersey dress draped across her tight body, strapless and so snug, it left absolutely nothing to the imagination, proving she was bare beneath it.

"What about you?" he countered, leaning against the door, refusing to venture nearer. "You don't call, you don't write…"

"Yes, well, that little misunderstanding with the responders left me cautious. I really hate being staked. It's a poor life choice."

"Yeah, I know all about having unwanted life choices forced upon you."

"Oh, don't be petulant. After all this time, you've not forgiven me? Haven't you found life as a vamp to be rewarding?"

"It wouldn't be my first choice, no." He advanced farther into the room, but made sure he faced her squarely, weight evenly distributed on the balls of his feet, knees flexed, hands clenching and unfurling at his side, ready for anything.

"Hmm." She tapped a long, glossy fingernail against her chin posing in indecision. "So, you would rather not be a vampire. Suppose…" She smiled beguilingly and patted the seat next to her on the couch. "Just suppose you could be human again. Would that win me your forgiveness?"

Matt felt as if an electric current had just shot through him. *Human again? What is she talking about? Nothing can reverse vampirism. Stay calm. This woman is a known psychopath. She'll say anything.*

"You want to make me human again?"

"Well, I've been thinking about it. I've been working on a party drug which negates the physical effects of vampirism. It's becoming quite popular. Maybe you've heard about it in your work?"

Matt thought for a moment. *What did Rick say about Catalina's warm thighs?* Certainly, he'd remember if he heard about something that mimicked mortality. He shook his head.

"It lasts four to twelve hours. You know, it's a thrill. It lets you go sail gliding during the day or whatever. Gives you that adrenaline rush, the possibility of death. You know who really loves it? Skiers and race car drivers! I can't sell enough to them! Anyway, by nighttime, you're a vamp again, fully restored."

"Uh-huh." He clenched his jaw to keep from screaming his frustration. "So, you want to give me a party drug that will make me human for a day, and you think it evens the score? I don't think so."

"Oh, now, Matthew…" She pouted again. "You didn't let me finish. Used in larger doses, the drug's effect lasts longer."

"How long?" He frowned, afraid to be as interested as he was.

"Well, the longest effect we've seen is six months. Most get about three months out of that dose. Just like any drug, it depends on one's body chemistry. I suppose if you really wanted to," she drew a breath, "I can't imagine why anyone would, you could invest in a way to make the change permanent." She patted the seat beside her again, and reluctantly, he sat.

"And you'd be willing to give me this…what…this…"

"We call it Humanité. Catchy name, don't you think?"

He squinted suspiciously. "You'd be willing to give me this Humanité? How much? For how long? What do you want in return?"

Her smile was saccharine. "As much as you want for as long as you like."

She ran her finely manicured hand up the inside of his thigh, and Matt gritted his teeth. He knew at least one thing she wanted.

"All I want in return is your forgiveness, legally, with the responders. I want that bothersome one-hundred-and-fifty-year sentence removed."

"I need proof," Matt said. "You prove you can make me human, and keep me that way, and I'll do whatever you want with the responders, but you'll prove it to me first, Veronique. And if you're lying to me, I'll fucking stake you myself and drag you off to Hades."

"Now, now," she soothed and opened the palm of her unoccupied hand to produce an ordinary-looking pharmacy bottle.

Inside were several small blue capsules. They could have been vitamins for all Matt knew. Hell, they could have been filled with silver. He opened the bottle and poured the pills into his palm. No burns. Unless they were shielded by something, they weren't silver.

"What?" He looked at her and gave an incredulous laugh. "You expect me to trust you and swallow one of these?"

"How else can you know?"

"I'll tell you what," he selected a pill from the center of his hand, "you take this one and I'll watch. If after an hour you're not dead, I'll take one myself. How long do these last, anyway?" He studied the small capsule.

"These are the short-acting form. They last about four hours." She took the pill he offered and swallowed it. "What in the world can we do as humans for four hours?" she baited seductively.

His stare bore into her. "There's always Scrabble."

"Matt, Matt, Matt. You've been around long enough to know there are many more exciting games."

"None I'd want to play with you," but he couldn't deny he was beginning to pick up the sound of a human heartbeat emanating from her.

He raised her arm and scented the blood rushing through her veins, felt the warmth of her skin, scented a human woman's arousal. *What if this is all true? What if she can make me human again?*

Steeling himself against his own excitement, he stared fixedly at the pills in the bottle. If one was poisoned, he had a nine to one chance of survival. To be human again, it was a risk he was willing to take. He shook the capsule out and swallowed it with a gulp. His slow vampire's heart began to race. He waited.

"If this is the short-acting form, where is the long-acting one?"

"In the hold."

She stretched luxuriously, making sure he saw the thrusting of her proud breasts through the slinky fabric of her dress. He remembered her beautiful tits, and she was as compulsive about sex as she was about blood.

Against his will, and with no effort at all, his phallus grew warm, blood suffused it, and he throbbed. These were non-vampiric, human sexual feelings of arousal. *Sweet lord, this stuff is working!* He swallowed hard, trying to ignore the warmth spreading through his body, the strong, steady rhythm of his heart and the intakes of breath now vital to his wellbeing.

"What do you want? What do you want to give me a lifetime supply of this stuff?"

"Just in case you asked," Veronique cajoled with a slow smile, "I have the documents right here." She reached for some legal papers and handed them to him.

It took all Matt's willpower to ignore the new sensations rampaging through his body and concentrate on the legalese before him. She wanted the charges against her dismissed, immunity from any further prosecution, and no claims upon her person or her future earnings. She must believe this Humanité would bring in the dough. Hell, he didn't care about all that.

Matt studied her. She amped up the sex appeal, and he doubted it had anything to do with affection for him. No, this was Veronique looking for a fast bunk-up, as usual.

"I'm not opposed to signing this," he agreed but held up a warning hand when she produced a pen. "When we've come to a complete agreement. I'll be writing a document of my own. My attorney won't be able to look it over, but I've signed enough legal papers to know it will hold up in a court of the Vampire Nation."

She sized him up in return. "What will it say?"

"It will specify that you will give me, free of charge, enough Humanité to keep me human for the next…ninety years. It will also state if, in the next seventy-five years the formula stops working for some reason, you will pay me…fifty thousand dollars per day, for every day it doesn't work."

She glared at him. "Fine. You can use the computer in there." She nodded at a doorway. "Draw it up, and I'll sign it."

"You don't have a conscription gang waiting for me in there, do you?"

"Darling," she smirked, "if I wanted that you'd already be in the hold."

Matt escaped into a fully appointed office and shut the door, trying to contain his delight, trying to think straight despite the surging physicality in every cell of his body. The room felt too cold, the seat too rough, the desk without the lights, too dim. His blood rushed, and his heart beat. He pinched himself hard and exalted in feeling the pain. He was human, at least for the next four hours.

After he emerged from the office, document in hand, he found Veronique standing next to the couch naked as the day she was born, pouring two flutes of champagne.

"What in Satan's name are you doing?"

"Celebrating." She looked up, smiled and re-offered the pen. "I have one more demand. Well, a request, really."

Matt raised a cautious brow. Veronique was nothing, if not predictable. "Yeah?"

"The night I turned you, we never got to…close the deal. Let's have that closure," she emphasized with a thrust of her breasts, her stiletto-shod feet sliding wide, revealing everything. "Now."

He stared at her for a beat. Veronique wanted not just his pardon, she wanted his sex. Matt felt zero desire for her, but he wasn't going to pass up the chance to get a little of his own back while securing the mortality he coveted.

"You sign the document first. Then we'll consider any…closure."

She shrugged and drew her knees closer together. "Fine." She laid both documents on the table, and then hurriedly signed.

"You and I need to go back to my place," Matt announced. "I have a copier there, and I want to be on my own turf – just in case."

She sidled close. "Copies can wait. Love now."

"Love?" Matt snorted. "Sure. Whatever you want to call it, but not here. My place or nothing."

She narrowed her eyes. Matt smirked. He'd been working with submissives a long time. He knew one when he saw one, and Veronique was submissive right down to her open-toed, spiked heels.

He didn't yield. "My way or the highway."

"Oh, very well." She fluttered her lashes, and Matt's stomach sickened. "But after that…" she moved closer. "The heart wants what the heart wants." She gazed at him, full-throttling her version of sex appeal. "Let me sweeten the deal."

As beautiful as she was, and she had always been stunning, Matt was revolted. What the hell, to be human again, he'd give her what she needed, though not necessarily what she wanted. She'd bring him those goddamn pills on her tongue by the time he was through with her.

He managed to hold her advances to a few hot kisses in the limo. She nailed him with another hot one just outside his door, grabbing his sex and rubbing until he couldn't help growing hard. Matt gritted his teeth. She wailed her protest when he dragged her hand away, but she was docile enough when he led her through the door and into his living room.

"You want me, Veronique?" he taunted, and she advanced on him eagerly, kicking off her shoes and dropping the slinky dress as she went. "Okay, only just screwing is too vanilla. I'm a vampire now—thanks to you— and my tastes have become a little more…exotic."

"Whatever you want." She purred.

"Good." His voice deepened into a Dom's growl, and he assumed a commanding stance. "Kneel."

"What?"

"Kneel. At my feet. And wait."

Matt pulled off his belt. It whistled through the loops. Snapping it together to make the leather crack like a whip, he walked a slow, predatory circle. Veronique flinched. *Yeah, this will work.*

"Give me your hands," he demanded, standing in front of her. He pulled a plastic wrist restraint from his pocket, acknowledging to himself the irony of always having one available.

Matt was excited, almost agitated, by the power he held over her. She wanted him to sign those papers, she needed him to recant his story to the responders. Having her in such a vulnerable state pumped exultation through him like nothing before.

Veronique nervously licked her lips. Matt felt her anticipation. She hesitated for just a moment before she offered her hands up to him as if in supplication.

"Very good," he praised perfunctorily and then secured her wrists together.

Matt wanted her miserable and realized vengeance was an emotion he'd never truly experienced before. The subs at the Gaoler thought he was a boring Dom? He'd prove them wrong tonight. Maybe it wasn't that he didn't want to be a Dominant, maybe he never encountered someone he genuinely wanted to submit. Now, he had the perfect candidate. He wanted Veronique to suffer as he had. He wanted to strip her of pride and hope as she had stripped him. If her flushed face and dilated eyes were any indications, she was ripe for humiliation. He continued snapping the belt around her like a whip, watching her cower from it.

"Straighten up," he commanded. "Stop flinching."

"Wha...what?" Her round-eyed gaze slid from the fixation on the ominous belt up to him.

"You're avoiding the belt. I decide if the strap strikes you. You have no say in it. Stop flinching."

Veronique swallowed hard. "All right."

"Eyes down," Matt ground out, "on the floor, and the proper response is yes, sir."

Veronique shook with desire. "Yes, sir."

"That's better."

He stalled, dragging out long moments without another word, making her anticipate and wonder. He studied her, walking around and around her in maddeningly slow circles. Desperation and lust poured off her like radiation from a nuclear meltdown.

Veronique was unacquainted with "no" and "abide." She'd lived in a world of "yes" and "now." When an answer was anything less than she desired, she forced the required response on hundreds, maybe thousands of unwitting mortals, just as she'd forced it on Matt. Well, now, she needed something—release from a jail sentence—and she'd be required to work for it.

"Are you wet for me, Ronnie?" Matt taunted in a voice as sultry and seductive as a rock star singing a ballad.

She moaned low. "Yes, sir."

"Yes, I thought as much."

Her moans grew louder.

"And your nipples," Matt demanded, "are they hard for me?"

"Yes."

"Pinch them." She did. "Hard." She increased the pressure. "Harder." She whimpered at the erotic pain.

"I said hard," he ordered harshly, and she squealed at the self-inflicted pain she delivered in an effort to please him.

Matt glowered at her, tsking as if she were unworthy. "Hmm. I need something…more…" he complained fractiously, frowning displeasure.

Veronique groaned. "Matt…"

"How about your clit? Is that little nub throbbing for me? Do you want me to rub it? Get you off?"

"Yes!" Her eagerness was sickening to Matt. "Please! Please, Matt! Make me come!" she pleaded, her entreaty ending on a keening note.

Matt watched her dispassionately. "No," he pronounced slowly and shook his head. He sliced his gaze down at her, displeased. "You know what? I'm just not feelin' it…"

"What? Why not?"

"I don't know." He pretended to consider. He opened his eyes wide as if he'd had an epiphany. "Maybe if you were…better somehow…you could make me want you."

Veronique's eyes grew wild. She squirmed with rage. "Better! What do you mean better? You bastard!"

"Ah, ah," he warned, a dangerous stare quelling her. "You don't want to challenge me, Ronnie. It will not get you diddled. It also won't provide you a get-out-of-jail-free card. Ask me nicely, and I might sign your agreement."

"Fuck you!"

Matt whipped his hand out bland dove into her long hair, gathering it tightly at the nape and tilting her head back in a posture that had to hurt. "Really?" He growled, watching her shudder with pleasure at his touch. "That's the best you can do? It's not very nice." He kneeled to confront her nose to nose. "Your freedom is entirely conditional on the Humanité. That's your only chance, Ronnie." He released her hair as if it burned his fingers. "Forget the sex. You'll never make me hot. Bring me the drug, that's all I want. Then, if it works, I'll sign."

"My God, Matt!" she screamed in frustration. "What are you doing to me?"

"Get up," he ordered, and after tearing off her wrist restraint, he threw the dress her way. "Put your clothes on, sit down and wait for me. I need a shower." He strode away without another word.

* * * *

Matt glanced at the clock as he left the bathroom and noticed it was twelve thirty in the morning, almost four hours exactly since he took the Humanité sample. He felt himself growing colder, his heart slowing, his vampire senses returning. There was no doubt about it. The party drug worked, at least for now. Who knew about long term? He knew this, though. If Veronique failed to live up to her end of the bargain, he'd more than stake her. He'd cut her despicable head off and watch her die.

He walked into the living room, wearing jeans and a forced smile. Veronique, dressed in her come-fuck-me dress and heels, sat composed, hands clasped in her lap, eyes down as he entered, looking no worse for wear. Her desires were carefully hidden again, for the moment.

"Are you convinced of Humanité's effectiveness?" she asked pleasantly.

"Yeah," he agreed just as pleasantly. "I want the drug sent over tomorrow. Does that give you enough time?"

She smiled and nodded slowly. "Tomorrow will be fine. I'll need you to sign the document after it arrives."

"I'll have it checked out, make sure it's actually the right drug, and then I'll be happy to sign and send you on your way for good."

"All will be as agreed. My attorney will present your new statement to the court, and by tomorrow night, we'll both have exactly what we want. Well, almost. Are you sure I can't persuade you to remain a vampire? We have great chemistry together, you know. We could be a power couple."

He studied her somberly. "Veronique, there are many vamp psychiatrists. You really should look into treatment." He opened the door to usher her out. "I'll expect your delivery tomorrow afternoon. If it doesn't arrive, expect to feel the wrath of the entire Vampire Nation on your ass by tomorrow night."

"It won't be a problem, lover. Until tomorrow."

She kissed his cheek before stepping into the hallway, jerking back slightly when he shut the door in her face.

* * * *

Cat leaned against the door, stunned to see the ravishing fire-and-ice brunette emerge from Matt's apartment. She thought she had dreamed the cries and moans, reliving the terror in the bank, or maybe from her childhood. No, she realized, they were real, and not cries of terror or pain, but rather cries of passion. How could she ever compete with a woman like that? No wonder Matt wanted to keep things platonic. Next to that exquisite, sophisticated beauty, she felt like a convent-sheltered hayseed. Well, she was headed for Brooklyn tomorrow, and probably out of Matt Brenner's life for good. He was just a guy, a unique guy, who'd been very kind to her once, and that was how it would have to stay.

* * * *

Veronique half-bribed/half-thralled the guard at the Park Central Building to let her onto the roof long past closing time. In 1922 this was the tallest building in LA, and a place she often visited to get her thoughts together. She needed clarity now.

Looking toward his condo building on Wilshire, Veronique considered the problem of Matt Brenner. She wanted him, now more than ever. He'd become a formidable Dom in the years since they'd last met. Even then, she'd recognized his alpha qualities, but now, she shivered. He'd come into his own. *Why did he continue to fight his vampire nature? He should be past all that by now. Why did he long to become human again?*

Humanité didn't serve her where Matt was concerned. If he were human again, he'd be useless in her plan to reunite them. She would have to do something about that. She would consult with her sire. Hadn't Papa said for decades that it was time she settled down, took a mate and became part of the family business? She knew just the vamp to fill the bill. She had eventually topped every Dom who had set out to tame her. Maybe Matt would be the one who finally mastered her for good.

# 8

Between the nightmares and disappointment warring for her attention, Cat tossed and turned the rest of the night until the alarm went off at seven. She couldn't get the picture of the gorgeous woman she saw exiting Matt's apartment out of her mind, nor banish the cries from her ears. *What must that be like to have such an irresistible, powerful man make love to you?*

She, on the other hand, was hopeless. What in the world was she thinking, anyway? She was going to have an affair with a vampire? Really? What, he was going to switch to some magical vegan blood, join hands with humanity and sing Kumbaya? They'd move to the suburbs, and she'd be Mrs. True-Crime Writer while he ran a bar in the neighborhood? This wasn't some fantasy. In real life, she paused for a moment, considering in her world real life contained the word vampire in a serious way. *In real life*, sweet little convent-raised virgins did not attract that kind of man, vampire or not. Maybe the sisters were right, and she should have given herself to God. It was a cinch no red-blooded (or cold-blooded) guy would have her.

On limbs made heavy by lack of sleep and paralyzing inferiority, she climbed out of bed and then into the shower. *I'll dress sensibly, pack, sign the police statement and be gone.* She and Matt would never have to deal with one another again.

* * * *

Matt actually brought an alarm clock into the mausoleum to be sure he awakened on time. He couldn't imagine being more hopeful or looking forward to the day with more glee. He'd grab a quick shower, and then get himself and Cat down to the police station. With any luck, her stay in Brooklyn would be briefer than she ever imagined.

*Slow down, buddy. Make sure this drug works consistently. You know how undependable Veronique is.* As soon as he got his hands on the stuff, he'd have it down to the lab for analysis. If it were possible to make this formula permanent, or at least something chronic, but manageable, they'd begin work on it immediately. God, he'd spend everything he owned or could borrow to make it happen.

And then? If he could make himself reasonably human, then what? He'd seek out Cat. He didn't have a whole plan, but he knew that for damn sure. He'd seek her out and make her his. *You must be crazy!* He grinned dementedly at himself in the mirror as he toweled dry. He barely knew the woman, but somehow, right down to the marrow of his bones, he knew she was the one for him.

And if, in the end, the Humanité didn't work? What then? That was why he had to be cautious. He couldn't let Cat know his true feelings, not until he'd had… a month? Yeah, a good solid month of humanity and some indications from the scientists this was going to be a permanent solution.

Until then, well, there was a visit to Brooklyn for Cat, and maybe a nice exchange semester at New York University. No, no, Columbia! Yeah, Columbia University was the place for her. An all-expenses-paid final semester at Columbia in their advanced writing program. She'd be in heaven, and safely sequestered away while he straightened out his mess of a life.

* * * *

Matt was perplexed by Cat's cool reception at the door. She was usually happy to see him, not today. She stood with her bags packed on the doorstep, arms protectively crossed over her chest, barely making eye contact. Any attempt at conversation netted him monosyllables in reply. *Damn! What's going on?* Was she merely drained by yesterday's events? His gut told him there was something more.

As they took the elevator to the garage, Cat let him have it. "You must have had a late night." Her gaze raked him. "I saw your friend leave." Matt shut his eyes and groaned inwardly. "Of course, that was after her cries woke me up. I thought I was having a flashback. Who knew it was just…" She searched for the word, and when she found it, acid dripped from it. "Romance."

*Crap on a damn cracker!* She'd seen and heard much more than he imagined during Veronique's little romp last night. What now? Without ever intending to, he'd cut her to the quick. Was he really that toxic for her? And, what the hell would he do about it?

"I know how this sounds, but it's not what it seems," he began and realized that sounded ludicrous. "There's a lot more to the story with that woman I'd like to tell you sometime. Just…not right now. Okay, Cat?"

"None of my business," she primly sniffed. She sorted through the contents of her purse as if he were irrelevant.

"So, uh…we've talked a lot about me and my past. How about you? You know, where did you grow up? Where's your family?"

Cat gave him a sullen glance and then relented with a cynical smile. "I'm afraid I have one of those Amityville family stories. I don't remember any of this, but when I was four, we were at a family reunion, and one of the sons went nuts and mowed down twenty-three members of my family, including my mom and dad. The only ones who survived were me—I was napping on a blanket in the backyard—and my great-grandmother, who was with me, asleep in a rocker."

Matt stared at her in horror. "I…Jeez, Cat, I don't know what to say."

"Yeah, I have a long history of people around me getting shot. It ought to make my friends nervous."

Matt reached over and squeezed her hand. "I'm not nervous."

She gave him a reproachful glance. "Yeah, well, you're a vampire, so I don't think you actually count."

He stared at her a beat, removed his hand and looked away, giving a single nod. "So, what happened after that? I mean, a great-grandmother is elderly."

"Sure. Since she'd been born in the 1910s, that would make her somewhere around ninety if she'd lived. Old as dirt."

*Whew! She is pissed!* Matt smothered a laugh at her jibe. "Sure, sure."

"I lived with Gram until she died when I was seven. Then, because there was the money of the whole collective family in my name, the private guardian decided to send me to a convent boarding school rather than putting me into the foster system. That's where I grew up. The Sacred Heart Boarding School for Girls was home for eleven long years."

"I went to a parochial school. Some of the nuns…" He broke off, unsure of how to put it diplomatically. "Like everywhere I guess, most were wonderful, and some were bullies with rulers."

"Most of mine were bullies with rulers, especially Sister Mary Immaculate."

"Sorry to hear that. Where is the school?"

"Up by San Francisco. After I graduated, I wanted to go somewhere warm and free, you know? So, I took what was left of my inheritance money, which wasn't much, applied for a scholarship at UCLA, and here I am."

"Working on becoming the new Jessica Fletcher, huh?" He grinned. "Maybe with a little more drama and sex for the new generation?"

She froze, iced-up on the spot. "I doubt it. I really don't know much about that. I'm sure you'd be the expert." He gave her an inquiring glance. "Dominants and submissives?" she reminded with a hiss at the end. "At least if your late-night guest was any indication."

He cleared his throat. How the hell should he explain this? She must think he was a total pervert, especially after last night. He actually caught himself swallowing in gulps while she surreptitiously watched him from under her lashes.

"You know, uh…" He trailed off nervously and cleared his throat again. "You know," he started again with more determination. "Inexperience isn't such a bad thing. It's a good thing to wait for the right person to come along."

"Matt, I'm inexperienced, not fourteen. You don't have to reassure me, but thanks for the sentiment."

Matt wondered if some of the Humanité lingered in his system. He could swear he was developing a tension headache. "So, here's the police station." He pointed needlessly. "Why don't you jump out and get started on your statement? I'll park the car, and then join you."

She gave him a long, pensive look. "Sure. The quicker the statements are finished, the quicker I'll be off to Brooklyn, and you can resume your regular activities."

"Enough, Cat!" he ground out in what was unmistakably his Dom voice, and she stared at him, a little intimidated. "Despite what you think you know about me and my activities," he drew a deep breath and gentled his voice, "I'm not looking to be rid of you, so I can --what do you think -- deflower virgins, engage in ritual sacrifices or something?"

Cold steel flinted her eyes. "Right. We can't have you deflowering virgins, now, can we?" Before he could respond, she unsnapped her seatbelt and then stepped out of the still-rolling car, making him stomp on the brakes. "I'll see you inside." She slammed the door with a resounding wham.

Their day together didn't improve after they signed their statements, identified the bank robbers' mug shots and gave samples of their fingerprints. Matt had to admit, he was relieved her lunch would be served on the company jet. He couldn't imagine trying to negotiate the minefield of a meal.

* * * *

Cat's depression plummeted into a deeper hole as she sat in the small terminal, hearing them announce the available flights. She watched Matt through her lashes while pretending to read a magazine. He was unsettled as if he was wrestling with something painful. He fidgeted, paced, checked with the scheduling desk, checked his cell phone, glanced at her, and then repeated the whole process.

Her flight was called, and he stood. She followed suit, primly extending her hand to shake. "I want to thank you, Matt, for everything you've done for me."

He looked condemningly at her outstretched hand. "That's how you thank me?" he asked quietly, hurt evident in his eyes.

She softened immediately. "I…how else can I…"

He reached out and pulled her against his hard-muscled body, enveloping her in a tight hug. He dropped his head and inhaled her scent, making her feel strangely cherished. Was he memorizing her fragrance, she wondered? She raised her head tentatively, leaning her neck back the long distance it took to look into his turbulent blue eyes. She read terrible longing in them, and her heart melted.

"I think I…" she began. *Love you* her heart screamed. She couldn't bring herself to say it. She absolutely would not make herself that vulnerable.

He stared at her intently. "What?"

"I think I…I…owe you…a…a…lot."

"You don't owe me anything." He wove his hands into her hair and drew her inexorably closer as his lips descended on hers.

He kissed her deeply, and Cat wondered if it was as meaningful to him as it was to her. She parted her lips under his onslaught, and he plunged inside as if trying to possess her with one kiss, trying to let her know the depth of his feeling.

For Cat, everything around them fell away—the activity in the terminal, the roar of the nearby planes, the loudspeaker announcements overhead -- all of it banished by his touch. Every sensation focused on the unexpected delight of Matt's lips on hers, tongue exploring her mouth, chest pressing into her suddenly hypersensitive breasts. An electric charge surged from point to point as their bodies met, knees grazed, hips crushed, and he enfolded her in a demanding, but gentle onslaught of passion. A soft moan escaped her as she strove to grasp the powerful emotions awakened by his touch.

Her mind swam, awash in the feeling of need clenching low in her belly, while his tongue delved deeply and thoroughly into her hungry mouth. His hips circled and pressed against her in what she was sure was a deliciously sinful rhythm. She shivered. With a single embrace, he brought her to life. She clung to him.

Gently, he ended the kiss and stepped back, his gaze locked on hers. "I owe you," he whispered and then walked out of her life.

* * * *

Matt glanced askance at the empty apartment across the hall, Cat's refuge for one night. It silently mocked him in her absence. How was it possible that his entire body cried out for more of her soft flesh against his? With clothing between them, how was it he felt her hungry ardor burning through to ignite his? She might be naïve, but she aroused him far more than any pro. His lips would hunger for her innocent taste until she was in his arms again, and he could do all those forbidden, carnal things he dreamed of, flesh to flesh. For the moment, he still had his vampire senses, but even when human, he'd never forget the heady aroma of her arousal as he heated her blood for the first time, or the thundering of her heart as she pressed desperately into him. It was going to be a long semester apart.

The ring of the doorbell jerked him from his erotic reverie, and he opened the door to a long line of sailors, delivering box after box of Humanité. Veronique kept her promise, arriving as the last box was stacked in his spare room.

He opened and examined each one, and once he was satisfied, signed the documents Veronique flourished. With the approval of the responders, she slipped out of Matt's life as quietly as she arrived, leaving behind more hope than he had in almost a hundred years.

The Humanité was stellar, perfect. His mausoleum became merely a lonely abode for spiders, an empty shrine to his immortality. For the first time in decades, Matt enjoyed all the pleasures of being human, and he took full advantage of it. He slipped into a warm, comfortable bed at midnight, rather than sunrise. He ate delicious food and drank beverages which didn't exist before he'd been turned. He went to the beach every single day and soaked up the warming, healing rays of the sun. He splurged on every human activity save one, not that he didn't have plenty of offers, but none of them was as valuable to him as Cat, and he wouldn't betray her. He'd endure until she could satisfy that particular human craving herself. Until then, he had a great fantasy life.

* * * *

Matt listened patiently for almost an hour as Dr. Noah Bernstein, the head biochemist at Consort Group International's pharmaceuticals branch, lectured him on the finer points of vampire biochemistry. Bernstein had been Matt's first stop after the formula arrived. Not only was he a brilliant biochemist, but he was also the master sadist at the Gaoler. Matt knew him well since he'd been forced to sit through more than one demonstration of Bernstein's 'expertise' with the subs. It always left him with the urge to strangle the bastard with his own whip, notwithstanding Matt understood the women who agreed to scene with Bernstein actually wanted his kind of brutality. Matt found the gawky, hawkish, bespectacled guy objectionable on just about every level, but if he could do something to enhance the Humanité or make it permanent, Matt would buy him his very own solid gold paddle.

"Are you coming to my demonstration of the violet wand tomorrow night?" Bernstein asked conversationally as they waited for the spectrum analyzer to give them a readout of the formula. *Fun with electricity?* Matt didn't think so.

"No, sorry. I'll be busy tomorrow night."

Bernstein looked him up and down. "You know, now that you're mostly human, you can stop your obsessive concern about hurting subs and just relax into your role as a Dom. A lot of girls at the club would love to spend some quality time with you."

Matt's smile was brief. "I'm overwhelmed with work right now." He really wanted to tell the guy to jam it but realized he could be antagonizing the man who controlled his destiny, so he softened his words. "It's a little different being human these days. Gets tiring. Maybe later."

"To tell you the truth, Brenner," Bernstein condescended, using his Dom persona, "I always thought your preoccupation with sub safety was…hyper-vigilant…at best. Take it from me, they're not that fragile."

Matt turned a cold gaze on the man and assumed a stance leaving no doubt Matt could and would kick his ass, vampire or not. "Since you've never been a vampire, and never had to resist breaking a puny human in half, I'm going to suggest you bugger off the subject. Are we clear?"

"Uh…sure." The big, bad sadist backed down without further questions.

"Good." Matt smiled tightly. "Now, you think this Humanité is something you can work with? Can you make it longer lasting or even permanent?"

The machine's buzzer sounded, and Bernstein studied the printout. "All the ingredients she used are pretty attainable. Everything, except this one." He pointed to the readout. "Betulina barosma, commonly called buchu."

"What's so special about it? You can get it, right?"

Bernstein nodded. "With time. It's heavily protected by the South African government so Consort Group will have to use its contacts and probably grease several palms."

"If money's an issue…" Matt began with the intention of offering his own.

"Not really it's more an issue with conservationists. We'll just have to convince them we're after it for a good cause. Actually, what we should do is find a sample somewhere other than South Africa and cultivate it away from prying eyes. We'll research that possibility."

"And the duration? Can you make it last longer?"

Bernstein nodded slowly. "I don't see why not. We'll investigate some enteric coatings, some stabilizers; we should at least get a formula that will last years instead of months. Permanent? I don't know yet, but I'll work on it."

"I'll leave you to it. And, Noah," Bernstein looked up from his computer, "your discretion, time and accuracy will be well rewarded. Anything else…" Matt left the threat unspoken, but his stare was direct, and he didn't have to be a vampire to know Bernstein's compulsive swallowing meant he got the message.

# 9

"See you then," Cat agreed and then clicked off the call.

This time tomorrow, she might well be with Matt, by the end of the week at the latest. It all depended on how quickly the trial went to the jury. He sounded so wonderful just now on the phone, apologizing for not being able to meet her at the airport. If it hadn't been for the District Attorney not wanting them to be seen together before they each testified, he would be there to greet her, no matter what was going on.

She toyed with her carry-on bag, so nervous she scarcely knew how to contain herself. Maria's trial, which started tomorrow, would be stressful, and she was certainly not looking forward to the drama, though she was determined to see Maria's killer put away. No, the real test would be an honest to God renewal of her relationship with Matt. In a way, a whole new relationship. Now that he was, at least temporarily human, what would happen between the two of them?

What would happen to her? Things had gone well for Cat in New York. She'd finished her semester at Columbia, and in a few weeks would graduate with honors. That was a nice feather in her cap, but that and five bucks would get her a tall latte, and that's it. She was working on a novel, one with an immortal hero, though not a vampire. Writing took time, and publishing took even longer. She needed a job. She was somewhat reassured by Rick's invitation to check out any of the companies that struck her fancy in the Consort Group. Still, what if the job she wanted and the man she wanted were in two different parts of the world? And what if, after he really got to know her, the man didn't want her, after all?

Not seeing Matt for almost three months seemed like forever to Cat, though she had to admit she probably learned more about him through their daily phone calls where the possibility of sex was non-existent. If they'd been together physically, well, they wouldn't have been talking. Sex was the elephant in the room. She had never really had a boyfriend, never had sex. And Matt, she supposed he knew everything there was to know about it. Could a relationship that unbalanced survive?

There were no vampiric barriers between them now, and she was terrified somehow she would screw up a human relationship. What in the world did she know about making any kind of relationship last? What example of family life had she ever seen? How did a mostly inexperienced twenty-one-year-old woman forge a lasting relationship with a one-hundred-and-twenty-year-old ex-vampire?

Her flight was called, and Cat took a deep breath. She would be with him again soon. She'd thought it over carefully, and she wanted him, vampire or human. Matt Brenner was the man who filled her every fantasy, and she wanted him. She hoped, over time, he would still want her.

* * * *

Matt strode from the Gaoler to talk with Jonesy and make sure everything for Cat's homecoming had been arranged.

"Mr. Brenner's office." Jonesy handled a call and looked up at him as she cradled the phone. "Oh, hi, boss. What's shakin'?"

Matt grinned. Jonesy was a woman fascinated by life in the twenties, and she was determined to live there as much as the modern world allowed. Her decorating efforts resulted in his Sam Spade-era private offices.

"Hey, kid. I just got off the phone with my girl. You got everything ready the way I ordered?"

"Oh, yeah. The cleaning company came in, got everything spit…spot. Food's in the fridge. The car's washed and gassed up. A dozen red roses are in a big crystal vase in her kitchen. I sure hope she's not allergic."

"You're the best, Jonesy."

"And you're a romantic, boss. I never would have guessed it. Wish I was the lucky girl!"

"Yeah, well, she may be taking on more of a challenge than you think. I appreciate the thought." He sighed. "I'm stuck with the suits until Rick can take over tomorrow. I get what a lucrative deal this is, but… You have everything arranged, right? It's crucial."

"Sure thing, boss. Rick gets back from Tokyo tomorrow morning. He'll be in the office at noon, then you're off until whenever. I know you have that trial thing first."

"Yeah. Good to know he's taking over. Cat wouldn't hear of me leaving under the circumstances. Damn, I wanted to be there to pick her up at the airport."

"Don't you worry, boss. I got ya covered. I ordered a big, fat stretch limo with champagne and chocolates to meet her. She'll think you're the bee's knees!"

* * * *

Matt sat on the dais in front of a crowd enthusiastic about BDSM anime and endured what felt like the hundredth sake toast. He wondered darkly if Jonesy was optimistic about Cat's response to his romantic gestures. Yeah, sure, finishing this financial deal was important to Consort Group, and by trickle-down effect, thousands of employee families. He still worried Cat was a little too willing to do without him tonight.

Matt knew a lot about her now. Knew they shared many of the same views on life; knew about her dreams and goals, and she knew about his. What if it wasn't enough? What did a vampire know about making a relationship work with a twenty-one-year-old woman? Now that Cat was home, he was counting the minutes until all his dreams came true. The hopefulness of that, after so many years without hope, terrified him.

* * * *

Cat didn't expect this trial to linger on. A long line of eyewitnesses, including her, preceded Matt to the stand. From the prosecution's point of view, he was their closer. They had a confession from both gunmen, with one absurd exception. Miguel Dominion, the man who killed Maria and the teller, claimed he was driven to murder by the trauma of seeing Matt turn into a vampire. Matt told her he looked forward to testifying and putting Dominion away. It would almost be fun.

The day outside the Los Angeles County Court House was sun-drenched and smog-free. It was easy for Cat to imagine the jurors profoundly wishing they were anywhere but here, listening to the ludicrous arguments put forth by the defense. It had to be obvious to everyone present that this scum bag,

Dominion, was guilty as the devil, and if anyone on the planet deserved the death penalty, he did.

Miguel Dominion was a toad of a man, no matter how his attorney tried to clean him up in a cheap suit and haircut. He was up to his tattooed eyelids in crime and innocent blood, and the jury was, to say the least, hostile, especially when they were shown pictures of the young bank teller and Maria.

District Attorney, Angela Hall, finished her re-cross of the Medical Examiner. "So, Dr. Blake, in your professional opinion, there's nothing that could have been done to save Samantha or Maria?"

"No. Both women sustained fatal injuries leading to their immediate demise."

Cat sighed with relief when the Medical Examiner left the stand. No more gruesome photos of Maria used as visual aids, at least for the moment. Well, it wasn't as if she could block out the mental images.

It had been mere months since Maria's death, but the trial started in record time. The public outcry, given the senselessness of the crimes, was enormous. D.A. Hall was trying the case herself rather than farming it out to an assistant D.A. She'd pushed hard to get it started with all possible haste. If things went well on this one, it might set her up for a Mayoral run. Thank goodness Dominion's public defender had political ambitions of his own and was all too happy to throw his scummy client under the bus for the sake of speedy justice.

Cat thought back to the day in the bank. She was so grateful for Matt's rescue. Now, she depended on him, loved him, which made their separation that much more painful. Because of him, she was alive to sit here in this courtroom, and so was everyone else in the bank. His vampire strength allowed him to overcome Dominion easily. Matt didn't share her perspective, of course. He couldn't see past the negative aspects of being a vampire, and the fact that the condition was forced on him. If his life had been lived and ended decades ago, she and a lot of other people would have paid a bitter price.

"The State calls Matthew James Brenner," the District Attorney said clearly.

Cat's head snapped up.

"Matthew Brenner, please step forward to be sworn."

The doors at the back of the courtroom opened, and Matt walked in. Was it Cat's imagination or did the gaze of every woman in the room snap to him with rapt attention? She smiled inwardly. She was used to that. He was always the focus of female attention, and why not? He moved with a power and grace which gave testimony to his lithe, muscular build and constant training. He was dressed in his usual—dark suit, dark shirt, dark tie. The combination could have been sinister on anyone else. On him, it was just…sexy. There was really no other way to describe him. She drew in a deep breath and let it out again. This was going to be interesting.

* * * *

Matt was sworn in and then took the stand. He nodded at the judge, who turned to the District Attorney. "Please continue, Miss Hall."

"Mr. Brenner," the D.A. began, "would you please look at the defendant and tell us if you know him?"

"Yes, I do," Matt said clearly, his deep baritone voice carrying easily.

"Would you please tell us what you witnessed on January 21st of this year, during the robbery of the First California State Bank?"

"Miguel Dominion killed Maria Gonzalez and Samantha Johnson. He shot Mrs. Johnson in the face, fired once at me, grazing my arm, causing a ricochet bullet to hit Mrs. Gonzalez in the head and killing her. I saw both women die of those wounds."

"You were an eyewitness to those events?"

"Yes."

"Was anyone else present when Mrs. Gonzalez and Mrs. Johnson were shot?"

"Yes." Matt's gaze swept over Cat. "Catherine Temple was with me during the incident, as were all the other occupants of the bank that day."

"Did you have any interaction with the defendant, Mr. Brenner?"

"Yes. I volunteered to take the place of a pregnant mother and her young son as a hostage."

"Please tell us what happened then."

"We were on our way out the back door of the bank when Miss Temple screamed. It startled Dominion, and he turned to fire at her. I was able to push his accomplice out the door, and then wrestle Dominion for the shotgun. I disarmed and incapacitated him."

"Are you aware the defendant claims he was terrorized by you into committing these acts of murder?"

Matt looked down at his hands folded in his lap and smiled wryly. "Yes, I've heard that," he admitted dryly and stifled his smile as he replied.

"Mr. Dominion stated…I'm quoting now…" Hall read from a file. "Brenner is a devil. A vampire." She smirked.

Matt let a smile creep out and bit it back. "Yes." The grin spread across his face as he looked directly at Dominion. "I understand that's what he says."

The D.A. smirked again. "Mr. Dominion states you revealed yourself to him as a vampire when you wrestled him for the shotgun." The courtroom buzzed with murmurs and stifled laughter. "So, for the record, Mr. Brenner, and remembering you're under oath, will you please tell us whether or not you're a vampire?"

Matt looked down at his hands, a relaxed smile on his face. "Not according to my mother, Counselor."

"I see," Hall continued, thoroughly enjoying the discomfiture of the defense attorney. "When you were sworn in, you placed your hand on the Bible, did you not?"

"Yes."

"Did it burn your hand or repel you?" The District Attorney inquired, holding the Bible up for the benefit of the jury.

Matt held up his hand and examined it. "I'm afraid not."

"If we order a pizza with garlic for lunch, will you be driven out of the room?"

Matt smiled. "Not unless you order anchovies, too." Muffled laughter rippled around them.

"There's a nice sunny spot here by the jury box, Mr. Brenner. I wonder if you'd oblige the court by standing in it."

Matt stood and strolled to the spot indicated. He turned a lazy circle, his smile sweeping over the jury members.

"I see you haven't burst into flames, sir. Would you mind holding this mirror?" Hall passed Matt a hand mirror, and Matt held it up, so the jurors could plainly see his reflection. "Can you tell us what you see in it?"

"A man who needs a haircut," he quipped as he finger combed a stray curl.

With a strangled cry the defense attorney stood. "Your Honor, the defense will stipulate that Mr. Brenner is not a vampire."

There was outright laughter, and the judge banged her gavel for order. She motioned for Matt to sit back in the witness stand.

"Sidebar, your Honor?" the defense attorney requested, and the judge waved the two attorneys forward.

Matt took the time during their discussion to consider how this little demonstration would have gone if he did not have the Humanité coursing through his system. He still could have handled religious items, garlic and the mirror with impunity. The sunlight would have been more of a challenge, but survivable. If all those superstitions had not been bogus, his kind would not have survived in society as they had for millennia.

The judge spoke again. "Court will take a brief recess while defense confers with his client. Please keep your seats."

Matt sat relaxed in the witness stand, caressing Cat with his gaze. He'd been unable to call her since she landed. Her clear blue-eyed gaze caught his from across the room, and she smiled faintly. He nodded imperceptibly.

Matt could barely restrain himself from vaulting over the witness stand to snatch her against him. He needed to show her he was here for her now, as he knew she was here for him. He fantasized about her for so many months. Now, the chance to actually hold her hand on the beach, or in a restaurant drove him to distraction. He would kiss her lips until they were swollen, and she was out of her mind with the need for him. He was certainly crazy with need for her. With annoyance, he willed his erection away. Yeah, that was all he needed, for the whole courtroom to know he itched to get hard and horizontal with their star victim. From her half-stifled expression, he knew she was hot and wet just looking at him.

The attorneys filed back in, and Matt was relieved when the judge waved him to stay seated, though the threat of having to stand had pretty much brought down the house.

* * * *

Cat followed him with her gaze as he walked from the courtroom, and Matt wondered with amusement if she knew he hid a fading hard-on. He presumed the judge would soon call a recess for the day. It was late, and he was sure the prosecutor wanted the jury to consider his testimony overnight.

Matt, his hands burrowed deep in his trouser pockets, hung around the courthouse hallway for a few minutes, praying for the opportunity to see Cat. And soon, just as he'd hoped, the courtroom began to empty. She exited while deep in discussion with D.A. Hall, but he felt her gaze seeking him the second she stepped through the door. Her head went up, and she homed in on him like radar. A smile teased her lips.

"Can you give me a minute? I need to talk to someone. I'll be right with you." Cat explained. Hall looked annoyed but nodded.

Matt smiled pleasantly, he hoped impersonally, as she glided toward him. His heart thundered wildly. He wondered if hers did, too.

Their gazes met and held. How could anyone look so beautiful in black? Sunlight caught her golden hair and illuminated it. Her tongue flicked nervously at full pink lips, and a rosy flush invaded her cheeks as she approached.

"Hi," she whispered.

"Hi."

"Good job on the stand."

He laughed softly. "Oh yeah? Was I convincing?"

"Shh." She looked around. No one was listening. She chuckled. "Well, I bought it."

"Yeah, but you were always an easy sell."

Just reflexively, as if nothing had separated them and time had never passed, she swatted his arm as a reprimand for the smart remark. Her blue eyes danced.

"Thank you for all you did, you know, the limo and flowers and all. I don't know what to say. It was all so much." She stopped babbling, looked around to be sure they weren't being observed and took his hand. "I've missed you so much."

"You know, Cat, I'm right here." His voice was suddenly a caress, and her eyes grew serious.

"I know. I just, I need to finish this, you know? For Maria. And then…"

"Then what?" Matt asked almost coolly.

"Then I'll call you. If that's all right?"

Another impersonal smile. "That's always all right."

"Cat!" Hall called.

"I…I've gotta go. Hall needs to talk to me. I…" She touched his arm and squeezed gently. "I want to talk to you. I have a lot to say. I just…"

He looked down at her hand and then back to her eyes, and the hungry, longing expression on his face drew a tiny gasp from her. "Me, too."

"The trial could be over tomorrow, depending on the jury. I'll call you as soon as there's a verdict, okay?" Her eyes pleaded with him for understanding.

"Of course."

"You understand, I need to finish this. It's like a commitment I have to Maria. I have to do this for her."

"I understand, Cat." He stroked her cheek with his fingertips. "I'll wait for you."

* * * *

Matt still cringed hours later. *I'll wait for you. Why did those have to be his last words? I'll wait for you. I love you. Without you, I might as well be buried in a box like Maria.* It was all pretty much the same sentiment.

In frustration, he stretched weary muscles that never used to ache, and then snatched bottled water out of the office fridge. His body felt wrong, colder than usual, his senses a little sharper, leading to concerns the Humanité might be wearing off sooner than expected. Still, Bernstein's work in extending the life of the drug was extremely promising.

Matt reached for the small metal vial in his breast pocket. It contained one emergency dose of the drug. He intended to keep it on his person at all times. A safety measure in case he was ever separated from his supply. A literal ton of the stuff sat safely in his spare room, so what the hell, he'd replace his "emergency" supply when he got home. Right now, when he was so close to consummating his relationship with Cat, he couldn't afford to slip into vampirism again, even temporarily. He gulped down the capsule and then slipped the vial back into his suit coat, determined to replace it as soon as he walked in his front door.

Resolving that work was fruitless, Matt closed his computer and decided to spend the remainder of his evening with Rick and his donors at the Gaoler. He stood at the door of Rick's private dungeon, and before he swiped his card for admission, bent over to tie his shoe. He was about to straighten when the door opened. The first thing he saw was a delicate foot wearing an ankle bracelet. As he slowly raised his head, he saw a gorgeous young woman with thick, silver hair drawn back in a ponytail, hanging long and glossy over one shoulder. She might have smelled fruity and delicious like some kind of tropical wet dream, but she was built for business. Her long legs rose to narrow hips and an impossibly tiny waist. Her shoulders and arms were lean but muscled, like a swimmer. Her complexion glowed with sun-kissed health. This, he thought with amusement, must be the new girl.

She smiled invitingly. "Cute. You must be the partner." Her golden eyes flashed.

Matt held out his hand. "Matt Brenner."

She shook it. "Georgia Gregoriev." There was enough of an accent to hint at exotic locales. "I'm new here." She ushered him into the room and gestured for him to take a seat opposite her on the couch. "The other girls will be here in a minute. They're with Rick. Everyone's very excited to see you."

Rick's private party adjourned to the dining room where Matt enjoyed a few drinks, and then dinner in the company of his old friend. It was a treat to eat the meals prepared by their gourmet chef. The donors ate like this every night, he thought with amusement. No wonder they never wanted to leave. While he ate heartily of stuffed salmon, Rick settled himself at the table with a twin donor on each side.

After dinner, Georgia stood and chatted with Matt while Rick took an urgent call. She took two steps into Matt's space, and keeping her eyes straight ahead, squeezed his well-developed backside. He started and looked down at her in shock.

"What are you doing after you leave here?" she whispered.

He still had enough of the early 20th century in him to be shocked. Georgia might make it as one of Rick's assistants, but he doubted she'd ever go further if she was willing to risk Rick's wrath with action on the side.

"Actually, I'm spoken for, but I appreciate the offer. If it was an offer."

Georgia gave him a sultry look. "Oh, it was an offer, all right."

Matt frowned. "You should know, Rick doesn't share…much, and I don't share at all, anymore."

Georgia shrugged an elegant shoulder. "What a shame."

Matt readjusted himself and glanced at her appreciatively. "If anyone can bring the dead back to life, it's you."

On the way home, Matt had to fight the compulsion to drive to Cat's place, bend her over and bang her like a screen door in a hurricane. Georgia had made him hotter than ever! Rick was going to have his hands full with that woman, and God bless her, Rick needed a challenge! Matt only hoped he could tame his own lust into submission for the sake of his sanity. He needed to get Cat beneath him—now. *She's a virgin for God's sake, choke back your dick long enough to finesse her. Where's the neighbor lady to turn a hose on me when I need her?*

The traffic on Wilshire was surprisingly light on this late June evening, and Matt enjoyed the feel of the city breeze tossing his curls. He tapped the Bluetooth on his steering wheel, answering the ring of the phone.

"You need to know something." Rick's voice sounded odd.

Matt's forehead wrinkled as he drove. "Hey, listen, if this is about Georgia—"

"No." Rick cleared his throat in discomfort. "I'm sorry to tell you this, dear boy. Your condo is on fire."

"What?" Matt snorted. "What do you mean…on fire?" Just then, his building came into view, hot flames licking around his unit's windows. "The Humanité!" An explosion blew out the walls of the penthouse and rocked the street like an earthquake.

"Matt?" Rick waited for a beat while Matt gasped in dismay. "I can see your building from the office. The entire top floor is on fire. Your whole place is gone." Matt stared numbly at where his penthouse used to be. "This had to be arson. I'm sorry, dear boy."

Ignoring the honking cars around him, Matt jerked his Jaguar to a stop, despair crawling deep inside him.

"That's not the worst of it. The bombers got to Consort labs too, and killed Bernstein, destroyed all his work, every sample, every note."

"Off-site backup?"

"I'm sorry, they were very thorough. It's all gone. Everything."

Matt slumped under the weight of the blow. He tapped the empty vial in his pocket that once held his emergency Humanité, the one he'd cavalierly taken earlier that night. He'd screwed the pooch on that one and knew it. *Just in case* materialized moments ago, and his own carelessness left him with nothing.

"Security at Consort got a look at the person who broke into the lab and faxed me a picture from the closed-circuit camera," Rick continued, interrupting Matt's agonized musing.

"Can you identify him?"

"Not yet. We're comparing all computer databases now. Matt, I don't think he's human."

Matt tried to imagine any vamps he might have angered. It didn't make sense. "Could Veronique have done this? Revenge for humiliating her?"

"I don't know. What does it matter? Whoever it was, knew you were creating a longer-lasting form of Humanité. You're gonna have to protect yourself, Matt. These vamps are badass mother fuckers."

Matt gritted his teeth and continued home to assess the damage, which was catastrophic. Rick had been right, it was gutted. Less than an hour later, he motored the roads, climbing to the hilltop ledge where Rick's concrete and steel mansion perched. He needed the perspective of the three-hundred-and-sixty-degree view. If he stayed at the Consort penthouse, he would be within blocks of his great loss, with the stench of ash in his nostrils. Yes, he could see the burnt shell of the penthouse from his seat by the pool, but the distance was his blessing tonight.

He spent an uneasy night tossing and turning in Rick's guest room. There had to be someone, or maybe a group, watching him. How else could they know Consort had developed a new formula? And why would anyone else care? It wasn't as if he planned to market the stuff.

Now, he was truly vulnerable. For the time being, anyway, he wasn't a vampire, which meant they could kill him any time they wanted if that was their desire. And what if it was? Hadn't he said he'd rather die than remain a vampire? It was ironic, though, that just when he'd found someone, he could love, and finessed the circumstances so he could do her justice, he was at the deadliest risk.

Still, they hadn't attempted to kill him, unless they'd expected him to be home at the time of the fire. There was nothing left to find of his records and notebooks. What if they took all the research before torching the place? Could anything be salvaged from the cloud? Corrupting the cloud would take the crime to the next level. He sighed, turned over again and considered the question bothering him most. What to do about Cat?

Wasn't the fact that he contemplated his own demise proof enough that his time with Cat could be short? He didn't have the luxury of waiting. If he was going to claim her, he needed to do it now. He was a selfish pig, he thought, condemning himself. It was unfair to her, but he would do it, anyway. It was time he and Cat started this relationship for real.

* * * *

Matt's cell phone rang the next morning as he packed a few of Rick's clothes into a bag to tide him over. He checked the caller ID, and Cat's cheerful face smiled up at him.

"Hi."

"Hi, yourself. I'm guessing you heard about the plea bargain?"

"Yeah, it was on the news. Life without parole, the best possible outcome."

"So, now that the trial and everything is over, I was thinking maybe we could get together."

"Oh?" Matt kept his voice calm, a little teasing.

"Yeah."

"Do you have any plans for today?"

"No. Except, I was going to ask if you'd like to have dinner?"

"I just happen to have one of our beach house properties for the rest of the summer." He said it in an off-hand way, but Cat caught the import and gasped. It was unprecedented that Matt would spend time at the beach during daylight hours. As a vampire, he'd never be able to tolerate the intensity of the sun by the ocean.

"Wow! A beach house in Malibu? I could get behind that!"

"Yeah. There was a little fire at my condo, so I'm using the beach house until the repairs are completed.

"A fire? You have a sprinkler system, don't you? You weren't hurt?"

"No. I wasn't even home. Just an inconvenience, really." He didn't have the heart to tell her the Humanité and all their efforts to prolong the formula went up in flames. "I'm getting ready to move over to Malibu right now. The keys are in my hand. Why don't you come by around four, and we can figure out what we want to do after that?"

"Time at the beach sounds lovely. Give me the address."

Matt zipped up his suitcase and then headed for his destiny. His humanity was a ticking clock. Engaging in a romantic relationship with this virginal beauty was not his sin. Matt's sin of omission was his failure to tell Cat about the destruction of his stockpile of Humanité. That was the tipping point that threw him from being a man in love to being a bastard. Well, if he was going to be a bastard, he might as well be in full-tilt bastard mode.

# 10

The Malibu beach house, one of Consort's vacation rental properties, was luxurious by anyone's standards, and it's cool tranquility soothed Matt's restless spirit. A deep breath and a gaze across the deck, the beach, and the ocean helped him find his calm. Cool off, he cautioned himself. Cat was on her way to join him in this idyllic setting. Life didn't get better than that, but if he didn't get a grip…

*You can't go all Neanderthal and jump her, you'll scare her to death!* No, Matt didn't want to panic her, but he did mean to have her. He shifted his loose linen shorts. His heavy cock thumped against his thigh. He hadn't felt the hot, wet silk of a mortal woman since 1922. Eager hardly began to describe his need, especially when the flesh belonged to Cat.

A quiver rocketed through him from the touch of the invigorating breeze. Matt almost laughed at himself, knowing the chill running up his spine was truly anticipation. He stood at the sliding glass door and secured the billowing sheer that broke away from its tie-down in the sudden gust, a metaphor for his soaring spirit. His hands shook with eagerness.

* * * *

Cat bit her lip in concentration as her ancient Toyota chugged up the Malibu cliff. She counted the streets, following the directions Matt gave her. She was close now, really close, and her pulse raced faster as each house number drew her into his web. Well, that's how she thought of it—right into the giant spider's secret lair where all those forbidden pleasures the nuns had warned her about awaited. What would he think of her, of her performance, or lack of it? She trembled with equal parts anticipation and doubt.

*You know him, you love him. Trust that.* She pulled to a jerky stop at the appointed address, and the car backfired. Cat gazed over the beautifully landscaped ocean-front lawn and shivered. Breathe. She drew a steadying breath so deep it was almost a sigh, and with shaking hands, checked her appearance in the rearview mirror. *C'mon, you coward. He's waiting. Remember your last kiss? Don't you want him to hold you that way again?* Yeah, she really did. She got out of the car.

* * * *

Matt was lost in his own delicious thoughts when the knock came. With effort, he jerked himself away from his erotic daydream and went to meet the real thing. He drew in a deep breath, blew it out forcefully, and then manfully limited himself to measured steps rather than a bolt across the room to tear the door open. His eyes feasted on her. She looked like a spring garden in brightly colored shorts and a crop top, and he longed to bury himself balls deep in that flowerbed and never leave. He smiled lazily instead.

"Hi," he said in a relaxed drawl he couldn't quite believe was his own voice.

"Hi," she responded in a low, husky murmur of her own and then incongruously laughed.

"Did I miss the joke?" His smile wavered.

She beamed at him. "No. It's just, I've only ever seen you in these dark, serious clothes, and today…it's Bob the Beachcomber! I like the new look a lot!"

"Well, thanks." He ushered her into the house and then closed the door on the outside world.

She jumped nervously when the lock clicked. *Easy, now.* Even without vampire sensitivity, Matt could read her uncertainty. What could he do about that? *Alcohol, a little alcohol, and a little patience and understanding.* What man needed a devil on one shoulder and an angel the other, when he had a dick that did the heavy thinking?

*Chuck out patience and understanding! Get out the booze!* He plastered on an interested smile and followed her into the room. Damn! Her tatas swayed much too naturally to be encumbered by a bra. *Touch them! Taste them!* His entire limbic system screamed.

Cat turned toward the deck and gasped at the fabulous vista confronting them through the open door. Matt got an up-close view of her sweet heart-shaped ass in those silky little shorts and wanted to come just looking at her. Surely, he could find a little more self-control? *A little more, not much.*

The sheer slipped its mooring again and danced joyfully in and out of the sliding glass door, beckoning them onto the deck and courtyard.

"My God, this place belongs to you?"

Matt shrugged. "It's a Consort property, actually one that Rick principally owns. He uses it as an investment property, rents it out to tourists for a phenomenal fee. He gave it to me at a bargain rate for as long as..." He stopped, sadness momentarily overtaking him. "For the summer or...whatever."

Cat looked at him inquiringly but didn't pursue a question. Instead, she gestured toward the ocean. "So, for these prices, do we have to stay inside, or do we get the use of the beach?"

His grin answered her, and he beckoned her out the door. "Lemonade with a little extra?" He led her to an outside bar holding a tall pitcher of ice drenched in lemonade and spiked with strawberry vodka. It smelled like a delicious fruit drink, but Matt had reason to know it packed a helluva wallop.

"Why not?" she agreed, as he poured the drink and then handed it to her. She tasted and smiled her approval, took another long, nervous drink.

"We have food, too, if you want?" He could barely force out the words but thought it was only right.

She patted her stomach gently and shook her head. *Butterflies?* She smiled, and he was relieved. Food was not what he was hungry for right now.

He clinked glasses with her to encourage her to drink. "Would you like to stay in the shade or sit in the sun?" he asked with an unaccustomed formality.

Cat smiled. "Are you a little nervous, too?"

Matt affected nonchalance. "Me? Nervous?" His voice was strained. "Of course not. Nothing to be nervous about." He scrambled to collect the container of drink stirrers he'd just overturned. He led her to the railing of the deck overlooking the ocean.

"God, you're so gorgeous!" Cat said. "What in the world are you doing here with me?"

Matt's startled gaze searched her face. He was touched and didn't know what to say. "Cat..."

She seemed to shake herself out of her gaffe. "Is that sunburn?" She started to reach out to touch the expanse of his chest where the wind blew his denim shirt back, and then thought better of it and withdrew.

Matt caught her hand and kissed her fingers. With his hand covering hers, he drew them both down his six-pack to his waist. "It's okay to touch me, Cat," He leaned in to plant a gentle kiss on her cheek. "I like it when you do."

She bit her lip and leaned back, her elbows resting on the railing. Matt groaned inwardly as her breasts thrust forward teasingly inside the light, glossy fabric covering them. He swallowed hard, saliva pooling at the back of his mouth.

He fought to keep track of the discussion and glanced down at his chest. "Could be sunburn, I spent the morning outside."

A simple conversation was becoming elusive. Matt slid aside his lustful thoughts and leaned into the wide railing beside her.

Cat tensed. She broke his gaze, turned her back to him, and Matt saw the pulse pounding in her neck. He'd had plenty of practice at that. She pretended to survey the picture-perfect expanse of beach and ocean, but he caught her surreptitious glance up at him. She took another gulp of her drink, and he encouraged it, taking another sip of his own and hoping she'd follow suit. She had to relax, or this was going to be a disaster. What the hell had the nuns told her?

He swallowed hard. He needed to relax a little too, but that wasn't easy when he looked at her. Any man, with or without a pulse, would admire the way her trim waist met her rounded hips and continued into perfect slender legs. She wasn't wearing a bra. Had she also foregone panties? Was she bare and wet for him in that colorful garden? Maybe, but he couldn't miss the quaking of her hand as she held the glass.

"Cat." He caressed her shoulders as he stepped flush against her back. "Why don't we take a walk along the beach?"

"Um…okay…"

"You know, being this close to a bed is too much pressure for me." *Pressure? I've got your pressure right here in my two friends!* Matt ignored his dick. He turned to Cat. "I found some beautiful sea glass this morning. Would like to look for more?"

"Oh! Sea glass, here? Wow! Yeah!" Cat swallowed half her drink down and left the glass on the railing. She took off down the steps, hair blowing wildly behind her. "The last one to the water has to do dishes!"

Matt watched her go, hands on his hips, shaking his head at her joie de vivre. Once she was released from the confines of impending intimacy, she was the natural beauty he'd fallen in love with. In each moment, he took a photo in his mind of her reaction to the seabirds and the breaking waves.

Cat's fingers sifted the sand, fishing for the opaque sea glass. She shielded the sun from her eyes as she squinted up at him. "Aren't you hunting for treasure?"

Matt grinned and crouched beside her, he reached an arm's length to tame untamable curls. "I've found my treasure."

Cat blushed. "I don't know how to hear that. I've never had anyone talk to me that way." Her hands stayed busy sorting the sizes and colors within her reach. She bit at her bottom lip as she processed his words.

Matt inched closer. "Well, they should have. Someone should have celebrated your gifts. I'll bet your grandmother told you how special you were every night before you went to bed."

Cat confessed. "I remember bedtime stories and kisses on my forehead. I remember the look on her face. But I don't remember those words." Cat held up the largest piece of green glass in her palm. Their heads bumped together, upsetting their balance. They dropped into the sand, laughing when she wound up in his lap.

His arm slid around her, hugging her sun-warmed body snuggly against him. "That's a pretty piece. Almost as pretty as you."

"Is this the way you talk to women?"

"What do you mean? That's the way I talk to you. You've complimented me."

"Well, yeah..." Cat looked him up and down meaningfully. "...but look at you."

"Baby, why would you think I'm any less attracted to you than you are to me?"

Cat shrugged. "I dunno. I never thought of myself that way. I'm not very good at this." She frowned and stared down the beach, avoiding eye contact.

"Good at what? How do you know?"

"I remember the snubs at the school dances with our brother school."

"They were adolescents, they were pigs, they couldn't appreciate everything you are. Can't you look at me, baby?"

Cat looked at him with surprise. "Pigs?"

Matt snorted. "Yeah, adolescent boys are pigs. That knowledge should be part of every young girl's curriculum. They're only interested in the most obvious girls."

"I guess I wasn't obvious, then."

"I'll tell you what I can't figure out. You've just spent four years in college, and while college guys are only marginally better than high schoolers, anyone as beautiful as you should have met one or two men of quality."

"I did. I met you, and I met Rick."

Matt shook his head. "I really despair for my gender. Some up and comer who was looking for a brain in a beautiful body should have snapped you up by junior year."

Cat stared at him in disbelief.

"Success in business is just that. When I've closed a big deal on an international level, what good is going home if I have no one to share it with? Cat, you could have been half of a power couple."

"Perhaps the Universe has brought us together? I mean, you and I could be the power couple. That makes you a lot less intimidating."

He nuzzled her cheek with his nose. "I'm intimidating? Have you ever asked a drop-dead gorgeous woman to spend time at the beach, alone?" He turned Cat in his arms.

Cat swallowed hard. "I…Matt, could you please hold me for a minute?"

"If hold you now, I won't be able to let you go." He leaned in his breath mingling with hers. "Are you ready for that?"

* * * *

A peace enveloped them and grew with each of their strides along the wet sand. Every few steps they stopped to watch their shadows kiss. Matt pulled out his phone and snapped a photo of their feet and their shadows. As they approached the beach in front of the house, she stepped into him, seeking his embrace. He bent his head for a kiss, gentle and soft, and light as a zephyr. Her disappointed gaze followed him as he leaned back again. He gave a short laugh. "Oh, you want more?" She didn't reply, but her eyes smoldered. "Yeah, I can do that."

Need took Matt and shook him, quickening his breath as Cat closed what little space remained between them. His embrace claimed her with stunning force as he deepened the kiss. His cock was granite hard against her pelvis. He tried to slow down a little, realizing it wouldn't take much at this point to push him right over the edge.

Cat burst from his grip, running to the deck. "The last one back cooks dinner!"

Matt stalked her with even, unrelenting strides. "What makes you think anyone's getting dinner?"

Cat giggled. "If you wear me out, you have to feed me."

"I'll get back to you on that." His kiss was searing, it took her breath away.

"You're either gonna have to lay me down," she purred against his lips, "or I'm gonna fall down."

He laughed and swept her up in his arms. She clung to his neck, pressing light kisses down his cheek and to the edge of his mouth until their lips joined. He carried her up the steps of the deck to the exterior shower.

"Let me get you a robe. You can throw your wet clothes over the wall."

Cat eyed the tropical shower stall and grinned. "This reminds me of the night we met." She stepped behind the thatched partition and disrobed. Matt accessed the cabinet near the shower and pulled out two downy ivory robes.

He pulled his shirt off and dropped his shorts. "Yeah, I was so hot for you that night!" He turned on the hose and dashed his lower body with the cold water. *Just like I am right now.*

"Really? I never got that."

Casting an incredulous glance her way, Matt drew on his robe. "You seriously have no sexual radar."

Cat turned and gave him a saucy smile. "Maybe you can help me tune that in!"

"Come out from behind that shower, and I'll tune you in."

The water stopped. Cat emerged from the shower wrapped in her robe, with the very edge of her kitten-pink tongue between her lips. Matt groaned. "Do you know what you do to me?" *Don't show me your tongue unless you're going to use it on me!*

"I don't know what I don't know. But I'm a good student."

Matt enveloped her in a second. "I will happily provide the highest quality of instruction."

"Will it involve textbooks, quizzes?"

He shook his head. "This is hands-on training in the trenches. We'll get down and dirty." Matt swung her over his shoulder, caveman style. At the canopied doublewide chaise, he playfully tossed her down. She landed against the cushions, and he followed. They fit together perfectly. He nudged her knees apart with one of his, his weighty, rigid cock wedged firmly against her untried mound.

"You know what goes where and why, right?"

She ran her tongue over her bottom lip. "I have a general idea."

He turned away for a moment to flip a switch and lower the canvas blinds providing privacy.

"Nice gadget."

"Handy." He was stopped dead by the look in her eyes when he turned back to her, half greedy anticipation, half innocence. "Hey." He stroked his hand reassuringly through her hair. "Everything's okay. I'm here."

"How crazy is this? When I lose contact with you, I get scared."

"Then," he lowered possessive lips to hers, "let's not lose contact."

Their kiss exploded, mouths and tongues insistent and mindless and frantic as all the repressed passion they had felt for months poured out between them. Cat might be inexperienced, but she was eager. They were both breathless when Matt finally lifted his head. He felt her frantic heartbeats racing against his own.

"I want to see all of you, Cat. Now."

He eagerly reached for the collar of the robe. Cat watched him, mesmerized, as he loosened the belt and spread the top wide.

* * * *

Cat's heart thundered out of control as Matt's admiring gaze burned over her. He reached out to caress her breasts, his mouth to suckle them. She gasped. His fingers branded her, and when his lips closed over one perfect peak and drew, the fire darted directly down to her sex, making her ache. She was overwhelmed with sensation, consumed in the blaze he'd created.

"My God! You're a glorious wet dream! Show me more."

Cat's gaze never left his, as she slipped out of the robe. A smile split Matt's face as he watched her.

"Oh, you're a naughty girl," he groaned. She smiled at his teasing. "I love that about you!"

He feasted on the sight of her laid out before him. "Mmm. Honeysuckle, lavender, vanilla and…" He dipped a finger into her wet folds, drawing a shocked gasp from her when he brought her essence to his nose, and then tasted her. She moaned. "Yeah. See what you do to me? You know I want you!"

Cat reached out an uncertain hand, nearly snatched it back, and finally laid it against the hefty bulge tenting his robe. Her breath stuttered. "I've never seen a man naked before," she admitted shyly. "Will you show me?"

"Oh, it would be my pleasure, yeah!"

He stood and quickly doffed his robe. Cat's gaze fluttered up to his as she checked him out, a one-sided grin played about his lips while he studied her reaction. She had no basis for comparison, so she had no way of knowing what a completely lucky woman she was. She did know she was staring at wide shoulders, an acre of his broad, firm chest, sprinkled with a liberal amount of curling black hair, a set of washboard abs that were fitness-commercial-perfect, and narrow hips leading into long, muscular legs. For a long moment, she simply stared. *He's so beautiful, like a breathing classic statue or something.* His long, thick cock stretched up toward his navel, the ropey veins pulsing insistently.

Cat drew in a long breath and raised a wide-eyed gaze to him. "May I touch you?"

Matt groaned. "Yeah, no problem." He joined her on the chaise, his hands shaking slightly. "Can't you tell? That's not a problem at all."

With her palms and inquisitive fingers, she traced the ridges of his abs, descended, following his treasure trail until she met his proud erection.

"May I…" She reached for him shyly. "Would you mind if I…?"

"Touch me." Matt groaned. She snatched her hand back. "That wasn't pain, baby." His voice was tight with need. "It…just…feels…really good." He put her hand back over his hot length and held her there. "Oh, yes, Cat, please touch me. Explore to your heart's content."

"You'll tell me if I hurt you, right? I've heard this is, well, a sensitive area."

He barked out a laugh and gritted his teeth. "Yeah, it's sensitive all right, but it feels freaking great! I feel like a guitar string." Instinctively, she pumped him, her grasp tentative. He shuddered, and caught her busy hands, placing them firmly on his shoulders. "We'll do more of this later. Now, it's my turn."

"Your turn?" she whispered in a tiny voice.

"That's right, baby. I'm gonna make this something you'll never forget."

He started with a kiss, deep, demanding, hot, and seductive. He swirled his tongue around hers, delved deep, nipping her full lips. Cat moaned.

Matt cupped her bottom, pulling her tight against him, letting her experience his hard cock notched against her. Her kisses and caresses, her throaty moans, inflamed him. *More!* Her euphoric body demanded. *More!* He broke away from her lips, showering kisses on her face, eyes, neck, and slowly, slowly down to her breasts.

Cat submerged into a world of swirling sensation and desperate need. She'd had no idea, making love to him would be like this. The nuns were right. This was dangerous, but if she was going to burn, she wanted to burn with Matt!

He teased her breast with his mouth and then clamped onto a sensitive nipple. With his tongue, he circled it, flicking the taut bud with its tip, then suckled hard. Cat threw her head back and moaned softly, chills racing through her. Matt groaned a reply. He moved to the other breast and continued the same gentle torment.

"You have perfect breasts. I've never seen any this ripe. Look how your nipples stand up and get rosy when I work them. I could stay here forever, just playing with them."

Unconsciously, Cat arched her hips up to him and parted her legs in unknowing invitation. Matt gulped. His chest rose and fell rapidly, and hers was right in step with him. His dick stood up rigid, proud and pulsing against her.

Matt slid his body over hers and slithered down, gripping her waist, arching her back up to him and watched her face. She had no idea what was coming, but she was willing to let him take her wherever he wanted to go. He placed tiny, nibbling, open-mouthed kisses down, down, down. She wriggled futilely in his strong grasp as he reached the hot triangle between her legs.

"You smell like heaven! I want to inhale you, Cat! I want to dive into you and make you explode!"

His body had already parted her, in another inch he'd be right there! Cat felt as if she were alive for the first time. Every nerve in her body screamed for something unknown.

He moved his fingers against her gently, running over the petals of her folds. Cat started, shuddered, but didn't try to evade him. Her heart beat wildly as he stroked her languidly, working his way deftly inward. She was so wet.

"Matt!" She cried out, arching against him, digging her fingers hard into his biceps.

Matt hummed his approval, the vibration of his chest so close it coursed through her. Cat shifted restlessly. He continued his delicate search, landing upon the small bundle of nerves at her delta. With a sure and expert touch, he stroked the receptive flesh that blossomed for him, engorging, and growing slick.

"You're so beautiful, baby," he praised. "You're beautiful here, too." She glanced down to see his admiring gaze appreciate her as he petted. "Cat, I want you so badly!"

Matt's thumb wound tighter and tighter circles around that tiny bundle of nerves, which Cat now understood was an incredible pleasure center. Soon, he was directly upon it. He slid two fingers inside her.

"God, you're tight." He groaned. "I'll have to fight my way in."

Cat had no clear idea what he meant by that, but it seemed a little ominous to her. He curled his digits up to touch her rough, sensitive G-spot. Cat bucked against him and panted, so overwhelmed, she felt entirely out of control.

"Breath, baby," he coached gently. "Just breathe. You're almost there."

A wildness coiled deep inside her. Her entire body tensed. Most of all, her clit throbbed, begging for…something…what was it? Cat shuddered and gasped, as he rubbed inside her. His thumb danced upon her clit, and she exploded.

Wave after wave of involuntary spasms crashed through her as she gritted her teeth and cried out her bliss. Matt kept up the pressure and movements, gentling them slowly as her shuddering became less and less frequent and finally died out altogether.

Cat, drenched in sweat, shook in reaction as he moved up to wrap her in his arms. He held her close against him, smiling down at her, kissing her hair and forehead and lips.

"That's your first orgasm," he smiled, enormously pleased with himself.

Slowly, her shaking stopped, and her flushed body cooled. She shivered slightly. He held her tighter.

"Will you warm me up again?" She reached out to touch him.

Their gazes locked while she fisted his hot, hard cock. Matt jerked as she explored him, tracing the veins along his scorching length. He closed his eyes and then grabbed her hand and exhaled slowly.

"Keep that up, and I'll come before I get inside you, and Cat, I want to be inside you. Now."

* * * *

Matt crushed her back beneath him, his knee parted her thighs while he gently stroked her waiting warmth and notched himself at her tight delta. As he breached her, his gaze held hers and he moved, gently pressing into her, gaining ground slowly. She wasn't only tight, after that blinding orgasm, she held her tension with fever grip.

"I hope you can relax, Cat," he coached tenderly. "It'll be so much easier if you are. It's gonna feel so good, baby. Let me love you." The effort of holding back rolled beads of sweat down Matt's back.

Cat shut her eyes, drew in a calming breath. Yes! Matt immediately felt her yield. Cautiously, but firmly, he pressed forward. Her silken folds welcomed him in a tight embrace. She mewled, surrendering.

"You're perfect, baby."

Her virgin barrier stopped his forward momentum. Okay, no matter what he did, there would be pain, but he sought to minimize what he could.

"Wrap your legs around my waist." She obeyed. Matt held himself still and gazed down at her beautiful face. Her eyes were passion filled. "Do you trust me?"

"Of course."

Her reply was so simple and filled with certainty his heart opened wide as she spoke. Matt anchored her, one round hip in each hand, and surged forward. Her maidenhead broke away, and he settled hilt deep into her. His virgin welcomed him unconditionally, hot and wet. As his thick length stroked her sex, his spine went rigid, and he fought to hold back a climax. *Dear God, she feels like heaven!*

She bit her bottom lip again. Was she stifling a cry? He covered her lips with a kiss, a loving distraction to the brief discomfort. He held her immobile beneath him, tasting and prodding and gliding his tongue against hers until she moaned and clenched her fingers into his back with need.

"I'm gonna make this good now, I swear."

She turned her trusting gaze up to him. He moved slowly inside her, relieved she was so wet. Matt wanted them to be as closely joined as any two people could get. He would use his body to show her how much he treasured her. He tilted her hips up, straining to glide the head of his cock repeatedly over her most sensitive spot. Cat moaned and met his angle, hungry for his internal caress.

"That's right. Feels good, doesn't it?" She nodded urgently. "Hold on."

Matt slowly picked up the pace as she caught the rhythm, and her body naturally responded. He kept moving, one endless glide after another. Cat quaked around him, rippling. He refused to come before he got another climax out of her.

"Yeah, Cat! You're so gorgeous this way, taking my cock, taking all of me." She ground against him. "Oh, fu…, baby, I'm gonna come so hard!"

He skated his hand from her hip to her clit, circling the little bundle of nerves with one insistent caress after another. Cat shook, threw her head back, gasping, and came, her velvet grip anxiously milking him.

Matt arched forcefully into her twice more and then erupted. This one climax emptied him of all the regret and pain and desperation he'd known for decades. He was home within her, Cat's acceptance left him pure and perfect.

Cat held him fast within her while she gasped for breath. Their hearts thundered a staccato rhythm together, and then gradually slowed as they relaxed into post-orgasmic bliss.

Matt heaved a fulfilled sigh and rolled them onto their sides, still joined. He brushed sweat-dampened locks away from her face with shaking fingers. He hardly dared breathe for fear this precious moment would evaporate into a dream. Cat nuzzled into his shoulder and gave a disappointed coo as their bodies uncoupled.

He held her close, stroked her face, feeling the smile on her lips as she turned her head to kiss his palm. "Hey, baby, how ya doin?"

She smiled again into his palm. "I feel…" Her words escaped on a sigh.

"Yeah?" he teased.

"Oh, yeah." Her gaze sought his. "I had no idea it would be like this I didn't know…" Tears brightened her eyes, and she was too overwhelmed to continue.

Matt nodded his understanding. "You're everything to me, Cat," he rumbled huskily as she watched him with heavy-lidded eyes sliding into sleep. "God help me, I mean to keep you." It was part prayer, part vow, and allowed him to join her in peaceful oblivion.

# 11

The moon had risen, and the stars were in full brilliance when Cat awakened and cuddled into Matt to escape the chill of the ocean breeze. He scooped her up, kissed her sleep-softened lips and carried her to bed. Her warm body welcomed his, molding into him as he caressed her everywhere, licked and kissed and tasted every inch of her skin, and slid slowly and patiently inside her. With devastatingly controlled strokes, he possessed her. His words and kisses seduced her heart, and his essence besotted her soul. She was his. He might not know that yet, she mused, hovering on the edge of sleep, sated and limp in his protective arms, but she knew. She was his.

* * * *

It was surrealistic. Sensations long lost overcame every bit of Matt's body, including that crucial eight inches. Vampires could not dream, they merely laid down and turned off. This was real. He didn't remember it like this. Had ninety-some years tarnished the exquisite sensations he remembered between a man and a woman? His newly awakened subconscious processed what he and Cat had shared by reenacting the tactility of their lovemaking in his dream. It was sublime, the taste and the touch, the warmth and the strength in her softness. It all surpassed his amped-up vampire senses.

After the Humanité ran out of his system, what sensations would he have left? He'd be as cold as a snake. Matt shuddered. He couldn't ask the woman he loved to go skin to skin with him. What joy is there in offering a cold, stony phallus to the one who warmed his heart? He would lose her. It was inevitable. He could not endure an endless life without her. Matt jerked out of the nightmare, eyes blinking to reorient himself in the middle of the dark night.

Cat slept on, cuddling next to him in her own dream. When she moved exceptionally close, the sound of her breathing was interrupted by a precious sigh, or was it a moan? Matt's arms reached out to hold her close, he caressed her sleeping form, and let the music of her even breathing lull him back to sleep.

* * * *

Matt reluctantly let the morning sun drag him away from sleep, the delights he remembered within Cat's body inspiring him to wakefulness. He raised his joyful gaze to hers and grasped her fingers. They smiled foolishly at each other.

Cat stretched luxuriously, placing her slowly hardening nipples right under his gaze where he couldn't fail to be enticed. She draped herself across his chest and gave him a lingering morning kiss.

"The nuns were right, you know. You are a wicked, wicked man to lead a virgin astray that way."

Matt propped a hand under his head and watched her smugly. "Oh? You don't like it? Because we can stop right now and find other entertainment."

"Uh-uh." She emphatically shook her head. "I like it just fine…probably too much." Cat ran her hand down the length of his chest -- soft, warm skin over firm muscle.

He chuckled, grabbed her hand and kissed her palm, and then her lips. "It's just going to get better and better, baby. Now that you're not so nervous, believe me, there's a lot more to come."

"Really?"

"Yeah."

He shoved his hand into her tousled blonde curls and rolled her under him to merge their lips and breaths together in a long, deep, wet kiss meant not so much to arouse as to bond them together.

As chaste as he'd started, their hunger for each other was like fire and gasoline, and before they could contain the inferno, they were a wildfire again. He needed to stop, or at least slow down. She'd been a virgin. She was bound to be sore. He needed to be considerate. Matt reluctantly pulled away from her hungry gaze and stood.

He thrust a hand toward her. "C'mon. Let's take a shower, and you can tell me more about the nuns' version of how all this goes."

After following him into the opulent en-suite bath, Cat grabbed the shampoo and bath gel off the vanity while Matt adjusted the water temperature and the multiple sprays of the shower. He extended a gentlemanly hand to guide her to him. She joined him under the spray and touched the pink marble walls with wonder.

She looked at him. "Rick never does anything halfway, does he?"

"Nope." After pouring shower gel onto a mitt, he lathered her gently all over. "So, uh, just for fun, what did the nuns tell you about," he dropped his voice conspiratorially, "s-e-x?"

"Well," Cat shot him an amused glance, choosing her hand instead of a mitt to spread the sweet-smelling gel over him. "Not much. You understand it's hard to comment on something you've never actually experienced."

Matt nodded.

"There was a lot of 'wifely duty' kind of stuff. You know, 'Close your eyes and think of England?' We did have Sister Mary Bernadette who'd been married before she joined the convent. She always talked about what a happy marriage she'd had, but there were the rumors she'd killed her husband in his sleep."

"What?" Matt choked, his hand arrested mid-stroke, but Cat only shrugged nonchalantly.

"Yeah." She said it matter-of-factly.

"My God, with your background, no wonder you decided to become a crime writer."

"Sister Mary Bernadette was from Scotland." Cat laughed. "And she'd say," she affected a Scottish accent, hands on her hips, "now, girls, forget your romantic notions about the physical side of love. Pleasure is for men. It's God's punishment for woman's original sin."

"Hmm. Harsh, and now that you've experienced the physical side of love…" He doffed the mitt and drew a slow finger across the suds-smoothed trail of one thrusting breast and down her belly to land tantalizingly on her clit. "Would you agree?" He rubbed softly.

Cat's breath hitched, and her eyes grew unfocused as fresh lust overtook her. Matt chuckled. "No." She gasped. "Not unless your bones dissolve…"

"They nearly do when I'm inside you. Let's see if we can prove Sister Mary…" he faltered, his mind focused elsewhere.

"Bernadette," Cat supplied automatically, then groaned deeply and leaned into him as he sank his fingers inside her. "I liked her a lot, but the nun was definitely wrong."

Matt swooped her up into his arms and sat her gently on the heated marble shower seat. Turning the shower setting to "cool rain," he dropped to his knees before her.

"What are you doing?"

His smile was wickedly lazy as he gazed up at her. "More. Open for me, Cat. Let me get to you."

He started at her shapely calves, running sensuous fingers lightly up the insides of both thighs, insinuating his body between them. Cat's breath hitched. Her eyes widened. Gradually, she opened her legs for him, and Matt placed her heels atop the marble seat, spreading her. His chest rose faster and deeper as his heated gaze devoured her.

"My God, you're beautiful, so pink and lush." He parted her with his thumbs and dove in with his mouth. He invaded her, using his tongue, with a dark succulent kiss delving inside her as seductively as he'd possessed her mouth. He traced all the curves and eddies of her sex, again and again, giving fresh, delicate attention to each until she writhed on her perch, and he pulled her legs onto his shoulders to keep her from falling.

"Matt!" Cat's cry was half plea and half demand. Matt chuckled, knowing a conflagration was about to consume her.

"Mmm. You're so wet, baby, so hot. Feel that?" He rubbed against one perfect spot inside her, and Cat shook. She nodded, dragging in a stuttering breath. "That's your G-spot. Really sensitive. I wanna own that spot. It's mine."

"Sure," Cat squirmed, "okay."

Matt grinned. God, he loved showing her all the wonders of two bodies playing together. Her sweet juice seeped over his fingers. His sac tightened with renewed need. He reached forward using his tongue to tease her hard, shuddering clit from its hood. A series of rapid-fire licks had her flushing all the way to the roots of her hair. He watched in fascination.

"You're ready, Cat. Come for me. Now."

And with a final lick and rub from his fingers, Cat cried out and shattered into ecstasy. She panted as her pulsing went on and on, encouraged by Matt's mouth and fingers.

Matt pulled her up to stand in his tight embrace, his mouth crashing down on hers for a deep, urgent kiss, and just as quickly he spun her around to face the shower wall.

"Bend your legs a little, baby," He grasped her hips and pulled her back against him.

In one quick, fluid motion his thick sex breached her, sliding smoothly and inexorably inside her, eased by her recent climax. Those newly awakened nerve endings roused for him again, the swollen tissues of her sex flowering open as he drove into her repeatedly, creating friction that had him gritting his teeth with need and the determination to hang on until she was ready.

She was so tight, oh, lord! A fine sweat broke out across Matt's chest and back as he continued to tunnel in and out of her; the need to come drawing his sac up to strangle all his noble desires. He fought down the urge and focused on Cat instead. Her legs wobbled. She reached back to grab his hips, anchoring them together. He leaned farther into her, his chest blanketing her back. He swept his hand around her, fingers gliding down her belly to tantalize her little buzzing clit. It pulsed under his caress.

"Matt!" She gritted his name, and then sang it like a prayer, low and sweet as she came. "Maaaatt!"

"Oh, fu...! Gahh, I can't..."

The insistent velvet fisting of her sex lured Matt into his own blinding release, so intense, if he hadn't been holding Cat up, it would have dropped him to his knees. Instead, he gently lowered them to the shower floor where they leaned against the seat, his body covering hers. The sounds of their panting mingled with the sound of rain in the little stall, which all at once was interrupted by her stifled sob.

Matt pulled her onto his lap. His gaze searched her beautiful face. "Are you okay, baby? Did I hurt you?"

"No. No." She hiccupped the protest around tears. "I don't even know why I'm crying. I just...I have all these feelings...I don't know...what to do with them."

"Oh." He heaved a relieved sigh and held her close, sliding a gentle caress down her back. "It's okay. Sometimes when an orgasm is really intense, it just...causes tears. Kind of a release of energy, you know?"

Cat nodded. "I feel like an idiot!" She half-blubbered, half-laughed, looked away. "I don't see you falling apart like some stupid...girl."

Matt pulled her face up to plunder her lips with a deep kiss. "That 'stupid girl' reaction may be the nicest compliment a woman has ever given me." He kissed her warmly again. "And just because I didn't well up with tears doesn't mean I didn't feel it too."

"You did?" Her question was as honest and sincere as everything else she'd given him. Her tear-brightened gaze studied him. "Matt?" It was barely a whisper.

He nodded.

"I think…I love you."

It was as if a stake pierced Matt right through the heart. No. No, she couldn't be saying that. She couldn't even think she was in love with him. This was bad. It was very bad. What if he wound up dead because of this damn Humanité? What if they couldn't reproduce it and he became a vampire again? No way, no. It was bad enough that he loved her. It wrenched his gut not to be able to court her with all the lovely words and emotions he felt. Her in love with him? Absolutely not. That would never do.

"Cat." Matt tread carefully, picking his way through a minefield. "I'm flattered you feel that way, baby, but it could very well be your reaction to all these new sensations."

"Do you think I'd give you my body if I wasn't sure how I felt?" The devastation of his non-response was evident in sharp relief on her face. "Don't tell me what I feel, Matt." She rose with silent dignity, and he released her, feeling helpless. Turning at the shower door, she stared him down. "It would be nice if you felt the same, but for now, my feelings are my own. I love you, Matt. Deal with it."

She left him a soggy, defeated mess on the shower floor. He looked at his reflection in the shiny marble wall. *I'm the top of the food chain*, he told himself, stinging from the irony.

She should walk out on him, Matt thought, as he washed quickly and rinsed. She should turn right around, drive home and never look back. He was a bastard, a son of a bitch who scored a woman's virginity and dashed it on the rocks. While he'd given intense thought to his uncertain future, he didn't consider her feelings. He didn't consider the love a virgin assigned to the man who took her maidenhead. Now, standing under the last of the cooling shower, he had misgivings and no choice but to seek Cat out and finish their discussion. Too many hormones spiraling out of control caused too many emotions to erupt from him.

* * * *

Cat was confident despite Matt's odd reaction to her declaration of love. *That'll get him thinking.* She combed her hair and watched the waves. He loved her. Why he was so reluctant to admit it, she couldn't guess. She didn't want to let his attitude stop her from expressing her emotions, but it did. Maybe some willingness on her part would show him confessing his love wasn't so frightening, after all. She wished it were true.

Matt approached cautiously from behind her. She turned and smiled, trying to relieve his uncertainty. He looked like a man waiting for the other shoe to drop. Cat's mood had lightened considerably in the few minutes it took him to towel off and join her on the deck. She stood with a bath towel wrapped around her slim form, letting her golden hair toss in the light ocean breeze. If she were honest, she'd admit she tamped down her emotions to keep things going a little longer. Since she had no answers yet, she decided to go with the flow rather than push.

"Um…no clothes? I mean, in broad daylight?"

Matt shrugged. "The neighbors have no view of the deck, and if someone offshore or in the air has binoculars, hey, let 'em watch."

She gave him a doubtful smirk. "Sister Mary Immaculate would give you demerits."

"How do you know? She might want to see more."

"Emm." She cuddled into him. "I wouldn't blame her for that." She gasped when his hands moved to the clip holding her towel, and then the offending cloth dropped to her feet.

"If I'm gonna get demerits, let's make 'em count!"

Cat laughed and rubbed against him. "I'm all for making it count, but not before some breakfast! I'm starving."

"Well, there's lots of food in the kitchen. You can make a gourmet breakfast if you want!"

"Uh-oh. I have sad news." She winced. "You'd have had better luck with me cooking if you were still a vampire."

"Vampires don't eat food."

"Exactly."

"So, you can't cook, princess?"

"Oh, I'm sure I could, if they print the directions clearly on the microwave box. You saw my teeny, tiny kitchen. Who learns to cook anything there?"

Matt laughed easily and then groaned. "Well then, it's a good thing I can cook. I come from a time before microwaves." He placed a kiss on her upturned face.

"No kidding? There was a time before microwaves?"

He looped a companionable arm around her neck. "Yes, Miss Microwave Queen, there was. You know those mysterious appliances you see in all the kitchens…the big square things that make fire?"

Cat nodded solemnly and suppressed a grin. "I've seen those."

"Well, at one time everyone used them for cooking."

"Really? That must have been a lot of work."

"All you have to do is decide whether you want omelets or cereal."

"That depends. How active do you think we're going to be after breakfast?"

He shook his head and grinned at her saucy come-hither smile. "Could be quite active. I considered hanging a trapeze in the living room."

"Ooh! Kinky!" She giggled before being smothered by his kisses. "I'm thinking something a little more fortifying than cereal then. Let me get my robe—"

Matt stopped her with a hand on her wrist, gentle but restraining. "No robes. No clothes. I want to look at you. I want to paint you, just like this."

"No…" Cat repeated numbly and swallowed hard. "No clothes?"

Matt shook his head.

"For either of us?"

Matt gave her a naughty grin and shook his head again while Cat considered a moment.

"Okay. As long as it's a level playing field because I wanna see you too. The, uh, painting…you won't show it to anyone else, right?"

Matt considered. "How about if you pose nude and I supply the clothes on canvas?"

"You can do that?"

"It will hurt, but for you…" He winked. "I'll see what I can do. I see fig leaves and vines."

* * * *

Matt took a few moments to acquaint himself with what a vampire thought a mortal's kitchen should contain. As usual, Rick overstocked everything. He'd probably had some famous chef outfit the place.

Cat rummaged in the fridge, catching Matt's leer as the cold made her nipples harden and peak. She shivered slightly as she went to the coffee cabinet, and he was unable to resist roaming in behind her, sliding a tantalizing hand around her waist, another over a firm breast to play with her beaded nipple. He slid the hand at her waist down her abdomen, hovering over her golden triangle. She dropped her head back onto his shoulder and moaned. His erection insistently nudged at her back.

Her voice cracked as she read off the coffee labels. "There's French mocha, cinnamon vanilla, and smooth Italian roast. Which one?"

Matt shrugged, teasing her folds. "Maxwell House?"

"No." She sighed the word as her knees quaked.

"You chose. Are there scones?" His voice got wistful as he idly toyed with her. "I love soft crescents smothered with cream." Cat groaned.

Giving him a saucy glance, she popped open the bread bin at the same time she drifted a hand back to fondle his tight balls. "There are, indeed, scones," she confirmed in a deceptively steady voice as they both pretended they were cooking breakfast.

Matt upped the ante again by running another finger into her folds, hooking it deep inside her, and then drawing it out to smear on her clit. Cat shook, breakfast forgotten for the moment.

"So, what do you want in your omelet? I can see you're hungry."

Cat swallowed hard. "I want you," She turned in his arms, watching his face. "You've spent so much time making me feel so…" she bit back words, "so wonderful." She dipped her head shyly. "I want to do something for you."

"Baby, you already—" he began, but she cut him off with fingertips to his lips.

"I've read…I've heard…"

"Yeah?" He watched her curiously.

"I know men enjoy oral sex…uh…blowjobs."

"Oh." Matt smiled, his eyes widening at the thought. "Yeah, that's true."

"Would you like me to…I mean, I've never…but I could learn."

"You want to go down on me, Cat?" His voice dropped a seductive octave and made her shiver.

"Yes."

"Yeah." He blew out a quick breath to keep himself calm. "I'd like that a lot. You want me to teach you?"

"Yes. Would you?"

She was so sincere, he stifled his laugh at her eagerness. "It would be my pleasure. Come into the living room. Your knees will get sore on this hard tile floor." *Not that you'll be there long.* His hard-on grew stiffer in anticipation.

Matt braced himself against the back of the couch, which he was certain he'd need for support before Cat was through with him. She dropped to her knees in front of him. Demurely, she fisted a hand around his cock, staring at the swollen head, bulging a deep red with need and excitement. She inched forward, experimentally tasting it. He shuddered. She looked up at him with wide eyes and met his ravenous stare. Encouraged, she licked farther, and then ran the flat of her tongue up and down his shaft several times, like a hot, erotic, velvet brush. He groaned. She kept her gaze riveted to his face as she swirled around the head. She tested him further, licking around the underside, watching him tense and shake.

"I think I understand," Cat whispered, enjoying this new-found power to reduce him to a shivering mess.

"Cat, stop, baby. Stop for a minute." He gasped.

"Something wrong?" she purred teasingly, going for another lick.

"Not a thing. You're doing great. Just some other things you need to know, and I can't tell you while you're making me crazy."

"I'm an empty vessel." She grinned. "Fill me."

Matt clenched his jaw. "You're asking about blowjobs...and...there's more."

Several minutes later, Cat proved to be an eager student. She sucked him intently, and Matt opened his eyes, dazed, to stare down into hers as she searched his face with such intensity, his heart melted right along with his self-control.

"Oh, lord, baby. You've got me where I wanna be when you look at me like that with my dick in your mouth...ah....ah."

Cat swirled along his underside, sucked, withdrew, took him deep again. With her teeth, she lightly grazed his head on the uptake and used her tongue to prod the bundle of nerves under his glans. She sucked him deep and hard, and Matt exploded, shuddering violently.

"Ahh…, fu… me!"

He groaned as he erupted from his impatient sac, and into the velvet furnace of her mouth. His eyes flashed wide open, still unfocused, as the blinding ecstasy overtook him. Finally, he relaxed totally, and his lids fluttered shut in sublime contentment. Time froze for a moment, and slowly a one-sided, grin crooked his lips, and he opened his eyes. He stared at her, feeling a sweet kind of reverence before bending to take her into his arms and hold her against him.

"Cat, baby, you're uncommonly good at giving head," he told her with a soft laugh.

She ducked her head self-consciously. "I just did what seemed natural, and I think maybe you needed it." He glanced away. A non-verbal confirmation of her guess. "Matt," her hands cupped the sides of his face, "I wanted to do that for you. I wanted you to feel even a little bit of the joy you've given me…I…I loved doing it. It made me feel so close to you."

"Yeah?" He cuddled her against him. "I loved it, too. You could probably tell." He laughed softly. "Aw, Cat…" He shook his head, wound a hand around the back of her neck and drew her toward a tender kiss. "I've never known a woman as open and receptive as you."

Cat playfully propelled herself against him, shoving at his chest and hurtling them over the back of the couch and onto its bed. "You've had a lot of experience with a lot of women," she chided. "If I had to guess, I'd say this was not the first time you've talked a woman through a blowjob."

Matt frowned. "No…" he admitted reluctantly. "I'm kinda the go-to guy at the club about that."

"I see." Cat arched a brow. "Then, I don't understand why you needed it from me so badly."

Matt looked uncomfortable. "One, you're not just any woman. Women aren't interchangeable, you know." He sighed. "And two, yeah, I've talked other women through it. I didn't say I was the lucky guy on the receiving end."

Cat turned a curious glance up to him. "I don't get it."

"I don't bed mortals. I don't take head from them, either."

"Why not?"

"Compared to a vampire, mortals are like glass. As a vampire, I could do real damage to a mortal woman. I won't risk getting so turned-on I'm out of control."

"Are you saying you haven't had sex for nearly a hundred years?"

Matt barked out a laugh. "I didn't say I was a monk! No, I've had sex with vampire women. We're on a level field there. Mortal women, no. I'll never risk that again."

"It sounds as if you risked it once. What happened?"

"Nothing we need to go into right now. You just need to know mortal/vampire sex, not a good thing." He shrugged and stood, depriving her of the developing intimacy. "So, getting back to breakfast."

"Not so fast." Cat's piercing gaze nailed him. "I'd like to know a little more about where I sit on the timeline. If you didn't have sex with donors, and you didn't let them give you oral, why do you own a BDSM club?"

"Let me get this straight. A day past virginity, and you think you're an expert on sex?"

Cat shrugged. "I don't think I have to be an expert to know something isn't right." She shot him a searching look. "You make it sound as if you were everyone's tutor and nobody's lover. The perennial wingman. That really doesn't fit with the guy I know."

"If I were still a vampire, it'd be exactly the guy you know."

"You mean, if you weren't human right now, we wouldn't be together?"

"Not if I was a vampire."

# 12

The weather turned the next day, and Cat worriedly scanned the turbulent, roiling clouds. Their sunny beach retreat suddenly came under attack by Mother Nature. The wind scuttled around them in a fierce howl, and debris hurled itself against the ocean-view windows.

The pop music D.J. who'd kept them cheerful company on the radio broke into the top one hundred with a warning. "Hey, surfers, time to beach the boards. We have the tail end of a bad storm heading in from Mexico, coming straight up the Five our way. If you're on the coast, batten down the hatches. If you're not, stay home."

Behind the safety of the beach house's thick windows, Cat watched walls of water rush the shore while the heavens cracked open, releasing torrents of rain. There was a gleeful kind of mean in the air that crackled with the whip of lightning and deafening thunder.

"His warning's a little late, isn't it?" Cat looked at Matt who drifted up beside her to wrap a protective arm around her shoulders.

The deck chaise's thick cushion, normally protected under its canopy, lifted and flew through the air like a paper napkin at a wind-crazed picnic. Cat gasped and made to slide open the door, intent on dragging it back. Matt's hand on her arm stopped her.

"Some things can't be saved." *Like us, in a few weeks.* "I don't want you to get hurt." *But I'm here anyway.*

"We made love for the first time on that chaise."

He tapped on her chest over her heart. "Every wonderful memory about that night will be right here, forever. If it's that important to you, I'll get it."

Cat shook her head. "You're right. I don't want either one of us to get hurt."

Matt's sigh dragged from the bottom of his soul. "It's inevitable. One of us is gonna get hurt."

Cat's heart clenched, and her alarmed gaze shot to his. "We're not talking about the storm now, are we?"

Matt led her from the outside turmoil. The bleakness of his face mirrored the melancholy in the air. He looked as if he was drowning in sorrow, and Cat's alarm escalated.

"I have to tell you something, Cat, and I'm afraid you're gonna hate me."

Cat's knees went weak, and not in that sexy, hot, good way. "Then, I guess you'd better tell me."

"The fire at my condo…it was more…serious…than I let on. My entire place was destroyed. It was arson."

"Who would do that? A business rival?"

"I don't think so. It may have been Veronique's sire, Papa Moreau. He isn't happy about the Humanité she's making. Within weeks of her giving it to me, he filed an official objection with the Vamp High Council. That makes it serious." Cat felt her expression darken. "I never thought it would come to this, but apparently Moreau's not shy about showing his opposition. This wasn't so much an attempt on my life as an attack against my choices." He couldn't meet her seeking gaze. "Cat, they destroyed all the Humanité. Not only that, they killed our research chemist and wiped out all the data from every source. I have no idea what was in it or how to recreate it, and I sure as hell have nothing left. All you and I have is now."

Cat was stunned. "I don't understand. You're human."

He shook his head. "That's an illusion. The drug simulates humanity. I'm still a vampire, and I took the last of what I had the day before you joined me here. I can live a few more weeks as human, at most. Unless we find Veronique and the drug, you and I, what we have, will be nothing more than a dream."

Cat stared at him in disbelief, and as the import of his words sank in, she couldn't restrain the rush of tears that overwhelmed her. She was speechless.

"Do you understand what I'm telling you?" His deep, rich voice penetrated her misery.

Cat shook her head. "This can't be happening. Not to us. Not now that we…"

Matt slid next to her, reaching to comfort, but Cat drew away. "We're working on it, baby. I have people all over the world searching for Veronique. Rick has our lawyers in Haiti trying to reason with Moreau. With any luck, we'll have our hands on the research again within a few weeks, but…" He left the sentence hanging and shrugged.

Cat's face felt as if it had turned to stone. "If not, what? I've been a really good sport?"

Matt drew a hand down his face. "C'mon, Cat…"

"C'mon, Cat! What? C'mon? Seriously? You make love to me, make me fall in love with you, and then…sorry?"

"Look, I can understand why you'd feel that way—"

"Oh, you can?" she sniped. "Well, that's mighty big of you! Mighty big of all of you!"

He watched her humbly. "What do you want me to do? Huh? What do you want me to do? You think I like this situation? You think this is how I want it to be? You think I don't…" he swallowed hard. "Care for you too?"

"Care for me? What, like you care for a…a…pet or something?" He watched her, his gaze wretched. "So, is this it?" She continued her rant. "Is this all there is?" She jumped off the couch, staring down at him, hands on hips.

Matt watched her warily. "You can leave, you know. I wouldn't blame you." He looked up at her, sorrow etched on every feature. "Let me ask you this. If I told you I'd be dead in a few weeks, would you leave me then?"

Cat gasped and felt the blood drain from her face so quickly, she thought she might faint. "That's not the same."

"It is the same. Don't you understand? In a few weeks without the Humanité, I will be dead—again."

"Un-dead."

"Worse than dead." He rubbed at the ache in his chest. "Not something I'll inflict on you."

"Even if you care about me?" she sneered.

"Especially because I care about you." He hung his head. "For more than ninety years, I've driven off every human I've ever cared about for their protection. You'd be no different. So, if you can live with now and walk away if I say so, I'll make these the best weeks of your life. If you can't, I'll understand, and you'll never see me again." He stood, and in strides that swallowed the space, was out the door and into nature's riot.

The rolling clouds plunged the world to black while thunder dealt retribution from above. Cat watched, knowing she was truly suspended between two worlds with precious little purchase in either. His words echoed in her mind. *If I told you I'd be dead...* She recognized that, whatever she believed, death was Matt's truth. If the question he put forth was literal, would she leave him? Of course not. Then, could she betray him now, and was any of this his fault? No. It was no one's fault. Well, maybe Papa Moreau's. She'd never leave him if given a choice. Her worst fear was he'd ultimately leave her.

Cat looked out the wall of windows, searching for him. Matt faced the treacherous ocean, head up, defiant, armed only with his own ferocity and guts. His hair blew wild, his shirt plastered wet against his strong chest. He stood at the edge of a jetty buffeted repeatedly to near ruin by nature's rage. Was he ready to let the storm claim him if her love wouldn't?

Cat called out, her voice ripped away by the callous gale. She ducked her head, and blinded by the blowing sand, felt her way toward him. Right now, an eternity separated them, but she wouldn't relent. Grit and determination brought her resolutely to his side. After she reached him, she threw her arms around him and offered the same shelter she sought from the storm.

"I won't leave you," she bellowed above the wind. "Don't you leave me!"

"Never." His lips captured hers in a desperate kiss. "Never."

* * * *

Rick turned his key in the front door while Georgia shook her head. "You don't know what we're walking in on. Can't you respect their privacy?"

Rick pursed his lips. "Privacy. The state of being free from intrusion or disturbance in one's private life or affairs," he quoted. "Even the constitution doesn't actually guarantee the right to privacy. Far be it from me to break with patriotic tradition. So...let's see what they're made of."

She shook her head. "You're a dick."

"That's my name! Hey, they need this news. Unless you want their 'privacy' to end in their untimely deaths?"

Rick toed open the door to silence. Not the silence of people grappling in sheets. The silence of vacancy. Georgia ventured in hesitantly, hiding her eyes, only to find the room bare.

"There, you see? No one's home."

Her gaze flashed to his. "How do you know that? Maybe they're in the bedroom."

He tapped his nose. "Nope."

"Well, I don't see how you can be so sure." She headed up the stairs, calling as she went. "Matt? Uh, Catherine?"

Rick followed in her wake, admiring the folds of her crepe de chine dress over the contours of her luscious hips. "I love an exercise in futility when it includes being this close." He caressed her bottom appreciatively.

"Stop it, Dick!"

"I'm telling you, they're not here." He drew in a quick breath, heading to the bathroom. "They've been here, though. God's nightgown, Matt! They've come, and they've gone, they've come, and they've gone..." Rick arrested on a footfall, hands clasped under his chin. Lifting his head, he spied the couple embracing on the jetty, the waves crashing over them.

Georgia picked up the silk sheet tousled on the bed. "There's blood on this sheet. She was a virgin? Surely not! The blood has to be from feeding?" She turned to Rick. "I thought you said he wasn't a vampire right now?"

"And...why?"

She gestured to the bed. "He fed on her?"

Rick crooked a brow. "He preyed upon her, but not in that sexy vamp way." He held up the sheet and drew in a deep breath. "I see saddle shoes, a plaid skirt, a white blouse..."

"Whoa! Not Matt!"

"Well, you're correct, but it would have been really clever." He winked.

"Clever?" A warning note sounded in her question.

"You're right. Too cliché." He lifted his head to the window view again. "Well, now that we've assuaged your curiosity..." With Georgia's back turned, he took off for the living room.

Rick arrived at the dining area just as Matt drew back the sliding glass door. Cat blew past him into the warmth of the house, struggling to close the door against the wind and rain.

* * * *

Matt lingered on the battered deck to secure the outdoor canopy and tie down the umbrella table. In the face of the gale, physical and emotional, he took a moment to relish that he was no longer alone. Against all the odds, Cat had rescued him, but could he fairly claim her? That was the moral dilemma plaguing him. Though she was young and foolish enough to believe herself invincible, he was humbled by a different reality. Their situation was perilous at best, life-threatening at worst. He would not lead her to destruction, even if she hated him for protecting her.

Through the wall of windows, Matt watched as Cat scrambled to the comfort of the fireplace, peeling off soaked clothing as she went. Item after item hit the floor until she came to rest on her knees before unlit logs. Her bare breasts tightened in the cold air, her thighs quivered. She turned the gas key to the right repeatedly, finding no success. Her hands shook with the cold.

With three silent strides, Rick was behind her, covering her hand with his, turning the key to the left and igniting tall golden flames, just as Matt slid open the glass door.

Cat screamed and covered her breasts. "When the devil did you get here?"

"Welcome to my home." Rick smiled expansively. "The emphasis on mine. Always good to see you."

Georgia tromped midway down the stairs in a huff. "I hate it when you do that…" Her words died on her lips as she spied Cat shivering before the fireplace.

Matt squelched a laugh as he entered the tense scene. "Hey, bud! What 'cha doin'?"

"What's he…" Cat's teeth chattered. "He was here when I came in! I didn't even see him. He rolls in like fog."

Matt was unnervingly calm. "Well, he is a vampire." He looked over Cat's huddled form, picked up the throw from the couch and strode to her. Bending, he lovingly wrapped its warmth around her, and then looked up at the stairs. "I see you brought a guest."

"She's not a guest. She's my new Renfield."

"How retro." Matt grinned.

Wrapping the blanket firmly around herself, Cat stood, gathering her dignity. "Rick, what are you doing here unannounced?"

"I thought I just announced myself." Rick raised a brow to Matt and Georgia. "Didn't I?"

Matt grimaced at his humor. "A call would be nice, Rick. Cell phones, we have them in the 21st century."

Rick winced. "And are most likely bugged, so I decided a visit was in order. Didn't mean to catch you in flagrante, dear boy."

"Sure, you didn't."

Rick shrugged. "You know me too well."

"If you'll excuse us for a moment," Cat huffed. "Matt and I aren't impervious to cold. We need to get dressed."

Rick bowed out of her way. "Of course."

Georgia headed down the stairs, her gaze assessing Cat as the young woman flattened herself against the wall to avoid brushing shoulders. Georgia headed for Rick's side.

"I can see the plaid skirt," Georgia said.

Rick shook his head and placed a judicious finger to his lips. Matt fixed him with an accusing glare on the way up the stairs.

* * * *

Matt's long V-neck sweater dwarfed her small frame after Cat jerked it from the dresser drawer, and then pulled it on.

"I have never been so embarrassed in my life!" she ranted, searching for something to pair with the garment.

Matt's lips quirked at her snit as she searched through the clothes. He pulled on sweatpants. "I can see why you'd feel that way, but..."

"But what?" She huffed and then turned, exasperated. "There is nothing for me to wear with this!"

"But...seeing your beautiful body is nothing to Rick. In five hundred years, the things he's seen... I mean, he's a Dom."

"I have to be honest with you. My comprehension ends at twenty-one years, and I don't think..."

Matt swept her into a firm embrace. "Breathe with me."

"What?" Her gaze flashed to his.

He repeated the command, low, deep, compellingly. "Breathe. Humans take breathing for granted." His command was resolute. Matt thought the irony was their time together might be measured in breaths. Cat's breath fell in line with his. She calmed instantly. "I feel better now. How about you?" he asked after a moment, waiting for her chagrined nod. "If Rick is here because the phones are bugged, then something's up. We have to be calm and find out what that is. Okay?"

"Okay," she grudgingly agreed.

"Put on some warm socks. You look great."

Cat rolled her eyes. "Sister Mary Immaculate would definitely give you demerits for this one!"

He winked. "I never could stay out of trouble with the nuns." He guided her out of the room, and then downstairs.

At the great room dining table, Georgia busied herself steeping tea while Rick enjoyed a Waterford tumbler of blood. She raised a challenging brow to the debonair vampire.

"What? She'd better get used to it now. Odds aren't in their favor that Matt will remain human."

Matt's foot hit the bottom stair heavily on Rick's remark, Cat close behind him. His voice heavy with concern, Matt headed for the table. "Clearly, you're not here for drinks. What's gone down now?"

"Maybe, you should have some tea before we start." Rick grimaced. "Maybe something stronger."

"Cut the malarkey." Matt hugged Cat to his side while she fearfully watched the discussion. "What is it?"

Georgia handed Rick a thick file. "The arsonists were definitely sent by Papa Moreau, who is Veronique's sire." He threw pictures onto the table from the file. "Seems Papa is deadly serious about Humanité being a threat to the Vampire Nation, and he has some very influential friends who agree—friends in the Vampire High Council. He's not thrilled with his offspring's behavior, and everybody else is paying for it."

"Okay." Matt's felt his face drain of color as he looked at the pictures. "Just how much influence does this guy have?"

"As much as any nine-hundred-year-old vamp," Rick replied grimly.

"Nine hundred, huh?" Matt winced.

"I don't understand," Cat whispered.

Rick turned a censorious glare her way. "If it were simple, I wouldn't be here."

Nearly ninety years of experience told Matt that Rick was right. A vampire's age equaled power, and a nine-hundred-year-old vampire was a superpower. He scowled. How could he justify dragging Cat into the middle of a fight with a vamp that age? To even have a chance at survival, she'd need a crash course on vampire lore, which could give away more information than he wanted her to know.

On the other hand, an effort to keep her ignorant would backfire and probably estrange them. Neither alternative seemed workable or protective. The smart choice was to send her away, now.

Matt stood, and Rick followed warily. It took everything in Matt to raise his gaze to the woman he loved and make his baleful determination. "Georgia, I need you to take Cat home. She needs to get out of here. Now."

"Wha…" Cat began.

"Now, Cat." His voice was cold. "You need to get out. Rick and I have to talk."

Georgia lowered her gaze. "If you think that's best."

Rick grabbed Matt's shoulder and spun him, so they were face-to-face. "Nobody asked me, but I'll tell you anyway. I don't think it's best."

"Thank you, Rick," Cat murmured.

"What… are you talking about?" Matt's glare was murderous. "You know what's about to happen. She can't be in the middle of this."

"You're in love with her. She's in love with you. You've had your 'honeymoon,' and now you're going to throw away the 'marriage?'"

"You know mortals and vampires are a fatal combination," Matt insisted.

"Not always."

"For me," Matt ground out.

Rick gave an exasperated huff. "Once, goddammit! Once. And you were a very young vampire." He sighed as Matt gave him a look of stubborn defiance. "Look, I don't know what will happen to the two of you in twenty years. Nobody has a guarantee of anything. Moreau could take you out tomorrow. All any of us have is today, despite the illusion of immortality. Let's get through today and let tomorrow take care of itself."

"I don't have to drag Cat with me."

"Neither of you may survive this crisis whatever you do." Rick strode to Georgia's side and propelled her toward the door. He turned to Matt. "You need to find a way out of this mess together. I'll expect you in my office tomorrow at dusk. Then we'll make a plan."

Matt scowled but nodded.

Rick paused before closing the door. "Don't try to be a hero, Matt."

The door closed. Alone, the reproachful silence was deafening. Ominous, threatening thunder crashed above them. The storm continued to rage, inside and out. Matt cast a cool, assessing gaze toward Cat.

"Well, that was quite a scene," she gritted, her gaze focused on the furious storm.

"Cat…" He reached toward her, devastated to hear her sniffing away tears.

She stooped to pick up her water-logged clothes from the floor, and then resolutely turned to face him. "I'll be wearing your sweater home. I guess 'never' was shorter than you thought."

"Don't…"

She cut off his words by picking up her purse and keys from the counter and then walking out the door. Of course, he followed, but what could he say? She'd heard his attempt to protect her as rejection, and he couldn't blame her. Nor could he escape the knowledge that protection for her equaled insulation for him. If Cat were no longer in his life, she'd be sheltered from Moreau's vengeance, and he'd no longer be faced with the need to turn her away when he inevitably became a vampire again. Not that either positive would heal the gaping wound in his gut over her loss. What joy would he have without her? How had he forgotten a mortal heart shattered so easily?

* * * *

Cat shoved her apartment's old wooden door open with a brutal thrust of her shoulder. She should have remembered what rainy weather did to it. How could the world remain so unchanged and yet seem so totally different? Indignantly closing it behind her, she was overcome by the scent of roses. Goddamn, Matt! Even when she escaped him, he continued to torment her.

They rested in their Waterford vase, taunting her from across the room— twelve velvet blossoms in various stages of bloom. One stubborn rose remained tight in its bud, its edges curled, dark maroon like dried blood. Would this have been her had she not spent the weekend with Matt?

She cradled the crimson gash of the broadest bloom, its petals wide open, its filaments reaching toward the light. She brushed her thumb over it as she admired the notion that it had seen the sun and given up its fragrance. Was Matt her source of light, and did she waste her precious fragrance on a man who plucked her only to callously toss her away?

Even the sky cried as Cat gazed toward her dingy window with unseeing eyes. Eventually, the rain and tears wore themselves out. In a decisive move, she thrust Matt's gift of Godiva chocolates under one arm and grabbed the neck of the champagne split. She snagged the wet stems of the twelve red roses with her other hand and shook them hard. Barely a petal fell. *Resilient bastards, aren't they?*

Rage echoing in every step, Cat stomped her way across the small apartment and headed outside, viciously whipping the long-stemmed roses against the wall, side to side, as she headed for the trash. The truffles made a smugly satisfying plop when she lobbed each injured one into the scarred wall of the Dumpster. Once she could only shake the tissue cups from the empty box, she turned her anger on the champagne. With a quick turn of her wrist, she upended the bottle to smash it across the edge.

"I christen myself, Independent." She tossed the broken neck into the rubbish.

Now that her anger had broken, she scanned the parking lot for observers. Did anyone watch her juvenile display? How foolish did she feel behaving like that? She longed for Maria to offer her motherly comfort, but now there was no Maria, no Matt, and no comfort. She was alone.

Sobs clogged her throat, choking the anger, reaching down to shred her heart. Cat wasn't quite sure how she made it back to the apartment. Chilled with anguish, she forced herself to take a scalding shower, which failed to truly warm her.

It was around noon of the next day when her whirling mind calmed. She'd analyzed every one of their conversations, ferreted out every nuance of meaning until she'd hit on the only hope she had.

*"You know mortals and vampires are a fatal combination,"* he'd told Rick.

*"Not always."*

*"For me."*

*"Once, goddammit! Once. And you were a very young vampire," Rick had replied.*

What does that mean? Is it the key to Matt's paradoxical behavior? Rick accused him of loving her, and though Matt hadn't denied it, neither had he admitted it.

What did her heart tell her? Without reservation, it said she belonged with Matt. What did her mind tell her? Something had to have happened to him to make him believe his undead nature endangered mortal women. They'd both alluded to it. She wouldn't let this relationship end without finding out what it was. Matt owed her that truth.

* * * *

Rick contemplated the clownfish and anemones drifting serenely amidst the other creatures in the expanse of salt water before him. He found the mammoth aquarium a relaxing counterbalance while he bartered for the fortunes of the Consort Group. His peace was rudely interrupted by his assistant's plaintive cry.

"You can't go in there, Miss…"

Her words died impotently as Cat threw open the ceiling-high walnut door and marched through. Her awed look showed her disorientation in the imposing room. Her gaze searched and finally lit upon Rick as he sat dwarfed behind the broad antique desk.

"Is this revenge for yesterday?" He asked.

"What?"

"I apologized for barging in on you then. Your reaction indicates you expected more."

Cat frowned impatient hands on her hips. "Really? I have no fucks left to give."

Rick grew uneasy. "Where's Matt?"

"That's not the question."

"Indeed? Then, what is the question?"

Cat marched up to him, leaned across his desk on splayed hands and riveted him with a glare. "What issue did Matt have with a mortal woman, Rick? Why is he so afraid of physical intimacy?"

"That's not my tale to tell." He rose.

"It's clear to me that it was tragic, and no one's willing to let me in on the big secret! I need to know!"

"Then, you need to ask Matt, and you didn't answer my question. Where is he?"

"After I walked out on him? I have no clue. Today, I realized he has some emotional problem involving mortal women. There's more to all this than getting rid of me."

Rick speared her with a stare that looked right into her soul. "So, does obnoxious, bratty behavior often get you what you want?"

Cat gaped at him. "I've never behaved like a brat in my life."

"I beg to differ. If you were my woman, I'd already have you across my knee with a strong hand on your red, sore ass."

"Right, because that would make me feel so much better!" She gritted her teeth.

"Maybe not, but I'd feel better, and maybe you'd listen instead of ranting like a petulant child. Because, Cat, right now, nobody needs a whiney child. Especially Matt."

Cat inhaled sharply. Her gaze dropped to the floor. "I'm afraid." She admitted.

"Ah! A shred of honesty, and truthfully, it is a frightening situation. You both have a lot to lose." He came around the desk, intentionally imposing, "the two of you are doomed unless you start communicating honestly and stop playing games. You're young." He passed a gentle hand over her hair. "And games come naturally to the young, but it's time to grow up or walk away. I could say the same for Matt."

Cat's voice was subdued. "What should I do?"

Rick linked his hands and stretched his arms out before him. "Well, I guess I'll have to put the two of you together in time out and see who comes back alive."

# 13

The last person on earth Matt expected to find under Rick's quelling gaze was Cat. His fear for her safety subsided after she left. Of course, departing worry had also left him empty and shattered. He halted mid-stride when he saw her and turned a questioning gaze to Rick.

"If you love them, set them free. If they return to you…" Rick intoned.

"Shut up, Rick." He turned to Cat. "What are you doing here?"

"I came to find out what happened to the other woman."

"What other woman?"

Rick rolled his eyes. "Oh, for God's sake. She's talking about Lilli." He grabbed their hands and joined them. "Go down to your playroom, and by God's bones don't come back until you've talked it all out and reached a decision. Get in or get out. In this situation, there is no in between. Am I clear?"

Matt, recognizing the wisdom in Rick's order, cast an assessing gaze at Cat. "If you want to know the story, I'll tell you, but it's an ugly truth. It's a truth you can't deny. If you try, I'll end this." Cat's eyes were huge. She nodded.

* * * *

Matt was consumed by his own unsettling thoughts as the elevator carried them into the depths of the building. The ride down to the playroom passed in a blur, and before he knew it, they were in his comfortable man cave. Cat glanced around the room, her gaze darting from object to object. She caught his look before he could hide his longing, and tears welled in her eyes.

"Why did you let me go?"

"Because I'm not selfish enough to ask you to stay."

"You love me."

"Immaterial. Move on."

"All right." Her level gaze bore into him. "What happened to you? Who did you kill, or see killed, or something, because you were a vampire and she wasn't?"

Matt stared at her a long moment, and when he spoke, his voice was hushed and initially solemn. "In 1922, a few months after I was turned, I met Lilli. She was one of Rick's donors, and we found we had a lot in common. Her family had all been cops, and so had mine. I'd been a cop until…and then I couldn't work anymore."

Matt sighed as the somber memory carried him back. His voice became animated. "She was a doll, a real dish, with legs that went up to her shoulders and big, big baby blues. Rick threw great house parties where the booze and dope flowed despite prohibition, and guests almost always ended up slinking off to the bedrooms for hot, wild sex.

"It had been a long, lonely, dry spell. Rick introduced me to some new women—ready and willing, but they were all vampires. Cold, clammy." He shuddered. "Dangerous. They played hard, too hard for pleasure, at least for my taste. So soon after being turned, I was having a hell of time adjusting. More than anything, I wanted to be mortal again, so I guess it was only right I wanted a mortal woman under me. Lilli was soft and warm and responsive, and I wanted to ball her like crazy. I had wanted to so bad for so long." He paced in circles as he spoke.

"That night, we were both a little high on coke. She'd sit on my lap, and I'd finger her while she snorted lines off a mirror. There are no words for the high of banging somebody while the blood in their veins circulates around you and gets you hotter and harder. Even before I bit her, I was cold steel." He ran a hand through his hair and risked a glance up to Cat to see how she was taking this. "Every time she did a line, that coke would go through her bloodstream, and I'd soak it up, just balling." Matt resumed his pacing, his gaze settling on her shocked open mouth and guarded eyes. Words swelled from his memories as he continued on brutally, unwilling to paint it prettier for her.

"Her pussy got so hot between the coke, the heightened desire, and our humping that I thought I'd lose my mind. It'd been way too long since I'd felt heat around my dick. I swear to God that sensation alone convinced me I was in love. We were both lonely, and she was everything I wanted. Maybe, if I'd known how, Lilli would be undead now, instead of…" He drew his restless hands through his hair again and then continued down his face to nervously rub his jaw and neck. He sucked in a tired breath to propel his words, his haunted gaze meeting Cat's.

"We started necking. She got off my dick and pulled me into bed, and I couldn't wait! She started with the fingernails and lips, riding my leg, drawing that long hair of hers over my chest. I was on fire. Then she rode me, arching that graceful neck above me, and I had to taste her."

"I wrapped my hand around the back of her neck and brought her down to me. She didn't resist. Well, why would she? I'd fed from her before. We both came so damn hard, and she tasted like champagne and love and forever, and my next thought was to ask Rick how I could make things permanent. She was begging me for more… moaning and making these sexy noises…and I thought we'd always be like this… I was drinking her blood…delicious…then…it seemed like only an instant…I looked into her eyes, and they were cold and…dead. Her lips were still warm, but there were no more kisses. Lilli was gone."

Matt sighed brokenly. "Without even knowing it, I'd taken too much." Cat dragged in a shaky breath. "Can you even begin to understand what it's like to kill someone you cherish during an act of love?"

"No," she whispered, a gentle hand reaching out to touch his arm. "I'm sorry, Matt." She paused and considered. "All I know is, I love you, and I trust you. I know you'd never hurt me."

"I'd never mean to, no." *A fat lot of help those good intentions had been to Lilli.*

"You haven't had sex with a mortal woman since then?"

"No."

"Rick does. Other vampires do."

"They're willing to risk it. Some are willing to turn their mortal partners if they go too far."

"You didn't know how to turn her back then?"

"Right. I didn't."

"You know now?" She prodded.

"In theory, yes."

"You've never actually done it?"

"I won't do it." His jaw tight, he clipped his words.

"Can you see where that's a problem? You're human right now, or close to human, or whatever. Maybe you can find the Humanité, and it'll stay that way. If it doesn't, and you're a vampire, and I'm mortal, we can still be together,"

"Really? You're willing to die if things go too far?"

"No, but there's no reason I should have to. If you can't join me in my world, I can join yours." She watched him quietly for a beat while Matt struggled to formulate an answer she could accept. Finally, she shrugged. "I guess that needs to be understood by both of us. I'm not sure you can live with that thought."

"You understand that becoming a vampire is dying, Cat? Except there's no streets of gold and meeting your maker. It's just more of the same. Forever."

"More of the same with you? Sounds like heaven to me."

"Oh, God, Cat! Why do you say things like that?" Matt dragged her into his arms and held her close to his heart, ridiculously touched by her faith.

"Because they're true. I don't begin to know how this will all work out. I just know somehow it will."

Experience showed Matt life wasn't that simple. He sighed heavily. "I can't fight both you and Rick." He forced a smile at her upturned face. "For now."

She frowned. "Didn't you and Rick say 'now' is all we have?"

"Okay, for now."

* * * *

Cat gusted a sigh and relaxed against him. She turned in his arms to visually explore the room. Filtered light struck bottle-green walls from geometric Tiffany lamps. Heavy, dark oak furniture stood like massive soldiers on guard along the walls. Tobacco-colored leather chairs sat atop a richly hued Persian rug, inviting conversation. In a secluded alcove, screened by blood-crimson drapes, sat a bed. Covered in deep chocolate and red silk, it invited her to disappear into its depths.

"This is your 'dungeon?'" she asked wide-eyed.

Matt frowned. "I prefer to call it the 'playroom.' Some Doms use what could justifiably be called a 'dungeon.'"

"Does Rick?"

Matt stopped and stared at her for a moment. "Why do you ask?"

"Well, I mean, it's all kind of…forbidden and dark. It's interesting."

"Are you saying you want to explore a Dom/sub relationship?"

"Me? No. I'm just curious, that's all. I…I looked it up on the Internet. It was…startling…some of it. I can't understand why anyone…" She shuddered slightly. "Some of it…looked…intriguing."

A broad smile split Matt's face. "I see." His lips twitched. "What specifically did you find…intriguing?"

"Um." Cat felt a blush creep up her chest to her face.

"Cat," Matt assumed a commanding stance and tone, "any satisfying sexual relationship requires honest communication. I can't give you what you want unless you share the information with me."

Cat giggled, not in the least intimidated by his demeanor and tone. "Okay. I can see that. So…it looks as if it might kinda be fun to be handcuffed, and you know, made to 'take' whatever your lover dishes out."

"So, if I did this…" In a flash Matt had her wrists pinned behind her back, held in his unbreakable grip, his leg positioned firmly between hers. "You'd find that a turn-on?"

"I guess so. I'm not really sure…"

"What else?" Matt asked. "What else seems intriguing?"

"I…uh." A long pause followed, during which Matt seemed perfectly content to wait just as they were until she worked up the courage to say it. "Um…the vibrators seemed…" She swallowed hard. "The girl in the video seemed to be enjoying…a…um…vibrator."

Matt grinned. "Yeah? Vibrators can be fun. How would you like to try some of that?" His voice was low and husky.

"I…uh." Cat felt weak all over but suddenly felt flush with arousal. "The nuns never mentioned this."

Matt laughed. "Let's broaden your sexual repertoire a little." He turned her to face him, her wrists still clasped behind her back. "As it happens, right in this room, I have handcuffs and vibrators." He kissed her deeply, sex appeal fairly oozing off him.

"You do?"

"I do." He drew her hard against his rigid length and ground against her, making her whimper. "Come with me." It was part invitation and part command. Cat went willingly.

Matt released her wrists. "Lose the clothes," he ordered, and Cat hurried to obey. She stopped her hand at the zipper of her jeans.

"Matt?"

He frowned, looking back at her inquiringly as he drew a manacle from the side of the headboard. "Is there a problem?"

"Just a little one." She bit her bottom lip.

"What is it?"

"It's just…the video reminded me, and I…should we have been using protection the past few days?"

Matt drew in a deep breath, slightly tilting his head back. He gave her a worried look. "Oh." He sighed out the breath. "No. No need to worry. Vampires are sterile. No vamp babies." He smiled sadly. That stung. Cat hadn't considered an inability to his child. "We don't carry disease either, so I guess that's a positive." He drew her partially bare form against him and nuzzled her. "So, if that answers all your questions…" She nodded. "Good. Then strip." There was a new bite to his command.

She giggled. "Yes, sir." She giggled again.

He grinned. "You make a terrible sub." Her panties fell to her ankles, and then she flipped them across the room with her toes. Matt growled.

"On the bed, brat!"

Cat obediently hopped onto the center of the bed and extended her arms to the side. "Like this?"

Matt laughed, hands on his hips. "I think you should be a little more intimidated."

"Why? I trust you."

* * * *

Matt shook his head. "Yeah, you do." He'd make this good for her, knowing the day approached when he'd have to let her go. At least before he broke both their hearts, he could give her this.

"Tell me how you feel when we're done," he growled.

Cat swallowed hard. "Why? What are you…"?

Matt lifted her against the plushly padded headboard, so she reclined comfortably, but still had a front-row view of all the wicked things he intended to do to her. With a dark grin cast her way, he clicked a soft, wide leather manacle around her left wrist. She swallowed again.

"What are you going to do?" Another clicked around her right. He didn't answer. "Matt?" A manacle secured her left ankle. "Aren't you going to talk to me?" The final manacle closed around her right.

"A true Dom wouldn't explain himself," Matt whispered against her ear. "Don't ask again. Just. Feel."

Cat's gaze searched his warily. He slid his little finger under the rim of each shackle, making sure none were too tight.

"How do you feel?"

"Helpless. How do you feel?"

"I feel really good," he admitted with a low, evil laugh. "Keep me posted."

Matt surveyed her spread-eagled body with relish. He saw the wild beat of her pulse in the arteries of her neck. Her skin flushed a rosy pink that he thought you really had to be a vampire to fully appreciate. She pulled at her restraints, just as every sub seemed compelled to do. She wouldn't be moving much. He gave a satisfied chuckle, stood and shed his clothes, taking great pains to maintain eye contact. *Let her sweat a little, heighten the anticipation.*

She turned her head in his direction as he opened and closed a drawer behind her, listened as he unwrapped a plastic cover, tensed with the metallic sound of batteries being loaded. He was back beside her on the bed.

"Matt?" Her whisper was low and needy.

Matt stretched out beside her. "I'm here, Cat. What are you feeling?"

Cat frowned, trying to identify the sensation. "Um…insecure…I guess."

"Okay." He ran a light fingertip from her chin, down her throat, between her breasts, and across her abdomen to her navel. He stopped there and kissed her belly. "Do you know why you feel insecure?"

"Because I have no control?"

He kissed her neck, dotting kisses and nips and licks along the same route his finger took but stopping at the valley between her breasts. "You only trust me if you have control?" He bathed the delicate skin under and along the side of her breast with his tongue. She shivered. He smiled. "Cat?" He repeated his sensuous bath on the other breast.

Cat shivered again. "What?" she squeaked.

"You only trust me if you have the power to escape me?"

"No. Of course not."

She shivered more violently as his mouth descended on one of her pink nipples. He watched it engorge and pulse with need. Lavishing attention there, Matt tugged with a gentle bite, suckling strongly, and then backing off to lick delicately at the tip, repeating the combination of sensations again and again. She moaned and arched up to him. He laughed softly and evaded her attempt to put him right where she wanted him. Instead, he went to work on the other breast.

Inspiration struck, and he rose to search the armoire. "I'm gonna work these gorgeous nipples until you come," he murmured, curling back against her, dropping a shiny object onto her flat belly. She strained to get a look at whatever he'd been after, but quickly abandoned the search as his teeth descended delicately on her aching nipples. "Mild tenderness can be stimulating during sex," he informed her cheerfully. He worked and stroked and plumped her full breasts, the prickly stubble of his evening beard abraded her smooth skin; he suckled her relentlessly, and soon, Cat writhed beneath him and moaned his name.

Matt plucked the thin chain from her abdomen. "Open your eyes, baby." Cat's lids fluttered languidly, her pupils were dilated. He held up the chain. "I thought tweezer clamps might be fun for you."

His words couldn't penetrate the muzzy cocoon of arousal he'd created. "Tweezers for what?"

"Nipple clamps."

These clamps were mild, not hurtful, but added plenty of stimulation. He sucked her nipple into his mouth, pressed it hard behind his teeth with his tongue and pulled. Cat groaned and squirmed under him. He grinned against her.

"Tell me how these feel." He closed the clamp over her right nipple and tightened it slightly. Cat gasped and turned huge, round eyes in his direction. She struggled against her restraints. Matt frowned. "Too much?"

"No." She shook her head emphatically.

He smiled. "Good. Let's try the other one." He attached the corresponding clamp, and Cat moaned. Matt held up the thin silver chain running between them. "Now, I put this chain around my neck," he continued. "If I tug on it," she gasped, "it tightens. Feel that?"

"Yes."

"You like it?"

"I-I'm not sure. It's…intense."

"That it is." Matt paused, waiting for her gaze to meet his. "And, Cat, you think this is intense? You haven't felt anything yet." She gasped and struggled. "Ah…ah," he admonished. "If you're going to struggle, I think we'd better take the chain off. The more you do, the tighter the clamps get." She whimpered, and he turned serious. "If anything, I do actually hurts you, I expect you to let me know. This is supposed to heighten your experience, not hurt you. Okay?"

"Yeah, okay."

The clamps should be losing their bite as she grew used to them. He reached behind her for something. Cat strained to see in her awkward position.

"No peeking," he admonished.

"Why?"

"Because I said so," he clipped arrogantly then softened his voice. "And because you trust me, remember? Eyes forward, gaze always on me." Cat sighed, snorted, but kept her gaze on him. "Good girl. Keep looking at me unless I give you permission to look around."

"You're enjoying bossing me around way too much!" She glared at him. "I don't want to play anymore. Let me go."

"Uh-uh. You're right where I want you, and I plan for you to stay there unless you specifically tell me 'no.' If you say 'no,' I'll stop, and we'll go home."

Cat hesitated. "I don't want you to stop. It's just that I want to touch you. I want to participate."

Matt chuckled low. "You're participating, baby, believe me." He dipped his fingertips into her wet cleft drew them out saturated with her fluids. He painted her cream over her throbbing nipple. "See?" he taunted. "You're participating plenty." He licked the slick fluid off her excited peak with relish, exaggerating his tugs and lip smacks until he was sure she understood he enjoyed himself. "You taste delicious."

Her gaze devoured him, and he thrust his fingers into her hair and drew her up into a hungry, plundering kiss. *What would he do when he was no longer human when he could no longer kiss and touch and love her this way?* Cat moaned and writhed under his lips, the look on her face telegraphing her longing. She panted and bucked up to him.

"Matt, c'mon. Untie me and let me touch you."

Matt grinned wickedly. "In a little while. When I'm ready. Until then…"

He slid down her body, using his tongue to pave the way, savoring the texture of her light golden skin, and the sweet saltiness of its taste. He ran his hands and sensitive fingertips over the rises and hollows of her slender form, relishing the grain of her skin, the feel of it sliding against his own.

Her gaze followed his single-minded fervor to taste and touch every part of her. She gave herself over to his ministrations, arching up as much as her bonds allowed, gasping when the clamps stung a little more on her nipples. Her body showed her willingness to please him.

"Aw, Cat," he groaned, "I wanna drink you in! Make you mine completely." He worked his way down to her spread petals. Her parted legs shook as he used his thumbs to peel back the vibrantly pink petals of her lips engorged with arousal, wet with passion. "Look at that," he crooned. "You're gushing for me." He licked suddenly dry lips. "Are you watching?" He glanced up at her, feeling the human blush of passion suffuse his face. "You make me so impossibly hot, baby."

"Matt!" Her cry was needy.

"Watch me eat you." He fell to his stomach between her legs. "I can lick you right here." He licked along the side of her clit, up and down on the right, and then the left. "Yeah, it's the left side for you, isn't it?" he observed, watching her reaction. "Fascinating how our nerves work, don't you think?" She twisted and cried out again as he went for that sensitive left side. He kept up his attention there until once again she was right at the edge, then he sighed and pulled away.

"Matt! Damn it!" She moaned in frustration.

"What's the matter, Cat?" he asked innocently. "You wanna come?"

"It would be nice," she gritted through clenched teeth.

"Well, why don't you?"

"Because you keep stopping just when…"

"Yeah, I understand." Matt teased her, running his forefinger over her clit with a touch so soft it was almost non-existent, but the response it generated in Cat left her shaking. "I should probably let you up in a little while, so you can get some relief."

"I-In a little while?" she stuttered in disbelief. "I swear to God, Matt, payback is a bitch! You remember that!"

"Hmm. Well, tell me how you feel about that after we're through." He rose off the bed. His engorged cock stretched up toward his navel, the thick ropey veins winding around it throbbing to the beat of his heart. "First, would you mind just giving me a little love?"

He crawled, straddling her body with his knees, and Cat eagerly licked her lips. She was more than willing to suck him into the hot cavern of her mouth. Matt groaned his delight as she licked, tongued his thick, ruddy glans, and then dropped her head to take him into her mouth. She inhaled him, engulfed him, drank him down to the point where Matt had to draw away or explode. Shaking slightly with pre-shocks, he freed her wrists. Cat followed him, wound her arms around him and sucked him into her mouth as far as she could.

Matt groaned. "I appreciate the thought, babe, but I'm not quite done with you yet." He backed away down the bed and unfastened her ankles. He picked up a tube of lubricant from a shelf behind her. Cat's eyes went wide.

"I…uh…don't think I need lubrication anywhere, do I?" Matt held up a clear plastic ring with something attached to it. "What's that?"

He chuckled wickedly. "You'll see. You mentioned you were open to vibrators."

"And?"

Matt slid back down her torso without answering. "Let's take these off."

He removed the nipple clamps one by one. Cat's eyes widened, and she squealed.

"That's the sting of blood rushing back in." He immediately caressed, licked and sucked what he knew was now exquisitely sensitive flesh. She squirmed beneath him.

"I'll make good use of this vibrator," he murmured, coating the inside of the plastic silicone ring with lube and then rolling it down his dick until it nestled in the riot of curls at his base.

"That's a vibrator?"

"Let me know what you think." He winked, and then deftly spread her flesh, notched himself and worked his way forward. She was ready. God, was she ready, ---deliciously hot and plush!

"Matt!" She shuddered beneath him. "I've been waiting to feel you inside me for hours. You're so hard and thick! You make me want to come just sliding inside me."

"You don't have my permission to come yet," he gritted, on the brink of losing control along with her.

"Yeah, well…Please?"

Matt choked out a laugh. Finally seated fully inside her, he flicked the 'on' switch and then nudged her clit with the vibrator attached to his throbbing cock. Cat keened at the intensity. She shook, every muscle in her body tensing, and he shook right along with her.

"Easy now," he murmured as he pulled back almost to the tip.

"Stop…" Cat wailed with frustration.

Matt stroked forward again and held for a few precious seconds, letting the vibe stimulate her once more. Then back. Then forward. Then back. Cat bucked wildly beneath him. Begged. Cried. He gritted his teeth.

"The vibe stimulates me too. The tight ring helps keep me from coming. I could do this all night." Sweat poured off him. He couldn't really do it all night, he knew.

"Oh, dear God, no!" Cat implored. "Please, Matt! I need to come! Please!" Her pleas rose to agitation.

"You need to come?"

"Yes! Please, Matt!" She was drenched in a mist of sweat everywhere.

Yeah, he needed to come too, Matt thought desperately. He drove deep inside her, held that wildly vibrating little toy in exactly the right spot and devoured her gasping mouth with his own.

"Oh, God!"

Her sex held fast on him in wild, strong spasms. The muscles of his abdomen went hard against her, his sac drew up tight just before he erupted inside her.

Their breaths came in hard pants as Matt collapsed against her. Cat was boneless, her body offered no resistance to his added weight. With his last vestige of energy, he rolled to his side, and then whipped off the little silicone ring, flipping the vibe off as he went. He tossed it to the end of the bed before he gathered Cat, shuddering, into his arms.

"Easy, baby," he soothed, running a calming hand down her spine. "You're okay."

Cat mewled and curled into him, her free hand clutching at his muscular biceps. She trembled as aftershocks quaked through her. Post-orgasmic exhaustion crawled over him, and he waited for it to hit her full force too.

"Oh, Matt," she murmured, finally beginning to meld into him. "That was good, but…"

He heard the tears clench in her throat. "Too much?" he whispered.

She nodded. "I wouldn't want to do it every day. The buildup is torture."

"So, no toys?" he teased with feigned disappointment.

"I obviously don't need anything more than you." She stroked his cheek and then down his chest, her small hand coming to rest gently on his abdomen.

"Yeah, me too, baby. All I need is you." He stroked her back. "I love you, Cat," he murmured quietly. She was already asleep.

* * * *

Matt glanced at his watch. It was two in the morning, and he stood in unbuttoned jeans, feet, and chest bare, hair tousled, talking with Rick on his cell. "In ten, yeah," he confirmed, looking up as he spotted Cat emerging from her shower. She was gloriously nude with a towel wrapped around her thick hair as a make-shift shower cap. He swallowed, his blood accelerating in a race to make his dick unbearably hard again. "Could be a little longer." He clicked off the phone without a goodbye.

Cat's smile hinted at a smirk as she held his gaze in the mirrored screen sitting beside the plush leather armchair. In the reflection, she unclipped the towel and shook her golden mass of hair free, letting it flow sensuously down her shoulders to curl teasingly against her slowly hardening nipples.

Matt eased up behind her as she reached to pull on jeans. He guessed she'd abandoned her panties because they'd been shredded during her last attempt to dress. Her brow arched at him as he ran a wide palm down the gentle swell of her belly, his lower lip between his teeth, his eyes hot as they watched each other in the mirror.

"I could take you right here," he murmured against the back of her neck, eying her reaction, feeling her shiver. "Bend you over in front of this mirror and let you watch me grind you from behind. You should see how your flesh swallows my cock, reluctant to let me leave." He moved his hand to her still swollen nipple and pinched. Her eyes brightened, fixed on the fingers toying gently with her clit.

"I wouldn't say no."

"Yeah, but." Matt shrugged casually, teasing her for teasing him. "Then, we'd keep Rick waiting, and you know how he hates that."

"He needs to learn to deal with disappointment."

143

Matt arched a wry brow. "Rick Hiatt accept disappointment?" He snorted. "Not likely, baby. So, get dressed." He gave her bottom an encouraging swat. "I told him we'd be there in ten. We can always resume our…activities…in the playroom at the beach."

Cat gasped. "There's a playroom there? I never saw that."

"You obviously never opened the closets in the guest room."

# 14

Refreshed and dressed, Cat was nevertheless oddly nervous as she stood with Matt outside Rick's dungeon door. From inside, she heard a soft whoosh, a snap, a muffled cry.

"Hmm." Matt frowned. "Sounds as if he's already started with his sub. Well, guess they'll have to adjust." He shrugged and slid his pass card through the reader. The lock clicked open, and he drew Cat inside.

At the other end of the room, Rick stood in front of a nude woman restrained to a large wooden X, her back to them, breasts pressed into the polished wood.

Cat gasped. "What in the world?"

"Rick's working with Holly, a sub in training." Matt's lips grazed Cat's ear in a whisper. "He's restraining her on a St. Andrew's cross."

"Restraining her so he can do what?"

Matt shrugged. "All kinds of things from simple necking and petting to—"

The swish and vicious snap of a bullwhip whistled through the air, followed by a shriek from the woman on the cross. Cat stiffened, squeezing Matt's hand painfully.

"Quiet, sub," Rick snapped, ignoring them. "Take your punishment with a little grace. Maybe if you do, you'll be rewarded."

Cat's jaw dropped, and she stared from the restrained woman to Matt. "Aren't you going to help her?"

Matt's patient smiled infuriated her. "I would if I thought he was actually hurting her, or if I thought she didn't want it. Cat, it's an exercise in trust."

The whip whistled through the air again, and just at the point when she was ready to constrain Rick's hand herself, Matt grabbed her arm in a firm grip.

"Look closely at her body," he instructed sternly. "Is the skin broken? Is she bleeding?"

Cat squinted across the room. "No, but…"

"Bullwhips don't have to hurt, Cat." Matt continued in that same stern, patient voice. "They can hurt and draw blood, of course, but I've seen Rick practice with a raw egg and never crack a shell. Believe me, when I tell you, he won't hurt her unless they both agree it's what she wants, and even then, it won't hurt much. He's helping her learn to trust and overcome her fears, and yeah, maybe fulfilling her need for some minor pain." His brow rose. "It depends on the sub."

"And she's just gonna stand there and let him whip her?"

"It's BDSM. That's part of the play or can be. Everyone has their peccadilloes."

"That's…that's crazy."

"I wouldn't be so quick to judge; didn't you say you found being restrained a turn-on?"

"Well, I know, but…"

"Everyone has different limits. This," he nodded toward the woman on the cross and Rick with his whip, "would be a hard limit for you. Trust me, there's a key for every lock, and Rick is very skilled with that whip. He has a list as long as your arm of women who want to submit to it."

"And he seemed like such a nice guy."

Rick coiled the whip in his hand. "I am a nice guy." He gave her a dazzling smile, then turned to the sub who hiccupped back her cries. "I'm leaving you here to pull yourself together and find your center." He caressed her whelp-dotted buttocks with a gentle palm. "Don't embarrass yourself."

"You could hear us?" Cat demanded as Rick strolled up to them.

"Vamp hearing." He gave her that knock-out smile again. "Much more acute than human."

"Oh." Cat couldn't take her gaze off the coiled whip he casually fingered as they spoke.

"Let's go somewhere a little quieter," he suggested amiably. "Meet me in the observation room."

Matt nodded and led Cat out the door, and then into an adjoining room. It faced Rick's dungeon with what, she now recognized, was a two-way mirror. Rick stopped by the restrained sub, offered her some ice water through a straw and comforted her with a tender stroke down her hair.

He walked through the door leading from the observation room into the dungeon. "So, what's the verdict? I'm on a timetable here."

"The verdict, is we'll stay together for now, but if at any time I feel Cat's in danger from me, I'll send her away, and she'll go."

"Wait!" Cat held up a warning hand. "I never agreed to that last part."

"Oh, God's nightgown!" Rick exploded in a low, threatening voice. "Go back to the beach. Enjoy each other for however much time you have—maybe a lifetime, maybe a month. I'm tired of hearing the two of you bicker!" Matt's face tightened. Cat glared, about to rebel.

"Listen, I have a modest lead on a medical research facility in Colombia. Our chemists think this place is doing research on Humanité. They've been trying to grow buchu. I need you to come to a party with me next month to check out the owner, Elliot Maynard."

"Is he a vamp?" Matt asked. "Why do we have to wait?"

"No, he's not a vamp, and he's out of the country right now. I don't think he realizes what experiments his people are doing. That would be Veronique's style—slip it in under the radar. Maynard's company does all kinds of medical research. The Colombian government isn't as squeamish about human trials as we are in the States." He smiled at Cat's hopeful look.

"Then you know we'll be there, brother," Matt confirmed. "I'll drop by tomorrow for the details. It's late. We're going to Cat's place to collect some of her things, and then back out to the beach."

"Good for you. I have to get crackin'. I have a sub who wants to dial up the pain."

Cat gaped. "She wants you to whip her more?"

"Yeah." Rick's smile was cheerful. "I haven't even drawn blood, yet." He winked. "Wanna stick around and watch?"

"I...no."

"Rick." Matt shook his head at the cocky vampire. "You're scaring her. Stop that."

"Don't worry, love," Rick cajoled, sweetly kissing Cat's cheek. "I won't permanently harm a hair on her head. I promise." He walked jauntily out the door and into the dungeon.

"He's going to draw blood, but not harm a hair on her head?" Cat's bewildered stare accused Matt. "How is that possible?"

Matt sighed. "Why don't you watch?"

"You mean, he can really do that?"

Matt nodded and gestured to the mirror. Cat watched with horrified fascination as Rick approached Holly. With a flip of a switch, Matt activated the sound.

"How about a little more water?" Rick suggested, placing the straw at Holly's lips, and Cat could now see the woman was maybe thirty, softly pretty, but very pale. He unfastened Holly's restraints and caught her as she sagged from the cross.

"You're telling me a woman who collapses like that isn't hurt?"

"Well, is she really hurt, or does she just enjoy being cuddled?"

"What?"

"Look, I'm not saying people can't be hurt during these games. I'm telling you Rick would never hurt a woman more than she could bear, or more than she wanted. Remember, every sub has a safe word. They say it, and all action stops. So…is she really hurt, or does she enjoy his attention?"

Cat was unconvinced but watched with a new understanding. Rick rubbed Holly's ankles and wrists as he snuggled her on his lap, kissing each limb sweetly as he went. He murmured to her, words they couldn't hear, and she nodded. Their resulting kiss was deep and earnest and somehow filled Cat with both longing and the uncomfortable feeling they were intruding on a private moment. Holly nodded, and Rick stood her on her feet while he turned a lever behind the cross and the X drew together into a solid post.

Rick turned to his sub. "You're sure you want to do this without restraints?" he asked. "You'll have to hold yourself up."

Holly nodded. "I want to try, sir, if you'll be there for me afterward."

"All right." Rick led her to the post and then wrapped her arms around it. "It's important that you not move. You get scared and suddenly change position, I'm liable to hurt you unintentionally."

"Unintentionally?" Cat whispered dryly. "Yeah, we wouldn't want him to hurt her unintentionally!"

Matt grunted. "Just watch."

Rick walked back a good six feet and then dispatched his silk shirt to the floor behind him. Bare-chested, he unfurled the bullwhip before he cracked it at his side, his muscles dancing in command of the length of leather. A tremor ran through Cat. She could only imagine what the woman clinging to the post felt. His arm now loose, he let the whip fly with a whoosh and crack that placed a long welt from shoulder to thigh across Holly's back. First one side, and then the other, and then again four more times in rapid succession. Each time Holly's cries got a little louder, and on the sixth stroke, blood coursed from the wounds as Holly sagged against the post. Rick threw the whip to the floor and then raced forward to catch her.

"Not hurting her?" Cat accused in outrage. "You think this isn't hurting her? Are you all insane? I'm calling the police!" She unzipped her purse, intent on finding her cell, when Matt restrained her in a painless, but unbreakable grip. He kept her back to his front, facing the mirror.

"Watch."

As she looked up, Cat saw Rick's eyes turn, his fangs drop long and razor sharp. Gracefully, he caught Holly in an embrace and lowered her gently onto her belly. He straddled the backs of her thighs, his body tense with anticipation as he bent over her weeping back. Cat gasped at what he did next. With loving focus, he lathed the welling droplets of blood from her slowly oozing welts. Healing strokes of his tongue stemmed the crimson flow and quieted her mewling cries.

Cat expected the worst as the vampire consumed more and more of the whipped woman's blood. Rick savored every drop. *Did he taste her pain? Was it delicious to him?*

As she watched Rick's ravenous consumption of his sub's life force, Cat wondered if he'd be able to stop. Holly was so pale already. *Am I about to witness a murder?* As horrified as she was by the thought, she couldn't deny there was something sensual in the way he worshipped Holly's body.

While Rick licked and kissed the sub, he drew his fingertips gently over her quivering body, comforting and stimulating her all at once. Holly bucked and moaned beneath him. The flow of blood stopped, leaving the whip's cleavage of her savaged flesh obvious under the harsh lights. Still, his lips and tongue paid homage to what he and his sub shared, rather than succumbing to the need to rip and drain. As he licked, he stretched the length of his muscled body over Holly's, holding himself centimeters above her as if separated by some imaginary force field. He whispered words into her ear, too low for Cat to catch.

Cat stood transfixed, watching Rick's lips move, watching Holly's back arch into him. Holly pinched her nipples eagerly as she absorbed the meaning of his words. He drew her with him onto their knees. Seeing her passionate swoon, he raised his knee for her to lean against, balancing her as she fought for focus.

Cat's shock intensified as Rick drove his wicked-looking fangs deep into his own wrist and held his bleeding arm over Holly's open mouth. The sub drank from him eagerly, her eyes going wide with the kick, and then dreamy with the high. Before Cat's unbelieving eyes, the marks from the whip diminished and finally vanished altogether. She turned questioning eyes to Matt.

"It's the vampire blood, even a small amount has the ability to heal human wounds."

"Oh." It was more a gasp than a whisper.

"And…" He chuckled, watching Holly's head drop back in ecstasy as she tightened one arm around Rick's neck to settle his lips at her breast. "It has some aphrodisiac properties." The sub rose to her knees, hands working eagerly to unzip his leather pants.

"Oh!" Now, Cat was uncomfortably shocked.

"Yeah, I think we'd better give them a little privacy." Matt clicked off the two-way access and then led her away from the mirror and toward the door. "Or, we may see more than you bargained for."

Cat couldn't resist a glance back into the dungeon where Rick had drawn Holly into his arms and carried her toward the bed. Yes, she definitely wanted to give them their privacy, didn't she?

# 15

A handful of weeks separated their affair at the beach from the practicalities of *real life*. Cat was on the phone when Matt walked in, juggling several bags of groceries from the Upscale Market, a little gourmet shop that was *the* place to shop in Malibu.

In the past weeks, life developed a rhythm, and he enjoyed every second of the normalcy. Grocery shopping on Wednesday, movie night on Friday, Thursday night poker with Rick and the guys while Cat did things with Georgia and the girls. Long walks. Long swims. Staying up late, making love, and then sleeping late and making love. Maybe, if they did it often enough, he thought irrationally, he wouldn't miss her so much when the inevitable happened, and she was gone—for eternity. He resolved to make love to her until she cried out for him to stop, which of course, she never did. *Hussy!* He chuckled.

"No," Cat said firmly. "I'm not ready to start yet, and I don't know when I will be." She paused to listen. "I need to take this time." She ran her fingers lovingly down Matt's back as he passed her. "It's a time that may never come again, and Mr. Hiatt and Mr. Brenner have given me their blessing to take as long as I need." She grinned. Matt knew their names worked wonders. "Okay. Okay. We'll stay in touch. Bye." She clicked off the phone. Matt arched an inquiring brow. Cat shrugged. "My obligatory weekly refusal to start work. That was the human resources manager at Consort Publishing."

"Ah!" He paused in putting away the groceries to stand behind her, caressing her abdomen in a soothing motion. "Are you sure this is what you want? You don't have to delay. You can start the new job if you want."

Cat whirled in his arms, grabbing his face between her hands. "Are you kidding? Leave you? Leave this? Do you want to go back to work?"

"No. But…"

"And neither do I!" Cat bit back tears and turned around with a sudden need to scrub the spotlessly clean sink. "I don't want to miss one tiny second of your time as a human."

"And when I'm no longer human?"

"I don't want to miss a second of that either," she said with unrelenting cheerfulness.

She turned her head to smile confidently, but there was an underlying sadness, rather as if he'd asked, *"And when the cancer comes back?"* It wasn't lost on Matt.

He shook himself mentally and refocused. He was human now. He reminded himself to live in the present, just as he had learned to do during the war. He might be dead tomorrow. He might have to disappear tomorrow. Those dire possibilities were not going to rob them of today. He shrugged off the feeling of impending doom with fierce determination and kissed her neck, drumming his hands lightly on her abdomen before turning back to stock the groceries.

"Mrs. Jenkins, at the dry cleaners, says she accidentally picked up one of your saucepans from cooking class."

"Is that where it went? Thank heavens! I thought I was losing my mind. That's a very expensive pan too…well, Rick's very expensive pan… I don't know how I'd make hollandaise sauce without it."

"You're really out to impress me, aren't you? I mean, meat and potatoes would have been fine."

"Fine isn't good enough." Cat hugged his shoulders with still damp hands before she stepped past him to get ingredients from the fridge. "When Emeril Lagasse invites you to join his cooking class…what kind of an ingrate would I be not to accept?"

"I hate to say this, babe, but don't you think his ambition to make that deal with Consort had a little something to do with your invitation?"

"Maybe, but why not take advantage of the opportunity? Live while you can, right?" The thought ate at Matt. "Besides, aren't you busy chasing that fuzzy little ball around a tennis court?"

"Yeah, I think I overdid it a little. My knee is giving me hell today."

* * * *

Matt extended his leave of absence from the Consort Group to spend as much time as possible with Cat. Their time in the Malibu beach house, or as she dubbed it, "Utopia Beach," continued, bringing days of bliss and nights of toe-curling passion. He converted the second bedroom, overlooking the ocean, into an art studio. He'd paint while she wrote, and in an effort to hold on to what they had, both of them scoured the Internet for every possible lead to Veronique.

Matt took it a step further and looked into the Darknet, a specially encrypted area of the Internet dealing in quasi-legal endeavors, and the VampNet, an underground Internet system maintained exclusively for the Vampire Nation. There were countless meetings and endless phone calls made to anyone with connections to the vanished Moreau arsonists. All their efforts led to zilch, and that, along with the continued absence of Humanité anywhere on the planet, left him in a state of dread.

Every bite of food, every moment in the sunlight, every night between Cat's honeyed thighs amplified his foreboding that he'd soon lose his human state, and along with it, the love of his life. The premonition inched itself inexorably closer and strangled Matt's tortured heart. The situation was impossible. He knew all resolutions not to touch her sexually would be worthless once he was a vampire again. He'd scent her inevitable arousal, and all those good intentions would evaporate. He wouldn't be able to help himself, and he wasn't willing to put her in that kind of danger. She'd fight his retreat and knowing that he was already making plans to drop off the radar. He'd do whatever he had to do to keep her safe.

* * * *

Matt watched the relentless march of the calendar with dread. The weather turned imperceptibly cooler, and the days got shorter. They walked hand in hand along the shoreline of the beach at sunset, enjoying the wind, sun, and waves. It'd become their end-of-day ritual. He felt the ominous stirrings of something else, something indefinable, within. He mourned it privately, unwilling to share his fear with Cat, but he sensed she'd noticed the changes. He sighed low, lost in thought.

"Hey, Laddie!" Cat greeted the yappy little sheltie who tore down the sand bluff to them, barking furiously. The dog delighted in trying to "herd" them as they walked along what he considered to be his stretch of beach.

"Hi, Cat! Matt!" his owner called and waved as they came in sight of the house. "Laddie! You come here and leave them alone."

Cat waved back. "Hi, Mr. Stanton! He's not bothering us."

Matt kept Liv-a Snap treats in his pocket especially to distract the miniature collie from his nervous obsession.

"Hey, buddy!" Matt greeted the dog, bending down to offer the treat. "How are ya? Huh? How are ya?" He scratched the little sheltie behind his silky ears and gave him the treat, letting him prance off proudly to enjoy it.

"Maybe, we should get a dog. What do you think?" Cat asked, watching them affectionately.

Matt straightened slowly and turned to her, his expression grave. "I think animals don't do well with vampires," he replied solemnly, and from the look on her face, felt as if he'd struck her.

"Of course. You're right, so…" Cat drew a deep breath, "what time is Rick picking us up tonight?"

"Eight, sharp. He says we're on a schedule."

Cat dismissively waved the statement away. "Rick's always on a schedule. Thank heavens, he's not human. He'd be eaten up with ulcers."

* * * *

Matt watched the horizon turn from red to purple. He stood on the deck, taking in the soothing view while he sipped his drink. The tux made him fidget. He ran a finger under the stiff collar and sighed. Cat said he looked fabulous, but he felt uncomfortable as hell.

He turned to watch her through the open bedroom windows. She dabbed some of the gingery perfume that drove him wild at her neck and between her breasts. She was always careful to use just a dot. They both despised overly perfumed women. With her golden curls apparently tamed to her liking, she picked up her tiny evening bag, and then snapped off the light.

While he waited for her, Matt turned back to his view of the ocean. He was relieved Rick was joining them tonight. He desperately needed to talk to someone undead. Rick would understand, had always understood his self-doubt and torment.

He frowned down at the drink he held. The taste was anemic, he thought irritably, not the rich fruit and smoke he was used to in the fine Glenlivet single malt, and he needed something strong tonight. He couldn't imagine a Malibu liquor store having the balls to open and water down their stock, but

154

this stuff definitely didn't taste right. Maybe it was corrupted at the distillery? All thought of the unsatisfying scotch fled when he caught sight of Cat framed in the arch of the sliding glass door.

"Hey, mister, lonely tonight?"

Matt grinned and caught his breath at how lovely she was. She was every inch an elegant lady in a black strapless sheath, her blonde tresses swept back in a conservative chignon, and a simple pearl drop at her neck. He would be the envy of every man at this stuffy do tonight and the undeserving bastard who took her home. A sudden tingle warmed him below his belt, and he smiled, knowing it was his name she would scream as she came.

"Why?" He strolled casually toward her, one hand in his pocket, the other holding his drink. "You know where there's a party?"

She rubbed against him, using his lapels to draw him toward her. "I think I do." She purred seductively, her tongue darting out to touch his ear.

"Mmm." Matt shivered. "I think I'd rather party with you than go to this thing with Rick." He kissed along her neck, overwhelmed by the scent of her perfume, surprised she'd used so much. He heard her heart thundering. He studied her, mystified. "Your heart's beating a mile a minute."

"Matt…I…" she hid her concern with a shrug and gave him a dazzling smile instead. "It's the way my heart always races around you, sweetheart!" The doorbell interrupted the conversation. Rick had finally arrived.

"I hate to hurry things along, dear boy," Rick announced to the half-open door, "but this little shindig is in our honor, so I suppose we can't be fashionably late." He urged them toward the waiting limo, giving Cat an admiring glance that made Matt growl low in his throat.

"Dick." Georgia shook her head in reprimand. "Can't we at least say hello?"

"Of course." Rick looked surprised and then spoke to his driver through the intercom. "Los Angeles Country Club."

Their foursome settled into the limo's plush seats, and Rick poured chilled Dom Pérignon into long, elegant flutes. "Here's to doubling the reach of Consort Group and sussing out Maynard's connection to Humanité in the bargain." They clinked glasses, and he smiled at Matt and Cat. "I think this dull reception tonight may suit all our purposes. If you're lucky, Maynard's Colombian facility will still be producing Humanité. And if I'm lucky, Consort becomes a major player on the world markets."

"We're already a major player."

"A whale then," Rick countered cheerfully.

Matt researched Maynard on the Internet but mostly drew a blank. The guy was more low profile than Rick B. Cohen, the billionaire grocery tycoon, and that was saying something.

He drew the fine embossed linen invitation from his pocket. "Elliot Maynard," Matt said, frowning at the card. "Never heard of him. Neither has anyone else, as far as I can tell."

Rick nodded. "He keeps an exceptionally low profile. He's a great big fish in the Midwest where he lives. Still inconspicuous, though. Definitely doesn't want undue attention." His brows drew together in concern.

"So, is Humanité the only reason Cat and I were dragged away from heaven to attend this little gathering?" Matt scowled at the weak-tasting champagne in his hand.

Rick shook his head. "No pressure, but the deal we're doing with Maynard is worth several billion dollars, and if it goes south, well, no more beach house." He frowned. "No more any house."

"No pressure there. If so much is riding on the deal, haven't you already checked this guy out?"

"Yes." Rick hissed acidly. "And we found…" he gestured to Georgia.

"Nothing," Georgia admitted.

"Nothing," Rick echoed, looking perturbed.

"Isn't that a good thing?" Cat asked.

"I don't trust 'nothing.' Nobody has 'nothing' in their backgrounds, especially not billionaires. There's something. We just haven't found it yet. That's why I want you two working on it. Use your special investigative powers or detective powers, or hell, psychic powers, I don't care what. I need to know I can trust Maynard before I sign those papers next week. And right now, I have nothing." He frowned and twirled the champagne flute between his fingers. "Now, there's the Humanité connection. He may know nothing about the party drug or vampires, or any of it, but what if he does?" Rick's question hung ominously.

"Consider it done," Matt promised with the hint of a snarl. "If he's hiding something, we'll find it," he disarmed with a grin. "Besides, I'm really fond of the beach house."

Rick shot him a sideways glance and smirked. Matt smirked back. Cat rolled her eyes at the both of them.

"And, Rick," Matt's voice was gravel. "If we find Humanité in Colombia, I'll owe you."

"You bet your life you will," Rick affirmed with a cocky grin. "Literally."

* * * *

Matt couldn't deny that Elliot Maynard understood hospitality. The party in their honor was held at the most exclusive country club in the city, which had been taken over for the night, especially for Maynard's use. Crystal chandeliers glittered above them while Italian marble floors supported the thick and colorful Persian carpets cushioning their steps. Priceless antiques that more properly belonged in museums held elaborate floral arrangements and trays of petit fours. The strains of a Viennese waltz lilted from a full orchestra in the adjoining room as they stood in line to meet their host.

Maynard didn't look like anything special, Matt thought, watching the man greet the rich and entitled. He was average height, balding, a little paunchy, with an open, smiling face. At his side stood his statuesque wife, dripping diamonds and sporting that wind-blown look hinting at a little too much plastic surgery. Definitely not vampires. And that made Matt curious. Rick routinely did business with non-vamps, but a deal this big? It had to be directly related to the Colombian facility, a fact that touched him deeply. For all his seeming indifference, Rick was quite a devoted friend. Matt and Cat would work the crowd tonight, gathering the names of as many of the bigwigs as they could in an effort to put together an accurate portrait of their new would-be investor.

* * * *

Matt and Rick managed to avoid detection in a secluded corner of the balcony, at least long enough to have a hurried exchange of information.

"He ought to be suspect just because of his half-baked friends!" Matt groused, watching the crowd disdainfully.

"I'd agree with that." Rick nodded. "You know, you've been to a lot of these parties with me. Have you ever seen such an accumulation of shallow know-nothings? Am I feeling my age, or is something different here?"

"Something's definitely different," Matt agreed. "Every society party has some hangers-on, but usually interesting people are doing worthwhile things. This group…" He paused and turned to Rick. "Why are we in bed with this guy?"

"Humanité." Rick winced. "The research being done at that Colombian facility is just too suspicious. It has Ronnie's scent all over it. And…money." He shrugged apologetically. "A lot of money."

"Cat and I are on it. If there's something more to find on Maynard, we'll find it. I suggest you take him out just because some people are too asinine to live!"

Rick snorted. "A little irritable tonight? What's the matter? The honeymoon over? A fight with the little woman?"

Matt turned and watched Cat as she worked the room, trying her best to be gracious. He could sense her distaste from there. He loved her so much, and the dread he felt over losing her had his gut in a knot.

"No." Matt looked down, and his face was a mask of pain. "I'm more in love with her today than ever, and I'm about to break her heart."

Rick frowned with genuine concern. "What are you talking about, dear boy?"

"Rick, I think the Humanité is wearing off. Things aren't right. I'm not right. My body feels…wrong."

Rick blew out a long breath and regarded Matt with a look of compassion. Matt thought he must really be in trouble if his predicament was pulling at Rick's heartstrings. "Okay," Rick reasoned. "You're about to turn again. How is that going to break her heart?"

"In a million ways. You should have seen her today when I told her we couldn't get a dog…as if I'd told a kid there was no Santa Claus. She's gotten used to me as human, and us as a human couple. I don't know if she can make the change back. I don't know if I want her to try."

"My dear fellow," Rick laid a hand on his shoulder. "I have to tell you I think you're worth a little more to her than a dog!" Matt snorted. "Look, this is a hyper-emotional time for you. You're about to lose the life you treasure and have wanted back for decades. Your body's about to transform, and who knows if you're going to feel as raw as a fledgling when it happens. Cat loves you."

"Yeah, but—"

Rick held up a hand. "Let me finish. Cat loves you, Matt. Please, promise me you won't make any decisions about your relationship until you're through the turn and thinking clearly again."

Matt drew in a deep breath and sighed it out. "I make no promises, but I'll try not to make any decisions until the change is over."

Rick nodded and clapped Matt on the shoulder again. "Now, safety. We have to be proactive. I think the two of you should move into the mansion with me as soon as possible. If you're together when it happens, I have the staff and security to keep Cat safe. None of us thinks a human is safe with a newly turned vampire."

Matt watched Cat and Georgia meet up on the balcony and head their way. He struggled to put a smile on his face. "On that, you and I agree completely, brother. She has to stay away from me. The trouble is, she's a little stubborn."

Cat took Matt's arm when she reached him. "Dance with us, gentlemen," she implored. "We've done our bit for business tonight." She smiled at Rick. "Now, there's an excellent orchestra playing, and we deserve a little reward, don't you think?"

Rick bowed to the women. "I wholeheartedly agree." He took Georgia's hand in his and led the way to the dance floor.

Cat relaxed into Matt's embrace and swayed to the music. "And if anyone tries to cut in, you have my permission to beat him up."

"That wouldn't be very gentlemanly."

"No, but it would be very satisfying." She sighed. "My feet hurt, and I miss the beach. When can we go home?"

"Rick and I were just discussing that. We'll cut out after this dance, and when we get home, you and I need to have a serious talk." She looked at him curiously but didn't push it.

A high-profile gathering with so many bigwigs required extra security, including guards with dogs patrolling the grounds. Limos came and went, and Matt waited impatiently for theirs to arrive just so they could get the hell out of there. He was briefly embarrassed when one of the dogs caught his scent and barked ferociously. Cat took a shocked step back, and when Rick and Georgia joined them, the guard dogs went berserk, barking and even howling, to the astonishment of their handlers. Rick and Matt ignored the cringing, growling dogs, but Cat's eyes went wide.

"Gosh," she glanced in Rick's direction, "I guess animals really are naturally afraid of vampires."

Matt smiled but said nothing. He wanted to get home and get this over. He was feeling less and less human by the minute.

* * * *

Cat watched uneasily as Matt withdrew further and further into a bleak mood. The drive seemed interminable by the time they dropped Rick and Georgia off, and then returned to the beach. Just as the limo pulled up to their door, Matt broke out in a profuse sweat.

"Cat, I need to tell you…" His steps faltered as they walked through the door. "Just let me sit down for a minute, and I'll be okay. Then, we have to talk."

As relieved as Cat was to be home, fear insidiously niggled at her. Something was desperately wrong with Matt. With the Humanité in his system, could he suffer human maladies? *Oh, God, please let it be that simple.*

"You want to come out onto the deck and sit? Get some fresh air?"

"Yeah, good idea."

She preceded him onto the deck and looked up at the stars, rubbing her arms to ward off the chill night breeze, or maybe it was the deep sense of foreboding.

"You want a nightcap out here to unwind?" she asked.

He pulled impatiently at his tie. "No, I'm exhausted. I'm going to bed."

She studied his face. He looked haggard and pale under his tan. "You said you wanted to talk. I'll come with."

She looped her arm through his, but he ignored her. He stopped next to the bed, stripping off his jacket, and then letting it fall to the floor. A very uncharacteristic thing for Matt.

"Matt." She reached out just as he fell like a dead weight onto the bed. He was ashen. "Matt! Matt!" He opened wounded eyes. "What's wrong, baby? Are you sick?"

"Yeah. Yeah." He rolled and curled into a ball. "I think I am."

Cat's nurturing instinct kicked into high gear. She felt his forehead, trying to decide if he had a fever, but no, he was cool, even clammy.

"Oh! I'm gonna be sick!" he declared, leaping up and staggering for the bathroom. He vomited up the entire contents of his dinner before he got to the door, and then sank weakly to the floor, looking around helplessly for a towel.

"Oh, Matt!" Cat was instantly beside him, seizing the wastebasket and placing it in easy reach. "Honey!" She brushed his hair back, and he stared up at her with blank eyes, opalescent eyes. "I'm here, Matt. I'm right here," she reassured him, touching him with gentle fingers, feeling anything but calm. Now, she knew what was happening.

# 16

Cat observed the unmistakable changes ravaging Matt with horror. A knowing part of her, deep inside, recognized his transformation, but was unwilling to acknowledge it.

"Get out of here, Cat! Please!" He growled sickly. "Get out! I'm dangerous! Call Rick. Please, if you love me, get out!" His plea seemed to have taken his last bit of strength, and to her astonishment, his body was suddenly out of control.

"Oh, no, Matt!" she cried, not knowing what to do to help him. "I'm calling Rick right now. I'll be back, baby. I'll be right back! Just hold on!"

She stripped off her soiled, expensive gown without another thought as she ran for the phone. It took her several agonizing minutes to convince Rick's assistant to put him on, and that this was Matt's emergency.

"What's happening, Cat?" Rick asked, using the speakerphone.

"Rick! Matt's sick... I think he's turning!"

"His biggest concern is for you. Get out of there."

"He's thrown up, and he's clammy—"

"And he's lost all control of his bladder and bowels, right?"

"Yes."

"He's turning. Very soon, he'll be ravenously hungry—for blood. I'm heading for the beach house right now. This is what I want you to do. There's blood in the freezer in the garage. You know the one I mean?"

"Yes. Yes." She shook so badly she could barely speak. "That freezer's locked."

"The key is in the right-hand drawer in the kitchen desk. I want you to go there and find it, now."

How could he be so calm when her whole world was coming to an end? She detoured through the bedroom on her way to the kitchen and found Matt still as she'd left him. He hadn't moved. She didn't know what terrified her more, his stillness, or the possibility of uncontrolled bloodlust. She tore open the kitchen desk drawer, and then closed her hand around the key.

"Yes. Yes. I have the key. Now what?"

"Good girl. Now I want you to unlock the freezer and get out three, no, make that four packs of blood. Do that now."

She dashed to the garage, and with fingers made numb by fear, she finally got the lock open. The freezer was stocked full of blood. She pulled out six units. It couldn't hurt to have extra.

"This blood is frozen solid, Rick."

"I know, I know, but it'll be okay for now." He continued on in the same infuriatingly calm voice. "Go to the bathroom, stopper the drains and fill the sinks and tub with hot water. After you've done that, put a pack in each sink, the others in the tub and get the hell out of the house!"

"What? You want me to just leave him here like this? With no help?"

"Yes, Cat. I want you to leave him there. I'm already on my way. I'm in the car. I'll be there as soon as I'm able. You'll have put blood there for him. You'll have done everything you can." He sighed, but his voice became sterner than she'd ever heard it. "Listen to me, Cat, get out of the house. He may have no more control than a fledging. He could kill you and not even realize he's done it. I can't let that happen."

"I'm not leaving him here alone, Rick."

"This isn't a debate!" he shouted. "It's what Matt wants!" The line went dead.

Cat hurried to the bathroom and then ran the hot water as Rick directed. She turned and bent over Matt. He was still out of it. Once the water was hot, she set the packs of blood into it to defrost.

Matt moaned and stirred behind her. "Matt!" She was on the floor next to him in a flash. His eyes opened, and his gaze met hers with dim, opaline recognition. "Hey, baby," she cooed softly, wiping damp hair away from his face. "I'm here. Rick's on his way. You're gonna be okay."

Matt's fangs descended, and he growled. Weakly, he tried to push her away. *How long would the weakness last,* she wondered. *Long enough for Rick to get there?*

"Do you think you can stand?"

His head fell back, and with an enormous effort and her help, Matt managed to lever himself up against the wall to a standing position. Together, they staggered toward the shower stall. Cat turned frigid water on full blast and stripped off his clothes as he rested against the cool marble walls.

Her touch was impersonal now, devoid of emotion. She needed to stay that way to keep from screaming her agony and falling apart completely. She grabbed the bath gel and used it liberally, washing off the filth covering him, washing his hair, and rinsing him completely. She hoped for his sake he wouldn't remember this tomorrow.

Matt caressed her cheek as she turned him to rinse his back. His gentle stroke was marred by long, claw-like nails tearing her delicate skin and starting a trickle of blood. She didn't feel the cut, but obviously, Matt smelled the blood. They looked down at it covering his fingers, and Cat touched her face, feeling the sting of the abrasion. He roared in a frenzy, the vampire within becoming fully engaged. She drew back, every limb quaking as she watched him.

He gasped, and when he spoke, his voice was rough and inhuman. "I'm begging you, Cat, get away from me."

Cat refused to leave. Instead, she wrapped him in a bath towel and spoke soothingly. "I have some blood thawing for you right now. Come on, let's get you into bed and you can have some."

Matt resisted her with a low growl and hiss. He was quickly gaining strength. His hold on her was now effortless and as strong as steel. He sniffed her neck as if scenting the tantalizing aroma of her blood. Cat froze. He'd told her once the neck was a dangerous place to bite. The wrist offered much more control. She knew without a doubt she was now in mortal danger. She had to be smart about this, had to minimize the danger if she hoped to survive the night.

"You want my blood, don't you?" Cat surrendered to the inevitable. He growled low and juicy, transfixed on her neck. "Okay. Okay. Let's sit here, and you can have it."

The monster inside him whined and cocked his head as though seeing her for the first time and settled abruptly onto the marble shower bench. His claws nearly pierced her skin as he drew her roughly toward him. Cat did her best to drape herself across his lap and lean against the cold marble wall. She prayed now. Prayed he had presence enough to hold her, so she wouldn't black out and hit her head against the unforgiving marble floor. She prayed Rick would get there in time, prayed Matt wouldn't kill her, blame himself and take his own life in remorse.

He was at full vampire's strength now, but his self-restraint disappeared along with his humanity. A sudden calm descended over Cat, and with a gentle sigh, she consciously decided to meet her fate at his hands, whatever that might be. Maybe, if she gave herself to him willingly, he'd remember it and not be devastated by guilt when he killed her.

"Here, baby." She spoke gently, as she would to the gravely ill. "Here's my wrist. You take my blood if you need to."

Matt sniffed her arm for mere seconds before biting fiercely into it. She was amazed that somehow, by the grace of God, he'd missed an artery. Pure instinct guided her now. He drew hard upon her wrist, great swallows and mouthfuls of blood, paralyzing the nerves from her shoulder to her fingertips, and making it feel as if her whole hand was on fire. She stifled a moan, knowing instinctively she must keep quiet, still, and wait for Rick.

She watched Matt's face and the intensity with which he fed. She couldn't help it, she knew she shouldn't move, but the man beneath the monster was still her Matt. She reached out with her free hand and gently ran it across his handsome cheek, now so distorted with his voracity to feed.

His bloody gorging slowed. He came to himself, briefly. His head twitched, and he looked at her. His fangs retracted instantly, though the vampire's roar reverberated against the stone walls. It was the bloodlust, Cat knew. He was close to killing her, but somewhere he must have found the will to resist. She closed her eyes and drifted away into soft oblivion.

* * * *

Matt was still the man who loved and protected Cat, and by some miracle, he managed to subdue the overpowering need of his vampire. He listened to her heartbeat, slower, fainter, but not fatal. Not yet. She swooned, and he held her fast, lowering them to the floor of the shower, her magnificent love-filled blood strengthening him. He didn't have the control yet to stop feeding entirely, so he concentrated instead on keeping his fangs retracted, letting the wounds naturally pool the blood up to him, taking small amounts. *Had she said Rick was on his way? Please, God,* he prayed, holding her tightly in his arms, *let him not be too late!*

* * * *

Rick tore into the room. "Matt! Where are you? Matt!" He steeled himself against the unmistakable and disgusting odors. Steadying himself against the door of the shower, Rick watched Matt, listening for Cat's heartbeat and her breathing. They were there. Not great, but not life-threatening. Not yet, anyway. "Dear boy." He spoke calmly, avoiding eye contact, careful not to inadvertently challenge a newly turned vamp feeding on his prey. "Cat called me. Looks as if she got you some help."

Matt looked down at the pallid, beautiful woman in his lap and held her against his chest, rocking her gently. His eyes were brightly human. He looked up. "Help us, Rick. We need help," he whispered before he lost consciousness.

Rick didn't hesitate. He grabbed Cat out of Matt's limp arms, taking her to the safety of the spare bedroom, and then laying her gently onto the bed. He stacked pillows under her feet and blankets over her in an effort to ward off shock. On his way back to Matt, he called the responders for help.

"I have an emergency." He gave the address to the businesslike woman on the other end of the phone. "We need blood transfusions of O negative. It's a human recipient." He listened to her response with irritation. "Yes, we're trying to save her! This is Rick Hiatt. You tell your boss if he's not here in fifteen minutes, he'd better look for another line of work because he'll be out of business! You got that? Very well, that's better…the door's open, tell him to come to the master bedroom."

Matt roused swiftly, his eyes opaline again, his fangs descended. Rick picked him off the shower floor and put him on the bench. He looked over at the sink. Two thawed units of blood floated in the water, four more waited in the tub. He smiled. Clever girl. Kept her head through this whole mess. He grabbed the thawed blood, and then drained the sinks.

"Here, Matt! Here's some blood until we can get you to the Gaoler for some fresh donors."

Rick tore the seal from one unit, letting Matt drink straight from the bag as he emptied the other into a glass. Matt drank ravenously, emptying the bag in a few gulps before accepting the glass Rick eagerly thrust into his hands.

Rick saw he was gaining self-control quickly now. He'd probably consumed at least four units of blood between what he took from Cat and the bagged stuff. Just to be sure, he planned to give him one more before they left. Matt's fangs retracted, his eyes normalized, and he stood on strong legs again. He voiced his first coherent thought.

"Where's Cat?" he whispered, dread suffusing every syllable.

The responders thundered into the bedroom, dressed in their innocuous blue jumpsuits. "Where's the woman?" the lead vampire asked without preamble.

* * * *

Matt fought panic, the dread inside him exploding. He resisted Rick's restraining arm, terrified of what he'd find, but desperate to get to Cat. The other somber vamps in the group of responders stood holding their high-tech cleaning supplies, respectfully out of the way of the unfolding drama.

"She's all right!" Rick answered them simultaneously. "She's all right. She's in the spare bedroom down the hall. She's had some blood loss, but with a transfusion, she should be fine." He turned to the vamp with the medical bag. "Thanks for coming. I know this isn't your usual case. Tonight you're Florence Nightingale in blue coveralls."

"Always available to help you, Mr. Hiatt." The man bowed formally, and then set off down the hall.

Rick turned to Matt. "I'll take you to her. She's unconscious right now."

"Oh, God!" Matt groaned.

"Unconscious, but unhurt. They'll have her patched up in no time. Just take it easy, you don't want to scare her, do you?"

"No, of course not,"

"Then, take it easy. Try to act as if this is normal procedure, okay?"

"Yeah. Yeah. Just let me go to her." Rick paced Matt down the hall, holding him to a walk.

The light from the hallway reflected on Cat's face as Matt entered the room. Her waxy, pale color nearly brought him to his knees. The responder clicked on the overhead light, deftly setting up the intravenous supplies and blood. Matt stood at her bedside, sucking in unnecessary breaths, hoping to calm himself. He listened to the slow, faint thudding of her ravaged heart.

The responder stood at his side. "Excuse me, Matt, I need to get in here to start the IV."

"Sure, Boris, thanks," he murmured, giving him room. "Humans need to have blood that matches their type," Matt reminded him.

Boris smiled reassuringly. "I'm aware of that. She's in good hands. Why don't you get dressed? She'll probably be coming around when you get back."

Matt looked down, suddenly realizing he was stark naked. "Yeah. Yeah, I guess I'd better." He allowed Rick to lead him back to the master suite.

The responders were already at work on the waste and vomit in the bathroom, the smell of disinfectant heavy in the air, a carpet cleaning machine running full blast. The stench was nauseating to Matt, and the noise deafening. Rick handed him another glass of blood and insisted he drink while he dressed. He was feeling better now, ultra-sensitive, but much more in control. Like his old self. His vampire self.

"I never should have let her come home with me tonight," he told Rick, anguished. "I suspected I was turning. Look at the injury I caused her because of my own stupidity."

"Ah, there's the Matt I know and love! Never one to miss a chance at self-flagellation!"

"You think this is funny?"

"No, but I also don't think it's tragic. Cat's going to be fine, and so are you. Although, God's nightgown, it could have turned out much worse." He sighed. "I told Cat to get out of the house. You told her to get out of the house. She wouldn't listen."

Matt nodded with the ghost of a smile. "Stubborn."

"Just so you know, and there's never any question, I'm not the one who stopped you tonight. Nor is she. You had already stopped feeding on Cat by the time I got here. She passed out. You stopped yourself, Matt, you wouldn't over-feed on her."

Matt released his breath in a heavy sigh of relief and looked up to see a responder in the doorway.

"Miss Temple is awake." He smiled. "She's asking for you."

The walk down the hallway felt a million miles long. Suddenly, confronted by her tender smile and rapidly improving color, Matt knew he owed her the truth. It might be the last thing he ever gave her, and she deserved to know she risked her life for a man who loved her with his whole heart. In an instant he was on his knees beside the bed, her hand held gently in his. She lifted her other to soothingly cup his cheek.

"Hey there, little donor!" Rick teased. "I see you followed my good advice to get out of the house."

Cat pulled the sheet primly around her, but never took her gaze from Matt's. "I heard your advice, Rick. I just chose to ignore it. Advice has to be reasonable. Leaving Matt like that, …just wasn't going to happen."

Rick shook his head in resignation. "Why do I waste my breath?"

Matt ignored their banter and continued checking her over, gently fingering the intravenous infusion, searching her skin to be sure the two deep puncture wounds on her left wrist were her only injuries.

"I'm sorry, baby." He tenderly kissed the ugly bite marks.

"Matt, stop it. You couldn't help it, and we both know that. Don't apologize to me again. We did what we had to do."

He leaned down to give her a soft, warm kiss. "I love you." The words he'd sworn never to say escaped his lips in a tortured rush followed by another more desperate kiss.

She smiled against his lips. "I love you, too." The next kiss was more ardent and deeper.

"Enough, you two. Don't make me turn the hose on you." Rick sounded more amused than squeamish.

Matt grinned and threw Rick a look over his shoulder. "Dad's getting restless," he murmured and smiled lovingly at Cat. "I may have to remove him before he gets overstimulated."

Rick smirked at him in return. "Someone needs to be the adult in this situation. Cat, I'm taking Matt home with me now."

"Ohh!" Cat protested, but Rick, now the one in control, held up his hand for silence.

When he spoke his words were clipped and implacable. "He needs at least two more units of fresh human blood, and since you won't be providing it, I need to take him someplace safe. Boris will stay with you until your transfusion is complete, which will take a few hours. Then, if you're feeling up to it, he'll bring you to my place. That is unless you'd rather stay here or go to your apartment."

Cat stroked Matt's cheek again, and he turned his face to kiss her palm, but in so doing, he could already smell the delicious scent of blood racing through her veins. Rick's judgment was sound. Matt wasn't thinking rationally but was instead in a chaos of emotions from love and devotion to guilt and remorse mixed liberally with a ravenous need to feed.

Matt almost wished Cat had been horrified enough by this experience to announce she was leaving for home, never to return. That was a vain hope, of course, and something she'd never do, but it would make their inevitable parting so much easier. Still, in his hyper-emotional state, he couldn't make himself send her away until he was certain she was truly unharmed. Then, the wrench would be intolerable. How could he return to the solitary, bereft existence he'd known for decades before she'd demolished his carefully constructed isolation? *How could he live an immortal life without her?*

"I'll come to your place."

Cat and Rick had continued their conversation while Matt had zoned into his own thoughts. Her words jarred him back to a reality where his heart leaped, and then plunged into despair.

Matt studied Cat's beloved face and then gave her one more lingering kiss before getting to his feet and letting Rick lead him away. This would be their last kiss. He looked over his shoulder once. She was pale and succumbing to the exhaustion of her ordeal. Her eyes closed before they reached the door.

"He loves me," she murmured contentedly as she drifted into sleep.

* * * *

Matt leaned his head all the way back, coaxing the thick drops of blood from a travel mug, compelled to drink and hating his need. Better to starve himself to death, which didn't work. He'd tried that decades ago. It merely resulted in a total loss of control and peril to every mortal in his vicinity. Someone would get hurt, and it wouldn't be him.

The powerful Maserati's headlamps cut a path up the fog-shrouded hills. Matt was agonized, staked by his own woeful decision. The wound might be self-inflicted and purely emotional; still, he couldn't imagine a physical stake being more agonizing.

"I can't allow Cat to follow me to your place, Rick," Matt decided grimly. "By this time tomorrow, I need her to be in New York City with no memory she and I ever met. Our chemists need to work with the responders and drug her and thrall her or…"

Rick took his gaze off the treacherous road long enough to stare aghast at him. "Dear boy, what are you saying? Only this evening, you agreed to wait to make any decisions."

"This evening before I almost killed her?" Matt ground out. "Yeah, great plan."

"Matt."

"By the time we're through, she'll forget me, forget about vampires and everything that's happened these last few weeks," he insisted. "For her own good."

"You must be mad if you think anything in the mortal or immortal world will make this young woman forget you."

"I'll do whatever it takes," Matt insisted, drawing hard on the blood in his mug, hoping it would somehow give him the strength to do what must be done. "This is her life, and she almost lost it tonight because of me. That's never going to happen again."

"This is a mistake, Matt." Rick insisted.

"You think I don't know I fouled up?" Matt swallowed hard against emotions that threatened to overwhelm him. "The mistake is mine—losing my head and involving her with me, with us. I won't let her pay for it again." He clenched his jaw against the searing pain, and his tone testified to his devastation. "You've said for centuries that a vamp/mortal romance never works."

"Maybe I was wrong."

"No. You weren't wrong. I nearly killed her, would have killed her if you hadn't gotten there." Matt turned his head to look out his window at the fog, unwilling to let Rick see his tears so close to the surface.

"I disagree," Rick insisted. "I told you, you'd already stopped feeding."

"How long would that have lasted? You really think I wouldn't have drained her once the bloodlust rose again? You know better."

"What I know, is I've seen a lot of subs, maybe thousands. Women who have schooled themselves to submit to their masters at whatever cost. I've never seen this level of devotion in any woman."

Matt almost vamped from fury. "This isn't some knock boots BDSM game!" He snarled. "She didn't 'submit.' She loves me, Rick. She was willing to die for me."

"Yes," Rick interrupted quietly. "That's my point. She's not playing a game. She loves you that much—and you love her. If you throw this kind of love away, you're the stupidest son of a bitch on the planet."

A galling silence traveled with them as the coupe wound its way up the switch-back. Finally, Matt acquiesced. "I agree. I'm a stupid son of a bitch, but I've wised up. If I were human…"

"Humanité might make you human again!" Rick exploded, and Matt was stunned. "You've adopted this idiotic stance against turning her in the event of another accident, leaving Humanité your only option. It's another mistake. She'd make a phenomenal vampire, and—"

Matt grabbed the steering wheel, skewing the car into a turnout area with a spray of gravel. He glared at Rick, deriding the elder vampire's suggestion with a look, his entire being going stone cold at the thought of turning Cat. Rick righted the steering wheel, and without a glance toward oncoming traffic, floored the auto back onto the treacherous road.

"You can't discount the possibility of the Humanité," Rick pressed, ignoring the irate driver who blasted a horn and flashed headlight behind them. "Now that we know about Maynard and the Colombian facility, there's real hope we can find more. Where is this defeatist attitude coming from?"

Matt studied his friend with a raised brow. "You know, I think you might be a little in love with her yourself," he accused.

"Maybe. A little. At least enough to know women like her come along maybe once a century, and you're willing to break her heart, break her spirit?" He ground his teeth, and his eyes flashed to opal. "If I have to be the one to help you clean up your mess, be goddamn sure about this. You give her up, you'll never have her again. I swear by your blood, I'll see to it!"

"I don't intend to give up. As soon as I'm sure Cat is taken care of, I'll be in Colombia searching for Humanité." He beat the travel mug a little too insistently against his leg, trying to free up the viscous fluid, needing it to combat the conflicts within and without. "What I won't do is involve Cat in this disaster any longer."

"So, you want to send her to some dorm in New York? You think anything can make her forget her college graduation? Maria's death? Never mind you. Are you crazy?"

"You're right," Matt agreed. After some thought, he added, "We need to invent a different reality for her. One that includes necessary details but eliminates me."

"Oh, I see, well…that makes absolutely no sense at all."

"It's not preposterous. It may be difficult. Get on the phone right now and have Boris sedate her. It won't be easy, but her whole life is about to be relocated to New York with a plausible explanation for how she got there, and a new job at Consort Publishing. As far as she's concerned, I'll be just a fantasy."

"You have a great deal of faith in our chemists, dear boy." Rick shook his head.

"Aren't you always saying they're the best? If this is too difficult for them, I guess I could call upon the Council for assistance."

Rick's arm cut through the air in his rush to negate that notion. "The Council will terminate her if you don't want her. Too much of a liability to the Family."

"Then, I don't see we have much choice. Unless you're willing to watch them eliminate her."

Rick jerked the Maserati into a furious one-eighty-degree spin as they entered the drive of the hilltop mansion. He yanked the emergency brake savagely and glared at Matt, his body vibrating with his transformation, his fangs dropping sharp and deadly.

"You expect me to believe you'd let them terminate her?" He demanded over a juicy growl.

Matt's vampire emerged at the challenge. For a fraction of a second, he was ready to take on his best friend. With a submissive whimper and a show of his throat, he withheld his inner beast.

"You know better," Matt turned his head to the window.

Rick sighed, shuddered and humanized. "I'll call the chemists," he capitulated. "First, we'll get some good, fresh donor O-negative into you. I'll put this in motion, hoping enough pristine blood will bring you to your senses. Maybe, we can find a virgin."

"It won't change my decision."

"I'll get Georgia to work on it," Rick grumbled, "You really are a cock-up, you know?"

# 17

Cat awoke slowly, as if from a perturbing dream. She squinted her eyes against the muted sunlight shining through mottled, leaded glass. The inevitable New York City street sounds filtered in through the window cracked for air. She glanced groggily around a pleasantly feminine, but totally unfamiliar bedroom.

On its tabletops and shelves, her dearest belongings now rested alongside foreign trinkets. Slowly, she pulled herself up against the padded headboard. The urge to shake her head to clear it was strong, but as she reached up to run a hand through her hair, her fingers encountered gauze wrappings, and she thought better of the idea. Her mouth and throat felt desert dry. She reached for the Waterford crystal tumbler at her bedside and nearly dropped it from shock. An exquisite manicure graced her nails. Manicures were not in her budget.

"Hello?"

"Ah, you're up!" A silver-haired beauty in royal blue scrubs greeted her from the doorway. "I'll call the doctor and let her know you're awake."

"Where am I? Who are you?" Cat demanded, struggling to speak over her parched throat.

The nurse, for surely she must be one, poured more water from a cut-crystal decanter and handed it to her. "I'm Georgia. What do you remember?"

Cat frowned, her fingers coming to rest on the gauze wrapping her head. "My…name is Catherine Temple."

"Yes."

"I graduated from college this year."

"Yes, that's right."

"I came back to Los Angeles for a trial…and…" Cat's memory faded into limbo. She frowned, struggling, and rubbed her forehead.

"It's very common, given your injuries, that you don't remember more," Georgia reassured. "You're in New York City, not Los Angeles. You attended Columbia your last semester." Cat nodded, remembering. "Do you remember the accident?"

"No."

"I understand you returned to the city shortly after the trial verdict. That was nearly ten weeks ago. You've been in guarded condition since then, in and out of consciousness."

"My head." Cat gently ran a hand over what she now realized was a bandage, her fingers identifying a two-inch line of stapled sutures running down the back of her head.

"The surgery was two weeks ago. You've made significant progress since the pressure was relieved."

"Where's Matt?" Cat asked with a gasp, the memories of him flooding her in a panicked rush.

"Matt who? Is he a friend or relative?" Georgia gently questioned.

"No…he's my…my boyfriend…he lives in LA. What is this place?"

"You're in your apartment. Mr. Hiatt arranged private nursing care for you at home, feeling you might recover more quickly in this setting."

"Hiatt? Yes! Richard Hiatt! Matt's best friend, his business partner,"

"Well, if that's so, I don't understand why only Mr. Hiatt has been here to see you." She paused, looking concerned and spoke gently. "Is it possible the person you speak of was killed in the accident?"

"I need to see Rick. I need to see him right now!" Cat insisted and watched in awe as a flurry of activity erupted around her.

Another woman, also dressed in blue scrubs, entered the room with medication. She was followed by the doctor, who frowned with concern. Georgia snatched a phone from her pocket and pressed an automatic number.

"Mr. Hiatt, please." she requested and then waited. "Sir? This is Georgia Gregoriev, Ms. Temple's nurse."

* * * *

Cat felt almost human again after she'd been helped to shower and assisted into fresh, soft pajamas and a robe more luxurious than anything she ever owned. Walking to the chintz-covered fainting couch, she reacquainted herself with legs that plodded heavily. She fisted and unfisted her hands to feel her arm muscles move. Georgia helped lift her legs onto the chaise when Cat's attention was distracted by the chime of the doorbell. *Matt?*

"I'm gratified to see you out of bed, Cathy." She glanced up to see Rick's slender, muscular silhouette dominating the doorway of her room. "They tell me they're cooking you something delicious for dinner."

"Where's Matt?" she demanded without preamble.

"Who?" He frowned as if in confusion as he advanced into the room to stand beside her.

"You know who." She searched her mind for Matt's last name. It eluded her. Cat snapped her fingers and then tapped her forehead in a vain effort to remember.

"Please, try not to upset yourself," Rick directed. He reached for the buzzer beside her and rang it.

"Matt!" she cried in frustration. "Matt…Matt." Her mind reached out for the name. "Tall, dark, immortal, your best friend." She lowered her voice conspiratorially. "A vampire."

A look of incredulity raised his brow almost into his hairline, but his voice remained calm as if he were speaking to someone slightly deranged. "I'm sorry, Catherine, they said you might have had some strong dreams. There is no Mack, and I know you don't really believe there's such a thing as vampires." Glancing around at the elegant furnishings with a satisfied smile, Rick made a sweeping gesture. "I took the liberty of moving you into the apartment you'd chosen before you left town. I hope the furnishings are to your liking."

If it hadn't been for the sedative damping her agitation, Cat would have turned on Rick with physical blows. "What do you mean no such thing as vampires?" she shouted. "*You're* a vampire!"

Rick gaped at her. "I'm a…" He broke off laughing. "Strong dreams, indeed." He lowered himself to a chair, and then took her hands. His were ice cold. Cat flinched, and he immediately withdrew his touch. "Cathy, now you know that's preposterous. I'm not a vampire. No such thing exists, and I don't have a friend named Mack."

"Not Mack. Matt. Matthew," Cat corrected, tears stinging her eyes. "I…" Her gaze darted around the room as if the answers to her questions were hidden there.

"Your doctor tells me you're recovering quite well," Rick encouraged. "Now that you're awake, it should be only a matter of days before—"

"Rick, how can you forget Matt? How can you forget everything we meant to each other?" she whispered in horror.

"Dear girl, though I've overseen your convalescence, you and I have barely met. I hear good things from my editors about your talent, but I'm afraid there is no Matt and no past between us."

She watched him shrewdly. "Then why would you do all this for me?" She gestured around the room.

Rick sighed. "The accident that put you here was due to an impaired driver from the Consort Group. I hoped, in some small way, to make up for our neglect."

*And to avoid a lawsuit.* She froze perfectly still. Thinking. Thinking. Was it actually possible? Could all she remembered of Matt, vampires, everything, be merely an injury and a drug-induced hallucination? *What other explanation could there be? Vampires?* She knew they were creatures of fiction, nothing more. Her mind whirled even as the sedative they gave her created a sense of indifferent detachment.

After she responded to his summons, Rick nodded to Georgia. "I'm afraid my visit has tired Cathy." He effortlessly lifted Cat and bore her to the bed. Georgia busily tucked the covers around her. "I'm going to excuse myself to let you rest. Later, they'll bring you something to eat."

The pull of the sedative became irresistible, and Cat succumbed to more induced sleep.

* * * *

Rick growled into the phone, his outrage barely contained. "It's not working," he snapped, "at least not completely. She remembers your name and our association. Clearly, the thralling and drugs have been only partially successful. It's just a matter of time before the whole damn thing unravels."

Rick's phone call was disturbing, to say the least. "I'm hoping we won't need much time. Just buy me a couple weeks. Can't you treat her as any other vampire witness? Denials and redirection might eventually extinguish her lingering memories."

"You don't have to lie right to her face. There are times I think you really *are* a monster for behaving this way."

"Yeah, me too."

Matt clicked off his cell, balanced unerringly on the slate parapet of the brownstone opposite Cat's window. The wind buffeted around him, howling its distress in a way strikingly similar to his own. Despite the swirling gusts, he was immovable in his determination to catch a glimpse of her. Longing for her kept him in place as the stars and moon moved above him, and minutes grew into hours. Still, he stood, watching her blurred image as she paced past the textured glass shielding the bottom half of her massive Queen Anne windows.

She'd undergone medication and thralling for only a couple of days, meaning that in reality, Cat was confined to bed for an abbreviated time. The row of stapled sutures in the back of her scalp were superficial and implied a serious procedure where there had been none. His knowledge that she was actually in excellent health, despite their deception, should have comforted Matt, but he found no peace in it.

Had this whole sham been in vain? He'd hoped to give her a fresh start. Instead, he led her to self-doubt. Time would tell if her obsession with finding him would fade from lack of confirmation, or whether they'd have to intervene again.

The gleam of Cat's ceiling light, flickering with the rotation of its slowly circling fan, was replaced by the softer glow of her bedside lamp. In the early hours, only the nightlight remained. Matt shrank back into the shadows reluctantly as the first rays of sun broke the dawn. The guilt he labored under was almost insufferable. Knowing he'd layered implied trauma over the emotional damage he'd already caused ate at him like acid.

* * * *

Rick flipped a switch and drew up the motorized shades protecting his penthouse suite from New York City sunshine. The light of day was unimpeded by anything surrounding the seventy-sixth floor of the Frank Gehry building. His New York home in the sky was ostentatious, yes, but he'd never shied away from a little glitz. The prestige of '*the tallest penthouse in Manhattan*' amused him. Those in the know were duly impressed he could absorb the six-figure monthly rent with a curt nod to his accountant.

Rick loved the spot for the nightscape that lay all of Manhattan, the East and Hudson rivers at his feet. He sighed in contentment as he gazed at the dying glow of the sun, dispersing itself into the Hudson. His favorite time of day, the magic hour, when the world was lit with gold, but with sunlight defuse enough to protect his vulnerable vampire hide.

The silk of his late summer robe whispered as he pulled it into place and secured it around his waist. He paused for a moment, considering the exact bouquet and finish he desired from his donor blood tonight. After making his choice, he reached across his desk for the intercom to order. As he moved, the sleeve of his robe nudged his computer mouse, and CNN popped up, showing the day's news.

Before his dismayed eyes, a news clip ran, showing a smoldering ruin where the Maynard Pharmaceuticals factory in Germany used to be. An online headline screamed *Industrial Terrorists Target Maynard Property*. In rapid succession, Rick watched with gritted teeth, and bared fangs as video of Maynard facilities in Germany, Colombia, India, Mexico, and Japan ran over the news report.

"A coordinated attack at noon Frankfurt time resulted in explosions at all Maynard Pharmaceutical plants, and the disappearance of Clementine "Cici" Maynard. The industrialist's wife was in Frankfurt to bestow awards at an Employee of the Year ceremony. A spokesman for Maynard Pharmaceuticals says Frankfurt police and Interpol are combing the area for clues…"

"Bloody hell!" Well, Rick guessed they'd been right about the Humanité. He cursed and grabbed his desk phone. "Get me Giles Paquet."

"Yes, sir," his assistant acknowledged, his tone surprised.

"Tell him my office in five minutes."

* * * *

Giles Paquet hadn't planned to end his day this way, but when Hiatt sent for you, it didn't matter that it was your anniversary. If Giles' wife wanted to continue her comfortable Manhattan lifestyle, she'd just have to understand. He skidded to a halt to collect himself outside Rick's home office, and then knocked respectfully.

"Come." The clipped response and swing of the automatic doors ushered him into Rick's presence.

Paquet swallowed down the unaccustomed nerves. "Sir?" he ventured with obvious concern. "Is there a problem?"

Rick gestured at the ninety-inch flat screen now broadcasting the story of the Maynard terrorist attack. "Why am I hearing about this from CNN?" he demanded. "Why wasn't my security team on top of it?"

"On top of…"

"This Maynard facility is a hole in the ground. What the hell is going on?"

"I…" Paquet cleared his throat. "I'm sorry, sir, I didn't realize your security extended to Maynard Pharmaceuticals." He turned a shocked gaze from the massive television to Rick.

"What?" Rick blew out a frustrated breath. "No…No, I'm sorry I was…abrupt…I…anytime there's a security breach of this magnitude it reminds me everyone is vulnerable."

Paquet guessed there was more to the story than Hiatt was telling him, but it did him no good to speculate. "Yes, sir." *What the hell else could he say?*

"Just double check everything, Giles," Rick instructed. "We don't want something like this happening to our own plants."

"Of course, sir." Paquet was nonplussed, but far too political to tell Rick he sounded like a paranoid crazy man.

"I want us on the highest level of alert until I tell you otherwise. That'll be all."

* * * *

Matt smelled charred flesh before the huge, ornately wrapped package rolled past the threshold of his suite. The concierge grimaced and offered a wan smile of thanks in exchange for the twenty-buck tip. Matt guessed it was poor recompense for such an offensive delivery. He eyed the package with dread, dismissing the attendant with a frown, and then hauling his delivery past the doorway in privacy.

He wheeled the shipping crate, large as a casket, to the bathroom's walk-in shower, anticipating oozing fluids at any moment. The top of the box lifted easily after the heavy poly-tape was cut. Matt wished it otherwise but suspected his discovery wouldn't be a pleasant one. He could never have prepared himself for what he saw.

Under a plushly upholstered satin casket blanket lay a woman he immediately recognized despite the mutilation. She was a vampire now, but when they last met, she'd been mortal and Elliot Maynard's wife.

She was staked through the heart, her mouth paralyzed in a scream of agony, which was understandable, considering the torture she'd endured. Matt removed the stake that tormented her, and it released its hold on her body with a sickening, sucking hiss. An infinitesimal amount of blood spattered from the finely polished spike, and hit his hand, causing immediate blistering. *Silver!* Somehow, her blood was permeated with it. Torture indeed, for any vampire. Matt hurried to the sink and attacked the few drops of blood with strong soap and heavy scrubbing before it could do more damage. He swallowed back dizziness and nausea, equal parts shock and silver sensitivity.

Satisfied he'd removed all the silver he could, he returned to his unfortunate guest and carefully drew back more of the casket blanket shielding her. Huge patches of skin on her nude body had all but melted away, revealing eroded tendons, muscles and bone like some sort of macabre anatomy model. This result might have been caused by the infused silver, but Matt guessed she'd been paralyzed, and then set out in the sun to burn before being sent to him. *In the name of God, why?*

The beeping of an iPhone secured to the side of the crate promised more answers. Matt clicked it on, and a man he instantly recognized as Papa Moreau appeared on the digital screen.

"I see you have received my package," Moreau began with a wicked smile, his accent heavy with the Haitian sing-song rhythm.

"You sick bastard!" Matt's eyes closed tight, then reopened slowly, "Why?"

"I felt I must impress upon you the seriousness of my objections to Humanité," Moreau intoned, steepling his fingertips. "Mortals who associate with the vampires creating it may find themselves in jeopardy."

"Maynard and his wife knew nothing about the Vampire Nation, they were innocents."

"Collateral damage." Moreau's hands rose in mock surrender, "Used to illustrate my point. You will cease your search for Humanité and the formula that creates it. To take away further temptation, you will terminate your association with your mortal lover, Miss Temple. If you do not, she will find herself in the same unfortunate position as the former mortal before you. Am I clear, Mr. Brenner?"

"Crystal, and if you've been monitoring us, you know my association with Catherine Temple is already over. I've gone to a lot of trouble to erase myself from her life."

"What I know," Moreau continued, "is you are not interacting with her. Never the less, you continue pining after her, watching her." He smiled a sinister smile. "You will not do so again unless you want…" He gestured toward the body in the crate. "It is time for you to move on."

"I understand," Matt bit out in impotent fury. "I'll leave New York today. No more contact of any kind. You have my word."

"Very well." Moreau's shoulders relaxed slightly. "On a more pleasant note, Mr. Brenner, let us discuss my offspring, Veronique. She is headstrong, as I am sure you know. She has always been so." He sipped blood from a Baccarat brandy snifter as he spoke. "Still, she is my delight, and I want her to be happy. You, she tells me, would make her happy."

Matt shuttered his appalled response and kept his features impassive as Moreau studied him through the screen and found him wanting.

"I have ceased to reason a woman's heart." He grinned demonically. "Many men find Veronique's spirit, and shall we say *joie de vivre*, appealing. She comes from a well-established and wealthy family, pillars as you would say, of the vampire community. You could do worse than to ally yourself with us. She needs a strong man to tame her. I would not object to you taking on that challenge."

Matt's response was cagey. He wanted no retaliatory punch to land back on Cat. "Your offer is tempting." He tried to smile pleasantly. "There's a great deal of unfortunate history between Veronique and me. I don't know if it can be overcome."

Moreau sipped from the snifter, and his smile wasn't so conciliatory. "You need to honor your lineage. Return to your sire and your blood family. I would appreciate your effort to try." It wasn't a request.

Matt stood his ground to the extent he could. "For now, let me say I get your message. I'll no longer search for Humanité, and my relationship with Catherine Temple is dead and buried." He steeled himself not to beg for Cat's life and betray his depth of feeling for her. Instead, he insisted, "No other innocent needs to become a living example of your demands." He spread his hands in supplication. "What else can I do to reassure you?"

"Nothing," Moreau drew out the word. "We will, of course, have you under surveillance." He leaned forward to cut off the call. "Consider the benefits of my offer." And then, almost as an afterthought, "If you are a kind man, as they say, you are, you will cut off the woman's head." The screen went blank.

For one horrified moment, Matt thought Moreau had instructed him to kill Cat, but as the moans of the pathetic creature in the crate permeated his awareness, he realized Papa suggested a mercy killing. Matt was a kind man, and so he did the only thing he could under the circumstances. He collected his katana sword, paramount for vampire self-protection, and with a murmured, "Forgive me," severed Cici's head and ended her pain. *Family? I don't think so. Papa Moreau's blood cannot possibly flow through my veins.*

Matt drew in deep breaths in an effort to calm himself as he sat on the edge of the soaking tub, dialing his secure burner phone. He waited for the New York City responders to answer.

"Your emergency, please?" the responder's voice was flat, impersonal.

"This is Matt Brenner at the Ritz-Carlton, the Consort suite, 1055." He listened to the clicks of computer keys as the responder confirmed the information. "Let me speak with your supervisor."

The young man's annoyance radiated over the phone. "I'm sure I can handle any—"

"Now," Matt's Dom voice erupted.

"Transferring."

"Matt?" Giles Paquet inquired after a pause and a series of transfer clicks. "Hiatt is crawling up my ass, and now you? What fresh hell is going on?"

As the Vice President of the east coast division of the responders, Giles was responsible for the safety and secrecy of every vampire in the area. He was doing Matt and Rick a huge favor by overseeing Consort Group at this critical time. Matt didn't especially want to piss off the guy who was helping them.

"I have two separate, but equally critical matters, Giles," Matt enjoined solemnly. "Thank you for handling things personally."

"What do you need?"

"First, you have a responder team protecting Catherine Temple?"

"Yes," Giles nodded. "We assisted Mr. Hiatt with medicating and thralling this young woman. She's coming along quite well. We should be leaving her on her own in the next thirty-six to forty-eight hours."

"You can't do that, you not only need to find a reason to stay with her another week at least, but you also need to assign a full security detail to watch her around the clock."

"There's reason to think she's in danger?"

"Your second task is the graphic illustration of the danger she's in," Matt confirmed. "You'll need to accompany your most skilled forensic cleaners to my suite at the Ritz-Carlton. I have a dangerous removal. The remains are badly contaminated."

"I'm sure they can handle that—"

"The body is saturated with silver," Matt warned, "I had to decapitate her to end her misery, but that's not all, Giles. This whole situation is a dumpster fire. Twenty-four hours ago, this woman was the mortal wife of a billionaire businessman named Elliot Maynard."

"Maynard?" Giles' concern was obvious in his voice.

"You've heard of him?" Matt asked, surprised. "There is a threat to do to Catherine what was done to Cici Maynard. An extremely powerful vamp is willing to compromise the anonymity of the entire vampire family to make his point."

"I see," Giles reflected on Matt's predicament. "This is grave."

"Yes, do what you have to do. Manufacture a threat Cat will believe, whatever, to ensure her cooperation with heightened security."

"I'll see to it. What about you?"

"I'm headed to the Consort Group offices now. Hiatt or I will be in contact when we have a firm plan."

Matt crumpled the burner phone in one frustrated fist before leaving his suite. It was a security measure to ensure the call could never be traced. He'd pick up a new one before the evening was done.

Giles Paquet was a trusted consultant. He'd handled Rick's east coast security for decades. Still, with the kind of money and power Moreau wielded, betrayal was always a possibility. Matt prayed he had a firm enough friendship with the stalwart Frenchman to protect Cat.

Matt's personal cell rang before he was halfway down the hall toward the elevator.

"Judas priest, Matt!" Rick came through the phone as every inch the business mogul. "What do you know about this Maynard thing?"

"How did you know? I'm on my way to the Group offices to brief you."

"About the bombing? I already—"

"What bombing?" Matt kept his information circumspect to thwart any listeners on his line. "A package involving Cici Maynard was just delivered to my room, compliments of Papa Moreau. It was a killer."

"Get your ass over here—now. The car's on its way to you. Call me when you're en route."

* * * *

Matt realized Rick's level of agitation was off the scale when the elder vamp met him on the plaza, pacing angrily outside the magnificent building's main entrance. Thrusting the video recording of his conversation with Moreau into Rick's hands would only add fire to the already banked flames, but Matt couldn't resist the drama of the statement. "We need privacy."

Rick watched Maynard's wife moaning in the coffin and shuddered. "I have two donors currently hitting the Glenlivet, ready to offer a little whiskey relief along with blood. I don't know about you, but I need that right now." Matt nodded.

Finally without onlookers and having had a little time to process the day's events, Matt turned to his friend, decision and finality suffusing his tone. "I'm going to find that bastard and eliminate him and the entire Moreau family, starting with Papa and working all the way back to Veronique."

Rick considered him for a long moment. "I don't think you'd get within a mile of Moreau. His protection is too good. No matter how covert your efforts, they'd spot you before you ever got near him. No, we only have one play here."

Matt shot him a raised brow query.

"I'll do it," Rick decided. "With a team, of course, but it has to be me. You have to be the diversion."

"What kind of diversion?"

"The loudest most flamboyant you can muster. Preferably involving Veronique."

"I'm seeing this," Matt agreed with a considering nod. "I make a splashy play for the princess while the dark knight sneaks up on the castle."

"Exactly," Rick agreed. "With some luck, he won't see me coming."

* * * *

Cat squirmed under him. The touch of his hands branded her with fire as he inched up from her knees to her thighs, his panting warm breaths searing against her sensitive skin. He parted her urgently, his tongue sweeping ahead of his long fingers to tease her saturated folds, and still, she couldn't move, immobilized by unseen hands holding her arms and ankles spread-eagled on the ridiculously huge bed.

Cat moaned in ecstasy, arched up to that pleasuring mouth, savoring the passion building within her. His tongue rimmed her opening, teeth, and lips gently nibbled her throbbing clit. She teetered on the edge of orgasm. With the gasp of her next breath, she found herself beside her bed, feet chilled by the wooden floorboards, adrenalin surging as she fought to reorient herself.

Her attention was immediately drawn to the dark figure peering in her bedroom window from the fire escape. Stupidly, she'd later admit, she ran toward the window to get a better look at the intruder. In the dark of night, with only a partial street light and her dim Tiffany-style nightlight to illuminate his ebony face, there wasn't much to see. Her reflexive scream of surprise alerted Georgia and sent her Peeping Tom thundering down the fire escape as the nurse threw open her bedroom door.

That started the onslaught of events, as Cat would come to think of it, but the intruder threat wasn't what captivated her attention. She was much more interested in the dream. How, she thought, could she dream of oral sex when prior to this moment, she had only been vaguely aware it existed? How could she have experienced bondage? How could she dream of luxuriating in her lover's caress, her body readying itself for orgasm, when she was a virgin? Wasn't she?

She had never known a man's touch beyond a few kisses and less than passionate groping, right? Right? Unless, as she knew in her heart, felt in her body, the ephemeral memories she glimpsed were real, and not drug-induced hallucinations as her caregivers claimed.

Overwhelmed by frustration and frantic to find the man who haunted her dreams, Cat racked her brain for a way to verify her sexual experience. What could prove that? A medical exam? Would that identify her as a woman experienced with sex? When she broached the idea with Georgia, her nurse was surprised, maybe a little annoyed, and less than encouraging.

"I think we should focus on what's really important tonight, Cathy," she lectured firmly. "A man tried to break into your home. Do you see how off-center your thinking is, that you want to focus on a dream instead?"

Cat crossed her arms over her chest in annoyance of her own and glared. "I have an alarm system. He may have been looking, but the chances of him actually getting into the house are remote."

"Just the fact that he was looking—"

"Georgia!" Cat's voice held a hard edge. "The police and security firm will take care of the Peeping Tom. I'm telling you, I'm dreaming about things I shouldn't even know, and always about the same man…Matt. I want a gynecological exam. Maybe that will give me some answers."

A glimmer of fear shone in Georgia's amber eyes for a fraction of a second before she looked away, her calm, competent persona back in place. "I understand your interest in this mystery, Cathy," Georgia soothed. "And, yes, an internal exam can verify that a woman's hymen has been ruptured, but nowadays, that's not evidence of lost virginity. Many women are born without a hymen, and so many girls participate in vigorous sports, they break theirs in completely non-sexual ways and never know it. We're not living in the Dark Ages, you know."

"Yes, I suppose so," Cat grumbled in agreement. "It just felt so real, and how else would I know all that?"

Georgia shrugged. "The subconscious mind is powerful. If you've read a steamy novel, or seen a racy movie, well, the mind extrapolates…"

"Oh." Cat conceded reluctantly. "Yeah, that's true. You could be right. Or, at least, there's no concrete proof that you're not."

"Exactly, now I've checked the window. It's secure. Would you like me to stay with you for the rest of the night?"

"No." Cat settled herself back under her covers, shivering slightly, more from the effects of the dream than the early morning chill. She just wanted to be alone to think. "I'll be fine. Sorry, I disturbed you."

"Don't be silly. I'm leaving your door open from now on. I'll be in the living room until morning."

Cat closed her eyes, but sleep eluded her. She could almost see him—almost, but not quite. Tall, dark. She couldn't see his eyes, but an inner knowledge told her they were beautiful and arresting. Matt. His name was Matt, and he was a vampire. Well, that was where the story broke down, wasn't it? A vampire? *Honestly, Catherine, what are you thinking? There's no such thing. Maybe he's a vampire who rides a unicorn and lives in Oz!*

She had actually gone so far as to look vampires up on the Internet, earning Rick's amused teasing and her own embarrassment. All she'd found there were fictional accounts of sparkly beings or fanged monsters with animalistic claws. Neither account fit with the Matt she knew -- or thought she knew.

Cat sighed. Everyone here had such valid explanations for her fancifulness and dreams. Surely, their explanations were substance and her's were shadow? So, why was that realization so devastating?

Most of her waking hours were spent longing for the love of a phantom, haunted by memories of a Prince Charming no more real than the fairy tale character. Tears of mourning choked Cat's throat and flooded her eyes. She could almost wish the dreams would stop, she suffered so afterward, but she didn't think she'd be able to bear it if they actually did and she was forced to live without her mystery man.

* * * *

Cat sat in the human resources office of Consort Publishing the following morning, wide-eyed and nearly speechless as Rick, Daphne Wise, the human resources director, and Giles Paquet, from security, outlined the threat against her. One more complication to make her life totally outrageous. Giles passed her five-by-eight, black and white glossies of sinister-looking men watching her building.

Cat was disconcerted. "What makes you think this threat is against me? Other people live in my building. At least ten others. Maybe these men are watching one of them?" She shuffled through the glossy prints again.

"Don't you think the man on your fire escape last night is enough proof?" Rick lectured tolerantly. "Georgia spotted these other lurkers and thought they might be a threat and reported them to Mr. Paquet."

"It turns out she was right to be concerned," Giles picked up. "This is a credible threat, Ms. Temple."

"You're crazy. Why in the world would anyone want to hurt me? I'm nobody," Cat shook her head, arms crossed over her chest.

Cat caught the look Rick, and Giles exchanged with irritation. What was going on here?

"We believe it's related to the auto accident," Giles continued unblinking.

"What?" She turned her bewildered gaze to Rick.

"The accident left you in a coma, but it killed your driver and a passenger in the other car. I told you before the Consort Group driver was impaired."

Cat nodded.

"As it turns out, the driver of the other car was also at fault, and he's a powerful mob boss. The Feds would love to nail him for his passenger's death. They haven't been able to put him away on any other charges. This would do it."

"Well, okay," Cat frowned, "but I don't even remember the accident. Why would they target me?"

Rick smiled. "We know that, but the Marino crime family doesn't. Until we can convince them you're unable to aid in Marino's prosecution, you'll need protection." He took her hand in appeal, "Cathy, will you trust us to know what's best for you in this situation?"

"Jeez, Rick, I just got out from under the thumb of a squad of nurses!" She turned to face Giles. "Now, I need bodyguards following me around? What do the police say about all this?"

Giles sat back in his chair. "My men will do their best to give you as much privacy and freedom as possible, Miss Temple. And the police, well, under the circumstances, the Marinos may be more accepting of our point of view if we handle this privately. The police will only make them more paranoid."

"Please, trust us," Rick encouraged again, and Cat fancied his charming smile had probably gotten him his way with women since he was in the cradle.

"I believe Mr. Hiatt and Mr. Paquet have only your best interests at heart, Cathy," Ms. Wise added. "You'll be safe when you're here at the Consort offices, but why not let the security team make sure you're safe in your off hours? You wouldn't want someone else injured because they were caught in the crossfire, would you?"

That did the trick. "No. Of course not," Cat turned beseechingly to Rick. "May I still, you know, walk around the Village and grocery shop and…" Her eyes filled with tears. "I need to be able to walk and…and sightsee, and…" She swallowed hard. "It helps me cope, Rick. I need to keep busy!"

Rick nodded, looking sympathetic, but adamant. "Shop, go out to lunch, see friends, visit museums, go see a show. Just know when you do, two bodyguards will be with you. Who knows? Maybe you'll all become friends?" Cat glanced at him with a look leaving no doubt about that remote possibility. "I'm just saying you're a friendly girl, Cathy. This doesn't have to be torture."

* * * *

Cat prowled restlessly through what, by New York City standards, was her spacious two-bedroom apartment which included a private park ringed on all sides by the surrounding brownstones. It was a shame, given the unprecedented amount of space and courtyard privileges she enjoyed, she should feel trapped. She peeked out the living room windows fronting the street.

There was her protector, keeping watch on her building from across the street. His partner was stationed in the courtyard bordering the park, unobtrusively monitoring the back.

She'd planned to meet with Father Mayfield that evening at the Catholic Center up the street, but her bodyguards discouraged it, so she'd finally canceled. And really, she was going to confess to a priest that she'd had a torrid affair with a vampire nobody else remembered? Yeah, that was sure to get her locked up in the loony bin. *Even if he believed her and who would?* He would tell her what priests always told people—pray, have faith. *Hadn't she already done that?* She'd prayed and cried and begged for God's help until she was exhausted. All that greeted her efforts was a resounding silence.

With a forlorn sigh, Cat wandered into the kitchen to check her soufflé. She flipped on the oven light—it was almost ready—and then stared in awestruck fascination. A soufflé. She, Cat Temple, made a soufflé. Not only that, she didn't even think about it, didn't consult a cookbook. She was so preoccupied with her thoughts of the elusive Matt she automatically whipped up an elaborate dish. There was only one problem—she'd never cooked one in her life. At least not that she remembered. So, she'd emerged from a coma with the sudden ability to cook?

The confection fell into something resembling a quiche when she snatched it prematurely from the oven, but Cat didn't care. She stared at it for awed seconds before breaking into sobs of frustration.

# 18

To ensure the most concrete evidence of their time together was permanently erased, Matt inspected the remodel of the Malibu beach house. Walls were torn down and rearranged. The kitchen redesign included the latest upscale appliances and a new island. The master bedroom was enlarged, eliminating the previous third bedroom/playroom. With the writing of a single check, and the admonition that time was of the essence and money was no object, the beach house went from California contemporary to Mediterranean modern within a month.

Matt waited for Rick's assistant to put his call through on video conference. Rick's face appeared on Matt's phone. "It took you long enough. How does it look? Will we make our money back?"

"And then some," Matt moved the phone's live feed around the living room. "It's a showcase. They'll be loading the new furniture in tomorrow, and your winter renters will follow next week, for twice what you charged before."

"Good. At least something positive has come out of this mess."

"How…" Matt swallowed hard. "How's Cat? No repercussions after Papa Moreau's late-night visitor?"

"No. Now that the 'nurses' are gone, Cat has a security team, but otherwise, she's on her own. She goes to work, shops, goes to church, lives. Moreau probably believes whatever threat she posed is over."

"Hmm. Well, I wouldn't trust that yet. Keep the team on her. So, how about friends or fun or dates? Is she lonely?"

"That's a hell of a question coming from you. You could be with her, you know, keeping her entertained and happy. We could all be in Los Angeles, for that matter, instead of this claustrophobic skyscraper hell."

"Rick." Matt heaved a sonorous sigh. "I'm no good for her. In fact, I think you should back away from her, too."

"Giving me orders now, are you?" Rick's expression went dark. "Guess again, Matt. This girl has lost everything. If you think I'm going to leave her without her only friend—"

"Cut the crap, old man!" Matt interrupted irritably. "She went to school there for a semester. I'm sure she formed friendships during that time." He leaned against the picture window that overlooked the Pacific, surveying the ocean with irritable, unseeing eyes. "She has that childhood friend in Brooklyn, right? There's no reason for her to be lonely. The longer you hang around, the more opportunity for memories to resurface. Come back to Los Angeles or check out Haiti, or hell, go to the moon, I don't care. Just leave her alone."

"Listen, fuckwit, you worry about your own activities, let me worry about mine. I'm sending you an email picture and a report from Paquet. I've had the responders working their little keyboards to the bone to find a connection between Maynard and…"

Matt opened the email, and his breath hitched as he studied the picture. "This looks like Veronique."

"Not just looks like. It is," Rick confirmed. "Giles got a bead on her. It seems our Ronnie's been spending time at Lust for Life, the vamp resort in Barranquilla, Colombia. Locale sound familiar?"

"Colombia, as in where Maynard Pharmaceuticals had a plant?"

"Yes, it was bombed, but oddly, the bomb was placed in an innocuous location. That plant is still running. It could be a coincidence, of course." Rick's tone was suspicious.

"Neither of us believes in coincidence. You think Veronique's in bed with Maynard?"

Rick shook his head uncertainly. "I don't get the sense Maynard knows anything about vamps or Humanité. My guess is his plant is simply convenient. The locals working there have a little action going on the side, but that's strictly speculation at this point. We need to further explore the connection."

Matt skimmed the info on the Lust for Life Resort. "I don't get the big draw. Why would vamps want to hang out at a resort in that much heat and sun?"

"One big reason—Alejandro Dias, the major player in the Cali drug cartel, is the owner of Lust for Life. He keeps a huge stable of donors he likes to dope up on coke or meth or opium and feed to his guests. Big high."

"Ah, I get it. A new kind of opium den? Vamp style?"

"Yeah, exactly."

"Could be unrelated to Humanité or Maynard, but Veronique's no dummy. Hooking up with a cartel for distribution would be great for business, wouldn't it?"

"That was my thought. For a while, Humanité was cutting into Dias' business in a big way. He'd want a piece of that action, and isn't it ironic that Veronique is the creator? If the two joined forces…"

Matt was thoughtful. "Well, if it cut into Dias' profits, wouldn't it also cut into Papa's? Is that the real reason he's so opposed to the production of Humanité?"

Rick winced, "The question now becomes, is Veronique wining and dining this guy for Papa or herself?"

"When have you ever known Ronnie to do something for anyone but herself? I'd bet money ole Alejandro has close dealings with Papa, probably running drugs through Papa's coffee exports. Coffee's a perfect way to disguise product from sniffer dogs."

"Neither Dias nor Papa will want to give that up. It's too profitable," Rick mused. "And I'm sure Ronnie wouldn't want to piss off Dias, either. She probably figures she'll be on Papa's blacklist, but she can wheedle her way around him. Daddy's little girl and all that."

"What else do you know about Dias?"

"He's dangerous, ancient, originally from Spain. We're still looking into him."

"I'll see what else I can find on the VampNet."

"It'll be interesting reading. Anyway, I see a trip to Colombia in your immediate future."

"I was thinking the same thing."

Rick stretched his muscles to ease their tension. "Now would be a good time to meet up and make nice with Ronnie and get a look at Maynard's plant.

I'll arrange a tour. A bonus would be diverting Papa's attention to something other than his personal security. That would help me out."

"And what will you be doing? Having dinner with Cat?"

"As a matter of fact, I'll be in Haiti. Someone has to eliminate Papa's threat to the Vampire Nation. Since a direct appeal to the responders would be tied up in politics and red tape for months, I guess I'll have to take action and beg forgiveness after."

"I'll be done erasing my footprints here tonight. Jonesy can book me on the next flight to Colombia."

"Have a great trip," Rick encouraged.

"Love the sun and sand." Matt snorted. "Listen, Rick, seriously, I want you to back away from Cat. Let's give her some space to make her own way."

"Dear boy, you may have chosen to abandon this beautiful woman 'for her own good,' but I have no such intentions. You want to give her up? Fine. There are plenty of willing suitors ready to take your place, me among them."

"Don't be an ass," Matt warned.

"Oh no, you don't get to drop your mess into my lap, and then dictate how I handle it. You want her, come and get her. I won't challenge you. You don't want her, you don't get to make demands on the rest of us."

"She needs a good normal life without vamps."

"Oh, what? We're the worst beings in the world, not fit to associate with mortals? You really hate yourself that much? Look, whatever, as far as I'm concerned, if you've tossed her back, the rest of us can bait our hooks with the tastiest worms in the can."

"That's rich coming from you. I thought you only wanted submissives."

"What makes you think she's not a submissive?" Rick countered.

"Rick, I swear to God, if you hurt her…"

"I'm not the one hurting her, Matt. You need to look in a mirror to accuse that man. Don't worry too much. I'm dropping by her office today to say goodbye before I leave for Haiti. Is that far enough away for you?

Matt frowned. "This is a side of you I haven't seen before. I don't think I like it all that much."

"Right back at 'cha, buddy." The videophone went dead.

* * * *

Cat drew her running jacket closer about her as the October chill crept in with the setting sun. She should think about getting some pumpkins set out

196

for the trick or treaters, she mused, wondering if kids in New York City actually did the trick or treat thing? She could dimly remember the ritual from when her grandmother was alive. Once she'd gone to boarding school, though, Halloween was just another day.

The early evening still brought out the wildlife, Cat thought with amusement as birds, who'd deserted the place in the warmth of the day, pecked about the courtyard, drinking from the flowing fountain and vying with militant squirrels for the scraps she'd scattered. The people in the neighboring brownstone had a half-grown ginger kitten they allowed out at night. She shook her head at the stupidity of expecting a kitten to stay safe in Manhattan, even if he did have a park to roam instead of the street. The kitten stretched luxuriously in his fading sunbeam, and then wound his way over to her for some attention.

"You wanna come sit with me, little guy?" she questioned his bright upturned ginger and white face. The kitten let out a terse *bruupp* and leapt onto her warm lap, circling and kneading into her thighs, until he was satisfied with just the right spot. "I wish I had some treats for you," she murmured, scratching behind his ears as he purred.

Unbidden, a scene leapt into her mind—walking with Matt along a stretch of beach. Laddie, a little Sheltie, he used to carry treats for him. *Hi... He's not bothering us.*

Everyone in New York had been kind, more than helpful. Rick wouldn't lie to her, would he? And yet, Cat couldn't shake the conviction everyone was lying. How could her memories of Matt be hallucinations or dreams? How was that possible? All right, they were disjointed memories, but she felt them, tasted them, saw them in her mind's eye, and they were evoked by everything from scents to music to stray scraps of conversation. Her dreams of him were vivid, and rather than diminishing with time, they were growing stronger, leaving her without rest at night and exhausted during the day. The entire issue was coming to a head soon, she knew it, could feel it, and now...

She had to get back to Los Angeles. Somewhere, there was a beach with a Sheltie named Laddie. Her enthusiasm flagged a little when she realized there were probably dozens of beaches with Shelties name Laddie, but she had to go back. She had to try. Cat wouldn't stop until she either found proof of her time with Matt or proved to her own satisfaction he was a figment of her imagination.

The kitten's purring grew softer and softer as he settled against her to sleep. Cat caressed him absently as she plotted.

* * * *

Cat thought the unseasonably cool weather the next morning worked out great! She layered clothes enough to have an outfit and a spare when she got to Los Angeles. Blessing her oversized Dooney and Bourke shopper, she crammed it full of needed underwear, cosmetics and an extra pair of shoes. It was the bag she always carried so her bodyguards wouldn't look twice at it.

They needed to be history, anyway. She spoke with Giles and tried to politely decline their escort, but he'd countered that Rick was still out of town, and until he returned, their orders were to stay with her. No one had lurked around the brownstone for weeks. It was time for her to become an independent woman again, and she meant it to happen today.

The Coffee, Tea and Tarot Bakery was one of Cat's favorite spots for a breakfast snack, so it didn't surprise her guards when she swung in there on her way to work. With rolled eyes, they nonetheless waited patiently for her as she purchased her abbreviated breakfast of a cronut, coffee light, and clairvoyant advice.

When she had time to spare, Cat often sat with the Romani woman, who had lent her heritage and Tarot-reading talents to the bakery's name. Lyuba, fifty-something with kohl-outlined black eyes and dark hair down to her waist, looked unfailingly exotic in her flowing skirts and gold embroidered headscarves. She'd been a welcome confidant in a world where every other person Cat knew was associated with Rick Hiatt in some way. It was great to talk with someone outside his influence, and though she felt like an absolute traitor for thinking it, she was glad to escape his long reach.

Lyuba's limpid-eyed gaze searched Cat's as it always did, delving straight into her soul. "You have come to a decision, no?"

"I have come to a decision, yes, I've been thinking a lot about what you said, that I'd had an old life, and now I'm moving forward into a new one?"

"This is so." The woman nodded wisely and withdrew from her pocket a deck of Tarot cards wrapped in satin. She shuffled the cards idly as she spoke. "Pick a card, *draga mea*, let's read what your guides see for you today."

Cat centered herself blew out a soft breath and engaged in the harmless ritual. She was startled to see the card she withdrew. Death, a skeleton riding a white horse, looked back at her.

"Don't be alarmed." Lyuba smiled. "Death doesn't mean physical death—usually. It means transformation, rebirth, change."

"Ah." Cat nodded. "I guess that fits."

"It does, indeed. There's more. The card is reversed. You see here?" Lyuba swept her hand over the ancient divination tool. "Reversal of the card means though you're on the verge of major change, you're resisting. Hanging on to the past will only cause you more pain. You must resolve the issues from your past which are tying you down. Only then can you soar."

"As it turns out, I'm about to do just that, Lyuba, if you'll help me? You see those men out there?" Cat nodded discretely to her bodyguards. "They're following me, intruding on my privacy, and they won't leave! Will you help me get away?"

"Of course, *draga*," Lyuba agreed immediately. "You must go into the back as if you're visiting the ladies' room, no? There are steps leading down to the cellar where our flour is poured. In there, another set of stairs leads to the back alley. Take it to Fifth Avenue and be on your way. I'll delay your friends."

Cat caught Lyuba's hand and squeezed it with gratitude and affection. "I owe you!" She grabbed her over-stuffed purse and then headed for the stairs.

Fifteen minutes later, Cat was on her way to Philadelphia on a Penn Station train. From there she'd catch a flight to Los Angeles.

* * * *

Lyuba turned expectantly to the two massive bodyguards hulking over her. It'd taken them five minutes longer than she'd thought it would to come looking for Cat.

"Where is she?" the first demanded.

"Who?"

"The girl you were talking to a few minutes ago. Where is she?"

Lyuba shrugged indifferently, and with a secret smile, turned back to stocking her pastry display. The second guard stalked down the hall to the ladies' room and pounded on the door. She heard his heavy footsteps descending the stairs to the basement.

"Goddammit!" His bellow exploded from below her.

Lyuba raised a brow at the guard before her. "Do you want a pastry or a Tarot reading?" she inquired pleasantly.

"No, thanks."

"In that case, I am afraid you'll have to leave. There is no loitering posted here." She pointed at the sign. "It is a rule."

"She's in the wind," his partner shouted into a cell phone as he marched back up the hallway. "Who the dafuq knows? Wherever she's going, she doesn't want to be found."

# 19

As he walked down the aisle to his first-class seat, Matt twisted his neck, trying in vain to release pent-up tension. He automatically filtered out the smell of stale air recirculating through the cabin and the wail of a baby in the economy seats. He hated the crush of humanity on a commercial flight, but sadly, Rick had the company jet.

It chafed to know Rick was fighting their battle with Moreau. Matt should be the one to end his reign of terror. He should be the one getting vengeance for Cat. Still, what the hell did it matter? Dead was dead. The important thing was Moreau would no longer be a threat to them. If the bastard hadn't played God with all their lives, he, Cat and Rick could have moved on with a little grace instead of the absolute cluster fuck it became.

One thing Matt could say for a long flight, first class gave a guy plenty of time for research. He studied every resource on Alejandro Dias, the Cali Cartel and the Lust for Life Resort, including the VampNet. He had a tour arranged at Maynard's plant the day after his arrival, but with luck, he'd be able to do a little reconnoitering before heading inside under his own identity.

Though Dias was considered a bad guy in the mortal world, vamps were much more sanguine about his activities. Mortal drugs had no adverse effects on vampires, aside from a nice party high delivered by donors, so they didn't care about human addiction, or the deaths resulting from illegal activity. It was a mortal problem. The advent of Humanité changed all that. Several hundred undead became dependent on Veronique's drug, which would be of keen interest to men like Dias, who already thrived on exploiting weakness.

No wonder the drug lord was sniffing around Veronique. So, what was her part in it?

Was she looking to make a deal with Dias behind Papa's back? Knowing Ronnie, that seemed likely. If it was true, Matt expected to see Humanité back on the market in short order.

He withdrew the small vial he still carried in his breast pocket, the one that had contained his last dose of Humanité. It'd taken him to heaven and hell. It had also allowed him a semblance of a human life with Cat, and though she'd been lost to him for weeks, he couldn't escape the longing for what had been.

Knowing it was purely symbolic, Matt opened the vial and peered into the emptiness. As empty as their hopes, as stark as the life he lived without her. For all his feigned enthusiasm for Cat's "new life," the truth was, he missed her like he'd miss a severed limb. Though he lived an unnaturally long time without her, he hadn't known joy until he met her, and now, he felt as desolate as nuclear winter with an absent sun.

Matt acknowledged again what he'd known from the moment their paths crossed. A relationship with him was the worst possible choice for Cat. Even if he were able to score a human lifetime's worth of Humanité, they'd never be able to have children. It was possible that though he appeared human, he wouldn't age, and she'd be left to deal with the insecurity of aging in front of a man who never left his twenties. It made no difference to him, he was in love with her, no matter the age, but how would she feel about that? Would she, in desperation, ask to be turned? That would not only rob her of her mortal life but potentially her eternal one as well. He wouldn't allow himself to be the instrument of her damnation.

Abruptly, he wished for the certainty of a priest, the certainty of someone who believed he knew the answers to all the eternal questions. It was something he and Cat would have to work through together if they were given a chance if Veronique resumed the manufacture of Humanité.

Despite all the risks and pitfalls, it was sure as hell worth buddying up to Ronnie to find out. There was only one way he knew to get Veronique's attention. It was too shameful to contemplate and too effective to ignore. He was going to have to rock out with his cock out and hope Dias didn't mind sharing. Damn it all, but they were all playing a dangerous game.

* * * *

Rick held a lightly fragranced Irish linen handkerchief up to his nose and mouth as he exited the airport at Port-au-Prince, Haiti. *Bejesus*, he hadn't been in this hell hole since he'd dealt with some French pirates in the 1730s, but as far as he could tell, nothing much improved. Cars and trucks replaced horses and wagons, the streets were paved after a fashion, but the people still lived in an unacceptable level of squalor. This part of the city had been further compromised by the tragedy of the 2010 earthquake, from which most of Haiti still had not recovered. If landowners like Moreau and his ilk had their way, the rich would continue to get richer, and the poor would starve.

He cursed Georgia when a neon green pickup truck pulled before him at the curb, and a jovial black man announced himself to be, "Wester, your driver and tour guide." Not that Georgia hadn't warned him about the odd taxis.

Rick sighed and warily eyed the smoking truck. "Will that thing make it to the hotel?"

*"Oui, monsieur,"* Wester replied with a crooked, toothy grin. "She'll take you anywhere you wish to go."

"Uh-huh. I'm meeting some landowners there, Wester," Rick told him with slightly more optimism as he climbed onto the dust-covered front seat. He watched with horror as his Hermes luggage was thrown into the truck bed as if it were bales of hay.

*"Très bien, monsieur,"* Wester nodded. You may count on my discretion in this matter."

"Ordinarily, I'd welcome discretion." Rick smiled. "Today, I have reasons for wanting news spread that I'm here and about to become the largest coffee grower in the country. Do you have family and friends who gossip?" He pulled several hundred from his wallet and fanned them before the astonished man.

*"Oui,* of course, *monsieur,"* Wester agreed and then hesitated. "You realize you are inviting trouble? Toughs and thugs hired by your competition will come after you if you announce yourself so publicly. And you," his smiling eyes were sorrowful, "do not look like a fighter."

Rick gave a self-deprecating laugh. "I might surprise you, and I'll risk it. You just spread the word."

"As you wish, *monsieur.*"

* * * *

Cat was unexpectedly annoyed by the Los Angeles heat. It was October and cool, verging on cold at night in New York, but it was downright hot in Los Angeles. Even the layered clothing she'd brought from the east was too much, and she stripped down to a cami and slacks as she waited for the agent to bring her rental car around. She'd lived in Los Angeles the greater part of four years, and yet the town felt foreign, pixilated, as though she could prick her finger on this version of reality.

Not knowing where else to start, Cat drove to the familiar, and then pulled up outside the apartment building she'd called home for so long. It looked startlingly faded and distorted compared to the structure she remembered. It had only been a handful of weeks since she'd seen it. How could it have changed so alarmingly, or was it she who had changed?

*Did loving the mysterious Matt transform her that much? Where was he? How could he love her and leave her in such hell? Were they just afraid to tell her he was dead? Do vampires die? And the ultimate question, was he really a vampire?*

Cat wanted to scream with frustration. The elusive answers dogged her every unguarded moment of her life. If she didn't find some concrete evidence one way or the other within the next few days, she intended to check herself into the nearest psychiatric hospital and beg for drugs.

It wasn't a long wait at the building's security-barred entrance before an older male resident let her follow along behind him. He didn't look familiar, but she supposed she didn't look like much of a threat, either. The man looked her up and down.

"Social worker?" he blurted.

"No."

"Don't be trying to sell nothing here."

Cat smiled in what she hoped was a disarming way. "No, I'm looking for a friend."

"You're not a cop?"

"No, definitely not," she said firmly, hoping she'd soon find a familiar face.

The miasma of mold and bad food choices permeated the building, and the light in the hallway was even dimmer than she'd remembered if that was possible. Rap music assaulted her ears from Maria's old apartment, but across the hall should be Amy, the young teen mother with twins. Cat knocked loudly, hoping she wouldn't wake the babies.

The door was thrown open by a large, intimidating man in gang colors. He snarled a hostile, "Whattaya want?"

Cat cleared her throat. "I'm looking for Amy? We used to be neighbors?"

"She's gone! Go away!"

"Sure, sorry to bother you. Uh, you don't happen to know where Amy went, do you?" she inquired meekly.

"No!"

The door slammed in her face. She remembered people here being friendlier. Now what?

Cat turned slowly in the hall. Everything was different, not just the residents. The baseboards were peeling, and the overhead fluorescent lights were flickering or missing bulbs. Things there were falling apart—just like her life, she thought dejectedly as she trudged back to her car.

* * * *

Matt watched the city streets and suburbs of Barranquilla, Colombia drift past the heavily tinted windows. The Lust for Life Resort sat high atop a hillside on the outskirts of the city, making the limo drive tedious in the high sun of the day. It was also a stone's throw from the remote location of Maynard's pharmaceutical production plant. Was it possible they were producing more than Humanité? What if Dias was running his drugs through it? Matt needed to get inside the facility.

Eventually, the stretch limo pulled under the generous, misted portico entrance where a handsomely dressed bell-staff rushed forward to welcome him. A bleached-blond beach boy in a jacket and cap gave Matt the once over and winked. Matt looked around for the source of the man's admiration, and with a shock, realized it was him.

*"Buenas tardes, señor,"* the young man welcomed him.

Matt looked at him askance. "Yeah, hi."

The bellboy switched to English. "Are these your only bags?"

Matt nodded.

"When you're checked in, ask for Juan. I'll be happy to escort you to your room."

"I bet." Matt grinned and shook his head. "See you in a few."

"I live to serve." The young man bowed.

"Okay, later then."

* * * *

Matt followed Juan inside the door of the frigidly cooled suite. "Seating for the dinner show begins in the evening at eight," the young man began. "Tonight's entertainment is a gypsy orchestra and an insouciant blonde, 2000."

"Isn't that a little young?" Matt asked, repulsed.

The man turned a bland look his way. "Welcome to Lust for Life, *señor*."

"Uh-huh. So, Juan, have you seen this woman?" Matt presented a picture of Veronique.

"*Si, señor*, That is *Senorita* Moreau. She is a guest of Alejandro Dias. They're in the Palacio de Oro."

"How do I get there?"

"Sadly, that residence is not accessible to all guests."

"That sounds like Ronnie."

"Though, she never misses a dinner show."

Matt put a friendly arm around Juan. "So, Juan, I guess Dias is pretty heavily protected?"

Juan's eyes clouded with suspicion. "Are you from the *policia*?"

Matt shook his head and gritted his teeth. "No, just a jilted lover."

Juan's eyes lit up. "Ahh. I understand the heartbreak."

Matt pounded his shoulder good-naturedly. "I knew you would. So, you'll keep an eye out for me, right?" He folded a crisp bill into Juan's breast pocket.

Juan bowed again. "I live to serve."

* * * *

Rick decided the Hotel Cul De Sac in the rural outskirts of Port-au-Prince was clean and hospitable if a bit rougher than his usual haunts. Georgia chose it precisely because each two-bedroom suite was a bungalow complete unto itself with its own ventilation and air conditioning system. It perfectly suited a vampire's needs, and a little extra coin made sure Rick had the most secluded bungalow on the hotel grounds, along with the most discrete staff.

* * * *

Rick did an interview with the state-owned radio station that afternoon. It provided the majority of the country's news. The radio spot was sold to two of the largest privately held stations as well. He surprised them all by

206

conversing in their Haitian Creole, a language in which he'd become fluent during the eighteenth century.

"Who's your largest coffee grower?" he demanded of the interviewer on the live broadcast.

"François Moreau," the commentator replied respectfully, knowing how to kowtow to one of the wealthiest and most powerful men in the country.

"Let the people know," Rick's Dom voice emerged, "by this time next week, all Moreau's workers will desert him to work for me. I pay twice what he does for half the work, and I provide decent housing for all my worker families—each with electricity and fresh running water. In six months, his coffee plantation will be abandoned, and his beans will die on the vine."

"Those are bold words, *Monsieur*. How can you be so sure of what you say?"

"Research my properties in Vietnam and Indonesia, see how the workers are treated," Rick challenged, knowing his computer wizards created an elaborate and totally fictitious presence on the Web, extolling his successes as Jean Martin, a coffee magnate. A search of the Internet, the DarkNet and, most importantly, the VampNet, should pique Papa Moreau's curiosity.

"Moreau's days are numbered. He and those like him, who think workers can be enslaved financially, will lose everything. I'll win because I know workers who are well-paid and well-treated are loyal and will give their all to the success of the company—for everyone's sake."

"There have never been complaints by Monsieur Moreau's workers."

"Of course not. If there are only a handful of employers in the country, who'd be foolhardy enough to complain? That doesn't mean unrest is non-existent. It's merely restrained by circumstance. Well, circumstances have changed." Rick grabbed the microphone and spoke urgently to the country's population. "I want every unhappy one of you to leave Moreau. Work with me, reclaim your lives."

The interviewer gaped at Rick, his expression a mask of horror and confusion. "Thank you, *Monsieur* Martin, our listeners will follow your endeavors with interest."

* * * *

Rick was amused by Wester's caution. "You are poking the barracuda, are you not, *Monsieur* Martin?" Wester frowned on the drive back to the hotel.

"Papa Moreau is not known as a generous or kind man. He is ruthless with his enemies, and you have intentionally made yourself that."

Rick shrugged. "We'll see, my man." They walked into the bungalow and were greeted by the solid wall of muscle and armament Georgia sent as Rick's security team.

"Ah, I begin to understand." Wester nodded. "You are not unprepared for the fight."

"Like a boy scout," Rick affirmed. "I'm always prepared." He handed a stack of business cards to the wide-eyed man. "These are my contact numbers. Tell your people one call will get them a job. Spend the rest of your day handing these out to anyone who's interested."

*"Oui, monsieur."*

"And, Wester," Rick's hand on his arm stopped the driver, "I need one brave man, someone who used to work for Moreau, preferably someone who was humiliated and fired. I don't care why. I want that person answering my personal phone. Send him to me here, and make sure everyone knows about it."

"As you wish, *Monsieur*. Perhaps I was wrong. Perhaps you are baiting the barracuda?"

"Perhaps." Rick grinned. "It makes life interesting."

* * * *

Cat had an intense longing for comforts of the past, so she headed for the student union of her alma mater. *Calories be damned*, she thought. She was hungry, and they had the best bear claws in town. She heaved a relieved sigh. This place, at least, consoled her with tempting aromas of all the smells that had brought on her freshman fifteen. After grabbing a tray, she pushed past the health-conscious, salad bar patrons and headed straight for a caramel macchiato and a warm bear claw, glistening with fresh glaze.

As she savored her treat, Cat pondered who she trusted enough among the university staff to disclose her totally impossible drama. Maybe, Professor Beatty would be willing to help her? He was conservative enough to be skeptical but open-minded enough to listen.

She was headed to the ladies' room to wash the glaze off her fingers when a startlingly handsome guy blocked her path, hands on his hips and eyes blazing.

"Bet you're surprised to see me out of the looney bin?" He smirked.

Cat's mouth worked, searching for words, and she finally fell back on the tried and true. "I beg your pardon?" She cautiously stepped around him. "Excuse me, please."

He caught her arm in a less-than-gentle hold but released her as if he'd touched a live wire as soon as she frowned down at his offending grasp. He raised his hands as if in surrender.

"Don't want to get your boyfriend upset again."

"Boyfriend?" She jumped on the word and then thought better of her optimism. This guy just admitted he'd recently been released from a psychiatric unit. What if he was just crazy? "Do we know each other?" her eyes narrowed at him.

"Well enough to dodge an accessory charge." His face was hard.

"Um…purses and shoes?"

"Oh, you're good. Really good."

"Listen, I'm sorry. I don't know what you're talking about."

"So, I guess your fanged friend got what he wanted and headed back to Transylvania?"

Cat's voice dropped to a whisper, and she steered the hostile man toward a less crowded area. "My 'fanged' friend?" She swallowed hard. "Could you please explain what you mean by that?"

"If you think I'm gonna spill my guts, and get sent back to the sanitarium, you're crazier than they think I am." He leveled her with a scornful stare. "You should just know, I'm watching you. One wrong step and I'll prove it's all true."

"What's true…" She was left talking to his rapidly retreating back.

* * * *

Cat thought it a wonder she actually had the wherewithal to get to Beatty's office and make an appointment to see him the following morning. She was consumed with the hint vampires were real. *Who was that guy? How did he know me? And who was the "fanged boyfriend?"* Her anxiety shot off the charts. Funny, she would have thought confirmation of her vague memories of Matt would be welcome. In fact, the thought that he was real and actually a vampire devastated her.

* * * *

Matt watched the Barranquilla night glow indigo against the infinitesimal horizon of southern Colombia. He studied the sunset as he savored the last swallow of his blood-laced scotch, thinking he had now or never to succeed with Veronique.

Rick wanted an ostentatious distraction for Papa Moreau, and Matt wanted Ronnie's access to Humanité. Well, he guessed he'd better be extra-convincing in his seduction tonight.

The drug-infused nights lured a misfit vamp population to the Lust for Life where they could live in luxury several lifetimes afforded them. At least, they did it in style. As he walked toward the music, Matt took a moment to admire the shimmer of pale light emanating from chandeliers suspended over the dark teakwood dance floor. A full orchestra played. Gypsy violinists, who generations ago played over the soundtrack of their lives, now played to spend a season in this rarified atmosphere of age and money.

It was no surprise Ronnie and her exotic date, Alejandro Dias, were the most arresting figures on the dance floor. Veronique had always been an unnatural force of sensuality. Tonight, she wrapped the drug lord around her finger with her usual ease. *Poor besotted ass*, Matt thought, blending into an ebony corner.

The violin's bow cried a low, long note as the soloist stepped into the spotlight. Matt didn't need one to see Ronnie toy with her ancient wealthy vampire. The guy couldn't take his gaze off her. Dusky, long-limbed and fluid, Veronique pulled the more reserved vampire into her arms, capturing him with her knee hooked around his hip as the music compelled them. There was no disguising the immediate bulge in his pants. How else could the undead cartel leader respond when Papa Moreau's insatiable daughter set out to vertically seduce him?

Her stiletto-clad feet drew her close to Dias; her inviting fingertips glanced over his cheeks. Veronique fascinated him; he dared not refuse the dance. The couple moved tentatively at first until her partner caught her fever.

The rumba beat led their hips to brush in tantalizing swipes, inviting a more brazen touch. Seeing her ruse stirred Matt's groin. He knew only too well where this was going. He needed to redirect the evening before Ronnie dragged Dias into her suite, shut Matt out and wasted precious time.

After beckoning a roving waiter with two fingers, Matt made sure his discretely folded currency found its way into the conductor's pocket. Once the rumba ended, the violins behind the soloist closed ranks within the spread of the spotlight and began a torrid tango.

* * * *

Rick listened intently to Giles' scathing report on Moreau's Colombian connections. It was just approaching midnight when a responder interrupted to inform Rick a man named Odney asked to see him.

"You worked for Moreau? You know him well?" Rick questioned, handing a chilled fruit drink to the man who sported a black eyepatch.

"*Oui*," Odney gritted, "I know him very well. He is mon père."

Rick's brow rose. That assertion was obviously impossible, but it was clear the man before him believed it.

"Your father?" Rick repeated.

"*Oui*, or so *ma mere* claimed. She was his mistress until I was six until he killed her."

Rick's mind spun with the possibilities. That made slightly more sense. God knew what a small child remembered. "I'd assume if he'd killed her, he'd be in jail?"

"*Non*," Odney shook his head. "Not in Haiti. The police looked the other way, and not a thing changed for him, except that he took an interest in me. A guilty conscience, I suppose."

"What makes you think he killed your mother?"

"The police said it was an accident in the warehouse." Odney's expression was bleak, his voice hollow. "An industrial accident. Except she never went anywhere near the warehouse. And what kind of industrial accident leaves a woman drained of blood?"

Rick shifted uneasily. The man didn't know they were vamps, but… "Your mother bled to death?"

"So they said. I never believed it. Moreau is a cruel man. I believe he slit her throat and left her there to die."

Rick gave a little sigh of relief. *Okay, probably a feeding accident. That or one of the vamps close to Moreau got carried away.* "How did you come to work for him?"

"As I said, he took an interest in me after Maman died. Made sure I went to school, and when I graduated, made me the manager of his import/export warehouse. Then, one day, I discovered our latest Colombian delivery had nothing to do with coffee."

"Cocaine," Rick surmised.

"Oui. I went to Papa and demanded answers. Instead, he told me to forget about what I had seen. I told him I would never do so, would never be part of such illegal activity. That was when he accused me of ingratitude and disloyalty. He ordered this." He tapped the eyepatch. "He ordered it as a warning to all. He would determine what his workers did and did not see." His jaw tensed as he recounted the day. "Within an hour, my family was thrown out of our home and off his property. He made sure we were pariahs."

Rick winced. That sounded like Moreau.

"That was two years ago. Since then, of seven family members, I've been the only one to find work. Now, I am an officer with the American Red Cross. Between that paycheck and our small farm, my family barely survives. If you have come to put an end to Moreau, I thank God for you, and I will help in any way I can."

Rick put a hand on the emaciated man's shoulder. "I'm sorry for your troubles, Odney, and yes, I will put an end to Moreau. This is how you can help."

The words were scarcely out of Rick's mouth when the phone rang. One of the security guards picked it up. "You're Moreau?" he clipped. "Just a moment."

Rick smiled slyly. "Take the phone, Odney. Tell him I'm not available, but I'll meet him here at noon tomorrow. Also," he smirked, "feel free to be as impolite as you wish."

Odney laughed and reached for the phone. Moreau refused the meeting, as Rick was sure he would. Maybe, he needed a little more motivation?

Rick turned to Odney. "How would you like to shut Moreau down for good?"

"Tell me how."

"My plane is waiting to take you to Miami. I have friends at the Drug Enforcement Administration. We won't only rid you of Moreau, but his entire operation."

Odney frowned. "I'm concerned not for myself, but for my family."

"Don't worry, your family will be right behind you. We'll settle you anywhere you like. I have work for all of you as legitimate coffee growers. What do you say?"

Odney hesitated, eying Rick distrustfully.

"Trust me, my friend." Rick extended a hand to Odney, who shook it with a look of bewilderment still on his face. "Give the United States authorities the ammunition, and by this time tomorrow, Moreau won't be a problem for anyone."

"I will do my best, *Monsieur*."

"If Moreau has bought off the police and military, are there a few honest members of the Haitian police? Is anyone brave enough to stand up to him?"

"There are a few. Not a lot."

"We only need a few." Rick handed Odney a legal pad. "Give us the names and contact numbers. I'll need five men here tomorrow morning. Can you make that happen?"

Odney considered, and then wrote down the names. "I'm giving you the names of only the most reliable. You can count on these men."

* * * *

Cat shivered with a foreboding chill despite the heat of the day, and the car melting in the California sun. Searching for some semblance of normalcy in her increasingly insane world, she fiddled with the sound system and then plugged in her iPod. She'd been grateful to find the tiny piece of electronics stuffed deep inside the pocket of her E-reader case. She didn't actually remember owning it or making the mix that comprised the playlist. Did it hold some secret message which would clarify her missing weeks?

She tapped "play" and prayed for a revelation. The car drove itself as Cat sang along while weaving in and out of traffic. The music served as a soundtrack to bits and pieces of memories or *fantasies? Vampires lived among mortals?* She struggled with the recollections. *Matt had been her boyfriend. She'd known he was a vampire, and yet, somehow not a vampire. He and Rick... Rick! Rick was a vampire, too!* She remembered she had been convinced of it the night she'd awakened at the brownstone, and he'd ridiculed the assertion as "a strong dream!"

"A dream, my ass," she muttered and headed in the direction of the Consort Group's Los Angeles headquarters.

If she'd hoped for some sort of epiphany when she saw the building, Cat was certainly disappointed now. She sat in the car, eying the elite traffic pulling into the shaded portico. Her heart pounded a drum beat staccato, and her spine felt like a string drawn taut with some invisible master plucking a deep tone within her. She'd never consciously been here before, but somehow she knew this building, knew Rick's office was on the top floor. Well, logically, wasn't that always where the boss's office was? She had been here with Matt before. She knew it, and things—unsettling things—had happened to her.

What the hell secrets did this fortress of power hide? She had to find out. She threw the car into drive, and then slid back into traffic, intending to give her car to the valet at the Consort building. At the last minute, she bailed and wound up circling the block several times as she struggled with the idea of actually going in. She avoided the turn into the portico, and she assumed there was a reason for that. She shouldn't chance it. In the end, she settled for the registration drive of the hotel on the next block.

An elegantly uniformed attendant opened her car door, calling her solidly into the present. "Checking in, miss?"

She couldn't afford this hotel, but the rental car intimated she could. Cat nodded and gave the key fob to the hovering man. "Yes. Yes, I am." Her voice strengthened with each word.

"Luggage in the trunk?"

Cat dodged the question. "Please, just park it for now, would you?" She smoothed her hair into a twist with a clip and then dug for tip money in her pocket. "I'll take care of the luggage later." *Much, much later.*

Without deliberate thought, Cat found herself inside the glass and marble structure that housed Consort Group International's financial headquarters. Icy air chilled the nervous sweat trickling down her spine as she observed the hive of employees clicking past her—strikingly dressed women in towering stilettos and serious men in black or pinstriped suits. She took a seat on one of the lush, low-slung leather sofas spaced across the lobby and watched the rhythm of the elevators as they ejected the anointed doing business with or working for Consort Group.

One particular elevator stood alone without the steady opening and closing which kept the others occupied, nor did it have the usual call buttons. At this one, only a card reader stood sentry. Watching it, a song from the playlist pounded in her brain, *Building a Mystery* by Sarah McLachlan.

Dark and dangerous and… irresistible… things happened on the floor that elevator served. Cat was certain of it, just as she was certain Matt initiated her into its mysteries—into a world where control meant everything in the right hands.

That elevator had borne her into a realm where one partner could hold absolute control over another and lead them into sweet, painful ecstasy. One partner could sense the other coming by scent alone if they were a vampire. Surety thrummed through her, and with it, the knowledge that wherever he was, whatever had happened to them, Matt introduced her to a world few humans knew existed.

Snippets of conversation flew by her as Cat dragged memories up from her subconscious. As if she could make it happen by willpower alone, she visualized the stainless-steel elevator door opening to reveal the face she knew only in furtive dreams. Matt's face. She longed to see the powerful build of the man she fantasized about when she touched herself in bed late at night. Bleakly, she acknowledged the sighting was unlikely.

*Being here is trouble. Love is trouble, and I am a fool. I need to get out of here.* She gathered up her shoulder bag and the sweater she carried in case of a chill and then headed for the door.

# 20

Matt loosened his tuxedo jacket as he strode masterfully onto the dance floor, keeping rhythm with the beat. He slid out of his coat with a flourish, and then hooked it over his shoulder, taking it with him for the few steps it took to approach Veronique.

He must become the ultimate alpha to wrest her attention from Dias's dominance. He summoned all his knowledge and control to accomplish the task. Once he reached her, he hurled the coat away. He caught Veronique's arm as it arched in a flourish. With one calculated snap, Matt yanked her from her partner's embrace and stole the dance.

Veronique's moss-green eyes widened when she found herself in the box of his embrace. A triumphant smile curved her lips. Before she toed back, she dipped and rose, sliding her pelvis past his, kindling arousal.

Matt splayed his fingers to comb down her bare arms, marking her flesh. She liked it when it hurt, he knew. Veronique's exotic eyes flashed in challenge.

Matt remained coolly impassive as he commanded the dance. Posed at arm's length, he grabbed a fistful of her dark silken hair and, in step with the score, drew her head back, revealing the café au lait length of her throat. His fangs dropped a tantalizing fraction. He summoned his fortitude. Had he ever demanded this much of himself? A quick lick against her mocha-colored throat was accompanied by a husky growl. Veronique shuddered slightly and eyed him curiously.

Matt knew submissives well enough to know if he bit her, sank fang into flesh right there on the dance floor, she wouldn't be able to resist him. She was doing a good job of playing hard to get, but in the end, he knew he'd have her.

Matt's audacious moves cleared away the other dancers, and the violins swelled. Wrapping her waist-length hair around his fist, he wound it end over end, arching her neck dangerously, and crashing their bodies together in an erotic rush. *You can't top me*, Matt's look insisted.

The violinist's bow trembled out a refrain as Matt brushed his lips over her cool flesh, deliberately amping up the pheromones. She struggled against his strength to return the kiss, yet he cruelly refused to satisfy her. She pouted. *"Let me love you"* all but pled from her pores. He yanked the fist he'd wound through her hair as he trailed the point of his tongue sensuously down to the crevice of her décolleté. His gaze stayed riveted on hers.

"Give in." He snarled.

She gasped and arched toward him, but Matt cast her away, sending her skirt swirling wide as she spun half the distance of the dance floor. Satisfied at her look of dismay, he circled her like a predator as her billowing skirt settled around her.

*I'm not as easy as you thought, am I?* Matt reflected triumphantly.

Veronique's disdainful ruby lips spat at him. He narrowed his eyes into a provocative glare while her hand rose, and their fingers interlaced. Matt's gaze locked on hers, beckoning her with a hint of desire, just enough.

Matt understood her hungry invitation. With a growl, he grabbed the back of her neck and snatched her nose to nose with him. She resisted him, pulling away and delivering a crisp slap across his handsome face. *A classic move for a woman trying to top from the bottom.* He would never allow it.

He countered by encircling her waist, lifting her to toss her away. Determined, Veronique clung to him, her hair whipping through the air, her laugh haughty.

Matt continued the battle for supremacy. He pried her loose. "You won't top me. Don't try."

He flung her away, and she landed on her perfectly rounded bum and spun to an elegant stop. She buried her face in her knees as if in defeat, her lush locks spread over her shoulders like an ebony cape.

Before he could react, her pointed toe darted out, and she vaulted to rise on the balls of her satin pumps. Veronique licked her lips, her chest heaving.

*Very un-vamp-like*, Matt thought, probably an indication of how aroused their battle of wills made her.

Matt stalked her, twisting her cape of hair into a rope. He felt her resistance waning. Pulling her into a deep dip loosed her hair and swept it along the floor as he bowed her spine.

Their furtive war played out to the music's counterpoint marking, their bodies moved gracefully. Clear, repetitive pulses measured their steps and drove them tightly together. A piano plumbed the lowest notes, mirroring the lust exemplified in the dance.

Once more, Veronique lifted to kiss him, and again Matt rebuked her by spinning her away. Weeping, she hid her face with her forearms, her hands covering her head in a defensive pose. He watched her submit, knew his goal was within his grasp. Their dance was more a battlefield than a seduction, but that worked for Ronnie. He fought the betrayal of his own body. Her surrender was incontestably erotic.

Stepping behind her, Matt caught her shoulders. He shook her, demanding she snap out of her piteous pose. She anchored herself in firm defiance for a millisecond, and then his strength overpowered hers. He watched her yield, feeling triumph surge through his body.

Their fingers clasped, and their foreheads touched ---Matt hissed out his frustration.

"What?" Veronique inquired innocently.

"You know what," Matt snapped, commandeering their steps.

"Why are you here?" she taunted. "Have you come for *me*?" Her eyelashes fluttered, instantly coy.

Matt's gaze bore into hers. "What man doesn't come for you?"

"Oh, Matt."

"Don't get cocky," he ground out. "We need to talk." Matt slid into the end of the dance, her leg between his, as he bent her back over his arm, nose to nose. "You've reneged on our agreement, you owe me."

He drew her upright, and with a twirl, escorted her off the floor. "It was a circumstance beyond my control."

"Really?" Matt was unimpressed. "Is that why you're here with Dias? Discussing something beyond your control?"

"Jealous?"

"Head out to the balcony. I'll show you what I am." He tucked her hand over his throbbing erection, and she groaned.

* * * *

Rick smirked. By the time the Drug Enforcement Administration completed the raid on Moreau's dockside warehouse the following morning, Moreau was only too willing to schedule the noon meeting with him. The authorities didn't have enough to charge Moreau specifically, but the entire event was unsettling enough to make the ancient vamp rethink his current incarnation in Haiti. The better part of valor might be to sell his interests and disappear to a more hospitable locale.

"There are some men at the hotel gate asking for you, sir," Giles Paquet informed Rick as he turned from the phone.

Rick looked up from the television coverage of the raid. It'd been conducted immediately before dawn and netted the Haitian Federal Police an estimated twenty-four million dollars' worth of cocaine.

"Odney's friends?"

"It would seem so, sir."

Rick nodded with satisfaction. "Give them directions." He looked around at the assault rifles laying in a row across the dining room table.

Five impressive men in uniform stood before Rick. If they were as loyal and competent as they appeared, this would work without a hitch.

"Moreau and three of his bodyguards will be here at noon," Rick informed the resolute men, who fingered their new rifles and watched him with interest. "We'll have the advantage of numbers and some uncommon weaponry. It's crucial you give nothing away in your manner. Are you good poker players?"

The men before him broke into broad grins. "*Mai oui, monsieur*, we understand how to keep our poker faces," Ricardo, their informal leader agreed.

"It's vital," Rick smacked his flat palm on the desktop. "My men will be outside, ready to trap Moreau and his guards." As he spoke, he counted and stacked several gold Krugerrands on his desk before each man as payment. "You'll be inside with them, armed with enough ammunition to stop them many times over."

Ricardo's eyes widened looking at the glittering stacks. "We will not let you down, *monsieur*, we're only to hold them here in this room?"

"Why? You want to do more?" Rick grinned. "You won't have a struggle for long, and they won't have weapons. Are you up for it?"

The ringleader laughed. "With the greatest of pleasure."

"All right then. When I leave you alone with them, the fun will begin."

Rick dared not give them more information. The fact that their automatic weapons would be loaded with silver bullets would be an eccentricity to these men, but equally as deadly as lead, from their perspective.

His security team had completed work on the suite's ventilation system long before sunrise. The powerful compressor, hidden in the lush foliage, stood ready to pump aerosolized silver into the air conditioning system. It would deliver more than enough to immobilize, if not kill every vamp in the room, including Papa Moreau. The beauty of it was it would have no effect on the humans. They probably wouldn't even notice it.

At the stroke of noon, Rick came face-to-face with Moreau. He considered he might have played a more dangerous game of "chicken" than he anticipated.

* * * *

Cat's leaving was arrested by a singular ding. As if summoned by an ironic goddess, that elevator opened to reveal a glamorous, black-haired woman dressed in a painted-on, black leather pencil skirt and vest, walking competently on shiny stiletto pumps.

The stunning creature was framed by the matte steel doors as if she were a living poster for a high-priced dominatrix. Suicide red lips pouted as she cautiously stepped out of the elevator's dim glow. A Venus of sorts in full-grain leather, she glided across the marble floor, secreting an item in her elegant hands.

Venus stopped in front of a vulnerable-looking twenty-something man, who stood behind a podium meant to signify his authority as a security guard. He might have been the least authoritative figure Cat had ever seen.

Cat spied on them, pretending to read a magazine as she watched them through her lashes. The beauty carefully placed a stack of keycards before Junior.

"These are for the initiates," her beautiful face was stern. "The ten o'clock event, got it?" She turned on her high heels.

Junior swallowed and straightened his shoulders, extending his five-feet-ten portly frame by almost an inch. "You bet."

Venus stopped in her tracks. She turned slowly, watching the dork pick up the cards. Eyes narrowed, she tilted her head, the ends of her long, black hair playing tantalizingly around the V of her leather vest. His gaze followed the caress of her locks.

"Rephrase," she demanded, her whisper dark and whiskey-smooth.

He gulped hard as his hands hovered over the cards. "I…I…mean, yes, Ms. Rawlings. The ten o'clock event. I understand."

In his obedience, he seemed ten times more awkward. Venus stared at him as if judging his performance, and with a curt nod, accepted his response and was gone, clicking back to the reserved elevator.

The inept man let out a shaky breath, shuffling the cards and spewing them in all directions. Cat reflexively sprang toward the podium, placing a foot over one of the cards which migrated away from the rest.

Cat took advantage of his flustered state. The guard was still grabbing up stray cards when she spoke. "Hello, I'd like to see Rick, please, if he's in?" She knew perfectly well he wasn't unless he'd stalked her to L.A.

"Rick?" Now the man behind the podium was flummoxed. He gaped at Cat and swallowed hard, his voice a nervous squeak. "You mean Rick Hiatt?" He held the unruly cards to his chest as he stared at her.

"Right." She maintained unblinking eye contact as she dragged the foot covering the keycard closer, hoping he didn't look down at her black patent pumps.

Wrestling the slippery cards below the podium prompted him to look down, and Cat struggled to keep his gaze front and center. Casually, she leaned her arms across the podium and rested her silky camisole and its contents within easy view. Predictably, he ogled her, the purloined keycard unnoticed.

"D-Do you have an appointment, Miss…"

His name badge read Brett. "No, Brett, I don't." She purred. He was entranced. Cat took a step back and shook her head. "You know what? It's okay. I'll call Rick, check in with him before I just show up." She tipped her purse and keys off the edge of the podium, aiming them toward the foot covering the card. "I'll get it."

Her bent-over position showed cleavage nearly down to her navel as a distraction. She scooped up the keycard along with her bag. Brett watched her hungrily, the contents of her hands the last thing on his mind.

*Success!* With a parting smile, Cat walked briskly to the door. She closed her eyes when the glass wall slid open. *Will bells and sirens ring when I step out the door?*

* * * *

Matt led Veronique toward a balcony door, Alejandro Dias stalking close behind them. Matt's hand on the ornate door plate was arrested by loud, slow clapping. He turned to find Dias glowering.

"That was quite a show," the elegant vamp said in perfect English, heavily laced with a Castilian accent. "I hope it was worth it?"

"This has nothing to do with you, Dias, so I guess it's not worth much," Matt's testosterone already boiled from the heat of the dance.

"You are wrong, my friend." White teeth flashed under Alejandro's black mustache. "It is worth your life, for dishonoring me."

Matt sneered his disdain. "Oh, go chase yourself, I'll have her back to you soon enough." His hot gaze licked Veronique's curves. "If you still want her, then."

"I do not take another man's scraps." Dias sneered in return. "This is now a matter of honor, regardless of the lady's intentions. You will agree to meet me, or I will come for you."

"No need. I'm happy to accommodate you."

"We meet at moonrise, then."

"Where?" *With any luck, I'll be well gone from this place by moonrise.*

"There is a field, very close by, often reserved for me and my…challengers." Dias snapped his fingers, and four burly, insistent vampires encircled Matt, cutting him off from Veronique. "You will be my guest until then."

"I have an appointment with the lady," Matt drew Veronique close and cupped her ass.

"I am afraid not," Dias countered darkly. "If you are lucky enough to best me…" He paused and chuckled as laughter went up from the surrounding crowd. "Then, you may see her."

"This is business, you jagoff," Matt spit back. "I'm not trying to beat your time."

"Until this evening." Dias bowed to Matt, and then turned to Veronique, planting a steely hand on her arm and tugging her away.

"Jandro," Veronique protested as he dragged her away. "He's no match for you with *facóns*, and it *is* just business."

"We will talk about what 'business' you have with this man in my suite," Dias countered in a quietly cruel voice.

*What the hell*, Matt wondered, *was a facón?* He sighed as one of the bodyguards pushed him forward to follow Dias. He hoped this was ostentatious enough for Rick.

* * * *

Rick held his pose while Moreau scrutinized him. He had the annoying feeling Moreau was not above suggesting they drop their fangs and measure.

"I do not know you, but you are obviously one of the family," Moreau accused.

Rick held steely eye contact. "Obviously."

"I don't recognize the name, Jean Martin. I should know you."

Rick shrugged casually. "I deliberately keep a low profile. All that should concern you is whether I have the money and whether I'm willing to spend it on your property. Of course," a smirk flirted at his lips, "from what I hear in the news, it's worth much less now." *Whose fangs are longer now, you bastard?*

Moreau glowered, his ebony face hard, his vampire's body wilting in the sun. He gestured his impatience. "A temporary setback in status. In a hundred years, it will mean nothing."

"It could be an uncomfortable hundred years," Rick countered smoothly. "Once you're on the DEA's radar, you're marked, aren't you?" His voice hardened. "Tell your men to turn over their weapons."

Moreau glared at Rick, as he nodded to his men. They relinquished semiautomatic weapons. Moreau turned to Rick expectantly and attempted to step in out of the sun.

Rick held up a warning palm. "Giles?" He turned to his head of security.

Rick's responder guards stepped forward from the shade to frisk the outnumbered bodyguards. Grinning, they pulled away stakes, machetes and silver-plated stilettos from the now murmuring Haitians.

Once he received the all-clear from his men, Rick gestured the other four inside. "Will you join me for champagne?" he asked cordially. "We have reason to celebrate."

"Women drink champagne, men drink Everclear."

Rick had anticipated the choice. For vampires, the one-hundred-and-ninety-proof Everclear actually packed a small punch. Champagne was a soft drink. He turned and nodded to his five mortal guards disguised as resort servers.

"Please see that *Monsieur Moreau* and his men have everything I can give them."

"*Oui, monsieur*. We'll do exactly that," Ricardo agreed with a bow.

"Let us talk business," Moreau suggested after he'd taken a large draught of his chilled Everclear. "What will you give me for the property?"

Rick threw prospectus papers onto the coffee table before him. "What will the sale include? There are a number of properties. I want them all."

Moreau nodded. "For all. What is your offer?"

"One hundred million." Rick's offer started high, and he knew it. What did it matter? Moreau would never collect.

It was a sham done for show, but Moreau felt obliged to counter. "One hundred and ten million."

Rick pretended to consider. "Your docks are old and need repair. I'm generous to offer a hundred. Take it, or…maybe you think you can get a better offer elsewhere? In prison, perhaps?"

He could tell it riled Moreau not to have the leverage to truly negotiate, but Rick knew the truth of it. The vampire needed to get out of Haiti with whatever he could salvage of his fortune. The clock ticked lazily, and Rick waited imperturbably until Moreau admitted defeat.

"Very well. I'll sign for one hundred million on the condition the money is immediately transferred to my account in the Cook Islands."

Rick lifted his gaze to the '*servants*' stationed unobtrusively around the room. "That's acceptable." He waited patiently while Moreau signed the papers and smiled with satisfaction as he eyed the signature ceding to him all of Moreau's property. "I'll step across the hall and alert my personal banker." He extended a hand to Moreau.

As soon as the words left his mouth, Rick was out of the room. Within seconds, he'd crawled up the exterior walls of the bungalow like a spider and positioned himself at the rooftop skylight. From here he would be able to see all the action inside and outside the building. The heavy wooden doors slammed shut on the living area, and as planned, his guards braced them closed from the outside. Trying the doors and failing, Moreau's bodyguards sprang toward the windows, but the heavy hurricane shutters clamped shut with a resounding clatter and were secured by iron rods.

Moreau and his guards looked around in shock to find the humans pointing assault rifles at them, and Rick knew they'd assume the weapons were loaded with silver bullets. This attack was too well coordinated for the wrong ammunition. The trapped men dropped their fangs, their eyes taking on the pearlescent glint of vampires ready to fight.

"Name your price," Moreau barked to the man nearest him. The mortals looked alarmed but stood firm.

"You don't have enough money," his jailer taunted.

The air conditioner kicked on, and Moreau and his fellow vamps coughed, but not so much that it stopped their deadly advance on the human guards. They hissed as they stalked them, their fangs glinting sharp and ominous, their skin blanched. Three of the terrified humans sprayed their weapons wildly, spending ammunition uselessly, and allowing the uninjured vamps to gain the upper hand.

Rick's heart sank. "God's bollocks! The damn thing's not working," he called down to Giles. "It's not strong enough. They're still fighting."

Giles turned immediately to the air compressor while machine gun fire rang out. Peering down into the chaos, Rick realized he couldn't wait for Giles to correct the problem. Delay might cost the lives of men who'd trusted him.

He opened the latch securing the skylight vent. "Latch this behind me," he instructed the responder beside him. "If Giles gets the compressor working, we can't allow an open window."

"You'll be trapped," his protector protested.

"A chance we'll have to take." Rick lowered himself through. "Though, I'd appreciate a rescue if things don't go my way."

With a laugh, he landed nimbly a few feet from Moreau. The silver seeped into his nose. He suppressed the urge to inhale. It wouldn't stop him, and it certainly hadn't stopped Moreau, who was nearly double his age and power.

Rick had the advantage of knowing the silver was airborne, and since breathing was unnecessary, he merely suppressed the instinct. The damn stuff stung as it touched unprotected skin, not enough to thwart him, but perhaps all the effects combined would hamper Moreau enough to give Rick an edge.

The commotion of the battle was mind-boggling, and Rick had been mentally prepared for it. He could only imagine the terror borne by the mortals in the room. Ricardo and Michael, the only mortals who'd remained conscious after fiercely battling the enraged vamps, emptied their supply of silver bullets into Moreau's vampire guards. The vamps lay immobilized on the floor, blood seeping with a smoking hiss into air which was becoming more silver saturated. Moreau faltered, and so did Rick, as it penetrated more and more into his nearly indestructible body.

Moreau lunged toward him, with a murderous ferocity. Rick staggered away, dimly hearing the report of Ricardo's weapon as he spent his one remaining round Moreau's way. Moreau shook off the shot that hit his shoulder but missed his heart. He stopped mid-lunge on his way to Rick and turned against Ricardo. In an instant, he'd immobilized the brave man, and gained sustenance from the clean human blood at Ricardo's neck.

With a raging surge of power, Rick called upon his last reserves to hurl the vamp away from Ricardo and against the bar. His desperate gaze landed on the two-liter bottle of Everclear they shared earlier. He smashed the remains over Moreau's head, spraying the one-hundred-and-ninety-proof liquid from head to toe. Moreau was momentarily stunned by the blow, just long enough for Rick to ignite his cigar lighter and toss it.

Moreau screamed when he caught fire. If Ricardo had not dragged Rick away, the three of them would have been consumed in flames. The two careened out of reach as Moreau flailed, setting the heavy drapes aflame in his quest for escape. Smoke billowed in the room, further compromising the mortals. Moreau's screams unnerved the responders to the point they opened the doors to see what the hell was happening. In the nick of time, they dragged Rick and the mortals to safety, just as the silver compressor finally kicked in full force. Those vamps who weren't dead already soon would be.

* * * *

Cat's hand shook slightly as she applied tinted lip gloss to her generous lips. It was almost the appointed hour. The opulent mirror in the ladies' room of the five-star hotel where she'd parked the car showed her ready. Hands clutched over her nervous stomach, she waited for the clock to click to nine forty-five. Before she could talk herself out of it, she headed for the Consort Group building and the forbidden mystery of the exclusive elevator.

*What if I get in there and can't get out?* Cat asked herself, eying the building's lobby. Though she didn't know what dangers the initiation held, her feelings at the sight of the lone elevator were an unsettling combination of erotic anticipation, unease, and disapproval. Though she couldn't draw out the reasons behind the feelings, she knew answers awaited her through those elevator doors.

A long line of initiates wound their way around the stanchions snaking from the elevator and running throughout the lobby. Cat joined the line, wishing she was more inconspicuous. Who would have guessed she'd be distinguished by black business slacks and a silky white camisole? Everyone else in line looked like members of some bizarre private investigator's club. The women sported teased hair, overdone makeup, and ridiculously high heels, while the men wore black slacks and slicked back hair. All were covered knee to neck with closely cinched trench coats. Well, she missed the memo about the dress code.

Finally, it was her turn in the crowded elevator. As they descended past the garage level, the lights dimmed to a blood red, and the thrum of a human heart pumped its way through the metal chamber. Cat shivered. *What the devil is this?* The doors opened to red leather walls and flickering carriage lights, and she gasped along with the rest of the awed elevator crowd.

A greeter ushered the excited occupants toward the locker room, but the titillated crowd were barely able to wait for their keys to find their personal lockers. They relinquished the conservative trench coats, revealing outrageously bawdy costumes. Cat struggled to keep a straight face while watching them.

A devastatingly attractive, twenty-something next to her played with a curl in the middle of his forehead and smoothed an oily hand down his bare, landscaped chest. Meticulously, he withdrew a hand towel from his locker, wiped and checked his manicure. With obvious pride, he adjusted the generous package in his sleek black trousers, and Cat gulped. *Is that thing real? Surely it isn't real.*

Not to be outdone, the curvy woman to her left divested her coat to reveal a naughty, French maid costume complete with a black ruffled skirt skimming her thighs. The least amount of movement lifted it even higher to reveal a sheer white lace thong, leaving nothing to imagine. Cat couldn't believe the woman could draw a deep breath in the obscenely tight bustier that barely contained her buxom breasts. All around her, one costume was more flamboyant than the next, and she struggled to keep her composure, thinking wildly that she looked more like a member of the wait staff than an initiate.

So, who was running the initiation? And what, exactly, were they being initiated into?

* * * *

Rick fought to stand and direct the chaos outside the bungalow. It felt like only moments before hotel employees were on site, garden hoses in hand, in a futile attempt to put down the flames.

"Let it burn," he told Giles. "The fire will hide most of the evidence. The rest we can remove before the authorities get a look." His gaze swept the area. "Where's Ricardo?"

Giles pointed. "He's bleeding badly but alive." One of the responders held a cloth securely against the senseless man's neck.

"Get him to a hospital." Rick teetered on the verge of collapse himself. "What about the others?"

"Three unconscious. One dead."

Rick staggered and fell. "I need blood." He gasped. His men carried him to the fallen body of a human guard.

"He's already gone, sir. You need it."

Rick gratefully fell upon the body of the dead soldier, siphoning what blood he could from the lifeless veins.

At last, he stood, strengthened by blood, and ready to make whatever explanations would satisfy the local police. The three surviving mortals were slowly brought around by his guards, and Ricardo, who saved his life, was in the hands of physicians. Rick heaved a sigh of relief.

"It was a great plan; too bad it didn't work."

Giles nodded. "The compressor nozzle was too narrow. It clogged with silver."

Rick sighed. "Make sure all the weapons are removed from the bungalow before the police get in there. And get those Krugerrands to the men. We need to commend their heroism to their commanders, make sure they're protected. The one who died, offer his family home and safe work in the States."

"Yes, sir." Giles was already on the way to carry out his orders.

"And see to it Ricardo recuperates in Miami and we pay the tab." Rick looked around as the roof of the bungalow disintegrated and collapsed in a shower of sparks. "We have had just about enough of you, Papa." He sneered as the rubble burned. Moreau and his petty dictatorship were dead. Ronnie was really going to be pissed about that.

* * * *

Matt ground the heel of his hand into his dry eyes, wondering where the hell Veronique was. This whole machismo knife and vampire show was in her "honor." The least she could do was give him her favor. It would be just like her to let him and Dias kill each other while she took up with the next in command. On the other hand, he was pretty confident he reignited her fantasies with his dominant display on the dance floor. She wasn't one to walk away from a fantasy.

A duel! *How bleeding archaic is this?* He tore away his shirt and eyed the oil Juan presented. "Really?" Matt snapped suspiciously.

Juan replied with all solemnity. "If the blade breaks, and you're forced to wrestle, it could save your life."

"I think… I'd rather … just die."

Reluctantly, Matt slicked his skin, watching Dias do the same. He gritted his teeth in irritation. He'd simply been doing what had to be done to attract Ronnie's attention. Now, he stood on his pedestal of masculine pride in mortal danger and pissed off his grand gesture was being ignored by the one person he'd sought to impress. *How poetic. How vampiric.*

Of course, Alejandro Dias had to go old world in his smackdown. Wasn't that exactly what a five-hundred-year-old vampire from Colombia would do? A fight to the death with twenty-inch double-sided blades innocuously called *facóns.* Matt would much rather have rumbled in a back alley until the other guy slapped the ground and cried "Uncle." That would have satisfied his honor just fine. Instead, he was faced with the risk of disembowelment, and then beheading at moonrise all to impress "the girl." Leave it to Veronique to inspire insanity.

Matt dialed back his mounting irritation. He needed to keep his eyes on the prize and move forward. He had to take this guy out, secure the Humanité from Ronnie, and get the hell back to Cat, or at least his twenty-first-century bloodsucker lifestyle.

The jewels in the elaborately carved hilt pressed into his palm as Matt weighed the heavy dueling knife. The wicked blade whistled through the evening air; he tested its arc and reach. Time ticked away what could be the last moments of his existence while he stood surrealistically stoic. What the hell, maybe he'd stake the bastard on his own blade, though he was always one to avoid killing if he could.

Of necessity, they were relegated to a literal field on the outskirts of the resort. Their barehanded strength would have destroyed the ballroom where the challenge was flung. In what was apparently an opening ceremony of sorts, the duel's mediator threw the twenty-six commandments of the South American field of honor over his proverbial shoulder. Clearly, these were rules with which the small crowd hovering on the challenger's side were familiar. There were no seconds. It was Matt and Dias until one of them was *à l'outrance*, headless in the dirt.

Matt eyed Alejandro's hostile supporters. He was no one to these people, and they had huge political motivation to cheer on his challenger, not the least of which was promotion within the cartel. Thumbing the sharp edge of his blade, he cursed Ronnie inwardly, and abruptly craved an end to this farce. He'd get nowhere with her as long as Dias survived.

The gypsy orchestra leader had been chosen to drop the silk, based solely on the merits of his outrageous mustache and his bright yellow pocket square. The lanky man fidgeted, waiting for the edge of the moon to crest. Matt and Dias sprang forward when the buttery silk spread on the earth.

Older, wiser in the ways of the *facón* duel, Dias took the initial advantage, driving Matt to the field's perimeter with a volley of thrusts. Each of them slashed at the other, neither catching so much as a fiber of clothing. The blades whistled with preternatural speed. The few observers shouted encouragement to Dias, certain the challenge would end soon with Matt staring wide-eyed and dead. He was determined to surprise them.

Longing to feel Cat's soft body alongside his once more inspired Matt to give his all. His calculated thrusts probed his opponent's fighting style, avoiding his strengths to capitalize on his weaknesses. The more experienced drug lord parried easily, smirking his disdain. Tension coiled in Matt's gut while he fought for his life. Rapid-fire slashes of their blades carved incisions which healed almost as quickly as they bled. Moonlight glinted on blood-encrusted steel as the knives flashed.

Matt gritted his teeth and set his jaw with effort. He'd been a goddamn fool to let himself be goaded into this madness! Whatever he thought of Dias as a man, he had to acknowledge his mad skills for dueling. This thing wasn't turning Matt's way, and he mustered all his grit and guts to remain in the game. He refused to succumb to the fear that he would never see Cat or Rick again.

Alejandro's blade clipped his ear as Matt whirled aside, spraying blood among the crowd chanting for his death. Matt spun on his heel and crouched, more limber than his aggressor. He gauged speed and space in the moon shadow and pivoted to trade places with Dias. The full moon cast golden shadows on his opponent's pale face, the hollow of his throat glistening as they fought. Matt swayed from one foot to the other, eluding one deadlier swipe of the blade.

A woman's shriek from a patio high above them echoed in the clearing. Startled night birds shivered out of the trees and soared en masse to swoop and swirl above the duelers. Distracted, Dias glanced up. Matt lunged forward, thrusting in close quarters, his double-edged blade catching the black plait at the nape of his opponent's neck and taking blood, tendon, and muscle with it. He retreated as Dias howled with pain and fury, then re-lunged to double thrust, his blade sinking deep into Dias's shoulder, but missing the throat.

Alejandro's eyes bulged with panic at Matt's unexpected advantage. In the next instant, Matt caught the ivory blur of a woman rushing toward them. Dias teetered forward, blood gushing from Matt's blade. Veronique crashed into the midst of the duel, oblivious to the carnage on her behalf.

"He's dead! *Ma Papa!* What have you done?" she wailed, her emerald eyes accusing Matt.

Dias used the momentary distraction to uppercut a thrust into Matt's gut. Gritting his teeth against the white poker of pain, Matt yanked his *facón* from the drug lord's shoulder bone. In seconds, fears converged, and destinies were sealed. Veronique's hands clutched her midsection in despair, Dias froze with the shock of his loss, and Matt capitalized on the temporary lull to drive his blade deep into the elder vampire's thick neck. Flesh parted like butter, and Matt's blade severed Alejandro's dark head.

Veronique shuddered with disgust when Dias's head rolled off his exquisitely sculpted shoulders and onto the bloody earth. Matt's glance raked her with disdain. She was now as she'd always been—totally absorbed in her own drama. Had she felt any part in two vampires dying? Did she feel any culpability in the body before her, or her own sire's death? No. They were all her pawns, and she was the queen.

* * * *

Cat knew the answers to all her questions were in the next room where a pleasant master of ceremonies, who looked more like the warm-up guy for a real estate seminar than an S&M master, motioned participants into seats.

"Welcome to the Gaoler, my friends," he boomed. "I'm Nicolai Pares, your orientation host. You may call me Nic. We're happy to see so many attractive, warm-blooded initiates joining us. Let's take a moment to go over precautions before we get to the fun part." The crowd vibrated with excitement. "I'm hoping all of you read your contracts and followed the listed suggestions?" He beamed at them as if he were discussing dental health. "Everyone prepped with vitamin C and B? Abstained from aspirin and Ibuprofen? Have to watch those anticoagulants!" He stopped to run his fingers appreciatively over the exposed nipples of a nearby fan who squeezed in close to the stage. She giggled invitingly. "You know what I'm talking about, don't you, baby? Everybody has their safe words, right?"

Heads nodded. *What is a safe word?* Cat wondered. Somehow, she felt she might need one. *Is it like a mantra?*

"I'm gonna assume none of you have fed a vamp before, though you may already know quite a bit about Dom/sub relationships. So, a couple more suggestions. Don't get scared and jerk away. All the vamps here are experienced and will make it good for you if you give them the opportunity, so don't choke up."

Inexplicably, Cat's left wrist throbbed, and she rubbed at the scar she was told was a result of the auto accident. Now that she looked closely, there were two ugly puncture marks. Could it be…

"If you feel light-head, we want you to speak up right away. We always have orange juice or something a little stronger for fortification. Last, but not least, stay with the vamp you're assigned to. Just like a school dance, it's bad manners to leave the one who brung you." He smiled charmingly. "The last thing we want is two vamps fighting over a donor. Naughty donors who cause trouble won't be invited back."

Nicolai turned once again to his giggling admirer. "Miss Angelica has offered to help me demonstrate the most popular feeding positions." He picked the delighted woman up as if she weighed nothing, and then settled them both on a fainting couch, draping her over his lap. He caressed her neck with his lips while he extended her arm to demonstrate. Cat shivered.

"Some areas, such as the wrist or arm, are considered the most casual, least intimate sites to feed upon." He winked at the crowd. "That's something you might see between virtual strangers; vamps and donors who are grabbing a quick eat-and-come in the lounge area."

In a single motion, he unzipped the demonstrator's bustier and let her tits spill out. The crowd buzzed excitedly.

"There are more intimate positions your vampire is more likely to reserve for the privacy of his or her dungeon. This area here." His fangs dropped, his face paled, and his eyes shone like opals. He licked sensuously along the woman's throat. "Yum…or this." He lapped at her nipples. "Is tasty." He winked. "The best." With lightning speed, he flipped the girl onto the bed of the fainting couch, spreading her knees wide, and exposing her completely to the gasping crowd. He rewarded them with a devilish grin. "Vamps are fast. The best place is here." Nic scraped his fangs between her legs along her femoral artery, and Angelica squealed.

Cat squirmed in her seat. *Okay, vampires are real.*

* * * *

Matt dropped the bloody knife from numb fingers and gaped at the grizzly tableau as the stunned crowd enveloped Veronique and Dias. Juan was at his side in seconds, drawing him urgently away before the mob could organize themselves to give chase.

"You are a marked man, senor. We run, or you die."

Matt nodded, dazed. His side hurt like a son of a bitch. Had Dias' blade been coated with silver? He clutched the wound and let Juan spirit him into the woods where the young man stripped. Now what? Matt wondered crossly.

"Your pants, *señor*."

"Yes, these are my pants."

Juan leveled a bold look at him. "Take them off."

Matt's look challenged his. "What?"

"Take them off and take these." He thrust his uniform into Matt's hands. "My motorcycle is in the employee parking lot, the only red Ducati. Here is the key."

Matt stared in surprise. Juan threaded his fingers into the longish hair at Matt's temples, and hard masculine lips covered Matt's. Outraged, Matt jerked away, his fist connecting with the young man's jaw. Juan reeled back, still upright.

"Sir, you have to hit me harder. Knock me out. Otherwise…"

A smile crept over Matt's face as he realized the young man's intent. "Goodnight, Juan, and thank you."

His uppercut to Juan's chin laid the boy out flat just in time. His bloodthirsty pursuers were on the hunt, though luckily moving in an adjacent direction. Matt circled back to the employee area of the resort, hoping Juan's gaudy aftershave permeating the uniform would disguise his own scent, and give him some lead time.

The bike started without a hitch, and Matt was confident he made a miraculous escape until ominous black SUVs surged past him headed toward the airport. Luckily, it hadn't occurred to them to identify the anonymous bellman on the motorbike. It looked as if the airport was out as an exit strategy, though. He'd have to use the docks, and he'd better get there fast, and onto a departing ship before they figured out where he'd gone.

* * * *

Matt's tribulation in the hold of a freighter, filled with coal, lasted for over seven hundred interminable nautical miles and two days. He spent the majority of the time pissed off that he'd was unable to access the Maynard plant. He was now certain Veronique produced Humanité there, and the cartel may have been using it for street drugs.

After the debacle with Dias, he was bound to be persona non grata, at least in Colombia, and probably with Ronnie as well. It was a misstep even the most polished seducer would not be able to overcome. *Maybe money? Veronique does like money. Would it compensate her for the loss of her lover and sire all in one night?* He doubted she had deep feelings for anyone but herself. Still, if she cast him in the role of villain, it would impossible to win her forgiveness. What would compel her to relinquish a substantial amount of Humanité to him?

Grubby, coal-coated, blood-starved and exhausted when he reached their club in Puerto Rico, Matt was snubbed by the socially acceptable. The looks he garnered in the tattered stevedore clothes he'd stolen en route made it clear he was a fashion don't. Hopefully, he'd be able to find something decent to wear before he headed home.

* * * *

Cat began to sweat. Memories converged on her, and all at once the chilly room was way too hot. It spun. Her breathing accelerated alarmingly, and blackness closed in on her from the edges of her vision.

The feel of an icy cold towel at the back of her neck and another against her forehead slowly brought her around. She blinked into consciousness and found herself lying on a tobacco-colored leather couch in a space lit by geometric Tiffany lamps and surrounded by bottle-green walls. Her heart pounded. She'd been in this room before.

Cat blinked to clear her vision. An elegantly tall man with chiseled good looks and a strong muscular body gazed down at her. He was impeccably groomed in tuxedo pants, a pleated shirt, open at the neck and an air of complete command.

Cat sat up slowly, catching the towel across her forehead before it dropped to the floor. She twisted it in her hands, reluctant to meet his gaze.

"Look at me." His voice was deep and sonorous and brooked no denial. Her gaze snapped up to his. "*What* were you thinking?"

"I had questions. I needed answers,"

His lips formed a straight line of disapproval. "Answers about what?"

"About Matt…me…us."

"So, you came here without him?"

His look was skeptical, but it gave Cat hope. Obviously, he knew who Matt was.

"I had to. He's gone."

"If Matt's cut you off, no one here will touch you." From the look on his handsome face, Cat could tell she was about to be shown the door.

Tears welled up in her eyes, but he remained impassive. "They won't even admit he exists or that vampires exist." She gasped through a sob. "They won't tell me anything at all."

His expression lost its chill, replaced by confusion. "Who is they?"

"Rick and Georgia, they told me I was crazy."

He sank onto the leather chair opposite her, his large hands steepled in front of him. "I think you'd better tell me the whole story."

Cat's stubborn chin jutted out. "I think you'd better tell *me* something first."

He eyed her speculatively. "What would that be?"

"Your name, and what you are to Matt and Rick. What you are to this place?"

She watched him fight to squelch a grin. "You may call me *Master* Adam. I am the manager of the Gaoler. Matt and Rick are the owners."

"Matt and Rick own a sex club for vampires," she muttered. "Well, I suppose that fits. Where is Matt?"

"Tell me your story,"

As Cat recollected her scraps of memories and feelings, Adam's demeanor softened. Once the pace of her confession slowed, she was wrung out. She stared at him dully, and Adam the Master became Adam, the Counselor.

"So, does Matt exist or not?"

"Yes, Matt does exist. At least, he did. I assume he's still alive. What happened, why he and Rick took the extreme measures they did...I will not begin to speculate, and I won't risk leading you down the wrong path." Cat drew in a deep breath and started to protest before he held up an arresting hand. "Don't ask me. It will get you nowhere. You need to go back to New York and talk with Rick. You can call him from my office."

Cat viciously dug her fingers into the sofa cushions, furious with the frustration she met at every tiny advance. "Oh, what, call the guy who lied to me for months, who denied being a vampire, denied Matt even exists? Call that guy?"

She clenched her hands in irritation, and it was on the tip of her tongue to suggest Master Adam chill out when her fingers closed around a scrap of silk. She pulled it up, ready to shake an admonishing digit at him when she stared at the lavender silk and lace in her palm. She was deluged by memories.

This was her thong. She and Matt had been in this room. They'd been fighting, and then loving...and... Her gaze flew to the bed, and within seconds, she was upon it, pulling out the leather cuffs still affixed to the bedposts.

She gasped and shook the cuffs at Adam. "I remember these! I remember Matt..." She shook as tears of relief flooded her eyes. "We were here. This is his room, isn't it?" She swept away his silence with a wave of her hand. "I know it is. He calls it his playroom. He doesn't like the connotation of a *dungeon*." Cat ripped the coverlet from the bed, and then snatched up the pillow below it. It still smelled of Matt, his singular fragrance, woody and sharp. She sobbed as she clutched the pillow to her as if she could absorb the comfort of his touch from it. "He was here with me…it was real. I'm not crazy. It was real."

Adam approached her cautiously. She watched him wearily as he settled next to her, and dragged in huge gulps of air, almost hyperventilating. He wrapped a consoling arm around her.

"I honestly don't know what's going on, Cat," he whispered, smoothing her hair with one hand and letting her cry against his chest. "The only ones who can give you the answers you're looking for are in New York. Go home."

"I'm afraid. I'm so afraid to find out the truth."

"Matt's a lucky guy. If he lets a woman like you go, he's an idiot."

She gazed around the room, every sight a memory now. "He brought me alive in this room. Awakened a part of me I didn't know existed."

Adam's gaze was profoundly serious. "Have you considered there are some doors better left closed? If Matt did everything, he could to remove your memories and hide your past with him, it was certainly for your benefit."

Cat's voice turned hard. "I don't see how."

Adam stood, held out his hand to guide her out of the playroom, his look implacable. "Then go back to New York and ask.

# 21

Cat luxuriated in the warmth of his body snuggled next to hers.

"No."

"No, never?"

The joy in his deep masculine voice reinforced his answer. "Couldn't happen in a million years."

He was warm, his flesh velvet over lean muscle. His morning stubble bristled against her neck, and the room smelled like sunshine after a long rain. His fingers played as his hands spanned around her waist, and she nestled into his awakening erection.

"Then what was it? Some cosmic thingamabob?" Cat smiled.

"It's not…" Matt's voice wavered as his interest diverted to the hill and valley of her hips and thighs.

"Then we can be…"

"Our lives together will be mortal. Our love will have no end, but…we'll age and gray and wrinkle."

"Until we look like the shuffling couples in Central Park? I don't understand." Cat dragged a nail down his forearm to watch the mortal changes on his tanned flesh. "Where are your fangs and opal eyes?"

"That was—"

She bit lightly on his bottom lip as she traveled her thumb over his long eyelashes. She noticed the dusting of pale freckles across his forehead, evidence of his time at the beach.

The broad bed and soft sheets caught their tumble. Flesh met excitedly only to retreat and return. Sweet sweat covered them as their play roughened.

It was a slow, comfortable screw, cooled by a soft dawn breeze, caressing their damp flesh.

Cat found some ironic joy in biting his shoulder, marking him, and watching it welt and redden. There was no instantaneous healing, no immortal transformation. On the verge of his climax, at the second when he lengthened just that much more, she was shaken.

"Miss, we're beginning our descent. You have to return your seat to the upright position."

The steward passed systematically up the aisle, his demeanor earnest and perfunctory. His words yanked her out of that yet-to-be-completed moment and thrust her back into limbo. Cat shook herself out of the dream, wishing she was back in the ecstasy of Matt's human arms.

* * * *

Cat huddled under the overhang outside the terminal, watching the rain fall in sheets. Cab after cab flew past her, favoring parties with luggage, splashing her travel-wrinkled pants with gutter water. She thrust her arm up higher, aiming for a more aggressive stance at the same moment her shoulder strap snapped, casting the contents of her tote bag into an oil-slick puddle. She screeched in frustration, finally opting for a communal limo rather than battling for a cab. Limo, huh! It was a van, whatever fancy name they tried to pin on it.

"The Frank Gehry building," she said, directing the driver to Rick's apartment.

The other passengers eyed her irritably. One groaned aloud.

"You know how much a detour like that will cost us?" a fellow passenger snapped. She ignored them, giving the lower east side address which would take many of them miles out of their way. She was determined to have her say with Rick at any cost.

The closer the limo came to her destination, the more apprehensive she became. What Cat feared most was exile. If Matt and Rick went to such lengths to keep her in the dark, what would they do when they realized her memory had returned?

Her watch read noon, and Cat reset it to New York time. That meant it would be a little past three in the afternoon when she walked into Rick's penthouse. He'd be getting an early wake-up call.

* * * *

Cat swiped the private access pass given to her by Master Adam through the penthouse keycard reader. The elevator doors slid open, and she stepped inside, making sure the security team saw her face clearly on the closed-circuit monitor. She wasn't surprised at the end of its rise when the doors opened to reveal Giles Paquet flanked by two of his responders.

"Gentlemen," Cat acknowledged briskly. "I need to speak with Mr. Hiatt."

"Mr. Hiatt had a late night," Giles stalled. "He's resting."

"Wake him up." Her voice was clipped and firm. "If you have trouble getting his attention, give him this." She produced a pack of folded papers and handed them to Giles. "Tell him Master Adam sent me."

"Ms. Temple." Giles bowed stiffly and then walked toward Rick's private rooms.

"I'll wait in Mr. Hiatt's office," she called after him, before heading for the massive double doors.

"I'm sorry, miss, you can't go in there without Mr. Hiatt." One of the remaining guards deterred her as she approached. He stood in front of the office, side by side with his co-worker, hands clasped formally behind their backs at parade rest.

Cat fixed both men with a determined stare, placed two fingers on each of their adjoining shoulders, moving them apart, and strode into the room. The automatic door swung shut behind her. She settled herself in Rick's desk chair. It was fine calf leather, ergonomically designed. She would expect nothing less from his decorators. Low-hanging clouds drifted their rain and haze past the seventy-sixth-floor windows as she folded her hands and waited. She didn't wait long.

"What in damnation is this?" Rick growled, storming into the room, fully dressed in his three-piece suit, the donor initiate contract in his hand. He appeared astonished to see her behind his desk and slowed his pace. "You've been busy."

"You mean busy for a mortal, or just busy?"

Rick wedged his index finger into his shirt collar and twisted his neck to loosen his tie, "What have you done, Cathy?"

"The name is Cat," she snapped. "And…really? That's how you're going to play this? What have I done? I remember everything, Rick. You, Matt, the Humanité, everything."

Rick stared at her for a beat. "Well, bollocks," he grumbled at last and sank into a chair, facing her. "So, what now?"

"You know, I asked myself that all the way back on the plane, and I think I finally know the answer. I want to see Matt. I mean, yeah, I'd like answers. I'd like to stake both of you for what you did, but more than anything, I want the truth. I want to talk to Matt. I want to talk to him now, and I want him to explain everything. No more smoke and mirrors. Then, I'll decide what to do about it."

Rick quirked a brow. "Do about it? What do you think you can do about it?"

"I don't know." She stood with great dignity. "I won't know until I get the answers. I know this much. I won't be a victim again." She held up a warning hand when he opened his mouth to protest. "No. Don't speak. Just find Matt. Let me know when you have."

* * * *

Cat found concentration impossible after her confrontation with Rick. She got to the brownstone, donned workout gear, and set out for the gym to burn off frenetic energy. Sweat and pain replaced her furious heartache and left her slightly more collected after her workout.

A soothing shower helped her focus, and immediately afterward, Cat began packing to move back to L.A. If Matt and Rick thought she was going to rely on a life and career built on their largesse, they were the fools.

She was a California girl and an uncomfortable transplant to New York. She had a degree with honors from UCLA and Columbia, and thanks to Rick, a few months of experience at Consort Publishing. She expected decent references from him, and that was it. She'd find her own job, and make her own way in Los Angeles, or wherever else opportunity presented itself. Whatever the outcome, tonight she'd be done with this lingering nightmare.

* * * *

Matt rested, oblivious to Rick's agitation as the older vampire swept past the guarded elevators at the Ritz-Carlton, keeping the doorman at bay with one juicy growl. He barged into Matt's suite without as much as a knock on the door.

"Get up!" he barked, throwing open the door to Matt's make-shift mausoleum so violently it banged against the adjoining wall.

Matt squinted at him, trying to orient himself after the rude intrusion. "What's going on?"

"Cat's back. She knows everything, and she's pissed." He threw Matt a robe. "Haul your bollocks over here. She demanded a meeting."

"She can't know everything." Matt rose slowly, drawing the robe around him. "You and I are the only ones who know everything."

"Let me clarify. She knows enough to be thoroughly pissed." Rick watched his friend with agitation, hands sliding deep into the pockets of his hand-tailored Armani slacks. "What do you plan to do with her?"

Matt drew in a deep sigh. "I plan to answer her questions." Frustrated, he ran a hand through his hair. "We've eliminated the danger from Moreau, and that's huge for her safety."

"Thanks to me." Rick rocked angrily on the balls of his feet.

Matt acknowledged with a nod and continued. "With him gone, and Veronique restarting production of Humanité… If I can get my hands on enough, there's a chance we'll have that human lifetime, after all."

Rick studied his friend. "Whatever you want to do, dear boy, that's fine with me, but Veronique hates your guts and mine. It won't be easy acquiring the amount you need. Besides, you don't know what this drug will do long term. There's evidence it's addictive. Why not just turn Cat or have a vamp/mortal relationship with her, though granted, those never endure."

"Life's a gamble, old man." Matt grimaced. "None of us can be certain of anything. I'm just grateful Cat's back in one piece." He headed toward the bathroom. "Give me a few minutes to shower and change. She's right. We need to talk, and I'm sure that'll involve a good deal of groveling."

"If she stays in the mood she was in when she got home, you bet your ass it will."

Matt's lips quirked up in a half-hearted smile. "Maybe, she'll take it a little easier on me when she hears the whole story."

* * * *

Matt watched the sun make its weighty plunge into the Hudson. Rick's car pulled up by the iron gates guarding the acre of a private park that adjoined Cat's building. He hopped the eight-foot brick fence surrounding the area without waiting for Rick to unlock the gate. Irritated, Rick followed, "You're going to get us arrested doing that."

Matt smiled easily. "Maybe someday. Obviously, not today. I thought the park might give you a private place to wait while Cat and I have our discussion. You start lurking around the halls, someone will call the police."

"Tedious fool," Rick grumbled as they walked toward a bench heavily laden with fallen brown leaves. "I own the sodding building, and I didn't want to come in the first place."

Matt's gaze snapped up when the heavy back door of Cat's building opened. He caught her scent when she stepped out, shaking a bag of cat treats.

"Here kitty, kitty, kitty."

A flock of alarmed birds suddenly taking wing startled her. Her head swiveled around, her blonde curls spilling over one shoulder. She hesitated mid-step, looking right at him.

"Cat!"

"Matt!" The kitty treats fell unnoticed from her fingers, and she froze, drinking in the sight of him.

Then, she ran down the stairs, and he ran too, his arms open in invitation. The flat of her foot landed, and then slipped on wet leaves littering the steps. Cat's momentum propelled her headlong down the steep flight of wide stone stairs. With nothing to temper her fall, her arms, and hands splayed wide to save herself.

Matt 'oh'd' a silent scream, Rick gasped, both suspended in momentary shock at the sight of Cat flailing in the air several yards away from them. Within seconds, they leapt toward her, pushing past lawn furniture. The crash of breaking glass was trumped by the dull smack of her head hitting flagstone, punctuated by the snap of her neck. Stunned, Matt and Rick froze over her, hands reaching, each fearing their slightest touch could be a death blow.

"Oh, God, no!" Rick gasped, his anguished cry echoing Matt's thoughts.

Entirely focused on Cat, Matt heard blood asphyxiating lungs which could no longer inflate, heard her heart faltering in its effort to beat in rhythm. She lay dying before them. He caught her up in an embrace, her limp arms and legs splayed over his own as he cradled her against his chest.

Her eyes said it all—astonishment, alarm, panic. Cat was completely paralyzed with only moments to live. No Emergency Medical Service could arrive in time.

"Our only option is turning," Matt murmured. *When nearest to death, the sire must drain the dying.* Someone's words chanted on a loop in his brain.

"Matt, you have to," Rick insisted, now down on his knees, hovering over Cat's still chest. She lay flaccid in Matt's lap, memorizing his features. Her blue eyes dulled as her life force withdrew.

Matt's conflict immobilized him, and precious seconds ticked away as he debated dooming her to an undead life versus losing her forever. Ironic that a week ago, he'd been willing to face oblivion himself to protect her. Now, would he surrender her to the unknown to do the same? There was no more time for self-indulgent angst. He must act or the light rapidly dimming in her eyes would go dark forever.

"Damn her to death, and you might as well torch yourself," Rick admonished.

"Brother, I...I can't screw this up." Matt relinquished her to Rick's arms, trading anxiety for hope as the experienced vampire received her.

Rick smoothed back the tangle of blonde curls from Cat's neck and his fangs dropped, ready for his unconventional emergency medical treatment. At that moment, her heart ceased to beat. Rick sank his fangs into her jugular in fierce desperation, almost tearing it in two in his haste to absorb and replace her dying blood with his own. He tore into his wrist, and then pressed it against her lifeless lips, sharing his precious red elixir. Endless seconds elongated further as they awaited a response. Matt fisted his hands, held his breath, lost in a dark pit of anguish.

* * * *

Cat's mind raced furiously, willing her limbs to move and getting nothing in response. She felt the pressure of being shifted from Matt's arms to Rick's, felt a crushing puncture at her throat, and then a pointed ache as her savior tore into her. The ripping pain morphed into a rolling sensation of chills, replacing every warm drop of blood. Still, this slide toward death wasn't unpleasant, as she had somehow expected it to be. It was... Her soul shuddered with the power of a cosmic orgasm. Hot arousal tumbled through her, she soared past stars that introduced new ecstasies as she brushed through them.

Curiously, in her new cosmic state, Cat found herself flying through stars, but still conscious of the sights and emotions gripping Matt and Rick back on Earth. She easily read their minds and watched with understanding and tenderness as they labored to save her.

*I can't look at her.* She heard Matt's terrified thoughts in her mind. *Please, God, damn me but don't leave me a final memory of her face frozen in fear. If you give her back to me, I swear to guard her soul forever.* She watched him stare at the ground and knew he strained to hear some sign of her continued existence, human or vampire. He looked up sharply. *Do I imagine it?* He listened for a long moment. *Thank -you, God! Thank -you.* His head bowed in prayer. *Please, bring her back to me.*

Cocooned in her nurturing celestial bubble, Cat felt transformed, as alien as a mermaid cast onto a welcoming shore in a most delightful sense of rebirth. Electric energy surged through her, animating her bit by bit, pumping potency and vitality into every atom of her being. Slowly, her spirit drifted back toward her body.

She saw Matt scrutinize her throat for movement. "Thank you, God," he murmured hoarsely, as he watched her unmistakably suckling from Rick's wrist.

Cat began to lose the unlimited senses, as more earthly ones took over. Now, scent told her who was beside her. She felt the love and desperation pouring from Matt, and the commitment and affection alive in Rick. Their emotions warmed her, filling her heart like a resurrecting sun.

Blood ran freely down Matt's arm, he had gnawed the flesh on his own wrist almost to the bone. Now firmly back in her body, deprived of cosmic awareness, Cat lifted her head, scented his blood and looked directly into his eyes.

"Let me have her." Matt reached, ready to receive her. The men nodded agreement before Rick gently turned her face to Matt.

"Feed her, Matt. I'll hold her."

Matt's wrist hung within an inch of her lips. He pressed the flow of his blood into her mouth.

Her body was still weak, but inside, Cat felt invincible, euphoric and full of life. Matt watched her intently. *Drip, drip, drip,* the first drops of his blood slid onto her tongue. *Drip, drip, drip,* she quivered as she accepted his sustenance. *Drip, drip, drip,* her lips pressed to him with more vigor.

"Cat, come back to me, baby." Matt moved his lips close to her ear as he pressed a gentle kiss there.

*Drip, drip, drip*, her throat stirred as she swallowed. *Drip, drip, drip* her hand caught his bleeding wrist and held it feebly. Time stretched on as her mouth widened, and she drew strongly against him.

"That's right, Cat, you're getting stronger." Rick encouraged holding her tighter.

Matt continued the feeding, a look of joy on his face as he glanced at Rick, who nodded reassurance. The strength of her lips amplified.

"I love you, Cat," Matt whispered while she nursed from his wrist.

She wrapped her hand around Matt's neck, and with blood-slicked lips sought his. Cat's eyelids flickered wide, and she wondered if they were opalescent. Something in his look told her they were. She smiled delightedly as she gazed up at him.

"Matt, they said you were a dream."

"My beautiful Cat." Matt smoothed the hair away from her cheek. "This wasn't what I wanted for you, wasn't what I had planned, but…I swear I'll never leave you again. We'll live this dream together, forever."

# 22

A Private Jet at Los Angeles International Airport,
One Week Later

Rick ground teeth threatening to inch into fangs as he watched Cat's latest tantrum. It was just one of many they were forced to endure over the past week.

"I hate you! I can't believe you're doing this again!" Cat stomped her foot in rebellion, the force of her vampire strength causing the plane to rattle precipitously, widening her eyes with a jolt of alarm.

"Cat, I told you this is for your own good," Matt reasoned in a calming voice.

"You can't just make decisions for me and expect me to obey!"

"We had to remove you from mortal stimulation," Rick clipped in a tone brooking no further discussion.

Cat opened her mouth to retort before Matt added, "Until you're adjusted."

"*So* you say." Cat clenched her hands at her sides. "How long before you have another excuse to order me around?" she screamed in frustration.

Glasses in the neatly arranged galley beside them shattered. Rick glared from the fractured crystal back to Cat. This was a rough transition.

Matt drew a frustrated hand through his curls. "Honey, please, be reasonable."

Rick speared him with a sardonic look. "I can see you've never been a parent."

"I am not a child!" Cat gritted, and rounded on her half sire, fangs bared.

"Maybe not, but one more word, and you'll be spanked like one over my knee," Rick thundered.

She stared at him in shaky defiance. "You would not dare."

Rick didn't answer, just fixed her with a penetrating stare leaving her no doubt he could and would. "Sit. Now." He growled.

Cat's eyes blazed before she wisely lowered herself onto a seat. "I'm not a dog either," she muttered under her breath.

"I can hear you." Rick took Matt's arm and steered him to the opposite end of the cabin where Matt immediately grabbed for the blood-tinged Everclear.

"Stop it!" Rick snarled.

Matt's hands froze above the bottle. He glared at Rick in astonishment. "What?"

"You've had ninety years of training in domination. This is the best you can do?"

Matt drew an unsteady hand down his face. "She's not my sub, Rick. I'm trying to find a better way."

"Well, one of you better grow a pair and correct this behavior, and I doubt seriously that the fledgling will." He surveyed Matt with utter annoyance. "If you don't take control of this, I will."

"Nobody controls me. I'm my own person!" Cat snapped from her seat at the back.

Rick stared Cat down until she squirmed under his unyielding authority. Matt slumped into a chair and stared morosely out the window. She fretted her lower lip and stewed.

Rick watched the two people who meant the most to him agonize with more sympathy than he dared show. "You two need to dial it down and stay away from each other on this plane. I need some peace and quiet. I have business to conduct. If you truly need something, ask me, otherwise…stifle it!"

Cat crawled into a sullen shell of angry compliance and studiously ignored them. It'd been a week since she was told the full extent of Matt's deception. She was both gratified and horrified knowing the degree to which Rick and Matt gambled their fortunes and lives for her. Still, the broad breach of trust they created turned their whole world to enmity. Today, she was a morass of seething anger. So, instead of enjoying Matt's company, she amused herself with games on her tablet until she succumbed to fatigue.

Matt didn't appear to draw a relaxed breath until Cat rested. He spent the majority of their ten-hour flight reviewing the literature about their destination—Serenity, a secluded vampire retreat renowned for their work with troubled fledglings and other vampire issues. Rick would never have anticipated her anger and rebellion. She said she would welcome being turned. How did it all go so horribly wrong?

The jet connected with a helicopter in Santiago, Chile, which took them the remainder of their journey. Cat had never been on a helicopter before, and curiosity and the thrill of the ride tempered her rebelliousness, as she gazed down at the stunning Chilean landscape.

Slowly, the congestion of the city gave way to the meadows of the countryside, slanting up to craggier ground, and finally the majesty of the Andes Mountains. The copter blades whined as they worked furiously to spin in the thin mountain air. Cat caught her breath at the sunset's glow reflecting off mountainous red rock towering over their elite destination. The copter zeroed in on the landing pad and then settled comfortably to the ground moments before the cabin door opened, blasting them with pristine subzero air.

A man so tall he dwarfed Matt and Rick held on to the cabin door swaying slightly in the wind. Rick studied his remarkably unlined, knowing face, framed by straight black hair. The man smiled invitingly at Cat.

"Welcome to Serenity." He did not raise his voice at all despite the racket created by the rotors.

"Hello." She greeted with a smile of her own in the most pleasant voice Rick heard from her in an entire week.

Matt glanced distractedly at Rick as he climbed out. "Will you stay and have a drink with us?" His invitation was sincere but felt perfunctory all the same.

Rick's eyes narrowed. "No." It was hard to let them go, but the cord had to be cut. "I have business in Colombia. You two go ahead. Get it figured out."

He jerked the door closed. Their small party retreated as the rotors kicked into gear, and the copter lifted away.

* * * *

Cat was glad to stretch cramped muscles and inhale clean air when they alighted from the chopper cabin.

"I am Khuno, your guardian during your stay." The tall man's graceful fingers caressed first Cat's left cheek, and then Matt's right as he stood between them. She sighed in relief at his touch. "May your treasures be revealed by the journey of your bodies and hearts." The gentle giant paused as his words sank in. "You must be hungry. Come with me to the lodge, and then I'll show you to your rooms."

"Rooms?" Matt bristled back from the gentle hand.

"The elders have agreed each of you need your own space."

"I'd prefer we stay together," Matt protested, his stance widened, his hands on his waist.

Cat shifted nervously. "You want us apart?"

"Uh…could I talk with you privately for a moment?" Matt petitioned.

Khuno's hand fell to their shoulders, and he lowered his voice almost to a whisper, his wise gaze seeking theirs, gaining their complete attention. "That won't be necessary, Mr. Brenner. This is a therapeutic decision. Modifications come with progress."

* * * *

Matt's mausoleum abruptly glowed with LED light. Only moments ago, he surrendered to an exhausted vampire's deathly rest. '*Bedroom*' in the vampire lexicon was something less than the padded, upholstered comfort of the best hotel suites. Stark-carved marble as a resting place would horrify any mortal, but their accommodations were plush by vampire standards. Matt rose on his elbows, slipping slightly on the high polish of his slab. He squinted into the sudden glare.

"It's midnight, and your first challenge begins," Khuno intoned gravely.

"*My* challenge?" Matt questioned. "I'm not the fledgling."

Khuno's brow rose, and he gave a transcendent smile. "Indeed?" He turned and led Matt from the room. "Nevertheless, you have a challenge."

With a soft "humph" of annoyance, Matt followed and could have sworn he caught another smile on Khuno's lips before he stifled it. He was led to a plain, but functional staging area with long tables where hiking paraphernalia, bedrolls and plastic pouches of blood were neatly organized.

"Please wait here," Khuno directed. "Miss Temple will be joining you shortly." He gestured to the long, low-slung sofa. "Refresh yourself, if you're so inclined."

*Yes, Sensei.* Matt worked hard to keep the sarcastic reply unspoken.

* * * *

Cat didn't stir when the lights flickered on above her crypt. Drawn and bone-wearied by the events of the past few weeks, only Khuno's gentle nudging woke her. He peered deeply into her sleepy eyes. She felt weak and weary.

"You must feed regularly, Catherine," he admonished. "You've been nervous, and upset, and that's distracting you from a fledgling's most vital duty. Without blood at steady intervals, you will not survive." Cat was wistful, and Khuno searched her heart. "Is this what you want, Cat? Do you truly wish to die? Are you angry you were turned?"

"No." Cat sighed. "I'm angry about what happened before. They lied to me, Khuno. Brutally. They made me think I was insane." Tears swam in her eyes. "I don't know if I can get past that and back to where we need to be."

"We may be able to help you with this, but the journey will not be easy." His smile faded. "Nevertheless, it begins. Come with me."

When they walked into the staging area, Matt was already sipping a cup of O positive and had another poured for Cat. She picked up the cup he proffered and sniffed disdainfully.

"What made you think I'd want O positive?"

Matt clenched his eyes shut, reaching for his last vestige of patience, and then slowly reopened them. "Sometimes, you drink what you have."

Khuno stepped between them. "Your words are walls, not bridges. Therefore, no more words." Matt's gaze flew to Cat's, and their shocked gazes met. "The elders will tell you when speech is allowed again. Until then, you will both remain silent." Cat opened her mouth to protest, but before she could form words, Khuno squelched her outrage with his finger against his lips. "Shh, you need silence to find your soul."

Cat blinked and remained mute, for a change. Matt cleared his throat with a tilt of his head.

Khuno turned to him. "Complete silence," he reiterated. "From both of you."

Cat's lips curved in a satisfied smile when Matt narrowed his eyes and shook his head in disbelief but complied.

Khuno drew his finger along a line in the wall, and a hologram appeared. A contour map revealed terrain of incredible depths and dizzying heights. Matt's look back at their meager survival gear was filled with doubt.

"Your journey will take you deep within yourselves, and far beneath both earth and water." Again, Cat made to speak, and again Khuno's look silenced her. "You must interpret what nature presents to you as well as the clues the ancestors have left. We've prepared your gear with exactly what you'll need." He gestured to the readied backpacks. "Travel but leave no trace. At the end of your journey, there will be understanding."

"A riddle, wrapped in a mystery, inside an enigma," Matt muttered, garnering a censorious look from Khuno. He sighed and drew his brows together pensively, as Cat worried her lip in confusion. "Look," he challenged Khuno, "Cat is no outdoors adventurer, and this is a long way from her convent upbringing. I have military training to help me. I can read a topographic map, which leads me to anticipate the worst on this little adventure. How do you expect me to guide a fledgling to success on such an arduous journey, without the benefit of words?"

Khuno surveyed him with deep disappoint and disapproval evident in his expression. "For a supposed 'Dominant,' Matt, you seem to have a great deal of trouble understanding and obeying orders. Silence is to be observed at all times."

Matt's lips thinned into a fine line of irritation as they followed Khuno along bustling hallways. The retreat came alive at midnight with the footfalls of sires and fledglings completing their own tasks. Finally, they emerged from a back exit and then walked toward a rustic dock.

Cat stopped, struck by the magic of the night. The air was alive with sounds of nature she never heard before. She heard low, vampiric whispers from behind the tree line, and the full moon illuminated the bright eyes of small animals too shy to come close to the vampire resort. A part of her wanted to share the wonder of this moment with Matt, a part of her wanted to escape him.

A sleek canoe waited for them in the water, lapping gently at the shore. Well, escape would be hard in that.

Khuno pointed. "Matt, there." He indicated a paddle toward the back, then pointed to the front. "Catherine, there." He untied the line before he tossed it into the canoe. "Work together. Maintain your silence. Return when you've attained your truth." He smiled serenely at their chagrin and waved as he shoved the canoe away with a sandaled foot.

Cat knew that, as a vampire, she wasn't supposed to ache. Still, she eyed the minuscule form of the island toward which they paddled, and knew they had to be hours away. She glanced at the horizon. How could they possibly make it before sunrise? Fear tickled at her throat. Once again, she'd be forced to trust Matt's superior experience and knowledge. Trust wasn't easy for her where he was concerned.

Matt's muscles worked to push them farther and faster toward the island. His strength and stamina far exceeded hers, and he must be working hard to beat the rise of the sun. Their tandem rowing became mindlessly repetitive and hypnotic and allowed her to ruminate over the past week after she understood the full extent of his betrayal. Certainly, he fractured her trust. Still, only a week ago he admitted to sacrificing her absolution in favor of her safety.

"I never actually expected your forgiveness," he'd said.

"What do you mean?"

"I never let myself count on us being together again. I tried to strangle that hope, all the while I was looking for a way to keep you safe. "

He had a complete and utter need to protect her, Cat realized. It was an intrinsic part of him, and always would be. Was that really so bad? The lengths to which he'd taken it in wiping her memory were extreme. Yet, given his tragic history, was it unforgivable? What *would* she have done if he simply cut off the relationship without all the drama? Was he correct in saying she would have fought his decision? Would her obstinance have gotten her killed as he feared?

Now, that he was her sire, and they were together again if she couldn't find a way back to trusting him, everything would be lost. Might she start the process by being completely honest and transparent herself?

Cat ran a tentative tongue over dry lips. Her exertion manifested as hunger long before she became fatigued. She was starving, but how could she stop paddling and let Matt see her weakness? She glanced back at him. He was head-down in concentration and effort. She studied the man she'd loved for nearly a year.

He was so outrageously handsome, even when furious with him, she couldn't deny his physical flawlessness. The black t-shirt he wore stretched over a muscled chest while he drove them forward, the cotton jersey of his sweatpants pulled tight across his rigid groin. In the dim light of the moon, his hair was thick ebony tangles curling around the sculpted curves of his pale face. Those huge, blue, soulful eyes glanced up at her, and a one-sided grin flitted across his perfect lips before she slid her gaze away. Cat's heart fluttered. How could she love him and hate him so passionately at the same time?

* * * *

Matt watched Cat, anxiety steadily building in him over her anemic color. Forbidden to speak, he gestured at their blood supply, urging her to refortify. Though vampires were always pale, she edged into waxy by her refusal to eat as she should—a way to defy him which ultimately only hurt her. She secured her paddle and then bent forward to the knapsack containing nourishment, every move lithe and undaunted.

God, he loved her so much. What if he couldn't make this work? She held up a bag in offering to him. Well, at least she still considered his needs. Matt refused, turning back resolutely to his canoeing and correcting their drift toward the small island.

Moonlight waned. The first faint glow of sunrise glinted off towering walls of white marble, surrounded by an aquamarine lagoon. After gliding toward a meager strip of land, Matt jumped into the shallow water and pushed the canoe ashore. Cat gracefully followed his steps to the pebbly ground. They both gazed upward, awed by the solid marble caves and hollows the water wore away over millennia.

Matt turned in the direction of an alarming skitter emanating from the cave. The sound of disturbed gravel alerted something primal within the caverns of the island, and in seconds, he heard a thunderous flapping of wings. He ducked away from the blur of darkness surging out of the nearest cave, and instinctively drew Cat against his chest, protecting her within the grip of his arms. She huddled under his chin and buried her face in the strong column of his neck. He splayed his fingers, protecting her face from thousands of leathery wings beating against the early morning air. Bats. Harmless, but frightening.

Gradually, Matt's protective hold on her weakened and fell away. Unable to speak, he looked into her eyes, irrationally hoping to find an answer there. *What would it take, for them to come to an understanding right now? Was this quest really necessary?* She'd already been through so much because of him. Couldn't he spare her this? For God's sake, if he loved her, surely he could shoulder the majority of the burden. Why did the *seeker* on this quest have to be Cat?

Dust motes danced in the morning light, their deceptive beauty belying the danger the sun's rays posed to a fledgling. Matt grabbed Cat's hand, and pulled her into shade, under a canopy of smooth, cool Parian marble marking the entrance to a shallow cave. It was a momentary reprieve. Looking up at the roof, he realized wide cavities dotted the ceiling, and would soon flood with sunlight. He jerked her into the recesses, worrying, even as they went, that the sun relentlessly followed. His gaze fell upon cave drawings, and he drew her to his side as he studied them.

She pointed at drawings of waves on the wall, then to the ones lapping outside. She whimpered and shook her head violently, backing away. *She can't swim,* Matt realized. Tears welled in her eyes, and she trembled. Immediately, it hit him that this was more than a lack of knowledge. Cat was phobic about water. He flashed back to her attempt to tell Khuno earlier. The cave drawings clearly pictured swimmers submerging in the lake.

Matt let her go momentarily to fully shoulder their backpacks. He needed to be ready for anything. He turned back in alarm as a tortured, stifled scream lodged in her throat. In the moments it'd taken him to secure their gear, Cat became engulfed in a shaft of sunlight, the pain of the burn paralyzing her movement. He grabbed her from the dangerous clutches of the sun's rays and plunged them directly into the icy waters of the glacier lake. She struggled against his grasp as soon as her hyper-heated body hit the water. It was all he could do to drag them deeper and hold her under as she fought in terror.

*How deep do we need to swim? How far under before we can break for ground?* Matt took a moment to get his bearings, trying to remember his glimpse of the ancient directions etched into the cave wall. Unable to assuage Cat's panic, he subdued her and propelled them down through the darkness. She fought like a wild thing. In an effort to calm her, he opened his mouth over hers and shared his breath with her. *Breathe with me, baby. Breathe with me*, he thought. He desperately wished his consciousness could somehow connect with hers.

Matt's cool breath revealed the truth, a truth he was sorry Cat hadn't had a chance to learn. She clutched at outmoded, human physical laws. They were vampires. Neither of them needed to breathe. She calmed as his breath entered her lungs.

Within moments, they were caught and drawn into an eddy of cobalt swirls. Minutes drew into eternity while Matt prayed he was right, and they would land in an underground cave. *Cat, Cat, somewhere past where we've been, is our place, hang in here with me. We can only do this together*. Once they finally reached safety, she was limp with the exhaustion of her pointless struggle.

In a final rush, the water gently lifted them against a dry white shore of fine powdered marble. Cat fell to her side, gasping for needless breath. Matt stood over her, pushing wet curls out of his eyes and assessing their location. They were safe at the entrance of a narrow underwater cave. Sunlight filtered harmlessly through the vivid turquoise water. The light was murky and low, but intense enough for a vampire's keen sight.

If he could, Matt would have reassured Cat. If he could, he would have told her she could do this, but his lips were forbidden, so instead, he questioned with his eyes, *Are you okay?*

Cat nodded and patted herself down, checking. She straightened her dripping khaki jacket and winced as blistered skin crossed the twill fabric. Matt frowned, raised her scorched arm to his lips and kissed it gently. She smiled softly.

*If our love has any sanction at all, why does every turn bring her pain?* The Universe didn't answer. Sighing, he reached for their blood supply and then opened a pack for Cat before placing it insistently in her hands. She nodded, sat and drank, but after a few swallows, she exhorted him with gestures to share. He shook his head and held her arm out to show her the slow and incomplete healing. Nodding her acquiescence, she finished the bag herself. She watched, appearing fascinated, as the rough, puckered skin of her arm knitted together.

Matt was studying another cave drawing when she looked up. This one pictured two pairs of hands far apart. *Their next step?* He placed his own over the painted ones closest to him. Catching on immediately, Cat placed hers in the corresponding positions. They pushed, and he quickly realized only equally exerted pressure would move the wall.

Slowly, it swiveled to allow entrance into a cavern. Matt grabbed two glow sticks from their gear, broke and shook them to light the way. They squeezed through the slender opening, awed by a chamber with vaulted ceilings and alabaster walls shot through with elegant veins of rose and dusty gray. The effect was breathtaking.

As they approached the far back wall, Cat found more cave art. She held her glow stick higher to illuminate it. There were erotic drawings, depicting a couple in various acts of love. A mildly hysterical giggle escaped her at the absurdity of the situation. Matt drew beside her, snorted at the cause of her laughter, then chuckled and finally laughed outright.

They embraced, relief at overcoming the latest crisis flooding their hearts. They fell into each other with laughter's joyful abandon. Cat slipped into Matt's sure embrace, and it felt to him as if she had come home. He'd missed her desperately. Stirred by their renewed unity, he grinned, drawing her willing body against his. He pressed his advantage, unwilling to wait another moment to reclaim her. He impatiently pulled soaked clothes from her cool flesh, his lips falling against whatever patch of soft ivory skin presented itself.

"Yes!" Cat breathed, breaking their prescribed silence first and clutching Matt's sodden jacket with fervor.

Matt gave her the slow, charming smile which always made her impossibly wet, and shrugged off his jacket. He destroyed the button fly of his jeans in his effort to get free of them. Vamp speed had its advantages when they could strip in a heartbeat. Within moments, the bedroll was out of their pack and then falling invitingly at their feet, cradled in the soft marble powder lining the cavern.

Cat paused to stand uninhibitedly naked, hands on hips, shaking her head at the erotic cave drawings. Matt's erection hardened, his abs tightened almost to the point of pain. The cavern's faint air current whispered against his sensitized cock. Seeing her now, so unconsciously natural and gorgeous, stimulated him past bearing. She cast him an ironic smile over her shoulder.

"Really? All this was about getting us to erotic cave art?"

Matt laughed, struggling to keep his voice steady. "I think it was about a little more than that."

He grasped her waist and pulled her close against him. His long, thick cock tantalized the soft slope of her buttocks, ramping up his desire. Matt nuzzled the back of her neck brushing sensuously against her. Cat groaned with need.

"I'm ashamed I hurt you, Cat," he apologized, his voice warm and deep. He turned her and pressed a loving kiss atop her damp crown. "I only wanted to keep you safe. I never meant to cause you pain."

She caressed his pecs and torso with her palms. His skin temperature mounted as her fingers traced the coarse hairs and his tightly puckered nipples. She smiled at his reaction. He shivered in anticipation.

"I believe you," she whispered into his chest. She sighed, pressing soft kisses to the nipple beneath her fingertips, worrying the tight kernel with the serrated edges of her teeth. Matt shuddered, distracted by mounting lust.

"Stop." He pushed her back a little to search her eyes. "Stop a minute. This is important. We can't lose the point."

"Yeah! Okay!" Cat teased, her fingers encircled the crown of his cock.

Matt stepped back out of reach. "Cat, this is serious. I hurt you. Tell me you know I'd never deliberately do that." Hopelessly drawn to her, he stepped into her reach, and their foreheads brushed. He licked sensuously at her lower lip. "I need you to forgive me. Please."

Cat's palms grazed over the peach fuzz on his tight ass. Her light fingertips drew down his thigh. "I think I understand better now why it happened. Why you thought you had to take such radical steps to protect me. I was mortal, you were a vampire."

Matt sighed with liberation and drew her down onto the flannel lining of the bedroll. "Then, for God's sake, tell me you forgive me," he urged, his voice gruffer and lower with desire than he intended.

She gazed at him, eyes limpid. "I forgive you."

He swooped in to overwhelm her with sweet, deep, drugging kisses, his tongue gliding against hers, claiming her mouth.

This time, Cat pushed *him* back. "We're the same now, Matt, both vampires, a level playing field."

"Yes," Matt acknowledged. He pushed his hand up from her ankle to her knee, widening her thighs, desperate to push inside her.

Cat's hips lifted. "The point is you can't *'protect'* me against my will."

"Um-hm." Matt massaged the silky wetness spilling onto her thighs.

"I'm not an extension of you. You have to let me make my own mistakes."

"Right. I promise," he avowed, carelessly tossing the thought off, his mind focused solely on the all-inclusive warmth of her waiting sex.

He pulled himself up short. This conversation could be the basis of their relationship for the rest of their immortal lives. Matt drew back and looked at her. When he spoke, his words were measured. "You have to know, Cat, your pain is my pain."

Cat stopped in the act of fondling him, sat up and took both his hands in hers. Her gaze searched his earnestly. "That's what a parent says to a child, Matt. I'm not a child. If I'm going to be your mate. I have to be your equal."

Tenderness suffused Matt and deluged him in a wave of love so strong, he thought he might drown. "You want to be my mate?"

"Of course, I do. That's what all this has been about. I love you."

His voice dropped seductively. He settled onto his side, head resting on his palm. A provocative grin teased her, and her pupils dilated, her nipples hardened.

"Well…exactly how equal do you wanna be?" he crooned, his fingers exciting her.

"On top half the time." She grinned, watching him watching her.

Arousal and need rushed over her face as he massaged her swollen sex. Her gaze shifted to focus on his every feature as he worked her. She bit back a groan, as he bent forward and found her clit with his tongue.

"Whatever it takes, baby," Matt's thumbs were restless against her soft petals. Cat caught his fire, and her skin flushed under his command.

"Oh, my love, Matt!" Her hips eagerly rolled against him seconds before a fleeting orgasm shook her.

"I love to watch you come," Matt placed two precise fingers at the perfect depth and pressure as he worked her with his thumb. "Show me again."

Cat panted hard, unable to resist. The flat of her palm cupped her breast. "I'm so hot!" Her eyes widened, and she shuddered at the exquisite sense of it all.

"That you are," he agreed with a soft wicked laugh. "And I can't wait to get my cock inside your sweet flesh!" Cat shuddered again while he notched himself at her delta.

"I didn't know I could still get hot!" she whispered, her flesh aglow.

"I'll make sure you're always hot, baby." He thrust home.

Cat gasped. She matched his power, her flesh encircling his. "God, I love you! I love this!" Her voice was throaty, her body as demanding as his.

His cock buried to the hilt, Matt arched his back while raw encouragement rumbled from her lips.

"There's more."

Matt drew nipple to nipple with her. The deep resonance of his groan vibrated his chest against hers. With a nudge of his cheek, he tilted her head to the side, bared her neck and bit down, releasing the exquisite bouquet of her blood. He sipped. She giggled. He chuckled.

"That tickles."

He drew more strongly, and she stopped giggling. Her fangs dropped spontaneously, her eyes shimmered opalescent, a fully aroused vampire. Matt's slow heartbeat surged. Determinedly, he bared his own neck to her razor-sharp fangs.

"Drink!" he commanded, and Cat did.

Through the magic of the blood transfer, Matt shared with her all his thoughts and feelings and received hers in exchange. She felt his pain over their separation and his joy at their reunion. She tasted his anguish over her rejection. He'd fought to protect her even to the edge of death.

Their bodies crashed together and retreated in a hungry effort to absorb all their spirit. Within their rich sanguine fluids and within their souls, they found a new understanding. Motives and fears were laid as bare as their flesh. Both wished only blessings toward the other.

Ecstasy claimed them. Rising on his palms, Matt surrendered to her bite. His flesh tingled and tightened under her control. With her blood on his lips, he labored against her. His cock twitched, his sac tightened, his length surged, as the fire in his belly spread. She tangled her legs around his hips, her clit collided with the tangle of curls at the root of his cock. Kicked into ecstasy, her greedy sex milked him. He gritted his teeth, groaned, and his lips drew over descended fangs. Urgency overtook him, release gave way to shivering relief. Her opalescent eyes flashed, and he cried her name like a prayer.

"Cat!"

Moments later, they lay melted into each other's arms. Something occurred in this connection that was indestructible.

"This is why Khuno sent us here, isn't it?" she whispered, turning her face toward his.

Matt watched her. "Maybe." He was pensive. "Probably."

"Did you know this would happen?" she probed.

"No," Matt murmured and rolled to cover her body with his own. "I'm grateful it did. I love you madly, Cat."

"Yeah?" Her sweet smile tugged at his heart, as she teased his sensitive fang with her finger. "I'm glad, because I'm madly in love with you, too." He gave her a supremely satisfied male smile, basking in her love. "I'd like to stay just like this forever." She stretched luxuriously, and Matt hummed an approving reply. "You're gonna get us out of this cave, though, right?" she challenged.

"Oh. Uh…okay." Matt glanced around, trying to engage his higher brain. He studied the cave drawings on the wall and then glanced her way. "So…it's not so bad…me taking charge…if I get us home…right?"

**The End**

# Blood Fugue, Tales from the Gaoler, Book 1

**Fugue:** [ fyoog ] *noun*

*Psychiatry.* A period during which a person suffers from loss of memory and often begins a new life.

*You think your memory stinks?*

Meet **Harry VanAlt**. An apex predator with fading memories of mortal life. Along with his memories, his exalted vampiric powers have faded to vampire-lite. *Great taste, less exciting.*

Along comes **Dr. Lizbet Mitchell**, a police profiler who has not yet opened the right door on her future. Thirty-four and questioning, when Harry rescues her from a rogue vampire, she invites him into her button downed life.

Her fascination meets his reticence as flashes and images from some other life intrude on his own. A 16th-century ceremony reveals Harry's memories and unlocks his powers.

When Lizbet challenges Harry and they take steps toward a new and powerful immortality, there are two flesh and blood details to reconcile. *Harry closes the door on 1951 and settles a score.*

# Appetite for Blood,
# Prequel to the Blood Trilogy

A revolution is roaring into the 1920s! Vampires, who previously killed to feed, now thrill to feed. The revolution is led by a four-hundred-year-old vampire, Rick Hiatt, and his newly turned ward, Matt Brenner. This is not the first time Rick has encountered the brutal treachery of the Moreau family of vampires, but he and Matt seek to make it the last.

Los Angelinos mortal and immortal are under attack by the entitled, remorseless Moreaus. Dragon-shifter Adam Lachlan and seductresses Venus and Luna, team up with Rick and Matt to put an end to the siege. Brute strength won't take these hellions down, but they might be hoodwinked into exposing themselves.

Read about the origins of the fast friendship between Matt, Rick, and Adam, and see how their BDSM empire grew from humble beginnings to an international conglomerate.

# Blood Emerald,
# The Second book of The Blood Trilogy

SDV (Single Dom Vampire) unknowingly ISO compassionate, sincere, spontaneous SMW (Single Mortal Woman). Extra points for patience, brains, and beauty. Handsome, powerful, Rick Hiatt has managed romance and sex within the roles of Dom/sub relationships for five hundred years. What if there is something more? What if the delicious Anna Curley, shielded from the world of dark sex games, can show him?

Rick returns to the helm of his international BDSM Empire after confronting a disaster within his vampire Family. His nemesis, Veronique Moreau, could destroy the fragile veil between the Vamp/Mortal worlds, leaving vampires exposed. He meets Anna, a guileless young woman with enough savvy to see trouble coming in the form of a vampire hunter.

Their worlds collide. Swept into the dangers of preternatural conflict, Rick and Anna experience exquisite passion, and heart-stopping peril. Is love enough? They could lose their lives as well as their hearts.

# Blood Dragon,
# The Third book of The Blood Trilogy

Adam Lachlan, a tall drink of scrumptious masculinity, has been exiled from his dragon-shifter clan for the past two hundred years. His bad-boy charm has been harnessed to succeed as a Master Dom in the mortal world. He's spent decades isolating himself emotionally.

Willow Greer is beautiful, intelligent and charming. Men have pursued her, but she's flown from them all. Willow has a secret burden. Adopted in infancy and having no explanation for shifting into a Pegasus at puberty, she's cloistered herself romantically. Without knowing the full truth of her nature, how can she commit to love?

When Adam's fire meets Willow's short fuse, flirtation is on! At the onset, secrets are guarded, but once their true selves are revealed, the complications begin. Can they overcome the problems of romance between different shifter species? Will they drop their emotional baggage and risk love's bondage?

# Other eBooks and Paperbacks
# by Amber Anthony

Arise, My Darling

Becoming Gabriel


Roman's Revenge, Roman's Adventures Book 1

Roman's Rules, Roman's Adventures Book 2

Roman's Return, Roman's Adventures Book 3


Appetite for Blood, Prequel to The Blood Trilogy

Blood Rising, The Blood Trilogy

Blood Emerald, The Blood Trilogy

Blood Dragon, The Blood Trilogy


Blood Fugue, Tales from the Gaoler Book 1